HUCKLEBERRY HEARTS

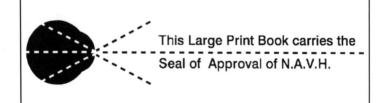

This Large Print Book carries the
Seal of Approval of N.A.V.H.

THE MATCHMAKERS OF HUCKLEBERRY HILL

HUCKLEBERRY HEARTS

JENNIFER BECKSTRAND

KENNEBEC LARGE PRINT
A part of Gale, Cengage Learning

GALE
CENGAGE Learning·

Farmington Hills, Mich • San Francisco • New York • Waterville, Maine
Meriden, Conn • Mason, Ohio • Chicago

LIBRARY OF CONGRESS CATALOGING-IN-PUBLICATION DATA

Names: Beckstrand, Jennifer, author.
Title: Huckleberry hearts / Jennifer Beckstrand.
Description: Large print edition. | Waterville, Maine : Kennebec Large Print, 2016.
| © 2015 | Series: The matchmakers of Huckleberry Hill | Series: Kennebec Large
Print superior collection
Identifiers: LCCN 2015045409 | ISBN 9781410485144 (paperback) | ISBN
1410485145 (paperback)
Subjects: LCSH: Large type books. | GSAFD: Love stories. | Christian fiction.
Classification: LCC PS3602.E3323 H829 2016 | DDC 813/.6—dc23
LC record available at http://lccn.loc.gov/2015045409

Published in 2016 by arrangement with Zebra Books, an imprint of
Kensington Publishing Corp.

Printed in the United States of America
1 2 3 4 5 6 7 20 19 18 17 16

HUCKLEBERRY HEARTS

CHAPTER ONE

Anna Helmuth glanced up from her knitting long enough to study the top of Dr. Reynolds's head. "Doctor, I can see your whole head from up here, and I'm happy to say that you haven't got any bald spots."

"That's good news," the doctor replied. "My maternal grandfather was as bald as a cue ball."

Anna sat on the exam table with one shoe off and one shoe on, knitting a baby blanket for the newest arrival in the Helmuth family, a baby daughter to her grandson Aden and his wife Lily. Anna's husband Felty sat next to her with a gift box in his lap.

The young, handsome doctor with the slightly crooked nose perched on his rolling padded stool, carefully examining the bottom of Anna's foot, and that was why she had such a good view of the top of his head. He worked his thumbs around the edges of the black spot the size of a quarter on the pad of her foot. She squirmed and tried not to drop a stitch while he poked at her.

"Sorry, Mrs. Helmuth," the doctor said, applying firmer pressure so as not to make Anna jump out of her skin.

"Call me Anna. We Amish don't go by 'Mister' and 'Missus.' "

One side of the doctor's mouth curled upward even as his eyes danced with good-natured humor. "Sorry, Anna."

His smile was one of the reasons Anna was considering him as a match for her granddaughter. Cassie needed a pleasant young man who would make her laugh and wasn't afraid to be laughed at. He had good teeth and a full head of hair, which made it more likely that Cassie would take a second look, and although Cassie wasn't Amish anymore, she needed a godly husband more than anything else. The doctor had a way about him that told Anna he was a man of God, deep down.

Anna's knitting needles clicked in an easy rhythm born from years of practice. "You're not married, are you, Doctor?"

Felty drummed his fingers on the top of the box in his lap. "You asked him that same question at our last appointment, Banannie."

Anna raised her eyebrows at her husband.

8

"It's been two weeks. I'm just making sure his situation hasn't changed."

Dr. Reynolds chuckled softly even as his fingers probed the bottom of Anna's foot. "Nope, not married."

"And what about a girlfriend? Do you have any girlfriends?"

"No girlfriend."

Anna winked at Felty as her smile grew wider. "You must be wonderful lonely yet," she said, starting a new row of stitches on her blanket.

The doctor let Anna's foot slip from his grasp and scooted over to the cart that held his computer. "I don't have much time for a social life. The hospital kind of owns me until I finish my residency. I live in a one-bedroom apartment with an ancient sofa and a turtle named Queenie. I don't get out much except to come to the hospital." He looked up from his computer long enough to give them a genuine smile. "But I don't mind. I've wanted to be a doctor for as long as I can remember, and I get to treat good people like you. You are the first Amish folks I've ever met."

"It's *gute* you met us first instead of David Eicher," Felty said. "He's a hard pill to swallow."

Anna nudged her husband with her elbow.

9

"Now, Felty. Be careful what you say. David's daughter is married to our grandson."

The doctor looked like he was doing important work on his computer and she hated to interrupt him, but she had to know a few things before committing to him altogether. "Do you like children, Doctor?"

"Children? I love 'em. I want a whole passel of kids someday." His lips curved as he typed away at his computer. "Which is probably why I don't have a girlfriend. Talk of kids tends to scare women off."

"Not if you're Amish. We're determined to multiply and replenish the Earth."

"Single-handedly," Felty added with a twinkle in his eye.

"Now, Felty." Anna looped the yarn around her needle and eyed Dr. Reynolds. "Are you a hard worker, Doctor?" Her *mamm* always used to say that being a hard worker was the best quality a son-in-law could possess.

The doctor stopped typing long enough to consider the question. "I hope so. You can't survive medical school without knowing how to work hard. My family owned a cherry orchard growing up. I used to work in the orchards with my dad. In the spring I pruned trees until I thought my neck would fall off. In the summer my brothers and I

10

memorized scriptures while we picked cherries."

"You memorized scripture?"

The doctor sprouted a crooked, unnatural grin and nodded.

That was all she needed to hear. God had put the doctor in Anna's path, and Anna wasn't about to waste the opportunity. There wasn't even time to consult Felty. She had to act fast.

The doctor rolled back to the exam table and took Anna's hand in his. Sympathy flooded his expression. "Mrs. Helmuth —"

"Anna."

"Anna, I'm afraid I have bad news. We got the results from the biopsy we did at your last visit. That black patch on the bottom of your foot is cancer. Melanoma. It will have to be cut out."

Anna furrowed her brow. "Does this mean I need to come back?"

Dr. Reynolds nodded gravely. "Several times. We'll have to cut out the bad part of the skin, and if it's deep, you'll need a skin graft. Someone will have to come to your house several times a week to change the dressing and check the site for infection."

Anna burst into a smile. "So we'll be seeing a lot of each other."

The doctor raised an eyebrow. "Not exactly the reaction I expected."

"God moves in a mysterious way, His wonders to perform." Anna deposited her knitting in the canvas bag next to her, slid from the table, and took the box from Felty's lap. "You'll be the one operating, won't you?"

"I could do it, but I'm on my dermatology rotation right now. You might want the plastic surgeon to do your skin graft. I've only done six weeks of plastic surgery."

"Stuff and nonsense. You're being humble." Anna pursed her lips and turned to Felty. "Another wonderful-gute quality in a husband."

The doctor's lips twitched. "I assume you want someone to operate on you, not marry you."

Anna pinned the doctor with the look she usually reserved for naughty grandchildren, complete with the twinkle in her eye. "*I* don't want to marry you, Doctor. Felty and I have been very happy for sixty-four years."

"I'm glad to hear it," Dr. Reynolds said.

"But I'll only agree to the surgery if you do it," Anna added, standing firm so that not even a team of Percheron horses could move her.

A grin played at Dr. Reynolds's lips. "I'll have to check with Dr. Mann first, but it should be okay."

Beaming like a lantern on a dark country road, Anna handed Dr. Reynolds the box. "I made these especially for you, Doctor. I know you won't disappoint me."

Dr. Reynolds opened the box and pulled out the navy blue mittens that went with the fire-engine red scarf and the red and blue beanie Anna had knitted, also in the box. "These are for me? Why would you knit a pair of mittens for me?"

Anna grinned. It was always gute to keep potential suitors a little off balance. "There's a beanie and scarf to go with it."

"It's an extraordinary gift for someone you barely know."

"My grandmotherly talents haven't led me astray yet. You're the one I've chosen to receive the special beanie."

The doctor looked as if he didn't quite know how to argue with that. Smiling, he picked up the red and blue beanie and stretched it onto his head. It fit perfectly over all that thick hair of his. "Thank you. It's very kind. Knitting reminds me of my mother."

"I want you to feel warm and cuddly when you think of the Helmuths."

Dr. Reynolds grinned as he wrapped the scarf around his neck. Anna had made it extra long. She didn't want a stumpy scarf to be the reason he wouldn't marry her granddaughter.

"Just in time for the coldest days of winter," he said.

Anna was sure he would have put on the mittens too, if he weren't still working on the computer. He finished whatever he was typing, took Anna's hand, and guided her to sit in one of the soft chairs. Felty, bless his heart, waited on the exam table — probably keeping it warm in case she needed to sit there again.

The doctor, with his beanie and scarf, rolled his stool directly in front of Anna. "I don't want you to worry about this. There's no reason we shouldn't be able to get all the cancer during surgery. You're going to be just fine. And have a killer scar on the bottom of your foot."

Anna waved her hand in the doctor's direction. "Oh, I'm not worried. The good Lord has a purpose for everything. Isn't that right, Felty?"

"Yes, it is."

She patted the doctor's hand. "But if *you're* worried about it, we should pray together. God will comfort you better than even my beanie can."

A shadow flitted across the doctor's face.

"I'm not worried. You'll be fine."

Anna didn't especially like that expression. "You're uncomfortable praying?"

"I suppose I am."

"But you said you used to memorize scriptures."

"I did. Out in the orchard." The doctor lowered his eyes. "That was a long time ago."

Anna scrunched her lips together. "Oh, dear."

Dr. Reynolds swiped his hand down his face. "The truth is, Mrs. Helmuth —"

"Anna."

"Anna, God and I aren't on speaking terms, but if you want someone to pray with you, I can call Marla. She's one of the nurses, and she goes to Mass every Sunday."

Cassie might not have been Amish anymore, but she still needed a godly husband, and someone who didn't talk to God would not be a godly husband. How could Anna have been so mistaken about this one? He seemed like such a nice boy. And *ach, du lieva,* she'd already given him the carefully knitted beanie and scarf. And mittens! Mittens were no small thing.

"Oh, dear," Anna said again. "Felty, I'm afraid I've cast my pearls before swine."

"No such thing, Annie."

Dr. Reynolds cracked a smile. "Am I the swine?" He pulled the beanie off his head, and wisps of his sandy blond hair stuck straight into the air. "If you'd rather offer this to someone more religious than I am, I completely understand. You had no idea what my relationship with God was before you gave it." His expression almost melted her heart. He truly held no hard feelings whatsoever. Maybe there was hope.

What kind of person would she be if she took back a gift simply because the young man might be unsuitable for her grand-daughter? "Of course not," Anna insisted. "Even if you are a swine, I gave that beanie freely. I want you to have it."

Dr. Reynolds chuckled as his eyes danced with amusement. "I guess I'm not used to the Amish customs yet."

Anna wrung her hands. "Oh, dear. I didn't mean to call you a swine. It's just an expression."

The doctor patted her hand reassuringly. "I know what you meant. And if it makes you feel better, you're not the first woman to call me that."

Felty always seemed to be able to get to the heart of the matter. "So you don't believe in God?"

Dr. Reynolds frowned in concentration.

"I'm not sure."

"That's better than a 'no,' " Felty said.

Anna tapped her finger to her lips. "So your faith is wavering, but not altogether extinguished. Felty can work with that, can't you, Felty?"

"I don't know what you're talking about, Annie."

"I mean that there's still hope for Dr. Reynolds," Anna said.

The doctor lowered his head to hide another grin. "Probably not."

"Just you wait," Anna said, nodding at the good doctor who'd misplaced his faith. "By this time next week, your faith will bloom like a cherry tree in springtime."

The doctor cocked an eyebrow. "What's so special about next week?"

Cassie was what was so special, of course, but Anna couldn't very well ruin the surprise. The doctor would take to Cassie like a fruit fly took to a mushy apricot. And Lord willing, he'd find his faith again.

Maybe the beanie was in the right hands, after all.

CHAPTER TWO

Weaving wildly from side to side was not usually the way Cassie Coblenz liked to drive, but it was the only way she managed to get up Mammi and Dawdi's hill in "The Beast." The Beast was what she affectionately called her 1993 Honda Accord. Affectionately, because that car, which she had scraped together every last dime to buy, had seen her through five harsh Midwestern winters, had nearly 240,000 miles on it, and hadn't complained about anything, even when Cassie drove it all the way to New York City to visit the Metropolitan Museum of Art.

Mammi and Dawdi's hill proved to be quite an adventure. The roads were plowed, but once Cassie ventured off the pavement and onto the lane that climbed up Huckleberry Hill, the way became icy and nearly impossible to navigate. A horse-drawn sleigh would have done much better than a car.

Cassie finally made it to the top of the hill and pulled The Beast in front of Mammi and Dawdi's house. There it was, just like she remembered it as a child: the wide covered porch with no chairs to sit on, the kerosene lamp that hung on a peg just outside the front door, the large kitchen window that faced the front of the house so that Mammi could see everybody who came up the hill.

Cassie couldn't remember a time when Mammi hadn't run out of the house to greet her when she came for a visit. Mammi wanted everyone to feel welcome and loved before they even set foot in her house.

Cassie turned off the car, closed her eyes, and leaned back against the headrest. She needed a place where she could catch her breath for a minute, a place where she didn't feel pushed or pulled or bullied or stretched.

Mamm would be disappointed that she had chosen Mammi's house instead of her own home to stay, but her mamm was one of the worst offenders in the pushy department. At Mamm's house, Cassie lived with a constant headache right between her eyes.

Mammi and Dawdi never lectured her about the church or baptism or hell. They just let her be.

She needed a place to be.

The tapping on the window startled her a bit. She jerked her head up and came face-to-face with Mammi grinning at her from the other side of the window. Of course Mammi would come out to greet her. She had the big kitchen window, after all.

Mammi stepped back so Cassie could open the car door. She jumped out and threw her arms around her little Amish mammi. Dawdi stood taller than the average Amish dawdi, and most of the Helmuth children and grandchildren had inherited their height from him, but Mammi was a puny little thing, no taller than five feet on a good day. Cassie wouldn't trade her mammi for all the paintings in the Louvre, but she was glad she'd gotten Dawdi's height. She clocked in at five-eight without heels.

Mammi gripped Cassie tightly around the waist. "Cassie, Cassie, Cassie. This is the best day in the whole world. We are overjoyed that you would spend your summer vacation with us."

Cassie giggled. It was January sixth and the temperature couldn't have been more than twenty-five degrees. Somewhere along the way Mammi had gotten her wires crossed. Summer vacation was a long ways away. "Well, winter break anyway," Cassie said.

Mammi's eyes twinkled like stars in the Big Dipper. "You know what I mean. This is your vacation, isn't it? You'll get to relax?"

"I'm supposed to be studying for the GRE, but I'll have plenty of leisure time. I don't really want to relax, though. I want to spend plenty of time with you and Dawdi, and I want to bake bread and fill the coal box and milk the cow. All the things I've missed since I've been away."

Mammi's whole face wrinkled when she smiled. "You want to do chores?"

"I want to do Amish things. There's something so calming about working with my hands and disconnecting from all the electronics."

Mammi winked. "Don't let your mamm hear you talk like that. Her hopes will soar to the moon."

"I won't," Cassie said in an exaggerated whisper. Mamm was not all that pleasant when she got her hopes up. She wasn't all that pleasant to begin with. "I'll be here to drive you to the hospital and help you recover from surgery and everything. Leave it all to me."

"I will," Mammi said. "I'll leave everything to you and the doctor."

"Is he a good doctor? Do you feel comfortable with him?"

A furrow appeared between Mammi's eyebrows. "There was some confusion about that at first, but Felty thinks we should give him a chance. I've already given him the gifts, and I don't think it would be right to back out now."

"I'm sure everything will turn out just fine."

Mammi bloomed into a grin. "If you're sure, then I have complete confidence. You always did have a sense about these things."

"I got it from you."

Mammi balanced on her tiptoes and planted a kiss on Cassie's cheek. "*Cum reu.* Let's get you out of the cold. Felty paid special attention to the fire this morning so the house would be toasty warm when you got here."

"Do you care if I walk around outside first? I kind of want to breathe in the whole place before I come in."

"Would you like some company? I wore my galoshes."

"Of course."

Arm in arm, Cassie and her mammi trudged toward the barn. Their breath hung in the air as their boots crunched through the snow. Mammi pointed to the house.

22

"We got a new roof in September. Your cousin Mandy's husband Noah did it for us. I think he and Mandy fell in love on that roof. Or maybe they fell in love in the barn. He'd go in there and lift heavy things, and she'd go in there and watch him."

Cassie opened the barn door, and the familiar, homey scent of hay and livestock and damp air filled her nose. She loved the pungent smell of a barn. It made her feel as if she were home.

She was as close to home as she would ever get.

Mammi pointed out the pulley system that Mandy's husband Noah had rigged up to lift hay into the loft. "He got tired of hefting it up there by hand." She talked about the horse and the chickens and cow. "If you milk the cow," she said, "be careful. Iris likes to stick her tail in the milk pail. She's ruined more than one perfectly good bucket of milk that way."

Cassie laughed. Cows could be ornery. She and Norman used to sing to them to coax them to cooperate during milking. Norman didn't have much success with the singing — his voice was too loud — but the heifers seemed to like it when Cassie sang lullabies.

A pit grew in Cassie's stomach when she

thought of her brother Norman. No one in her family had been happy about her leaving the community, but Norman and Mamm had been the most vocal about it. Being two years older than she, he felt it his duty to keep her on the straight and narrow path. He took it personally when she decided to stray.

They left the barn and walked under the beautifully pruned peach trees, then the empty trellises that would be laden with grapevines in the summer.

Mammi laid her hand on a plastic barrel that sat against one wall of the barn. "Your cousin Aden built us this composter. You put kitchen scraps in and nice black soil comes out in a few weeks. He says we're helping to save the Earth, which seems like a good project. It feels like a bigger job than just Felty and I can do, but we're doing our best. We wouldn't want the Earth to die because we didn't do our part. And we wouldn't ever hurt Aden's feelings."

"Aden is passionate about the environment."

"But I don't think everybody is doing their part," Anna said. "Aden's own father-in-law refuses to get a composter. And if you mention 'recycling' to him, he holds his breath and turns blue. He's not going to save the

Earth with that attitude."

As they walked back to the house, Cassie's gaze turned down the little path that led to the other side of the hill where the huckleberries grew. Some of her fondest memories were of huckleberry-picking frolics. "Did you get a lot of huckleberries this year?"

"*Jah.* Every year."

"I'm sorry I missed it."

"February is maple sugaring time. You can help with that if you like."

"I'd love to. That's almost as fun as huckleberry season."

Cassie walked to her car and pulled her purse and large blue suitcase from the backseat. "Thank you for letting me stay."

"*Nae,* thank you. We are looking forward to a very entertaining winter."

"I don't know how entertaining I'm going to be, but I'll do my best to be a good houseguest."

Mammi stopped in her progress up the porch steps. "Nae. You're not a guest. Guests are acquaintances that you put out the good towels for. You are our granddaughter and closer to our hearts than any guest could ever be. But I'll still put out the good towels for you." She patted Cassie on the cheek. "You are family. Never forget that."

Cassie's eyes stung with tears. It had been so long since she felt at home anywhere. It was a sure sign she desperately needed a break from the real world when one kind word from Mammi nearly made her melt into a puddle of water right here on the porch.

Mammi hadn't been kidding about the warm house. They were hit by a wall of heat as soon as they walked into the kitchen. Dawdi had probably been feeding the stove in the cellar all morning.

The kitchen table to her right was crowded with platters of cookies. "What's all this?" she asked.

Mammi, always genuinely happy, seemed to turn on a sort of fake cheerfulness in her voice. "We can't celebrate your homecoming without eats."

Cassie set her suitcase on the floor and took a deep breath. The great room was just as she remembered. Even Sparky, Mammi's curly white dog, didn't seem to have moved in the last four years. She lay asleep on the rag rug in front of the sofa. Dawdi's recliner sat in the place it had been for twenty years, except it wasn't the same recliner. He'd probably rocked the old one down to dust.

A new LP gas stove sat where the trusty cookstove used to be. More than once over the years, Cassie had heard Mammi swear by that cookstove. She had always put a stop to any talk of getting a new one because she felt more comfortable cooking on the old one. Not that anything was cooked *well* on the old cookstove — Mammi was famous for being the worst cook in Wisconsin — but Mammi liked it better, so Dawdi hadn't been inclined to get her a new one. Cassie smiled to herself. Dared she hope that the new stove had improved Mammi's cooking? She might volunteer to do all the meals while she stayed here. She could only gag down so much bad food before she was sure to develop some sort of digestive condition.

Mammi saw where Cassie's gaze fell. "The new stove was Felty's idea. He used it to lure Noah Mischler into the house so he would fall in love with Mandy. I'm willing to make any sacrifice if it will help one of my grandchildren find love."

Cassie smiled and wondered how someone could be lured into the house with a stove. Dear Mammi. She was legendary for her cooking, her knitting, and her matchmaking. Thankfully, there was no risk of Cassie becoming Mammi's next victim. Mammi only matched her Amish grandchildren with good Amish mates, and Cassie wasn't Amish anymore. She was safe.

Dawdi came bounding into the great room with the energy of a sixty-year-old. He never seemed to tire. "Well, bless my soul, it's my long-lost granddaughter." He drew Cassie in for an embrace, and the unruly hairs of his beard tickled her chin.

"Hi, Dawdi."

He nudged her to arm's length. "Let me have a look at you. You cut your hair. I like it."

"Mamm won't," Cassie said, taking a deep breath in anticipation of Mamm's reaction to the chin-length hairstyle she'd been sporting for over a year.

"Now, who says she won't like it? She'll love it."

Cassie kissed Dawdi on the cheek. "It's wonderful gute to be here. Thank you for letting me come."

"The Lord's timing is perfect," Mammi said. "How often do I get melanoma on my feet?"

"I'm glad I could be here." Cassie took off her coat. "Can I help make dinner?"

Mammi looked at Dawdi, and Dawdi eyed Mammi. "You didn't tell her?" Dawdi said.

Mammi shrugged. "I didn't want to spoil our lovely stroll."

Dawdi smoothed his beard, a sure sign he mulled over something serious. "Cassie, I have some good news and some bad news. Your mamm caught wind that you would be arriving today, and she's invited herself to dinner."

Cassie's smile suddenly felt as if it were plastered onto her face. "Is that the good news or the bad news?"

Dawdi thumbed his suspenders. "Jah."

She sank into one of the chairs at the table. "I had hoped to have a little more preparation before I saw Mamm."

Mammi plopped next to her and patted her hand reassuringly. "I tried to think of a good fib, but your mamm caught me off guard. She even insisted on bringing the food. I couldn't think of a good way to say no. Sometimes it's tricky being the mammi. I'm always getting myself into trouble."

"It's all right, Mammi. I knew I'd have to face them sometime. I was just hoping for a good night's sleep first."

"Your mamm loves you very much," Dawdi said in an attempt to make her feel better.

Cassie slumped her shoulders. "I know. She can't help herself. When we get together, she feels a certain responsibility to lecture me on the evils of the outside world.

I just wish she weren't so ornery about it."

"She thinks you're going to hell," Mammi said. "That makes her a little testy."

Even though her lungs felt as if The Beast were parked on her chest, Cassie couldn't help but giggle at Mammi's nonchalant attitude about where Cassie would or would not end up in the afterlife. "Everybody in the community thinks I'm going to hell. It kind of puts a damper on things."

"I guess it does," Dawdi said, pulling out a chair and joining them at the table.

Mammi shook her head. "I don't think you're going to hell, dear."

"I know," Cassie said. "But I don't understand why. You are two of the most dyed-in-the-wool Amish I know."

Dawdi snatched a cookie off one of the plates and took a bite. "There are eight billion people on this planet yet, and I have a pretty hard time thinking that God created all those children just to send them to hell because they're not Amish. My job is to live my life the best way I know how and leave the judgment to Him." He leaned back in his chair and pushed his lips to one side of his face.

Cassie laughed. "Be careful, Dawdi. That's pretty radical talk."

"I usually keep it to myself."

"Felty, you are so smart," Mammi said. "I had no idea there were that many people in the world."

"No smarter than you are, Annie. You know how to make gingersnaps without a recipe. And they're so tasty."

Cassie eyed the gingersnaps on the plate. They looked like maple-brown golf balls. How bad could they be? Mammi would be pleased as punch if she ate one. It made Mammi so happy to see people enjoying her food, or rather pretending to enjoy it. No one but Dawdi actually enjoyed Mammi's cooking.

The second Cassie picked up a cookie, she knew it was a mistake. Not only was it the size of a golf ball, it was as hard as one too. She'd break her teeth if she tried to bite into it.

Dawdi's teeth scraped against his cookie like fingernails against a chalkboard.

"Have you got milk, Mammi? I like to soak my cookies in milk to make them soft." Would Mammi get suspicious if Cassie's cookie was still soaking at midnight? That thing would never, ever get soft.

"Of course I've got milk," Mammi said, going to the fridge and pouring Cassie a generous glass. "Iris is a good milker."

Cassie took a sip of creamy milk before

31

dropping her cookie into her glass. The milk made her feel somewhat better. She could handle Mamm okay. Better today than dreading a meeting later. "I'm glad Mamm is coming. I've missed her. It will be nice to have a chat, just the four us."

Dawdi leaned forward and took another bite of his cookie. "I have some good news and some bad news."

Cassie's heart sank.

"Norman is coming and so is Luke."

Cassie made an attempt to sound more enthusiastic than she felt. "Well. That will be nice. I haven't seen the baby for a year."

Cassie had seven siblings, all but one older than she. Her oldest sister Sarah married before Cassie had even been born. Sarah's daughter Beth, Cassie's niece, was older than Cassie.

Norman and Luke were the siblings closest in age to Cassie. Norman was two years older and Luke just a year younger than Cassie. Luke tended to keep his opinions to himself, but Norman was more than happy to call Cassie to repentance on a regular basis. He was one of the reasons she came home so infrequently.

Mammi tilted her head as if she were listening to something that no one else could hear. "They're coming." She leaped to her feet and went straight to the door. "We should probably move all those goodies so the table can be set."

Heedless of the cold, Mammi opened the door and charged outside to greet the new group of visitors. Cassie self-consciously smoothed her hair before helping Dawdi move the seven plates of rock-hard cookies to the kitchen counter. Luke would probably eat them. Luke ate everything.

Cassie's mother came in the door first, even ahead of Mammi, who was busy hugging one of her great-grandchildren. Mamm's measured gaze immediately pierced through Cassie's skull, as if taking stock of Cassie's deepest desires and the condition of her soul. Her assessment must not have been favorable. She narrowed her eyes and shook her finger at Cassie before she even took off her coat.

"What have you done to your hair? You look ridiculous, like a peacock with all those curls flying around your head."

Nothing like, "Cassie, it's so good to see you. I've missed you so much." Cassie sighed inwardly. She really hadn't expected a warm greeting, but a little kindness would have been a pleasant surprise.

"I'm sorry, Mamm," was all Cassie could think to say. She certainly didn't want to argue or make a scene in front of her grandparents or her siblings. It always went this way. She'd say anything, make any concession, apologize for things that weren't her fault, just to keep the peace. She'd been apologizing to her mamm for two decades.

Mamm was a wiry yet sturdy woman of sixty-five years with salt-and-pepper gray hair and deep worry lines around her mouth and eyes. As the oldest of Mammi and Dawdi's thirteen children, she'd learned how to be bossy at a very young age, and she'd never grown out of it. Cassie's *dat* had passed away when Cassie was ten years old, and Mamm's bossiness had only gotten worse. As a widow, she hadn't waited for the community to help her out. She'd rolled up her sleeves and taken charge of her life, finding ways to support her large family without burdening the community. Cassie had always admired her strength, the way she charged through obstacles and made a good life for her children without relying on anybody but herself and God.

But being such a fighter, Mamm was also vocal and opinionated, which meant she usually got what she wanted because no one dared cross her.

Except for Cassie.

Cassie had done the unthinkable when she

had decided not to be baptized. Of all Mamm's children growing up, Cassie had been the most compliant, never mustering the courage to poke a toe out of line in Mamm's well-ordered household. Her decision to leave the community had thrown Mamm completely out of her predictable routine and had made Cassie the target of all her wrath and frustration.

She thought her youngest daughter was going to hell. Such fear might make any mother frantically desperate. Especially an Amish mother.

Her brother Norman strolled into the house with his youngest son Paul propped on his hip. Norman and his wife Linda had three children. Priscilla, their oldest, was barely four years old. Jacob was three, and Paul had turned one on Christmas Day.

The last time Cassie had seen any of them was at Christmastime a year ago when she had come home for a short visit, made shorter by the fact that Mamm had ordered her out of the house until she humbled herself and chose to be baptized.

Without a word of hello, Norman planted himself next to Mamm as they studied Cassie's unacceptable hairstyle. They looked like two stone pillars tasked with holding up the *Ordnung* all by themselves.

"Are you wearing makeup?" Norman said.

It's good to see you too, Norman. I sure have missed your constant disapproval.

"Hello, Norman. Paul is getting so big." Unable to resist a baby, she reached out and took Paul from Norman's arms. Neither Paul nor Norman opposed her. Cassie might be a heathen, but they all knew how good she was with babies.

Norman's wife Linda came next, with Priscilla and Jacob each holding one of her hands. "Cassie, how nice to see you."

Linda was a petite woman with chestnut brown hair and a constant smile on her face. It didn't seem to matter how her husband felt about Cassie, Linda had always treated her with kindness. Whether she thought Cassie was going to hell remained a mystery.

Cassie kissed Paul on his velvety soft cheek. "Oh, Linda. He's beautiful."

"Almost twenty pounds," Linda said. "As solid as a tub of lard." She hefted little Jacob into her arms. "Do you remember *Aendi* Cassie, Jacob?"

Jacob shoved his finger in his mouth and eyed Cassie as if he'd never seen her before. Nope. He didn't remember.

"What do you think of her hair?" Norman asked Linda.

"A lot of *Englisch* girls wear their hair like

36

that," Linda said, apparently unwilling to say anything good or bad about it.

Resisting the urge to defend herself, Cassie handed Paul back to Norman and squatted next to her niece. "Priscilla, you have grown so tall since last Christmas."

Priscilla remembered her. She threw her arms around Cassie's neck for a hug and then pulled away and twined her finger around a lock of Cassie's hair. "Pretty," she said.

Mamm took Priscilla's hand and tugged her away from Cassie. "*Nae,* Scilla. It isn't pretty. It's vain. Vanity is a sin, and don't you forget it."

Cassie longed to point out that unkindness was a sin too, but Mamm prided herself on always telling the truth and in her mind she was only protecting her granddaughter from the influences of a wicked world.

Cassie winced. The pain of her mother's condemnation still stung after eight years. Still, the hurt wasn't the open wound it used to be. And she always had Mammi and Dawdi who loved her no matter what.

Cassie's younger brother Luke entered carrying what must have been their dinner. With a pot holder wrapped around each handle, he hefted one Dutch oven in each hand. Luke, tall like Dawdi and sturdy like an oak, was the one the family called on for heavy lifting.

"Stew and cherry cobbler," Luke said, lifting each Dutch oven in turn and giving her a half smile as if wanting her to know he was happy to see her but not wanting to offend Mamm by being too happy.

"It's wonderful gute to see you, Luke. You're getting blacksmith arms."

He didn't even try to hold back the grin that overspread his face. "I hope so. Nobody trusts a scrawny blacksmith."

"She cut her hair," Norman said, refusing to let his indignation die a welcome death. The Apostle Paul said long hair was a woman's glory, and Amish women didn't cut their hair from the day they were born to the day they died. That Cassie had cut and styled her hair understandably upset her letter-of-the-law brother.

Luke fell silent and stared at her with a mixture of affection, pity, and irritation in his eyes. Cassie wasn't altogether sure if he was directing the irritation at her or Norman. Maybe it didn't matter.

Mammi didn't let them wallow in the uncomfortable silence. "Let's eat. I'm starving."

Some sort of wall seemed to come down,

and everyone moved to get dinner on the table. After setting the Dutch ovens on the stove, Luke went to the cellar and brought up four extra chairs and the leaf to the table all at the same time. Cassie and Priscilla quickly set plates and silverware, while Linda opened a bottle of chowchow and heated up some green beans and Mamm stirred the contents of one of the Dutch ovens.

Despite the disapproving looks Mamm gave her every time they passed, it was the kind of activity Cassie remembered fondly — the whole family working together to get dinner on the table. The Englisch were worried about getting ahead at the expense of precious relationships. A gaping loneliness yawned in the pit of Cassie's stomach as it always did when she thought of her Amish roots. She didn't belong here, but nowhere else seemed like home.

She sat between Dawdi and Mammi as the others took their places around the table. All except Mamm. She stood next to her chair as if waiting for someone to pull it out for her.

"I ain't never found it very comfortable to eat while standing," Dawdi said.

Mamm squinched her eyebrows together and glared at Cassie. "This is disgraceful, and I won't sit until it's made right."

Dawdi rubbed his hand down the side of his face. Cassie tensed. Just what specifically did Mamm find unacceptable? Cassie had left the community without being baptized, so the strict rules of shunning didn't apply to her. While shunned members were required to sit at a separate table to take their meals, she felt comfortable eating at the same table with her family.

"Is there something wrong with the stew?" Mammi said. "Did you use Mary Schrock's recipe? She adds too much paprika."

"I refuse to pray at the same table with Cassie unless she puts on her prayer covering."

Cassie pushed down the hurt, pressed her lips together, and stifled the urge to sigh.

Mammi's eyes twinkled with amusement as she reached over and patted Cassie's hand under the table. "Very well," she said. "I don't mind if you stand."

Norman's chair screeched against the floor as he pushed it back and stood. He'd probably forgotten for a minute how indignant he should be and had accidentally sat down before consulting Mamm. "I would like Cassie to wear a covering too, as an example to my children."

Mammi scolded her eldest daughter with

her eyes. "We discussed it earlier and decided that eight billion people are not going to hell."

Mamm frowned. "It's not seemly to pray uncovered. I fear for Cassie's soul."

"Maybe you should fear for your stew," Mammi said. "Mary Schrock is a dear girl but doesn't know the first thing about using paprika in moderation."

The tension in the room felt like a gas leak that only needed a careless spark to ignite. Linda stared faithfully at her plate while Luke's glance darted between Cassie and Mamm. Only baby Paul was oblivious to the drama. He sat in his high chair and banged his little hand on the tray.

Cassie didn't want to be responsible for ruining dinner. She'd certainly brought her mamm enough heartache. If donning a prayer *kapp* would cool Mamm's temper, she'd gladly agree to it.

It had always been that way. She would have done anything to keep the peace — except for the little matter of her leaving the church.

"It's all right, Mammi," Cassie said. "I like paprika. And I will put on a kapp if that's what Mamm wants."

"It's not what I want. It's what God wants."

Cassie didn't feel the need to respond. She could still hear Mamm lecturing her as she went into Mammi's room to find a kapp. Mammi surely had three or four extras, and hopefully she wouldn't mind if Cassie rummaged through her drawers. After finding a kapp in Mammi's top drawer, she pinned her short hair into an awkward bun and placed the kapp on her head. She didn't mind wearing the prayer covering. It reminded her of happy days on the farm when Dat was alive and Mamm hadn't disapproved of everything she did.

Mammi's maroon dress hung on a hook by her bed. Should she put on the whole outfit for good measure? Mamm was bound to complain about Cassie's jeans and cardigan. Might as well wear Mammi's extra dress and a pair of black stockings and quit offending people.

The dress was a tad short. After all, Cassie stood eight inches taller than her mammi. Mammi measured wider than Cassie so the extra material added a little length to the dress. She tied a black apron around her waist and hoped Mammi didn't mind that Cassie played dress-up in her clothes. The outfit sagged in places, but Mamm would probably be satisfied.

They were waiting patiently and quietly

for her, except for baby Paul who had added squeaking to his banging. When Cassie ambled down the hall looking like a proper Amish girl, Mamm smirked, as if Cassie had finally come around to her way of thinking. Cassie sighed inwardly. Did she make matters worse by giving in to Mamm's demands?

Mamm sat down without another word. Norman sat too, although he looked as hostile as ever, as if he allowed Cassie at the table reluctantly.

They followed Dawdi in bowing their heads for silent grace. Cassie nearly chuckled at the thought that Norman would probably peek to see if she closed her eyes like everyone else. No doubt he thought her a heathen now, even though she attended church faithfully every Sunday. Just not Amish services.

Once they'd said grace, Mamm dished up the stew from the Dutch oven. Mamm wasn't a great cook, but she wasn't bad like Mammi, and her stew was one of the best things she made. Cassie's stomach growled. In her haste to get out of Chicago, she hadn't eaten anything since breakfast.

"When do you have to be back to school, Cassie?" Linda asked while blowing on Jacob's bowl of stew.

43

"School?" Mamm scowled. "All she does is look at naked pictures all day."

Cassie felt her face get warm at Mamm's stubbornness. Cassie had explained her major to Mamm several times, but Mamm chose to deliberately misunderstand her because it gave her something else to beat Cassie over the head with.

Cassie pressed a carefree smile onto her lips. It felt so stiff, she thought her face might crack. *Avoid contention at all costs.* "You're such a tease, Mamm. My subject is art history."

"Art history," Mamm growled under her breath. "Will art history help you make bread or sew dresses or have babies?"

Cassie waited patiently while Mamm dished out stew. She was going to make a point to serve her last. "I'm finished with my bachelor's degree," Cassie said, just in case anyone cared. Well, anyone besides Mammi and Dawdi. "I graduated in December."

Luke looked as if he'd like to smile wider, if only he could get Mamm's permission. "Congratulations, Cassie. That's a great accomplishment."

Mamm harrumphed. "A boy wants a girl who can cook and give him babies, not one who doesn't have any skills."

Dawdi placed a comfortable arm around Cassie's shoulder. "When I married Annie, I didn't care if she could cook or sew. Good enough for me that she was the prettiest girl I'd ever laid eyes on."

"Now, Felty," Mammi said.

"It was extra gute that she was also feisty and smart and stubborn. I feel like God favored me over every other boy in town."

Mammi giggled. "Now, Felty."

Mamm finally got around to filling Cassie's bowl with stew. "You're my daughter. You about broke my heart when I heard you were staying with my parents instead of with me. You don't even have the decency to come home. What have I done to deserve such an ungrateful child?"

For the sake of keeping the peace, Cassie remained silent. If Mamm didn't already know the answer to her own question, Cassie wouldn't enlighten her.

Mammi skewered some green beans onto her plate. "She's going to be here at least three months to help me out after my surgery and to study for the G test."

"The G test?" Luke said, trying to show interest and look disinterested at the same time.

"It's the GRE test. I want to work for a year, go to graduate school, and be a museum curator someday." It sounded so important. So lonely. Was it strange that Cassie had left the Amish way of life but longed for some of its joys, like marriage and motherhood? Her school friends were positively horrified when she had told them she wanted six or seven kids.

Mamm set the lid back on the Dutch oven. "More naked pictures, that's all."

"There's a benefit haystack supper in two weeks at the old warehouse," Luke said. "You should come. Everyone would love to see you again."

Not really.

Mamm wagged her spoon in Cassie's direction. "But don't come in Englisch clothes. You'll embarrass the family."

"Now, Esther," Mammi said. "Cassie hasn't embarrassed the family yet. Menno Zook poked himself in the face with a ruler and got a black eye. Perry Bontrager left his shoes in the stove to dry and ended up cooking them. *That's* embarrassing."

Norman raised his head and glanced at Mamm. "Elmer Lee will be there. He's selling a pair of plows."

Cassie nearly choked on a potato. It seemed that every conversation with her family somehow got around to Elmer Lee Kanagy, the boy most likely to lure Cassie back to the fold.

A year before Cassie had left home, immovable, dependable Elmer Lee had started coming around, paying her weekly visits, taking her on buggy rides, driving her home from gatherings. She had liked him for his quiet, steady manner, but even at seventeen, Cassie had felt herself being called in a different direction. She could never have been the ordinary Amish girl Elmer Lee wanted. She warned him six months before she actually went away, but he hadn't stopped coming around until the day she left for good.

Mamm smiled for the first time since she'd set foot in Mammi's house. "He's not married yet, Cassie, and he's got his own farm."

"And tall," Norman added. "I'll bet he's grown four inches in the last eight years."

Cassie took a long drink of water. "I'm glad. Eight years ago, he was only five and a half feet."

"Some boys are late bloomers," Mammi said.

"He bloomed mighty gute," Mamm said.

Cassie gave her mamm a smile because that was what was expected. "I'll come to the benefit supper," she said. "But Elmer Lee has certainly lost interest." Mamm didn't need to know that Cassie had absolutely no interest in Elmer Lee whether he had lost interest or not. If she'd been interested, she wouldn't have left years ago. Let Mamm scheme all she wanted. How hard would it be to fend off Elmer Lee and any other Amish boy Mamm wanted to foist on her?

Mamm acted like a balloon ready to pop. "What's his favorite color? Does anyone know his favorite color?"

Cassie put her head down and pretended to concentrate on buttering her bread. She'd hold her head high, go to that benefit supper, and come home without a boyfriend, and Mamm wouldn't be around to nag her about it. It was why she'd chosen to stay with Mammi and Dawdi. She could retreat to the safety of their home without the fear of having any unwanted boys pushed on her. Mammi and Dawdi wouldn't dream of trying to match her with some unsuspecting Amish boy. They understood her better than that.

Thank goodness for her grandparents.

She was safe.

CHAPTER THREE

Zach Reynolds pulled into one of the reserved parking spots at the hospital, slid the new beanie onto his head, and wrapped the bright red scarf around his neck before jumping out of the car. Living in Wisconsin was a daily reminder of why he liked California so much. The traffic might have been horrible, the property values inflated, and the crowds suffocating, but the weather felt like being in paradise 365 days a year. So far, this Wisconsin winter wasn't nearly as severe as a January in Chicago, but compared to California, Shawano seemed positively frigid.

"Good morning, Dr. Reynolds."

Stacey, one of the nurses at the hospital, strutted past him on the way to her car. Zach smiled to himself. He loved being called "doctor." He'd waited for the title all his life, and now he deserved it. His dad would have been so proud.

Stacey slowed and trained her eyes on him, letting her hips sway in a wide arc as she passed. No doubt she did the hip thing for his benefit. If she had attempted that much swing in the hospital, she would have knocked over every cart, IV stand, and orderly unfortunate enough to be standing in her path.

"Hey, Stacey. Just get off?"

"No more night shifts this week. I'll be sitting at home bored out of my mind if you want some company."

Zach merely flashed a smile and looked away as if he had somewhere very important he needed to be — which he did. Stacey was cute, a little forward, but cute. He just didn't want to expend all that emotional energy on her.

He knew what his mother would say. *Zach, you've got to save yourself for that one special girl.* He shook his head. If only she knew. He was already beyond saving, in more ways than one. College could do that to a guy. What fraternity ever encouraged something as old-fashioned as morals?

He still occasionally heard his pastor's voice in his head whenever he contemplated doing something sinful. Sometimes, even now, his upbringing and what he used to believe got in the way of his life.

Even with Anna Helmuth's beanie pulled tightly over his ears, he heard soft crying coming from somewhere behind him. Following the direction of the sound around the corner of the building, he discovered a little girl standing alone on the sidewalk that ran alongside the busy street behind the hospital. She couldn't have been more than four or five years old. The tears trickled down her face, and she shivered violently with cold. A black scarf covered her head, and her chestnut hair was gathered into a bun at the base of her neck. She wore a thin black coat over a pastel yellow dress with long black socks and black tennis shoes. She must have been Amish. Normal kids didn't dress like that.

The minute she caught sight of Zach, she began wailing in earnest. He was, after all, a stranger, a male, and a terrifying giant to someone so small. "It's okay. It's okay," he said in the most calming voice he could muster.

Her screaming dropped a few decibels in volume. She still cried, but at least she hadn't turned from him and bolted into the street. He'd hate to have to push her out of the way of a speeding bus. He'd rather not be run over this early in the morning.

He took three steps toward her. "I'm not

51

going to hurt you. I just want to help. Are you lost?"

She didn't answer, so he took a few more tentative steps. He didn't want to terrify the poor thing. She was certainly frightened out of her wits already. Getting close enough to kneel next to her, he took the scarf from his neck and wrapped it around her shoulders. It was thick and extra long and would lend her a little warmth until he could coax her inside. He immediately felt icy dampness from the sidewalk seep through his pant leg. Since the recent snow, the sidewalks had been shoveled and salted but they were still wet. He'd have a nice damp spot on his knee for the rest of the morning.

"Are you lost?" he asked again. "It's cold out here." He held out his hand. "Do you want to come inside? I'll help you find your mommy."

Zach didn't know what he said, but the girl's uncontrollable sobbing began again in earnest. He considered picking her up and carrying her into the hospital, but he'd probably be accused of kidnapping and sentenced to five years in prison.

"It's okay. It's okay. I just want to help. Let's go inside and find your family. What's your name?"

Her distress reached frequencies that only

dogs would have been able to hear. It seemed there was no reasoning with her, which Zach hadn't really expected from a young child, but he felt at a complete loss for what to do next.

"Can I help?"

Zach turned to see a cute blonde coming toward him.

No, not cute. Stacey was cute. Smurfs were cute. This woman was a beauty. She seemed to glide across the parking lot, every movement a graceful dance. The very air around her seemed to shimmer.

Zach rubbed a hand across his eyes. He must be working too hard. The lack of sleep had made him a little stupid.

He looked again. Okay, no shimmering air. Just a woman. A woman who carried herself like a queen.

No, that wasn't exactly right either. Queens tended to be divas. Zach had dated enough of them to know that this woman was no diva.

More like an angel.

She seemed familiar to him, but he couldn't place where he'd seen her before. Probably in his dreams.

Her wavy yellow hair fell just below her chin and framed her face like a halo. Her eyes were the color of the ocean at sunrise.

And those lips. Zach's mouth twitched just imagining what it would be like to kiss her.

Yep. An angel.

He sincerely hoped angels gave out their phone numbers.

She wore a puffy white coat with blue jeans tucked into her chocolate brown leather boots. Thin and on the tall side, she wore a Christmas-red knitted scarf around her neck — an almost perfect match to the one Anna Helmuth had given him.

He would have stood up and flashed his best smile at her — in cases like these he should pull out all his best weapons — but he didn't want to turn his back on the little girl and risk her running away. It was that aversion to getting mowed down by a bus again.

He stayed on one knee and turned his face slightly in the angel's direction. "I think she's lost, but she won't tell me her name, and I can't get her to come inside. I don't want to frighten her, but it's pretty cold out here."

The angel squatted next to the little girl and laid her hands on the girl's shoulders. *"Vas iss vi nawma?"* Zach had no idea what she said, but the little girl quieted down immediately.

"Rose Sue," she said.

"Bish du ferlora?" said the angel.

"Ich con net my mamm finna," the girl said.

No wonder he hadn't been able to get anywhere. How was he supposed to know the child spoke Amish? The angel spoke Amish too. An angel with an attractive foreign accent.

Angel pulled a Kleenex from her coat pocket, held it to the girl's nose, and instructed her to blow. She said it in Amish language, but the meaning was clear enough.

Angel fingered Zach's scarf still draped around the little girl's shoulders. The girl said something else in Amish and pointed to Zach. His heart pounded in his chest as the angel finally turned her crystal blue eyes to him. He fully expected a dazzling smile of gratitude for giving the little girl his scarf. It *had* been a pretty nice thing to do.

Instead, the angel did a double take, as if noticing him for the first time. Her eyes narrowed, the air around her stopped shimmering, and a shadow darkened her expression.

He ignored her suddenly cold demeanor. Her reaction certainly couldn't be because of him. He'd never met a woman who wasn't immediately charmed by his good looks and slightly crooked nose. "I wanted

55

to keep her warm," he said, just in case she needed some encouragement to like him.

"Oh," she said, which considering the color that crept up her face was probably the most coherent thing she could think of.

What had he done? He'd only said about four words to her. He certainly couldn't have offended her that quickly, could he? Maybe she didn't like his nose.

The angel lowered her eyes and pulled the scarf tighter around the little girl's shoulders. Standing up, she said something else to the girl in Amish and took her hand.

He had to drive that shadow from the angel's face. "I hope I didn't frighten her. I just wanted to help."

Angel seemed to recover slightly from whatever shock she took from seeing him and sprouted a weak smile. "It was good of you to stop. She might have wandered into the road."

"Can I help you find her mother?"

Her smile grew in strength, as if she'd decided to overlook whatever deformity he had. "You are very kind, but I don't think it will be too much trouble locating them. They're probably just inside at the clinic. A lot of Amish come to the clinic."

Her temperature seemed to be hovering just above freezing. Could he coax her to thaw even more? He stuck out his hand for a handshake when he really wanted to kiss her. Even though she was a complete stranger. Even though she might not like crooked noses. "I'm Zach."

She avoided his eyes. "And I should get Rose inside. Her mother is probably worried sick."

"So," he said, playfully cocking an eyebrow, "you don't want to tell me your name."

"You're a complete stranger."

"Not a complete stranger. You know my name."

"That's not a good enough reason to tell you my name."

"I know a lot about you. You own a white coat and brown boots. You do not paint your nails, and we have scarves that are eerily similar to each other. And" — he held up his hand to stop her from protesting — "you speak Amish."

She bowed her head as a smile crept onto her lips. "You haven't been in town very long, have you?"

"I got here in July. I'm doing rotations at the hospital."

The fact that he did rotations at the hospital didn't seem to impress her in the least. "The language is called Pennsylvania

Dutch, or *Deitsch,* if you actually speak it. It's a distant cousin of German. Most of the Amish can trace their roots back to Germany. They fled to America to avoid religious persecution."

One side of Zach's mouth curled upward. "So if I call the language 'Amish,' I'll broadcast my complete ignorance and lose all credibility."

"Pretty much." She spoke with a barely discernible accent. Zach found it irresistible.

Who was this girl and would she give her phone number to a guy with a crooked nose?

Without another word, she gathered the little Amish girl into her arms and trudged toward the front of the building. He couldn't let her get away that easily.

"Do you live in Shawano?" he asked, having no problem keeping up with her as she made a beeline for the main doors.

She didn't even break her stride. "No. I'm visiting family."

Zach's throat dried up as he considered a horrible possibility. She spoke Amish . . . er . . . Deitsch. Maybe she *was* Amish. He'd heard that Amish teenagers got to go out into the real world before they joined the Amish church. They wore normal clothes and did normal things. Maybe his angel was one of those. She was definitely past her teens, but maybe she'd been sowing her wild oats for longer than usual.

"Family? Are you from here?"

"Yes. Originally."

He almost dreaded the answer he'd get to his next question. "Are you Amish? I know you don't dress Amish, but are you going through that Rumpelstiltskin thing the Amish teenagers do?"

She stopped in her tracks, stared at him with those amazing blue eyes, and seemed to smile in spite of herself. He'd made her smile. Best day ever. "Do you mean *Rumschpringe*?"

"That's it," he said, returning her smile with a devil-may-care grin.

"I suggest you brush up on Amish culture, Dr. Reynolds, or you're going to alienate half the population of Bonduel and Shawano."

Dr. Reynolds? Had he told her his last name?

An Amish woman rushed out of the main doors of the hospital. "Rose Sue," she squealed when she caught sight of the girl in Angel's arms.

The little girl threw out her hands. "Mama!"

The girl's mother took her from Angel and

held her as if she would never let go. She rocked back and forth, whispering unintelligible words of comfort into the little girl's ear as the girl sniffled into the crook of her neck.

With relief evident on her face, the Amish woman looked from Zach to the nameless angel and back again. "Thank you. I turned my back, and she disappeared."

"The doctor found her wandering by the road."

A spark of recognition ignited in the Amish woman's eyes as she looked at Zach's angel. "Cassie?"

The angel nodded while Zach secretly rejoiced. A name. He had a name.

"I hardly recognized you with your hair like that," said the Amish woman. "How long has it been?"

"At least six years since we've seen each other."

The woman clicked her tongue. "*Ach, du lieva,* Cassie. You shouldn't stay away so long. It breaks your mamm's heart."

Cassie the angel turned as white as a lab coat. Zach felt sorry for her, but didn't quite know how to fill the silence that overtook them.

After a few awkward moments, the Amish woman seemed to remember her reason for being there. "I should take Rose Sue inside. We have an appointment." She looked relieved that she had an excuse to be somewhere else. "It was gute to see you again, Cassie. Tell your mamm I will have the quilt squares finished by Monday. And *denki* again for finding Rose Sue."

As if she couldn't escape fast enough, she hurried into the warm building with her daughter in her arms.

With her face to the hospital, Cassie stood as if her feet had been frozen in place.

"Your mom's Amish?" Zach asked. Maybe she'd feel better if she talked about it. Maybe he had no idea how she'd feel. Maybe he wanted to do something, anything to make her smile.

She glanced at him and made a valiant attempt at nonchalance. "My whole family's Amish."

A lump stuck in his throat as the fear bubbled up inside him. It would be just his luck if she were doing the whole Rumpelstiltskin thing. For a girl like her, he might be tempted to convert. "Are *you* Amish?"

She looked at him as if she were reluctantly surrendering every little bit of information she gave him. "No. Not anymore."

Zach almost passed out with relief. "Now that wasn't so hard, was it, Cassie?"

She flashed a genuine smile, even though he could tell she didn't want to. "It's pure luck that Mary Fisher happened to come by and let my name slip."

"But now you can't consider us strangers."

"Yes. I can."

"I'm trying to bring my A game here, Cassie," he said.

"What do you mean?"

He felt heartened by the befuddled look on her face. She didn't completely have the upper hand. "I can usually get a phone number out of a girl with just a smile. Do I have something stuck in my teeth?"

She probably blushed all the way down to her toes. "No. I've always thought you had very nice teeth."

"See? A stranger would never ask you to examine his teeth."

"He would if I were a dentist." She started walking again, faster and with purpose, as if she were trying to break some speed record to the main doors. But he hadn't been a three-year starter on the UChicago soccer team for nothing. With his long legs, he could easily match her stride for stride without even breaking a sweat.

"I'm going to be treating a lot of Amish people in the next few months. I could use a tutor who knows about the culture."

"There's lots of good information on the Internet."

"Come on, Cassie. What do you say?"

"About what?" she asked, obviously fully aware of what he wanted.

She was the first girl he'd met since high school who hadn't fallen at his feet and fawned all over him like he was some Greek god. He'd gotten used to his status as a Greek god. She seemed to be oblivious to the fact that he was irresistible. He didn't quite know what to do with that. Girls didn't often play hard-to-get with him.

He found her resistance both frustrating and exhilarating. He'd never chased a woman this vigorously before. Literally. He enjoyed the chase, especially when he knew she'd eventually relent. He pulled a few steps ahead of her and turned around. "Come to dinner with me?"

She stopped and eyed him as if trying to work out a calculus problem in her head without scratch paper. "You want to take me to dinner?"

"I'm a fun date."

She folded her arms and seemed to grow more and more agitated the longer they stood there. "I'm sure you are."

"I'll take you to the fanciest restaurant in

Shawano." Which might have been the Mc-Donald's for all he knew. "All I need is your phone number. Just a phone number."

She looked down at the sidewalk, over her left shoulder, and finally up to the sky before she spoke. He knew she'd refuse before the words were even out of her mouth. "I don't think I'd better. But thank you anyway."

Ouch.

Rejection stung like a ninja wasp.

He'd never been stung before.

She studied his face. A glint of surprise flashed in her eyes before her expression softened. She kind of looked like she felt sorry for him, as if she felt terrible about dashing his hopes on the rocks of despair.

He didn't like being felt sorry for, even if his disappointment was so thick he could have captured it in a cup and swallowed it. He shoved his hands into his coat pockets and tried to think of a way to make a graceful exit.

"I'm . . . sorry," she stuttered. "I'm sure you don't really care about me in particular. There must be plenty of other girls willing to . . ." She turned bright red as her voice trailed off into nothingness.

Oh.

She thought he wanted to make a conquest.

He had no idea what he expected, but when it came to the angel, a conquest wasn't what he wanted at all.

Lowering his eyes, he made his escape into the safety of the hospital. He'd be forced to perform surgery with wounded pride and a soggy pant leg. At least he hadn't been out in the frigid air long enough to get frostbite.

He looked down and groaned. That little Amish girl had made off with his scarf.

And the angel had made off with his ego.

CHAPTER FOUR

Outside through the glass, Cassie watched Dr. Zach Reynolds get onto the elevator. When the doors closed behind him, she counted to twenty before venturing into the lobby. She would have been mortified if they'd been forced to wait for an elevator together.

How in the world had she had the misfortune of running into Zach Reynolds in tiny Shawano, Wisconsin? Weren't there five million other places in the world he could have been assigned to do his residency?

She hadn't expected him to remember her. It had been four years, and he'd only actually spoken to her twice when they were both going to the university in Chicago. The first time they had met had been at a loud party with lots of flashing lights and zero visibility. She'd been passing through the crowd on her way to the exit when he had stopped and asked her name. She'd given it to him, but only because he'd caught her off guard. The second time she'd had the misfortune of coming in contact with him, she and Tonya had been standing at the threshold of his apartment, soaking wet from a torrential downpour outside. She had looked more like a drowned rat than herself. Of course he didn't remember her.

But she remembered him. Vividly. A good-looking, athletic senior like Zach Reynolds tended to turn the heads of every wide-eyed freshman girl on campus. But that wasn't why she remembered him.

He had been one of those arrogant, devil-may-care premed students, like all the other arrogant premed students who treated girls as if they were as disposable as Kleenex.

She'd rather not spend another minute rehashing her bad memories of college fraternities and heartbroken roommates. She could certainly steer clear of Zach Reynolds for a few weeks. It wasn't as if they'd be running in the same circles.

Guys like Zach Reynolds could be incredibly charming. It was a testament to his powers with women that he'd been able to make her smile, even when she hated the very sight of him. It wasn't in her disposition to be mean or sarcastic — but sometimes she wished it was. Her old roommate

Tonya would have scolded her for not having the courage to put Zach Reynolds in his place with a clever insult.

But was it so bad to try to be nice to everybody? She had worn a kapp and a Plain dress for her mamm in the name of harmony. Trying to get along was not a character flaw.

Cassie took a deep breath and tried to think charitable thoughts about the doctor. He'd been wearing a very nice, homemade beanie and an expertly knitted scarf. He probably had a sweet grandmother somewhere who loved him dearly and knitted him ties for Christmas. If some cute little old lady could find it in her heart to love Zach, then he couldn't be all bad.

He had seemed very concerned about Rose Sue Fisher, but maybe it had all been an act. Cassie took the scarf from around her neck and stuffed it into her purse. As a doctor, he was paid to care.

She decided not to risk the elevator. Mammi and Dawdi were only one flight up. She had dropped Mammi and Dawdi at the front before parking the car and encountering the arrogant and handsome Dr. Reynolds. She wouldn't be caught off guard again.

When Cassie got to the second floor, the

nurse at the desk directed her to the room where they were prepping Mammi for her surgery. Mammi sat in a leather recliner wearing her prayer covering and a hospital gown and knitting, and Dawdi sat next to her reading *Sports Illustrated.*

"Look at this tattoo, Annie," he said, turning the magazine so Mammi could see it.

"Oh," Mammi said. "He's got a spider crawling up his chest. Very nice."

"Is everything okay?" Cassie asked.

Mammi laid her knitting in her lap. "Fine, dear. When they brought us back here, I worried you wouldn't find us."

Cassie took off her coat and hung it on a hook near the door. "Parking the car took longer than expected."

"I'm glad you made it. You look so lovely today, and I was afraid you'd miss the doctor. He's coming in to say hello before he cuts the cancer out of my foot."

"Are you nervous?"

"Of course not. I gave birth to thirteen babies, all at home. Nothing scares me."

Dawdi turned the magazine sideways and carefully examined one of the photos. "Is that a fish or his mother?"

"I think it's his arm, dear." Mammi folded up her knitting and placed it in her canvas bag. "Cassie, this is very important. I want

69

you to be the one to hear all the doctor's instructions. Ask lots of questions."

Cassie sat on the chair next to Dawdi and reached over to squeeze Mammi's hand. "Don't you worry about a thing. I'll make sure I get all the important information."

"And be sure to mention his nice hair. He's very proud of it."

Mammi occasionally said peculiar things that didn't make a lot of sense. "Whose nice hair?"

"The doctor's. He doesn't have any bald spots."

"Oh. Okay."

They heard a quick tap on the door. Mammi's eyes got wide, and she squeaked in delight. "It's him."

Cassie didn't know why Mammi was so thrilled about seeing the doctor, but her enthusiasm made Cassie smile. To Mammi, every minute of the day was an adventure. Her persistent excitement made her seem younger than her eighty-four years.

The door swung open, and all of Cassie's internal organs plummeted to the floor. This couldn't be happening. Not when she'd been so careful to avoid the elevator.

Zach Reynolds was Mammi's doctor?

The doctor's eyebrows nearly flew off his face as he caught sight of Cassie. He halted

in his tracks and stood in the doorway staring at her as if he'd walked into the women's
bathroom by mistake. He looked even more
surprised to see her than she was to see him.
His face grew decidedly pale, making Cassie wonder who would be the first of the
two of them to throw up.

He seemed to have to pry his eyes from
her face. Clearing his throat, he smiled like
Mammi was his favorite patient. "Mrs.
Helmuth —"

Mammi beamed at the doctor as if he
were her best friend. "Anna, please."

"I'm sorry, Anna. I keep forgetting," he
said, seemingly unable to catch his breath.

Mammi reached out, slipped her hand
into the doctor's, and tugged him forward.
"Dr. Reynolds, I want you to meet my
granddaughter Cassie Coblenz. She's visiting with us for only a few short months,
and she is a wonderful-gute girl."

"I should have guessed," the doctor stammered. "We have matching scarves."

She hadn't even realized it earlier. Of
course Mammi had been the one who had
made the doctor a scarf. It was almost
identical to Cassie's. She tore her gaze from
his stunning aqua blue eyes. No way would
she get caught up in those.

71

"But the little girl ended up with mine," he said.

"What little girl?" Mammi said. "Do you two know each other?" She seemed almost disappointed.

Cassie played with an errant thread sticking out from her coat. "We . . . uh . . . we met by the busy street behind the hospital. Rose Sue Fisher wandered out there by herself. Dr. Reynolds wrapped his scarf around her to keep her warm."

Mammi turned to the doctor. "The one I made for you?"

The doctor nodded.

"What a nice young man you are. I knew it right from the start."

"I'm afraid I accidentally left it around her shoulders," Dr. Reynolds said.

Mammi smiled. "Not to worry. Cassie can fetch it from the Fishers and return it."

She'd rather not. But she couldn't be cross with Mammi. Mammi was only trying to be nice, just like Cassie should have been doing.

Mammi smoothed a crease from her hospital gown. "Cassie just graduated from college in art history. She looks at a lot of naked people in her studies. You two have that in common."

Cassie coughed violently as what was left

of her pride lodged in her throat. Mammi patted her on the back with no inkling that anything she'd said had nearly choked her granddaughter.

Dr. Reynolds's lips twitched upward. "Matching scarves and similar lines of work," he said. "I like your granddaughter already."

Cassie lowered her eyes as her face got warm. He was teasing, but in a way that wouldn't shame her or hurt Mammi's feelings. She hadn't actually expected him to be nice.

"She graduated from the University of Chicago, which I hear is a very big school with lots of important people who go there," Mammi said.

"Hey, I went to UChicago," Dr. Reynolds said. "You do look familiar. Maybe we ran into each other at the library or something."

"Maybe," she said.

"I did both undergrad and medical school there, but once I got into med school, I was usually buried in the Reg trying to make sense of biochemistry. I didn't have much of a social life."

Maybe not in medical school, but his social life had thrived during his senior year. Cassie frowned. Four years ago and she still remembered as if it were yesterday.

Zach's roommate Finn McEwan had started a club with some of the other senior guys. The goal of the club was to see how many different coeds they could sleep with before graduation.

Cassie didn't entirely blame the senior boys for the success of their little club or the notoriety it gave them. The girls on campus participated knowingly and even started a club of their own to keep track of their hookups. To Cassie, an ex-Amish girl with an old-fashioned sense of right and wrong, the whole thing seemed sordid and low.

Cassie's roommate Tonya was fully aware of the club but still felt shocked and hurt when Finn dumped her. She had talked herself into believing Finn loved her and that their relationship was different from all the others. He, on the other hand, had just wanted to increase his tally.

Poor Tonya.

And everyone at school said *Cassie* was naïve.

On a rainy night, Tonya had begged Cassie to go with her to Finn's, to plead with him to take her back. The attempt was nothing short of pathetic, but Tonya had been inconsolable until Cassie had agreed to go with her, more to save Tonya from herself than anything else.

Cassie could still smell Zach and Finn's aged apartment. It stank of stale pizza and sweaty boys. She and Tonya had stood dripping wet just outside the door because Finn wouldn't invite them in. Finn, with his wavy bleach-blond hair and diamond-studded class ring, told Tonya not to cry about it, that it was nothing personal against her, but that she had just been part of the contest. He even thanked her for helping him take over first place.

Cassie had tried to pull the sobbing Tonya away from the door so Finn could close it, but Tonya had wrapped her fingers around the doorjamb and held on like a barnacle.

At that point, Zach — who had been studying at their kitchen table — joined Finn at the door and started yelling at Cassie. She hadn't done anything wrong and certainly hadn't felt she deserved his disdain, but she got it anyway, along with some shockingly horrible words from the future Dr. Reynolds.

"Don't go sleeping around if you can't handle the rejection," he had said.

"Don't go starting a club, Dr. Reynolds, if you can't handle jilted girls showing up at your door."

Of course, she hadn't actually said that to

him. She never would have dared say anything even remotely snarky. Not to superior Zach Reynolds.

She and Tonya had walked home in the rain, wrapped up in an extra-large blanket, and drowned Tonya's sorrows in two pints of Ben & Jerry's ice cream while listening to a Beyoncé CD.

If you like it then you shoulda put a ring on it.

Cassie glanced at the doctor. He stared at her as if expecting her to say something, as if he wanted her to reconsider giving him her phone number. She folded her arms and smiled politely.

He cleared his throat, again. He must have found the air in Wisconsin very dry. Sitting on the stool, he gave Mammi all his attention. "Now, Anna," he said, "we're going to cut the cancer out of your foot and take a few lymph nodes to make sure the cancer hasn't spread. After that you will have to stay completely off your feet for three weeks. We'll give you a scooter so you can get up and go to the bathroom, but that's it. We're also going to send you home with a wound vacuum to help keep the site completely dry and infection free."

"They don't have any place to plug it in," Cassie said.

Dr. Reynolds looked up and smiled. Curse those brilliant white teeth. It made a girl forget why she disliked him so much. "This is a battery-operated wound vacuum, so there shouldn't be any problem. We'll have a home health nurse come every other day to change your dressing. After three weeks, we'll do a skin graft. Then it's off your feet for six or seven more weeks. You're going to be spending a lot of time in bed."

Mammi nodded. "Cassie will be with me."

That aggravatingly attractive smile again. "Then you're in good hands."

"Yes, I am."

Dr. Reynolds pulled out his pen. "Let's talk about medication."

Mammi waved him away with a mischievous glint in her eye. "I really don't have the patience for it, Doctor. Tell Cassie what I need to know." She picked up her knitting and acted as if she couldn't care less what happened to her foot.

The doctor smiled, scooted closer to Cassie, and focused his attention squarely on her. She wished he wouldn't have. It was all she could do to keep from fidgeting under his intense gaze.

He told her about the medications Mammi would need and promised to write explicit instructions for everything. Good idea. She wouldn't remember half of what he told her. No wonder immature college girls fawned over him. He was too good-looking to be a doctor. He'd prove a distraction to all his patients.

He pulled a card from his pocket and wrote a number on it. "If you have any concerns or questions, don't hesitate to call me. Here is the number for my answering service." He cleared his throat once. Twice. "I know Anna doesn't have a phone. I'll need . . ." Three times. "I'll need your phone number so that I can call and check on your mammi tonight, if you don't mind."

Cassie thought her face might burst into flames. He had tried very hard to get her number in the parking lot, and she had been clever enough to evade him. But now she'd have to give it to him for Mammi's sake.

Her only consolation was that Dr. Reynolds seemed as uncomfortable about it as she did. She had refused to give him her number. Under normal circumstances, he didn't seem like the type of guy who would keep hounding her about it.

"If it makes you feel better," he said, glancing at Mammi, "I feel like a jerk asking for it."

He cracked a smile. She did too.

She repeated her number, and he punched

it into his phone and grinned. "I promise I'll delete this at the first sign of temptation."

"Temptation?"

"If I'm ever tempted to call and ask you out."

Mammi looked up from her knitting. Dawdi didn't budge from his *Sports Illustrated.* "Oh, how nice," Mammi said.

Why was her pulse racing? This was Zach Reynolds, for crying out loud. She lowered her eyes and put her hand to her cheek to hide the blush. "Thank you."

A smile played at his lips as he fell silent and briefly tinkered with his phone. "Okay," he said. "I need your phone number again."

"What?"

"Just now I was tempted to call and ask you out, so I deleted your number, just like I promised."

Cassie had never blushed so much in her entire life. She had to remind herself that all the doctor wanted was another notch on his bedpost. It was all guys like him ever wanted.

"Is it okay with you if I change my promise a little?" he asked.

She nodded doubtfully.

"I promise to call you only if I need to discuss something about your mammi's condition."

"Okay," she said. Only after she said it did she realize she'd been holding her breath.

He smiled and turned his full attention to Mammi once again. "Are you ready, Anna?"

"Did you give Cassie your phone number?" Mammi said, as if the doctor's phone number were more important than her pending surgery.

"Yes, and she's got all the instructions."

Mammi put her knitting away for good this time. "Can I call you tonight, Doctor?"

"Yes, call me anytime you like, and I'll call to check on you too."

Mammi reached over and took Cassie's hand, then grabbed Dr. Reynolds's hand as well. "And when will you come and visit us? Felty, do you have a piece of paper?"

Dawdi looked up and smiled at Mammi. "Sorry, Annie. Didn't bring any."

"I've got to have something, Felty dear."

Dawdi tore a corner out of one of the pages in his magazine and handed it to Mammi. "Is this okay?"

Mammi took the paper, wrote on it, and handed it to the doctor. "Here is our address. Just plug it into the map on your phone, and you'll be able to find us."

"I don't think I can do that," Dr. Reynolds replied.

Mammi furrowed her brows. "Don't you have the map on your phone? Cassie tells me everybody has one."

The doctor squeezed her hand reassuringly. "I don't usually make house calls. But you can always reach me on the phone."

Mammi squeezed the doctor's hand. She must have really been serious. Cassie could see her knuckles turn white. "Doctor, I would feel so much better if you came to visit me. What if my foot falls off? What if I die and leave my children bereft of a mother? What about my sixty-four grandchildren and hundred and three greats?"

Dr. Reynolds didn't lose that gorgeous, reassuring smile as he tried to divert Mammi's attention. "Sixty-four grandchildren. That's amazing."

Mammi would not be sidetracked. "One thing you need to know about the Amish is that we really need our doctors to visit us."

Cassie stiffened. Mammi had seemed so confident only a few minutes ago. Maybe the fact that she was about to go into surgery had just hit her. Mammi didn't often talk about her own death. Cassie leaned across Dawdi, still looking at tattoos, and patted Mammi's hand. "It will be all right. I'll take good care of you."

"I'm sure you couldn't have a better caretaker," the doctor said.

Dawdi pried his gaze from the magazine. "It's no use trying to work things out right now, Annie Banannie. There's plenty of time after your surgery."

Mammi shrugged and seemed to sigh with her whole body. "You're right as usual, Felty. I've got two months to recover. We've done a lot more with a lot less time."

"Yes," said the doctor with a wink. "Everything's going to be fine. And those sixty-four grandchildren are going to get a big kick out of your scar."

Mammi still held Cassie by the left hand and Dr. Reynolds by the right. She brought her hands together and placed Cassie's hand in the doctor's. A bolt of electricity traveled up Cassie's arm at the mere touch of Zach Reynolds's skin. Surely her face glowed a lovely shade of purple-crimson.

"Right now," Mammi said, "the only grandchild I'm concentrating on is Cassie. And I know neither of you will disappoint me."

"We won't," Dr. Reynolds said, chuckling and looking as if he were surprised and pleased to be holding hands with her.

When the doctor didn't seem all that inclined to let go, Cassie slipped her hand from his and attempted a carefree smile to match the doctor's. "I won't disappoint you either, Mammi."

Mammi grinned like a fat kitty swimming in a bowl of cream. "I know you won't. I'm never wrong about these things."

CHAPTER FIVE

With bowl in hand, Zach sank onto his threadbare secondhand sofa and propped his feet on the short metal filing cabinet that also served as a coffee table. He had to stretch a little as he reached for the three remotes sitting on the arm of the sofa. One remote to turn on the TV, one to change the channel, and one to work the volume. He wasn't quite sure how he'd ended up with so many remotes, but at least the ancient TV worked and the cable box didn't spark and hiss like the last one.

Not really interested in watching, he turned on the TV more for background noise than anything else. With his fork, he twirled the long, curly noodles in his bowl. Oriental-flavored ramen noodles with hot dog slices probably had as much nutritional value as a shoebox, but they were easy to fix and tasted pretty good after a long day at the hospital. His grueling schedule over the last few years had made him less picky about what he put into his mouth.

Still, what he wouldn't have given for a thick slice of Giordano's Chicago-style pizza at this very moment.

And maybe another look at the angel.

The most beautiful girl he'd ever laid eyes on, and he couldn't even talk her into a date with him. There must be something fundamentally wrong with him. She'd looked past the straight teeth and the crooked nose and the doctor title. Had she been able to see into his heart? Could she tell just by looking how flawed and confused he was? And how angry he felt?

It wasn't just that she was pretty. If she'd been merely pretty, he would have been able to walk away from her rejection unscathed. There were lots of pretty girls who would jump at a chance to date Dr. Zach Reynolds. Her bearing, the way she carried herself had made Zach look twice, but the way she'd cared about the little Amish girl, the deference she paid to her grandparents, the kindness with which she treated him even though she didn't want to date him, were all astonishingly attractive qualities.

Earlier today, Zach had walked out of surgery to see Cassie engrossed in a conversation with Cheryl, the grumpiest nurse in the hospital. She didn't like anybody, and she complained about everything, but there Cassie had been with her arm around the prickly nurse, listening to her problems and offering kindness and sympathy. Cassie was like a one-woman ministry.

Sweet, unpretentious, kind people like her were pretty rare.

Why would a girl like her ever give a guy like him a second glance? Girls like her dated . . . Who did girls like her date?

Navy SEALs? Saints? Archangels?

He didn't know, but it was a sure bet they didn't date mere mortals like Zach Reynolds.

With bowl and fork in one hand, he slipped his phone out of his pocket and scrolled to her name. Cassie Coblenz. Pretty, smart, determined. Very good to her grandparents.

And completely uninterested in Zach Reynolds.

Dr. Zach Reynolds.

It took him about ten seconds to memorize her number. He wanted to commit it to memory just in case he lost his phone or accidentally deleted it.

He'd never accidentally delete it. Someday she might change her mind about him. He'd be ready.

He laid his phone on the sofa and stuffed another bite of ramen noodle with hot dog into his mouth. He wouldn't hold his breath for Cassie. His face would turn fluorescent blue before she would ever agree to go out with him.

He had almost secretly snapped a picture of her with his phone after Anna's surgery this morning, but he had thought better of it. He might have felt a twinge of desperation when he thought about not going out with her, but taking a secret picture was kind of creepy, and he wasn't the stalker type.

Maybe he could look her up on Facebook.

Lots of people did that.

Maybe not.

He picked up his phone again and resisted the impulse to scroll to her name. Instead, he checked his messages. Only one, from Blair saying she'd be in Stevens Point at the first of March. Did he want to get together?

Not really. He'd broken things off when he'd graduated from medical school. He hadn't invested enough in the relationship to make it work long distance when he'd never seen it working out long term anyway. Blair was a career woman through and through. There wasn't anything wrong with that, except Zach wanted kids, lots of kids, and Blair practically broke out in hives at the mere mention of children. But the real problem was that Blair didn't seem real, as if she put on a mask every morning when she got out of bed and never showed her true self to people. She acted out a part, and Zach was just another cast member in the movie of her life.

He didn't want to be a cast member.

His phone vibrated and lit up with a picture of Mom. His mom seldom called him. When he left for college, she had told him that she didn't want to be one of those annoying mothers who called three times a day to check up on her son. But she had gone overboard and hardly called him at all. She had told him that she didn't want to hover. The only times they talked were when he called her, two or three times a week. He liked to think that she needed him, but it was definitely a lopsided relationship. He wasn't too proud to admit that he still needed to hear his mom's voice every once in a while, and he wanted her advice and encouragement now more than ever.

"Hey, Mom. Is everything okay?"

"Relatively," she said, which wasn't an answer at all. "How did your surgery on that Amish lady go today?"

"It went good. Dr. Mann says I have

steady hands."

"It's all those years of piano."

"Or maybe all those years of picking cherries."

A pause on the other end of the line. "You're never going to thank me for those piano lessons, are you?"

Zach smiled. Mom had forced him and his two older brothers to take piano lessons until they were in high school, predicting that they would thank her later. At about age twelve when Zach had started to eat and breathe soccer, he had promised his mom that he would never, ever thank her for making him play the piano. It was a running joke, especially since he and his buddies had formed a band in high school with Zach on the keyboard. Mom wouldn't let him live it down.

Zach took a bite of ramen. "I *will* thank you for signing me up for soccer."

"Am I interrupting your dinner? I can call back."

"I can eat and talk," Zach said.

"Mac and cheese again?"

"Ramen with hot dogs."

"Have you found any good restaurants in Shawano yet?"

"Nope. I don't get out much."

"Well," Mom said, "you need to find a

surrogate mother to feed you a home-cooked meal."

Other moms might have told their sons that they needed to find a girlfriend, but not his mom. He liked that she never once asked him if he was dating some nice girl. She never mentioned grandchildren or tried to make him feel guilty for not going to church. She was just his mom, who loved him no matter how much she thought he was screwing up his life.

She and Dad had taken him to church faithfully for seventeen years. He'd memorized fifty scriptures at Bible study camp. He'd even taken a purity pledge before high school. But he just hadn't had the heart for all that fluff after Dad died, and Mom had witnessed his fall.

Of course she thought he was screwing up his life.

"So," Mom said, "what I've called to tell you is I've broken my arm."

Zach nearly spilled his noodles all over his thirty-year-old sofa. "What? Mom, what happened?"

"I tried to clean out those stupid gutters and fell off the ladder."

"Mom, I told you not to do that yourself. A woman your age shouldn't be on a ladder."

"Oh, for goodness' sake, Zach, I'm only fifty-five."

"Too old to be on a ladder," Zach said.

"Just wait until you're fifty-five. You'll be embarrassed that you thought I was old."

Zach gave up on his noodles and set them on the filing cabinet. "Mom, I'm coming home in June. Save all that stuff for me to do."

"You won't want to come home if all I do is make you work."

For the thousandth time since he'd left California for college, the guilt and anger slammed into him. He should have gone to school closer to home. He should be there for his mom. If God hadn't taken his dad, Mom would have someone there to take care of her.

His brother Drew lived in Japan with his wife and baby boy, and his brother Jeff was in Saudi Arabia with the State Department. Zach was the closest one to home. "Maybe I can get a little time off next month. I could spend a few days."

"You'll do no such thing. Stay there and finish your residency."

He ran his fingers through his hair. She was right, but it didn't make him feel any better. "What did the doctor say? How bad a break is it?"

"I don't know. Eight weeks in a cast. It's not a very convenient time. I have to finish the decorations for the auxiliary bazaar."

"Maybe you could turn it over to someone else."

"I'm not too bad with one hand. I don't want you to worry. I debated about telling you at all, but I figured someone would post it on Facebook eventually, and you'd be mad that I kept it a secret."

"I wish I could help from two thousand miles away."

"I know, but I can't imagine you'd be very good at tissue paper roses," Mom said. "Paper roses made by me with one hand will probably still look better than paper roses made by you."

"You're probably right."

"I could use a few prayers," Mom said, almost as an afterthought. She didn't often bring up religion with Zach, but this was an emergency. She thought prayers helped.

"If it will make you feel better, Mom, I'll send a prayer up tonight."

"It will." She paused, as if letting the idea of prayer soak in a little. "You can do something else."

"What?"

"Find someone in Shawano who needs you. If you do something nice for someone else, the good karma is bound to get back to me."

Zach chuckled. "One minute you're a Christian, the next you're a Buddhist."

"Christians believe in karma. 'Cast your bread upon the waters and you shall find it after many days.' "

"Okay, Mom. I know better than to get into a Bible discussion with you."

"Get some sleep, Zach, and find a restaurant that will serve you a few vegetables."

"This ramen contains parsley flakes."

"Good night, son."

"Love you, Mom." When he finished his residency, he'd find a practice close to home so he could look out for his mom. He'd see to it that she never had to climb a ladder again.

He'd lost his appetite. He slowly picked the hot dogs out of the noodles and popped them into his mouth. The grocery store was still open. Maybe he should go buy a head of lettuce or something. He imagined himself eating a whole head of lettuce like an apple. That had to be three or four servings of vegetables right there.

His phone vibrated again.

"Hello, Dr. Reynolds? This is Patti Gordon from the answering service. You know that Amish woman you did surgery on to-day?"

"Yes."

"Well, I think she called me. She told me her name was Anna and that she really needed to talk to you. I told her I'd have you call her, but she said she really needed you to come to her house."

Zach thought of Anna's granddaughter and smoothed his hair with his fingers. "Did she say what was wrong?"

"No. I told her if she had an emergency to go to the hospital, but she hung up the phone. I tried calling back, but no one answered."

"Thanks, Patti. I'll see if I can reach her."

Even though he had it memorized, Zach opened the address book on his phone and scrolled to the forbidden number. He stared at it, picturing the blonde angel with the red scarf. Would she be mad if he called?

Blonde angel or no blonde angel, Anna wouldn't have tried to contact him unless something was wrong, and his first concern had to be for his patient. Anna had come through surgery well, but she was eighty-four years old. Age was always a risk factor, no matter how routine the surgery.

His fingers shook, actually shook, as he highlighted Cassie's number and pressed the screen to connect. He cleared his throat. It wouldn't do anything for Cassie's confidence in him as a doctor if he sounded like a lovesick teenager.

The phone rang and rang. And rang. What? Cassie didn't even have voice mail? He hung up and tried again. Three times. Had a burglar come and tied them all up? Or had there been a fire, and they were all out on the front lawn watching their house go up in flames?

Anna was supposed to be at home, and someone responsible *with a phone* was supposed to be with her at all times. Where were they? Had they gone to the emergency room and left Cassie's phone sitting on the kitchen counter?

Zach stood and paced the room a couple of times before trying the number again. No answer. If Anna were a normal patient, he would have given up by now, figuring she'd call back if she really needed to talk to him. But Anna was not a normal patient. Zach didn't know enough about the Amish to decide if he should be concerned or not.

It only took him about ten seconds to make the decision. He'd feel much better if he knew for sure that Anna was all right. Besides, Anna had her heart set on a visit from the doctor. Mom would say it was good karma.

He shoved his hand into his back pocket and pulled out the ripped corner of the magazine that Anna had written her address on.

Huckleberry Hill, Park Road, Bonduel, Wisconsin.

What kind of an address was that? Maybe Huckleberry Hill was an Amish old-folks home. He looked it up on his phone. No listing for an old-folks home in Bonduel under Huckleberry Hill. He hoped this wasn't a wild goose chase.

Or a wild huckleberry chase.

He couldn't be sure which.

CHAPTER SIX

"Dawdi, have you seen my phone?"

Cassie glanced around the great room. She didn't really want to spend a lot of time looking for her missing phone. It would turn up. It couldn't have gone far. She remembered having it when she came into the house. For all she knew, Mammi could be sitting on it.

Cassie swept the floor as Dawdi washed up the dinner dishes. Her cousin Moses and his wife Lia had been kind enough to bring dinner for them tonight after they came home from the hospital. They had brought fried chicken, green beans with bacon, Jell-O salad, and the flakiest, most buttery rolls Cassie had ever tasted. Lia was a very good cook. She'd made enough for an entire houseful of Amish folks. They'd be eating leftovers for days.

Mammi relaxed in Dawdi's recliner with her feet propped up, dozing on and off while

Dawdi and Cassie finished cleaning up. A tube dangled from Mammi's tightly wrapped foot and connected to a small appliance about the size of a toaster. Dr. Reynolds had called it a wound vacuum. It sucked moisture from Mammi's surgical site to help it heal for a skin graft in three weeks.

Dr. Reynolds had been so kind at the hospital today that Cassie had almost started to like him. He hadn't pressed the issue of wanting to go out with her, and he hadn't tried to make her feel guilty for saying no. However he felt about her, he had treated her with uncommon courtesy and had been more than attentive to Mammi. He hadn't talked down to her grandparents like some doctors did with old people. Mammi and Dawdi were both still sharp as tacks. Sometimes Cassie felt like they were the only family she had left. She had a soft spot for anybody who treated her grandparents kindly.

Even Dr. Zach Reynolds.

Cassie's lips curled involuntarily when she remembered the look on his face when he requested her phone number that last time. He had been sincerely reluctant to ask. She found his unexpected hesitation kind of cute.

And what was it about his nose that made

his face so attractive? Being a little crooked meant it had probably been broken sometime in the past, but judging by that devil-may-care grin he usually wore, Cassie could just imagine that he'd been doing something wildly reckless and incredibly fun when he had broken it.

"Is everything all right, yet?" Dawdi asked.

"Oh, jah, everything is fine. Don't I look fine?"

"Well," he said, with a spark of amusement in his eyes, "you're sweeping the dog."

Cassie looked down. She was indeed brushing the broom back and forth across Sparky's back. The unconventional fur cleaning hadn't disturbed Mammi's little white dog in the least. She remained fast asleep in the corner next to the stove.

Cassie pulled the broom away and gazed at it as if it were a foreign object. What had she been thinking? How could the thought of a crooked nose distract her so thoroughly?

The recliner squeaked as Mammi shifted in it.

"Are you okay, Mammi?"

Mammi opened her eyes. "The pain medicine helps my foot, but it makes me feel like I'm floating away on a cloud. And I can't steer a cloud. I think I'd rather have control of all my faculties. There's still so much to be arranged. Who's going to do the arranging?"

"You just need to concentrate on feeling better, Mammi. Everything will still be here when you're on your feet again."

"The doctor won't. How am I supposed to work things out with the doctor if I can't even steer my cloud?"

Dawdi dried his hands before sitting on the sofa next to the recliner. "You've arranged things just fine yet, Annie."

She smiled and patted Dawdi's hand. "I suppose I have. But I'd rather not sleep through all the fun."

"I'll wake you if anything exciting happens." He turned and looked at Cassie. "But right now, she's just sweeping."

Cassie made her expression as earnest as possible. "I promise if I do anything exciting, you'll be the first to know. But studying for the GRE is about as boring as watching paint dry."

Someone knocked softly on the door as if they didn't want to be heard. Sparky, who hadn't woken up when Cassie swept her, immediately lifted her head and barked.

Mammi seemed to perk up as well. "No need to wake me, Felty. I'm ready for the excitement."

Cassie propped the broom against the wall

and answered the door. The sight of Dr. Reynolds standing there with a crooked nose and a bright red scarf tied around his neck almost took her breath away. It was a good thing she wholeheartedly disliked him or she'd be in some danger of being pulled in by his good looks.

He eyed her doubtfully. "I'm sorry to bother you, but I had to make sure every-thing was okay. Your mammi —"

"Tell him to come in," Mammi called from across the room.

"Oh," Cassie said, stepping back and holding on to the doorknob as if it were a trusted friend. "Please come in, Doctor. I didn't expect to see you."

Pulling the beanie off his head, he stepped tentatively into the room. "I apologize."

"No apology necessary," Dawdi said, jumping to his feet. He strode across the room and shook the doctor's hand vigor-ously. "Anna will feel much better now that you're here."

"I know this is unconventional," the doc-tor said, "but Anna called and the answer-ing service said it sounded urgent, but no one answered when I tried calling back. I got worried. If she were my mom, I would want the doctor to come and check on her."

"Mammi called you?"

He glanced at Cassie as if asking forgiveness for every bad thing he'd ever done. She was nearly inclined to give it to him. Darn that crooked nose!

"Come and let me have a look at you," Mammi said.

Dr. Reynolds gave Sparky a pat before walking past Cassie to the recliner. "Is everything okay? They said you sounded very upset over the phone. How is the pain?"

"She's on a cloud," Dawdi said. "I think she's feeling fine."

Zach nodded and got on one knee next to the recliner. "Can I do anything for you? Are you drinking plenty of liquids?"

"I'm feeling much better now," Mammi said. "There's nothing quite like a doctor to make everything better."

Cassie sidled near Mammi's recliner. "When did you call the doctor?"

Mammi pulled Cassie's phone from her apron pocket. "About an hour ago. I hope you don't mind that I used your phone."

"Of . . . course not," Cassie stammered. Mammi had stolen her phone to make an unnecessary call to the doctor? "I'm sorry, Dr. Reynolds. We really were trying to make sure that she rested comfortably."

His smile made her feel warm all the way to her toes. "It's okay. I was concerned when I couldn't get hold of you. I'm not sure what the Amish protocol is. But I was happy to come over. It's my first time in an Amish home."

"You're wearing my scarf," Mammi said, smiling as if she were floating on a cloud.

"Rose Sue's mom dropped it off at the registration desk."

"Here," Dawdi said. "Let me take your coat."

"I'm not going to stay," the doctor said, standing up. "I just wanted to make sure Anna was all right."

"Well, of course you're going to stay," Mammi said. "I counted on it."

"Thank you anyway, but I've imposed on your privacy long enough. I'll see you next week."

"Felty, make him stay," Mammi said with a mixture of amusement and scolding in her voice.

Although Cassie was eager for the doctor to leave, she would have done anything to make Mammi happy. "Have you eaten dinner, Dr. Reynolds?"

He nodded as a smile slowly formed on his lips. "Ramen and hot dogs."

"That's a sad excuse for a meal," Mammi said. "No one goes hungry in an Amish home. One thing we know how to do is to

103

feed people."

Cassie raised her eyebrows. "We've got cold fried chicken and homemade rolls."

"I couldn't impose," he said halfheartedly, wanting her to talk him into it.

"And Cassie made chocolate chip cookies," Mammi said.

Cassie was already halfway to the fridge. "If a doctor went to your mom's house to check up on her, she'd feed him."

He chuckled. "I suppose she would. She'd say it was good karma."

"Let me take your coat," Dawdi said.

The doctor slid his coat off his wide shoulders — not that Cassie noticed things like wide shoulders — and handed his hat, scarf, and coat to Dawdi. "I hate to impose," he said one more time.

Cassie retrieved the food from the fridge and a plate from the cupboard. She put a hearty piece of chicken on the plate as well as a scoop of Jell-O salad, green beans, and a golden brown roll. She motioned for the doctor to sit at the table where she deposited the plate and utensils, three cookies, and a tall glass of milk.

"I hope you don't mind that it's cold. We don't have a microwave, although I could warm up the beans in a saucepan, if you like."

"This is perfect. Thank you," Zach said, flashing an enchanting smile. "I don't eat this well at Thanksgiving."

"Mammi and Dawdi, do you want anything?"

Dawdi sat on the sofa and seemed to make himself very comfortable. "Not a thing."

Mammi laced her fingers together. "We'll sit right over here and not make a peep."

Cassie smiled to herself. Mammi would do anything to make her guests feel at home, but Dr. Reynolds probably would not require complete silence during his meal.

She dished herself a small bowl of Jell-O salad and sat next to him at the table. She didn't want him to feel awkward eating alone.

Dr. Reynolds took a big bite of chicken, and by the expression on his face, Cassie would have thought he'd died and gone straight to heaven. "Do the Amish always eat this well?"

"They take their food very seriously. Food is a way to bring families and communities together."

He held up a spoonful of Jell-O. "Did you make this? It's got cool little squares of gelatin inside of it."

"No, my cousin's wife Lia made it."

He picked up a cookie and took a bite.

"But you made the cookies."

She nodded.

"They're the best I've ever tasted."

Cassie refused to blush. How could they be the best he'd ever tasted? She shrugged off his praise. "I can cook, but I'd rather draw."

"Thus the art history major."

Cassie's cheeks got warm. "And for the record, I don't look at naked people all day."

He chuckled. "Neither do I." He relished another bite. "Do the Amish allow drawing?"

"My *onkel* Perry paints farm scenes on milk cans. We don't do portraits, but outdoor scenes are permitted."

"Did you want to do portraits? Is that why you left? Or is that too personal a question?"

He seemed so troubled about offending her that Cassie gave him a reassuring smile. "I don't mind," she said. "I couldn't see living this way for the rest of my life. It's a good life, but I wanted to get an education. I wanted to see more of the world than the twenty square miles that most people here grow up, live, and die in."

"But she isn't going to hell," Dawdi interjected from the sofa.

"Felty," Mammi said, "we're not to make a peep."

106

The doctor studied her face. "You looked sad just then. Do you regret your decision? Are you afraid you're going to hell?"

"My mamm and brothers think I am."

He bent his head to look her in the eye. "Too personal?"

Absentmindedly, she tapped the spoon against her bowl. "Sometimes I regret what I left behind. Life in an Amish community is predictable. It goes on pretty much the same as it has for decades. And there may be strict rules, but the people don't often let you down. They adhere to a set of values, and they try to live their religion."

"It's very admirable."

"Too many people don't believe in decency or self-control. Out there can be a very ugly place." She clapped her mouth shut. She'd come dangerously close to accusing Dr. Reynolds to his face. She didn't ever want to have a confrontation with the doctor. Let him live in blissful ignorance.

Besides, she sounded bitter, like a sour old preacher who resented other people's lives and begrudged them their happiness. Cassie didn't want to begrudge anybody anything.

Something subtle shifted in the doctor's expression. "It sounds like maybe you've had some bad experiences."

"Amish boys aren't like other boys. I never had to wonder about why boys wanted to take me home from a gathering. And I didn't have to be suspicious if they asked to take me on a drive. When I got to the university, I was pretty naïve."

He finally averted his eyes and skewered a green bean with his fork. "Now I know I've crossed the 'too personal' line."

She felt herself blush again. "I sound terribly disillusioned."

"No. Sooner or later we all figure out that the world is an unfriendly place."

"Now *you* sound disillusioned."

"I do, don't I?" He sprouted a crooked grin and took another hearty bite of chicken.

"I'm not sorry I left," Cassie said. "I sometimes forget that the grass isn't always greener on the other side of the fence, especially since I've been in that particular pasture before."

Dr. Reynolds had nearly devoured everything on his plate. "I don't mean to sound like some hardened cynic. There's a lot of good in the world, and I guess we all have to realize that even though people will disappoint us, we can't lose faith in the entire human race."

Cassie nodded. "You're right. Good doesn't exist exclusively inside our little

Amish community."

"There are eight billion people out there," Dawdi interjected from the sofa.

"Now, Felty," Mammi scolded. "Not a peep."

The doctor turned and grinned at her grandparents. "Some of the finest people in the world are right here in this room."

A warm liquid traveled through Cassie's veins. Dr. Reynolds was making all sorts of points with her tonight. Was he doing it on purpose?

Loudly scraping her chair out from under the table, she stood and marched to the fridge. "Would you like more chicken, Doctor?"

His eyes widened as if he'd found an extra present under the Christmas tree. "There's more?"

She stifled a giggle and pulled two pieces from the plastic bag. "Do you like drumsticks?"

"I would die for a drumstick."

This time she did giggle.

He smiled back at her. "Have pity on me. I haven't had good fried chicken in a long time."

"I think you'd better come over more often, Doctor," Mammi said, breaking her own rule. "Your mamm wouldn't want you to waste away to nothing."

Cassie laid both drumsticks on Zach's plate. He picked one up and offered it to her. "I don't want to hog all the food."

She raised her hands and backed away. "I wouldn't dream of it. I'd rather not see you cry like a baby."

It wasn't fair, the way he smiled and made Cassie's insides feel like they were doing a square dance. "You're right. I would cry like a baby. This is just like my mom used to make."

"I will have Felty get you a bottle of my peaches for you to take home," Anna said. "There's nothing like home-bottled fruit to warm your insides."

After Cassie made sure there was no danger of his trying to give her one of the drumsticks, she sat back down. "Does your mother live in California?"

Furrowing his brow, he paused mid-bite and gazed at her. The emotion didn't last long, whatever it was. He put down his half-eaten piece of chicken. "She still lives in the house where I grew up. In Gilroy, the garlic capital of the world."

Cassie raised her eyebrows. "Garlic capital? I didn't smell anything when you came in."

He chuckled. "I bathe regularly."

"What about your dad? Do you have brothers and sisters?"

"My dad's gone, and I have two older brothers. They both work out of the country doing big and important things."

"Your mamm must be very proud of you," Dawdi said.

"Of course she's proud," Mammi said. "Her son's a doctor. Isn't that a wonderful thing, Cassie?" Mammi and Dawdi obviously wanted to be more involved in the conversation than they pretended they did.

Cassie curled her lips and glanced sideways at Dr. Reynolds. "Wonderful gute, Mammi."

"Does she live by herself?" Mammi asked. "You said you hoped a doctor would check on her just like you wanted to check on me."

A shadow flitted across his face. "As soon as I finish my residency I'm going back there to be close to her. She called me earlier tonight and told me she broke her arm falling off a ladder."

"Oh no," Cassie said. "That's terrible." And it truly was. She could see it in his face.

"She wanted to clean the rain gutters. I keep telling her to save the hard jobs for me."

"I'm sorry," she said. "I'm sure it's difficult being this far away. I wish there was something we could do."

His expression softened. "I wish there was something I could do. She's got all these paper roses she's supposed to make for some bazaar, and she's only got one hand. I even offered to fly home and help, but she thinks I'd make a mess of them."

"I could knit a cover for her cast," Mammi said.

"That's very kind, but I don't think —"

Mammi sat a little taller as if ready to start knitting at that very moment. "I've got weeks and weeks to do nothing. I'd be happy to knit a cast cover for your mamm. I would knit a beanie, but I know it doesn't get cold in California. And a cast cover will protect her arm if she bangs it against the wall."

Cassie smiled to herself as she pictured the doctor's mom pounding her cast against the wall just to test out her cast cover. Dr. Reynolds's eyes danced as he glanced at Cassie. She smiled and nodded, encouraging him to accept Mammi's offer. They'd all be happier if he did.

"That's very kind of you," he said.

"Wonderful gute," Mammi said. She took a small notebook and pen from her apron pocket. "What is her name and address? I'll mail it to her as soon as it's done."

"Julie Reynolds, 1420 Montoya Street, Gilroy, California."

Mammi carefully jotted down the information. "What is her favorite color?"

"Uh, I have no idea."

Propping on one elbow, Mammi reached down and retrieved her knitting bag from the floor next to the recliner. "I have some pink left over from a baby blanket I made for the auction. I'll use that."

"Auction?" Zach asked.

Mammi took an empty set of knitting needles from her bag. "There's an auction next week to raise money to help pay Miriam Sensenig's medical bills. She was in a car accident three weeks ago and her neck is a mess."

The corners of Zach's mouth drooped. "The Amish don't have insurance. That's one of the first things they told me at the hospital."

"It's all right," Mammi said. "We're tough. We can handle it."

"I'm sure you can. But tell me more about this auction. Do they raise enough money to even make a dent in the bills?"

"Jah," Cassie said. "Lots of Englisch come, especially when we have a haystack supper."

"Wait. Haystack supper? Englisch? Those

113

aren't terms I've heard before."

"You really do need a tutor." Cassie felt immediately sorry for opening her mouth. It wasn't very nice of her to remind him that she'd flat-out refused to be his tutor.

"I really do," he replied, teasing her with a look of mock longing.

She returned his smile, glad she hadn't offended him then quickly wiped the smile off her face. Why was she enjoying his company so much? This was Zach Reynolds, frat boy, party animal, and leader of Finn McEwan's little hook-up club. If she showed any chink in her armor, the charming Dr. Reynolds would try to seduce her faster than an Amish mammi could knit a pot holder. She'd be just another one of the many girls who had been taken in by his good looks and movie-star smile.

Mammi pointed the sharp end of her knitting needle at him. "Dr. Reynolds, you must come to the auction next Saturday. Everybody will be there, including Cassie's family. You really should meet . . ." She seemed to reconsider whatever it was she was going to say next. "You really should meet the bishop."

"Oh," Zach said, "does the bishop need to approve me?"

"Something like that," Dawdi offered at

the same time that Cassie said, "No, not at all."

Zach's gaze traveled from Dawdi to Cassie and back again. "Is it permitted for me to come? I'm not Amish." He forced her to make eye contact. "I'd really like to come, but I don't want to make anyone uncomfortable."

"Stuff and nonsense," Mammi said. "We'll feel downtrodden if you don't come."

"Downtrodden and depressed," Dawdi added, though he seemed more delighted than anything else.

Zach shrugged and flashed a cocky grin. "I'd love to."

Cassie gave him a polite smile. What did she care if he came to the auction or not? He could be as persuasive as he wanted to. She would never sleep with him.

"Of course, I won't be going, with my foot the way it is," Mammi said. "But Felty can show you around."

Zach reduced his chicken to a pile of bones on his plate. "That was delicious. I can't tell you how much I appreciate it." He scooted his chair back from the table. "Now that I've eaten my weight in chicken and rolls, I'd better get going. I've got a long day of acne and warts tomorrow. The life of a dermatologist."

"Is that the kind of doctor you want to be?" Cassie asked.

He shook his head. "A pediatrician. I love kids."

She hadn't expected that. Zach Reynolds didn't seem like the kind of guy who had any use for children.

Mammi held out her hand. Dr. Reynolds immediately went to her and took it. "Denki for coming, Doctor. I'll be able to sleep much better tonight seeing how well things are going."

Zach patted Mammi's hand reassuringly. "If you need anything else, Anna, call me." He took a business card from his pocket and wrote something on it before handing it to Mammi. "Here is my direct number. Call me anytime. If I'm with a patient, I won't answer, but I'll be in touch as soon as I can."

Cassie's heart leaped to her throat. "Oh, no, Doctor, that isn't necessary. We'll be fine. Mammi won't need to call again."

"Jah, I will," Mammi said. "Several times."

"But you're tough, Mammi, remember?"

"Not that tough. It will do my heart good to see the doctor again."

Cassie turned to Zach. "It's really not necessary, Dr. Reynolds. We can't ask you to —"

"Miss Coblenz, please don't worry. I want to make your grandmother as comfortable as possible."

Miss Coblenz. It sounded so distant, as if there were a wide, yawning chasm separating them.

And that was the way she wanted it. He wouldn't dream of trying to make her one of his conquests if they were on opposite sides of the universe.

Dawdi handed Dr. Reynolds his coat and beanie. "We'll see you at the auction, Doctor."

Dr. Reynolds acted as if he were looking forward to it. "You will, Felty. What time should I pick you up?"

Cassie's heart leaped in alarm. "You don't need to do that."

"It's my pleasure, unless you'd rather not. I'm not putting any pressure on you." He cleared his throat and looked at Dawdi. "Maybe it's best if I meet you there."

"Pick them up at four o'clock," Mammi said.

Dr. Reynolds eyed Cassie as if waiting for her consent, but she couldn't very well tell him no. It wasn't as if it were a date or anything. Mammi and Dawdi were the ones who had asked him, and it wouldn't be very nice to refuse the doctor's offer. She managed a weak smile and nodded.

He returned her smile and put on his coat. "Okay. Four o'clock." After an awkward silence of him staring at Cassie and Cassie staring at the floor, Dr. Reynolds leaned casually against the door. "Miss Coblenz, I know it's cold, but do you mind coming outside for a minute?"

She had to concentrate very hard to keep from choking on his invitation. Certainly he wasn't going to ask her out, was he? She studied his expression and saw nothing there to give her alarm. He'd behaved himself very well tonight. She'd trust him as far as the porch.

He must have sensed her hesitation. He curled the corners of his mouth upward, showing a hint of bright white teeth. The look suited his face very well. "I don't bite."

She forced a casual laugh. "Yes, I know."

I know? Oh sis yuscht, *what a stupid thing to say.*

"Good-bye, Anna, Felty. Call if you need me."

"You can be sure we'll need you," Mammi said.

Cassie followed him outside, not even bothering to take her coat. The cold would force him to keep the conversation short.

Earlier, Dawdi had lit the lantern that

hung on the peg outside the front door. Zach took it from the peg and trudged down the porch steps to the dark shape that must have been his car. Or was that her car?

Two identical Honda Accords, same silver color, same style, and as far as Cassie could tell, same year sat side by side in Mammi and Dawdi's lane.

Dr. Reynolds motioned to her car, which she could tell was her car by the sparkly crystal angel that hung from her rearview mirror. "Your car, I assume?"

Cassie's jaw dropped. She inclined her head in the direction of the other Honda. "Yours?"

He chuckled at the look on her face. "My dad bought this car brand-new twenty-one years ago. All three of us boys drove it to high school. It hasn't been in one accident, and considering what a bad driver my brother Drew is, it's kind of a miracle."

"I can't believe we have the exact same car."

"We have matching red scarves and matching Honda Accords. It's spooky," he said, his eyes dancing in the lantern's glow.

She gave her car an affectionate pat. "My air-conditioning doesn't work anymore."

"I've reupholstered the driver's seat with duct tape."

Cassie folded her arms around herself to ward off the cold. "It was a struggle getting up Huckleberry Hill."

"Me too. I almost drove backward down the hill and gave up." After gently setting the lantern on the top of his car, he gave her a tentative smile, shrugged off his coat, and wrapped it around her shoulders. She tried to refuse it, but he shook his head and backed away. "I don't want you to catch cold."

Surrendering to the welcome warmth, she tugged the coat tighter around her, catching a whiff of cologne that still clung to it. It smelled earthy, like the mossy woods on a rainy morning. It was all she could do not to bury her face into the folds of fabric and breathe it in. Better to escape to the safety of the house.

"Thank you," she said, "but I really should go in."

Frowning, he shoved his hands in the pockets of his jeans and studied one of the footprints they'd made in the snow. "Can I ask you something?"

"Okay." *Just don't ask me out. If you ask me out I'll have to refuse you again, and I'd really rather not ramp up the awkwardness between us.*

He lifted his head and studied her face.

120

"While I drove up here in between moments of sheer panic on the icy roads, I remembered something that happened this morning." He massaged the stubble on his jaw. "You knew my last name before I told you."

Cassie's throat dried out like a puddle in the desert. She lowered her eyes and gazed at the same footprint Zach had been so interested in. "I don't remember that."

"You also knew that I'm from California. I don't think I shared that piece of information with you earlier." He propped his foot on the bumper of his car and leaned his elbow on his leg. "Miss Coblenz, will you look at me?"

She didn't want to have this conversation. She just wanted him to go. No confrontation, no discomfort. It would be easier if they could both pretend nothing had happened. But it wasn't likely he'd let her get away with "easier." Reluctantly she raised her eyes to his.

"I'm looking," she said.

"Your mammi said you went to UChicago."

She nodded.

"We had some sort of encounter there, didn't we? I don't know why I don't remember you. I can't imagine ever forgetting your face. But you remember me. I probably did something vile, and you've carried it with you all these years." His intense gaze pierced hers until she thought she might melt.

He took a step back and curled one side of his mouth upward. "Or maybe you've seen me play soccer and think I'm a terrible player. Is that why you didn't want to give me your phone number?"

"You're an . . . excellent player. Like a brick wall in the backfield."

"I'm making you uncomfortable."

"It doesn't matter."

He winced. "How can you say it doesn't matter? I've completely ruined my chances with the most beautiful, fascinating girl I've ever met, and I don't even know why."

She tightened his coat around her. Oh, how she hated confrontation. She'd rather spell it out in a nice long letter than say anything to his face. "Can I send you an email?"

He slumped his shoulders and frowned as if his mom had broken her leg as well as her arm. "That bad, huh?"

She swallowed hard. She should give him a chance to defend himself, even though there wasn't any possible justification for what he'd done. It would be pretty mean to make him wait for an email.

"My freshman year. Your senior year," she

stammered. "My roommate Tonya helped Finn McEwan get elected president of your little club."

He drew his eyebrows together. "My little club?"

"You premeds thought it was so fun, and I'm sure you had plenty of laughs over it, but a lot of girls got hurt."

Even in the dim light of the lantern, she could see a scowl form at the corners of his mouth. "Did you . . . you and Finn . . . ?"

Her stomach clenched when she realized what he was asking. "Me? Never. How could you think . . . ?"

"I'm sorry. I didn't mean to —"

"Yes, you did mean to." Cassie trembled with indignation. "Finn was a jerk. Tonya was devastated, and Finn only cared about the points. Tonya cried her eyes out while you stood there and yelled at us."

She pursed her lips together. Had she really been so bold as to say exactly what she was thinking? The doctor would probably be so offended that he'd jump in his car and drive down that hill so fast he'd break the sound barrier.

Deep lines etched themselves on his face. "When did I yell at you?"

"Girls aren't people to you. They're objects to be used for bragging rights. It's despicable."

"Girls were lining up to be in the club." Zach yanked the beanie off his head and ran his fingers through his hair. "I can't believe I'm defending Finn McEwan, but believe me, the girls were not the victims. They wouldn't stop calling him. It shocked me at how many willing girls he recruited."

Cassie turned away from him. "Shocked? Really? And how many girls did you recruit?"

Zach growled in frustration. "Finn McEwan was an — okay, Finn was a jerk. He was my roommate, but we weren't friends. I'm no saint, Miss Coblenz, but I was never a part of that club."

She didn't know if she believed him or not. Why should he be any different than all the other college boys she knew?

Sensing her skepticism, Zach lowered his voice and leaned toward her. "My mom wouldn't have liked it." He tensed the muscles of his jaw. "Which isn't to say that my mom would like a lot of things I do, but Finn's club was way out of line."

Cassie deflated like a balloon and leaned on the hood of her car. "Oh."

He looked at her out of the corner of his eye. "And you've hated me ever since?"

Her chest felt heavy, and she found it an

effort to breathe. "I guess I made some unfair assumptions about you. I should have kept my mouth shut."

He folded his arms across his chest. "I'm glad you said something. It's better than being rejected and not ever knowing why."

"But what do you think of me now, a woman who professes to be a Christian but can't even forgive you for something you did four years ago?"

"Something I *didn't* do four years ago."

"Exactly," she said.

"What do I think of you? I think you have really pretty eyes."

She ignored the quickening of her pulse. That was unprofessional and uncalled for and he had completely sidestepped her question.

He furrowed his brow. "Tell me about the time I yelled at you."

"It doesn't matter."

"Uh-uh. Don't rob me of the chance to apologize."

She sighed in surrender. "It was our fault anyway. We shouldn't have come over."

"No one deserves to be yelled at unless the house is on fire," he said.

"Tonya asked me to go to your apartment with her so she could talk to Finn. We stood out on the doorstep in the rain while Tonya begged Finn to take her back. He was pretty cold about it. Tonya made enough noise that you came to the door and started yelling at her to shut up. She was desperate, and I was humiliated. I had to pry her fingers from the doorjamb so you could close it."

"At least I didn't slam her fingers in the door." He smiled weakly at his own joke and then sobered. "I don't remember yelling at you, but I'm sorry."

"It was four years ago. I should be over it by now."

Frowning, he scrubbed his hand down the side of his face. "I must have made quite an impression on you. This really isn't a good reason, but I lost patience with more than one of Finn's girls. I was already annoyed with him for starting that stupid club, and I had a hard time studying with girls coming around all hours day or night, either wanting in on the club or whining that Finn had used them."

Cassie nibbled on her fingernail. "I suppose I remember it so well because it was my first taste of what the outside world is really like. I was fresh from Bonduel with the silly notion that people believed in things like virtue and purity and self-control."

"A lot of people believe in those things."

"In college, it was hard to find anybody who believed in those things. By my third year, I wasn't shocked by much of anything."

"So I destroyed your faith in mankind?"

She looked away. "Not single-handedly, no."

He furrowed his brow. "Is there anything I can do to make it up to you?"

"It's not your fault. It's not even Finn's fault. I made the choice to leave the protection of my community. I can't return to blissful ignorance, no matter how badly I'd like to. And sometimes I sorely wish I could."

She had definitely said too much. He looked at her as if he knew her, as if they shared some intimate connection that only friends could understand. No matter how polite or handsome or sensitive he seemed to be, Cassie didn't want to be friends with Zach Reynolds. Even though she liked him better than she had just a few minutes ago, she knew he'd only disappoint her in the end. They always did. "You're shivering," she said, sliding his coat off her shoulders. The cold air immediately attacked her and chilled her to the bone. "You should put your coat on."

He refused to take it from her outstretched

hand. "You wear it. I'm trying to keep you out here talking as long as I can."

"It will be a very one-sided conversation if you freeze to death."

"A small price to pay for your company." His grin froze when his eyes met hers. "On the other hand, I probably should get going. I've got an eight o'clock patient tomorrow."

Had she hurt his feelings? Not likely for a guy like Dr. Reynolds. But she had shaken his aggravating confidence. The doctor was very good at picking up on her nonverbal cues, and she appreciated that he wasn't the pushy type, at least as far as she was concerned. How many guys at school even knew how to take "no" for an answer?

He took his coat, put it on, and pulled his keys from the pocket. "Thanks for feeding me."

"Thank you for dropping by to see my mammi. She acts cheerful enough, but I know she's worried. She probably mentioned your name a dozen times after we came home from the hospital. She has a lot of confidence in you." She let a wisp of a smile play at her lips just so he knew there were no hard feelings. "And so do I."

Her praise seemed to make him happier than a whole plate of fried chicken. "I'm glad to hear it. I'll do my best to live up to it." He took the lantern from the roof of his car, handed it to her, and unlocked his car door manually with the key. His automatic lock was probably broken like hers. It had been that way for years.

"You locked your car? In Bonduel, Wisconsin?"

He gave her a wry grin. "Old habit. I'm from California, remember?"

"If you start to slide, turn your tires in the direction the back of your car is sliding. That might help you arrive without wrapping yourself around a tree."

"Fifi."

She arched an eyebrow.

"That's what I named my car," he said.

"Mine's The Beast."

He rested his arm on top of his open car door. "Fifi and The Beast. Sounds like a grunge band."

"Or a Disney movie."

He chuckled. "Is your key the basic kind like mine?"

She took her key chain out of her coat pocket and jangled it in front of his face. "The automatic lock doesn't work anymore."

"Me too. How have we survived this long?"

The keys slipped from her hands and into the snow. Dr. Reynolds bent over and picked them up then paused to examine the acrylic charm dangling from the ring. "What's this?"

"Oh, nothing. Proof that I'm an art history geek. It's a painting by George Frederic Watts."

The doctor held it up for a better look. "A knight in shining armor."

"Sir Galahad. One of my favorites. Watts captures the essence of Tennyson's poem. 'My strength is as the strength of ten because my heart is pure.' " She cleared her throat and took the keys from his outstretched hand. No need to bore Dr. Reynolds to death. "I should be going in now."

The doctor smiled. "See you on Saturday, Miss Coblenz."

Rational or not, she found herself looking forward to it. He shut the door and started his car, which made the same high-pitched squeaky groan that Cassie's did when she started hers.

She had no problem with Dr. Reynolds coming to the auction on Saturday. He was charming and funny, and her expectations were so low that he couldn't possibly disappoint her. Besides, he was coming because Mammi wanted him to, not Cassie. She might be able to spend much of the day at the auction without his really noticing her.

She marched to the house with all due speed. Something told her that she wouldn't escape his notice that easily. Her rebellious heart pounded with anticipation.

CHAPTER SEVEN

Cassie lifted her arms and pulled the dress over her head. All things considered, it wasn't too bad. Mamm, in a flurry of excited meddling, had brought it over yesterday. She had told Cassie that she wanted her to be in Plain dress for the auction so as not to shame the family. That was most of the truth. The other part of it was that Mamm still held out hope that Cassie would fall in love with an Amish boy, specifically Elmer Lee Kanagy, and return to the fold so she could marry him.

Cassie sighed. Sooner or later Mamm would have to come to grips with the fact that Cassie wasn't coming back. But not today. Mamm had sewn Cassie a new dress. Cassie could humor her mother for a few weeks. It didn't hurt anybody for Cassie to wear the dress, and Mamm would sleep a thousand times better tonight because of it.

The new dress was of the Plain style, with

hem well past the knees, fabric cut high at the neck with no buttons, long sleeves, and a loose waistband. Simple, as expected. But her mother had actually taken her by surprise with her choice of color.

The dress was pink. Pretty, pastel, baby-soft pink.

In other circumstances, her mother would have called it a "peacock" dress, but she had let slip yesterday that Elmer Lee loved seeing girls in pink. No doubt Mamm hadn't been able to resist.

Cassie used several extra bobby pins to secure her hair into a bun. It was harder to keep in place cut this short. She slid the crisp white kapp, another gift from Mamm, over her hair and deftly secured it with straight pins. She didn't own a pair of sensible black shoes like so many Amish women wore, so she opted for black stockings and her black flats with the silver buckle on the toe. She looked Plain enough. Lord willing, no one would be offended by her shoes.

Except Mamm. Sometimes Cassie's very existence offended her mother.

She took one last look at herself in the round hand mirror that Mammi kept in the top drawer. It was about the diameter of a DVD. Even though the Plain people considered it vain, Cassie definitely preferred the full-length Englisch mirrors, where she could actually see all of her face at the same time.

She didn't look awful. Dr. Reynolds probably wouldn't consider her repulsive. Why did her pulse quicken at the very thought of Dr. Reynolds and his boyish grin? She had no interest whatsoever in impressing Zach Reynolds.

He wouldn't look twice at a girl in plain Amish clothes, even if her dress happened to be pink. He probably had a preference for sequins, glitter, and conspicuous cleavage. Why he'd even been interested in asking her out in the first place was a mystery. She wasn't exactly the flashy type.

She heard someone knock on the door and scolded herself when her heart clattered around in her chest and a ribbon of warmth snaked its way up her spine. It wasn't as if she'd never seen a good-looking guy before.

"Come in," she heard her mammi call from the recliner.

Cassie strolled down the hall into the great room. It hadn't taken Mammi long to create her own little space around Dawdi's recliner. Early in the week, Cassie had pushed the end table closer to the recliner so Mammi would have a place for her medicines, a glass of water, and a plate of cookies in case she got hungry. Cassie had made a big batch of oatmeal raisin cookies this morning, and Mammi had a generous plateful ready at her left.

A bag of yarn sat at Mammi's feet, within reach in case Mammi needed to snatch another color. To Mammi's right, also within easy reach, Dawdi had set up a wobbly card table for all of Mammi's knitting projects. A pair of needles stuck out of the beginnings of a blanket, and a skein of salmon-colored yarn waited to be made into a pair of baby booties. Mammi didn't seem to mind all the time off her feet because it gave her a chance to get caught up and even ahead on her knitting.

And then there was that box of tissue paper hiding behind the recliner for a special project Cassie and Mammi were working on together.

Cassie walked past Mammi, who was working on pot holders for her closet. She often gave visitors a pot holder or two when they came over as a way of being extra hospitable. Since every visitor got a pot holder, Mammi constantly had to replenish the supply in her closet.

"*Ach, du lieva.* Oh, my goodness," Mammi said. "Cassie, you look as pretty as an orchard full of cherry blossoms."

"Yes, you do," Dr. Reynolds said. He'd let himself in and was leaning against the doorjamb sporting a dazzling smile. The room seemed to brighten like the sun peeking out from behind the clouds.

Cassie almost fanned herself to keep the blush from traveling up her face. The doctor really shouldn't look at girls that way. It made them feel goofy and stupid and rendered them incapable of forming a complete sentence. "Hello . . . are you . . . the welcome . . . auction."

He stepped into the room and shut the door behind him without taking his eyes from Cassie. "You are . . ." He stared at her for about five years as if he were stunned speechless, until he seemed to remember himself and snap out of whatever daze he was in. "You are matching," he finally said.

"Excuse me?"

He sprouted a twitchy grin and took off his coat to reveal a light pink button-down shirt that looked as crisp and flawless as if it had been starched and ironed three minutes ago. The light color accented the tan in his face and made him look like he'd just stepped out of a fashion magazine. His light brown, short-cropped hair was tousled, as if he'd just returned from saving a whole litter of kittens and puppies from a windstorm and hadn't had time to comb his hair but it hadn't mattered because his hair was perfect anyway.

He looked casually handsome, like he didn't care about his appearance even when he couldn't help being so good-looking. It made him all the more attractive.

Oh my.

She did that incoherent babbling again. "Pink . . . I didn't expect . . . how did you . . ."

"I guess great minds think alike." That smile was so mesmerizing. "I know I shouldn't say this to a patient's granddaughter, but you look stunning."

"Stunning? In this dress? I think my mamm hoped for plain."

"I don't know what your mamm hoped for, but you look like an angel."

Cassie didn't know how to reply to such praise. "I don't think angels wear pink."

"They do," he said, before clearing his throat and looking away as if he'd just realized he'd been staring. "Was I supposed to dress Amish?"

"No," said Cassie, finally able to string a few words together. "My mamm asks that I dress like this when I mingle with the community. She doesn't want her daughter to shame her in front of her neighbors." She tried to keep her expression unemotional, but her eyes must have betrayed a glimmer of sadness she always felt when she thought about her family.

He looked truly sorry for her. "I can't imagine she'd be ashamed of you."

"It's okay. I'm wearing makeup as a protest."

"Power to the rebels," he said, pumping his fist in the air.

His expression teased a smile to her lips and heat to her face.

He strode across the room and knelt next to the recliner. "Anna, how are you feeling?"

"Very gute today, Doctor."

Mammi grabbed one of Cassie's cookies from the plate to her left. "Have a cookie, Doctor. Cassie made them this morning."

The doctor took a hearty bite. "Mmm," he said, with a pleasant smile on his lips. "You made these, Miss Coblenz?"

She nodded, way too hopeful that he'd like them. She tensed, even though she knew they tasted okay. She'd had three of them at lunch.

"Cassie's a very gute cook," Mammi said.

"They're like a little bit of heaven," he said. He finished it off in four bites. Cassie stared at the floor so the doctor wouldn't see her gratification. She appreciated a man who could appreciate good food. The two times she'd seen him eat, he had relished every bite. He probably didn't eat very well at his apartment.

Taking Mammi's hand, Zach asked, "How is the pain?"

"I hardly feel a thing."

"Are you staying off your feet?"

Mammi held up her knitting for the doctor to see. "I've got plenty to do right here in this chair."

The doctor took her hand. "Good. Did the home health nurse come this morning to change the dressing?"

"Jah," Mammi said. "She is a very nice girl. Very thorough. But it wonders me if you couldn't be the one to change my dressing. I'd feel better if you did it."

The doctor glanced at Cassie, probably wondering if there was some Amish protocol for this.

"Nae, Mammi," Cassie said. "The nurse does a fine job. We can't impose on the doctor that way."

"The nurses are actually better than us doctors when it comes to stuff like changing bandages," Dr. Reynolds said.

Mammi dropped her knitting and put her

hand over the doctor's. "We'll feed you."

He glanced at Cassie, for her rescue or her approval, she couldn't tell. "I don't know. It might be all right. I can talk to the powers that be. What do you think, Miss Coblenz?"

She momentarily lost her train of thought just imagining what a stir he'd make at the auction. Handsome Englischers in crisp pink shirts didn't show up in Bonduel all that often. Well, never. He'd be the center of attention without even knowing it.

Her heart fluttered. People would think they were a couple, dressed alike as they were.

The doctor peered at her doubtfully, then turned to Mammi. "She doesn't think it's a good idea."

"I'm sorry," Cassie said. "Did you ask me something?"

"He wants to know if he should come and change my foot," Mammi said. "Since he's going to be dropping by often, we don't need the home health nurse."

"He'll be dropping by often?" Cassie said. Had she missed something?

"Yes, dear. To change my foot."

The doctor sprouted a tentative grin. "If your granddaughter says it's okay, I'll check with the hospital."

"It's not my decision," Cassie said, chastising herself at how pleased she felt about the prospect of seeing Dr. Reynolds three times a week.

His expression grew serious as he studied her face. "I think it is your decision."

Mammi slid another completed pot holder off her needles. "Of course it isn't her decision. It's my foot. I want you to come."

"Only if it won't make Miss Coblenz uncomfortable."

Cassie couldn't decide whether to die of embarrassment or float off the ground at the way he looked at her. His expression was casually cheerful, but his eyes glowed with restrained determination. Was he just being nice or did he truly want to spend his scarce free time with an old Amish couple and a boring art history graduate?

The look in his eyes told her that he wasn't just being nice.

But why? She'd made it perfectly clear that she didn't want to date him. Why would he waste his time?

Maybe he wasn't ready to give up.

That thought both thrilled and terrified her. She'd definitely softened toward Dr. Reynolds since Thursday. Who wouldn't thaw a little under the warmth of one of his smiles? But if he wanted to use her the way

Englisch boys always used Englisch girls, would he be mad at her when she refused to behave like a plaything?

The door opened, sparing Cassie the need to answer. Dawdi tromped into the room bundled in his heavy black coat. His cheeks glowed bright red, and ice crystals had formed on his eyebrows and beard. He leaned against the wall as he slipped off his work boots. "Cold day out yet," he said. "If temperatures stay low, the sap won't run until March."

Dr. Reynolds closed the distance between him and Dawdi in three strides. Lithe, athletic, soccer-player strides.

Not that Cassie noticed.

"Felty," he said, holding out his hand. "What have you been doing out there? You look like a snowman."

Dawdi removed one of his heavy nylon gloves. It seemed Zach nearly jumped out of his skin when his hand touched Dawdi's. "Your hands are like ice."

"I just milked the cow. The milk's on the porch," Dawdi said. "It's a little cold in that barn yet."

Zach's mouth fell open. "You milked? By hand?"

Dawdi's eyes twinkled. "I only got one cow. Doesn't seem economical to buy a

142

milking machine."

"Felty, you're eighty-six years old."

"Eighty-five."

"You're eighty-five years old. Most men your age are sitting in a rocking chair sucking dinner from a straw."

"I wasn't never much for rocking chairs. And why would I want to eat from a straw when Annie is the best cook in Wisconsin?"

Zach's lips curled. "I hope I'm as young as you are when I'm eighty."

"Eighty-five." Dawdi swiped his hand down his horseshoe beard, clearing the ice that had formed there. He smiled at Cassie. "Why, you're as fresh as a field of sweet clover, Cassie girl."

"Or an orchard of blossoming cherry trees," Mammi volunteered.

"A pink, breathtaking sunrise," the doctor added, taking her breath away with the way he stared at her.

She blushed, no doubt looking like a pink parfait with a bright red cherry on top.

Dawdi clapped his hands together. "Are you ready to go to the auction?"

"I'm looking forward to it," Zach said, as if he really was.

"Okay," Dawdi said. "I'll go change my coat and put on my shoes."

An awkward silence took over the room

when Dawdi disappeared down the hall.

Well, awkward for Cassie.

The lack of conversation didn't seem to bother Zach in the least as he seemed content to stare at her and say nothing. The door saved her again. She said a silent prayer of gratitude that someone always seemed to be buzzing in or out of Mammi and Dawdi's house.

Cousin Titus burst through the door, as comfortable walking in as any beloved grandchild had a right to be. Titus was two years younger than Cassie, and she had many fond memories of her younger years spent playing with him on Mammi and Dawdi's farm. Titus had always been as skinny and as tall as a light post, with a cowlick in front that made his white-blond hair fall in all sorts of unruly tufts over his forehead.

And a toothpick. Cassie had rarely seen Titus without a toothpick clamped firmly between his lips.

"Cassie!" he said, pausing long enough the pull the toothpick from his mouth before gathering her into his arms for a bear hug.

Cassie laughed at the pure joy of having a cousin who liked her so much.

Titus nudged her to arm's length to get a

better look. "I've missed you something wonderful."

"I've missed you too."

He took off his coat and hat and hung them on the hooks by the door. "I like the pink. You look like scoop of strawberry ice cream."

Cassie smiled. Titus always had food on his mind. "Mamm made it for me. She doesn't want me to embarrass the family."

Titus's lips vibrated as he blew air out from between them. "Who's embarrassed?"

Dr. Reynolds folded his arms across his chest and eyed Cassie and Titus. After a brief hesitation, he extended his hand. "I'm Zach Reynolds," he said, with a hint of uncertainty in his voice.

"This is the doctor who did surgery on Mammi's foot," Cassie said.

The corner of Titus's mouth twitched slightly as he took the offered hand. "I'm Titus Helmuth, Cassie's cousin."

"My grandson," Mammi called from her recliner.

"Your favorite grandson," Titus said.

"Definitely one of my favorites."

Zach blossomed into a full-blown smile as he let out a breath he seemed to have been holding for a very long time. "I thought for a minute you might be Cassie's Amish boy-friend."

Titus returned his toothpick to his mouth and thumbed his suspenders. "Not me. I'm scrawny compared to Cassie's boyfriend. He could pick me up and heft me twenty feet into the air."

Zach's smile withered.

Cassie cuffed Titus on the shoulder, certain that it was impossible to get any red-der. "I do not have a boyfriend."

Titus shook his head. "That's not what Elmer Lee thinks."

"I thought Elmer Lee and Hannah Mary were dating," Cassie said.

"He was just biding his time until you came back."

"That's not true, Titus. I made it perfectly clear when I left that —"

Titus held up his hands and backed away. "All I know is that he carved your name in the aspen in front of the school. Sounds like true love to me."

"Me too," Zach said, with a tease in his voice.

She ignored him. "Elmer Lee carved my name in that tree fourteen years ago, Titus. I was ten."

Titus looked puzzled for a minute. "Really? That long ago? Are you sure?"

"Yes. And he got in big trouble."

Titus shrugged. "He's going to the auction. He wants to see you."

"No, he doesn't." Did Elmer Lee still hold out hope for her? The thought made her want to toss her oatmeal raisin cookies.

Zach studied her face, his expression guarded. "We don't have to go to the auction, if you don't want to. We could stay here and play Amish games."

Titus perked up at that. "Do you know how to play Life on the Farm? It's my favorite."

"It's okay, Dr. Reynolds," Cassie said. "You came all this way to see the auction. You should see it."

"All this way? It's twenty minutes from my apartment." He looked into her eyes. "I feel bad that I got you into this. First the dress and now the boyfriend. We don't have to go if you'll be uncomfortable."

At his tender look, her whole body felt warm, like drinking a steaming cup of hot chocolate next to the fire. The sensation spread all the way to her toes.

"I feel like I maybe talked you into something you didn't really want to do," he said.

She laid a hand on his elbow. Surprise flashed momentarily on his face. "It's all right, Doctor. I want to go. Troubles don't

147

get better by avoiding them."

"An old boyfriend might."

He looked worried. Worried about her encountering that old boyfriend, or worried that she had an old boyfriend in the first place? Either possibility sent a whole fleet of skater bugs skipping down her spine.

Titus's gaze darted from Cassie to Zach. "Did you know you're both wearing pink?"

Zach stifled a smile. "Yes, we did."

"You look like a couple."

Zach winced. "Is that a good thing or a bad thing? For Cassie, I mean."

Titus narrowed his eyes and let his toothpick bob up and down between his lips. "*Are* you a couple?"

Cassie wanted to roll her eyes and say something clever, but she was too busy breaking some sort of blushing record. Zach caught her eye, and she managed to give him a wry smile, just so he knew everything was okay.

Titus didn't wait for an answer. "It's good to dress like a couple if you are a couple because that tells other interested boys and girls to stay away. If you're not a couple, it still gives everybody something to gossip about. They love the gossip. It's the only excitement we get around here."

Dr. Reynolds winked at Cassie. "We're not

a couple, but if you think it will add some excitement to the auction, I'll be sure to take off my coat so people will see my shirt."

Titus leaned closer to Zach, as if sharing a great secret. "Do you know Norman and Luke?"

Zach shook his head.

"My brothers," Cassie said.

Titus nodded. "They're like badgers when it comes to Cassie."

Zach cocked an eyebrow. "Badgers? Sounds dangerous."

Titus pressed his lips together and nodded eagerly as if anticipating an epic confrontation. "They won't like her being with an Englisch boy. And they really won't like her being with an Englisch boy in a pink shirt. I don't want to hurt your feelings, but it's not manly. They'll mock you, but maybe not to your face." He pulled his toothpick from his mouth and pointed it at Zach. "But they'll definitely make fun of you in private. Don't let them hurt your feelings."

"I won't," Zach said. "If anyone questions my manhood, I'll roll up my sleeves and flex my muscles."

Cassie's breath caught in her throat. That was something she'd like to see. She coughed and put that notion right out of her head. She must be losing her marbles.

"And don't be overconfident. Norman's made me cry before," Titus said.

"We were kids, Titus," Cassie said.

He put the toothpick back in his mouth. "When we were kids, sure. But Norman made me cry two weeks ago. He said my brain was the size of a pea and that it had rolled out of my ear when I was a baby."

Mammi lifted her eyes from her knitting. "I'll have to give Norman a talking-to. He was raised better than that."

Cassie gave the doctor a weak smile. "Norman means well. He's just a little overprotective. He's trying his best to save my soul."

She thought he might laugh, but his frown cut deep lines into his face. "Because you're not Amish anymore?"

Titus nodded. "He thinks she's going to hell."

Zach's frown degenerated into a scowl. "Who is he to judge?"

She had to wipe that unpleasant look off his face. He certainly didn't need to concern himself with her family's problems. She went to Mammi's cookie jar, retrieved an oatmeal raisin cookie, and handed it to him. "Have a cookie. You look like you're going to bite Titus's head off."

Giving her a sideways glance, he cracked

a smile and relaxed his shoulders. "Anything for one of your cookies."

Dawdi came down the hallway wearing his lighter black coat and leather boots. "Are we ready to go?"

"Ready," Zach said, polishing off his cookie in three bites. He turned to Titus. "Are you going with us?"

"Nah. I came to sit with Mammi so Cassie and Dawdi could go to the auction."

"Don't let your mammi get into any trouble today," Dawdi said.

"Oh, get on out of here, Felty," Mammi said, waving her knitting needles as if she were flagging down a car. "Titus is going to tell me all his hunting adventures, and I am going to teach him how to knit."

The toothpick slipped from Titus's lips as his jaw fell open. "You are?"

"Jah, and we're going to have a wonderful-gute time."

"Mammi," Titus whined, "I don't want to learn how to knit. It isn't manly. Next thing you know, you'll have me dressed up in pink shirts like poor Dr. Reynolds."

Mammi's eyes sparkled with good humor. "We'll make blue pot holders. You won't even have to touch the pink yarn."

Cassie giggled at Titus's crestfallen look. He didn't want to knit, but he would do it

151

for Mammi. He could never refuse his mammi anything.

Zach grinned and laid a hand on Titus's shoulder. "If it would make you feel better, I'll come back and knit with you."

Titus shook his head. "You're wearing a pink shirt. You probably already know how to knit. You probably crochet pink baby blankets in your spare time."

Zach chuckled, grabbed his coat, and pulled it over his broad shoulders. "There's no shame in pink baby blankets."

Cassie grabbed her coat, but before she could put it on, Zach took it from her and helped her into it. A little butterfly flitted in her stomach. Amish men didn't know how to be gentlemen. Neither did Englisch men, for that matter. She liked it when anyone displayed even the most basic of manners. "Thank you," she said, not looking him in the eye, just in case she was blushing again.

They walked outside and stood on the porch while they fastened their coats. Before Cassie could follow Dawdi down the steps, Zach turned to her. "Will you make sure I don't offend the entire community today?"

"What exactly are you going to do?"

"I might say something offensive without knowing it. Is it acceptable to shake hands with Amish women, or is that considered inappropriate? Should I kiss the bishop's ring? Will I be shunned for wearing pink?"

She smiled and batted her eyelashes. "Norman will definitely shun you for wearing pink."

"As long as he doesn't make me cry."

The flippant expression on his face made her giggle. "I'll protect you."

"Thanks. I don't want tear stains on my new shirt."

Cassie caught her breath. "Oh. I almost forgot." She ran into the house, snatched Zach's red scarf from her room, and ran back out the front door without a word to Mammi and Titus. Zach was right where she'd left him. "You left your scarf here last Thursday night."

Leaning close, she looped it over his head, twisted it around itself, and pulled it to fit snugly around his neck. She gave his chest a pat. "There you go. I don't want you to freeze."

Only when she raised her head did she realize she was close enough to catch a whiff of his clean, fresh scent and see the kaleidoscope pattern in his shocking blue eyes. He inclined his head to her so that their faces were mere inches apart. His expression was cloudy, guarded so that the only hint she got of what he might be thinking was a barely perceptible twitch of his lips.

She held her breath as the earth seemed to stop spinning. Or maybe it spun faster. Maybe she'd get dizzy if she held his gaze longer.

"I hate to tell you this, but I'm not getting any younger just standing here," Dawdi called from where he waited by Zach's car.

The connection between them snapped. Zach laughed as if trying to dispel a tense situation and bounded down the porch steps. "And I'm not getting any fatter. I'm eager to find out what a benefit haystack supper tastes like."

Slightly dazed, Cassie followed Zach down the steps. He unlocked the car, and Dawdi slid into the backseat. Zach jogged around to the passenger side and opened the door for Cassie.

Before she got in, he gave her a blindingly bright smile and whispered, "No matter what Norman says, pink angels do not go to hell."

Her heart hammered inside her chest. She would probably never be able to breathe normally again.

CHAPTER EIGHT

Zach expected to stick out at the auction. Being tall with an athletic build, he stuck out a lot of places he went. But a tall non-Amish guy with no hat, no suspenders, and a pink shirt was bound to draw attention. He didn't mind the attention as long as it didn't make Cassie uncomfortable.

He relaxed when he walked into the warehouse. Several — what had Cassie called them? — Englischers milled about, looking at auction items, mingling with the Amish folks. He wasn't all that out of place.

They lingered near the double doors and surveyed their surroundings. Four or five space heaters were scattered throughout the warehouse, making the inside feel almost balmy. At least seventy degrees. Zach took off his coat and handed it to an Amish woman who piled it next to dozens of other coats on a table by the door. Tables and benches were crowded into one side of the warehouse while auction items stood at the other end. People milled around the far end of warehouse, looking at things for sale.

"What do you think?" Felty said.

"I'm surprised that the entire place didn't fall silent when I walked in. Nobody is even staring at me."

"They will," Felty said, "as soon as they catch sight of that shirt."

"Oh, Dawdi," Cassie said, smiling at Zach. "See? Lots of Englisch come to these things. Nobody thinks twice about it."

Pots and platters of food sat on three long tables. Amish women served heaping spoonfuls of rice and sauce from the steaming pots. An orderly line formed at the head of the tables where an austere-looking man with a snowy white beard took money. Another man handed out paper plates. Sounds of voices echoed off the high metal ceilings.

"This is all to help pay someone's medical bills?" Zach asked. How many other communities anywhere in the world would do such a thing to help out a neighbor?

Felty smoothed his beard. "The real big auctions are on Mother's Day weekend and Labor Day weekend. We do it in a big field and set up big canvas tents. You should see all the quilts for sale."

Cassie's eyes shone. "Everybody comes together to help people in need. The men take days off work to help raise a barn or put up a pasture fence. Just last week my brother Luke fixed a leaky roof for one of the shut-ins in Bonduel with Freeman Kiem and Elmer Lee Kanagy."

"That was nice of them," Zach said, a little jealous of the admiration evident in Cassie's expression, especially since she'd mentioned Elmer Lee in the little group of do-gooders.

"Amish men know how to do just about anything, and if they don't, they learn right quick. They fix cars and machines that they don't even use. My dat was a farmer, a lumberjack, a schoolteacher, and a carpenter. They're all so smart."

Zach folded his arms across his chest. What did he care if Cassie admired all the stuff Amish men could do? Most guys couldn't dream of making it through biochemistry or gross anatomy, let alone medical school. Elmer Lee probably didn't know how to give someone a shot.

"Cassie, there you are."

Zach looked around. It was hard to tell where the shrill sound came from, but pretty easy to guess that the woman marching resolutely toward them owned the piercing voice.

157

The woman was thin but of a solid build, standing an inch or so taller than Cassie. The wrinkles lining her forehead and lips made it look as if she'd spent years frowning. Her salt-and-pepper gray hair peeked out from under her white Amish kapp and looked coarse enough to be wire instead of hair. Was she one of Cassie's relatives?

One thing was certain. From the way she marched through the crowd, brushing any and all obstacles aside, this woman was accustomed to being in charge. And if looks proved true, she was also used to getting exactly what she wanted when she wanted it and wouldn't put up with any opposition whatsoever.

He glanced at Cassie, who although uncertain, also acted genuinely happy to see this woman.

The woman stopped a few feet from Cassie, propped her hands on her hips, and looked Cassie up and down as if doing an inspection. "You should have told me you didn't have shoes, and I would have let you borrow a pair of mine."

"I didn't think about shoes. I'm sorry," Cassie said. She bowed her head slightly and tried to look contrite. Zach sensed that Cassie had learned how best to appease this woman. Arguments unlikely ever changed her opinion.

He peered at Cassie's shoes. Plain black with a silver buckle on top. Cute but nothing fancy. What did this woman not like about them?

The woman sighed in exasperation. "But the dress is nice. Pink suits you."

"Thank you."

"And hardly nobody will be able to tell your hair is so short under the kapp. I did good stitching on it."

"Mamm," Cassie said, gesturing to Zach. "This is Dr. Reynolds. Doctor, this is my mother, Esther Coblenz."

Her mother? The woman looked old enough to be Cassie's grandmother. And grumpy enough to be an Army drill sergeant. He could see it now, though. Esther had Felty's eyes.

"It's very nice to meet you," Zach said. Should he offer his hand? He'd never gotten that Amish protocol lesson from Cassie.

Cassie's mother seemed to notice Zach for the first time and turned all her attention to him, like pit bull ready to attack. "Who is this boy, Cassie? Why is he here? Elmer Lee is coming."

Zach tensed his jaw. Titus had warned him that Elmer Lee would be here. Why should the mere mention of his name make Zach so edgy?

"Mamm," Cassie said in a voice of perfect mildness, "Dr. Reynolds is the doctor who operated on Mammi's foot. He wanted to see an Amish auction."

Felty must have felt the need to intervene. "It's always gute to see you, daughter," he said to Esther. "A good turnout for the supper today."

Esther ignored her father, pinched her lips together, and gave Zach a once-over, making no attempt to hide her hostility. "You shouldn't have worn pink. You two look like a couple."

"We're not a couple, Mamm."

Esther pointed an accusing finger in Zach's face. "He wants to be."

Whoa. Cassie's mother could tell that just by looking? Maybe. The impulse was pretty strong on his side.

"Mamm," Cassie said. "He's Mammi's doctor. We are very grateful that he's taking care of Mammi."

Esther narrowed her eyes and frowned. She seemed to dislike the very idea of Dr. Zach Reynolds.

"The risk of living among the Englisch is that you soon become like them," Esther said. "They lead you into all sorts of wickedness."

Cassie bowed her head again, that submissive posture that she must have hoped would appease her mother. It made her look even more like an angel than ever. Wow, but she was beautiful. But he didn't necessarily like the whole submission thing.

"He is a great comfort to Mammi, to all of us," Cassie said.

Zach's chest swelled with tenderness. Even though Cassie was trying to placate her mother, her words were sincere. Maybe she didn't despise him as much as she used to. Maybe she didn't mind him hanging around so much. He hoped not, because he was dead set on hanging around.

Felty stepped in front of Zach and hooked his arm around Esther's. "Help your old *fater* get some supper, will you, Esther? I don't think I can do it by myself."

"Oh, Dat," Esther said, softening up a little. "You don't need help. You skip around town like you was seventy years old yet."

"It wonders me why I need a reason to want to eat supper with my daughter."

Esther grunted in disapproval. Or maybe it was a grunt of approval. She slid her hand over Felty's. "Let's go eat, then."

She turned to Cassie even as Felty tried to tug her away. "Promise me you'll talk to Elmer Lee." When Cassie looked as if she would protest, Esther said, "I went to all the trouble to make you a pink dress. It's the least you can do for your mother."

"He won't want to —" Cassie said weakly.

"I need a promise, Cassie."

Cassie laced her fingers together and shuffled her feet. "I promise."

Zach hadn't ever heard anyone say anything with less enthusiasm. He wanted to gather her in his arms and kiss those lips into a smile, almost as badly as he wanted to give Cassie's mamm a set-down she'd never forget. He'd known her for two minutes, and she already had his blood boiling like a steaming pot of McDonald's coffee. But he knew that calling out Cassie's mother in the middle of Amish country during a festive Amish event would be a big mistake. He closed his mouth and bit down hard on his tongue.

Esther glared at Zach one last time — probably needing to fill some sort of quota. "Don't ever wear that pink shirt again."

She turned and walked away, leaving Zach quite speechless. Had she really just ordered him not to wear this shirt?

Cassie looked as if she wanted to crawl into a very small hole. "Dr. Reynolds, I'm . . . I'm so sorry. My mamm . . ."

His anger evaporated, and he wiped his

hand over his mouth to suppress a smile. She stared at him, eyes round with curiosity. Despite his best efforts, the smile escaped and then the laughter bubbled up inside him like a volcano about to explode. He struggled to subdue his mirth, so as not to draw attention to himself, but it was no use. He had to get out of there.

Not wanting to leave Cassie guessing, he grabbed her hand and tugged her around three or four people standing by the side door and outside into the below-freezing temperatures.

"Doctor, what are you —"

No sooner had they stepped outside than he let go of her hand and burst into great belly laughs that shook his whole body and left him panting for air.

Cassie wrapped her arms around herself to ward off the chill, and her eyebrows seemed to fly off her face. "You're not mad?"

"Shocked," he said.

"That wasn't funny," she said, a smile already well in progress on her face.

"I get the feeling she doesn't like me."

Cassie pressed her fingers to her lips to push the smile away. "My mamm isn't known for her tact."

"This shirt really was a terrible idea. I

should know better than to trust *GQ*. They said pink was in this year."

"I'm just glad you aren't angry. My mamm has high hopes that Elmer Lee will fall head over heels in love with me the minute he sees me in this pink dress."

"It wouldn't matter if you were wearing a burlap sack. Seven or eight guys are going to fall in love with you today. You're that pretty."

The tinge of cherry-blossom pink on her cheeks proved incredibly attractive. "Don't tease me. No one is even going to look twice."

"They're all going to look at least twice."

She laughed. "You are incorrigible."

He couldn't resist slipping his hand into hers. Her cheeks got pinker, but she didn't pull away. He savored every moment of her feather-soft touch. It couldn't last much longer. Not only was she turning redder by the minute, but it was truly frigid out here. "What I really want to know," he said, "is what you think of my shirt. Because if you're embarrassed, I'll put my coat back on and keep it zipped tightly around my chin."

How red could those cheeks get? "To be honest . . . I think you look amazing."

Her compliment made his heart beat

double-time. "In that case, I'm tempted to never take it off."

She laughed. "You'd stink after a while."

"Probably. Will you still like me when I smell like a dead animal rotting along the side of the road?"

"I would still like you, but from a great distance."

"So you admit you like me?"

Her lips quirked upward, and she pretended to think about it. She still hadn't pulled her hand from his. "Well, you're very good to my mammi."

"That's something."

"And we have matching red scarves and matching silver cars and matching pink outfits. I suppose I like you well enough."

He'd be smiling for a whole month. "I can work with that."

She let go of his hand and opened the side door. "Whatever you want to work out, let's do it inside. It's wonderful cold out here."

"I'll follow you anywhere," he said, with an eager twist of his lips.

She rolled her eyes. "Don't follow too close. I'd rather not be seen with a guy in a pink shirt."

He laughed and walked with her into the warmth of the sturdy warehouse.

CHAPTER NINE

With his hands in his pockets and his sleeves rolled up to his elbows, Zach strolled around the perimeter of the warehouse, watching people and waiting for the auction to begin.

Cassie had sat across from him at supper, which suited Zach just fine. It had given him an opportunity to stare at her without being too obvious that he was staring at her. Pink was fast becoming his favorite color. Cassie made it look so feminine and appealing. His fingers had practically itched to reach across the table and caress her cheek, but he had fought the urge by clutching his fork in one hand and his knife in the other. He'd broken four plastic forks that way. Cassie had gone to the serving table and brought him back a whole pile of forks as a precaution. She'd told him she didn't want him to starve for the lack of a fork.

Amish haystacks turned out to be rice

topped with chicken and a white gravy-type sauce plus a variety of toppings like lettuce, tomatoes, chili, olives, and corn chips — just about anything Zach's heart could desire. He could get used to this down-home Amish cooking.

After supper Zach had offered to help with the cleanup, but the old Amish ladies looked at him as if he were a bright pink alien from another planet. He'd helped set up benches and folding chairs for the auction and then strolled amongst the items for sale with Cassie. He would have stayed glued to Cassie's side all evening, but he realized early on that his presence made her Amish neighbors suspicious of both him and Cassie. He saw that she'd do much better reconnecting with old friends if some Englisch guy in a matching pink shirt wasn't her constant companion.

Of course, that didn't mean he'd separated himself from her entirely. His eyes followed her every move, drank in the grace of every gesture, and although he never ventured too close, he hovered as if he were in orbit around her. When she moved one way, he did too. When she stopped, he stopped and pretended to gaze elsewhere while keeping his attention squarely on her.

He had never met anyone like Cassie

Coblenz. She was tender and gentle, resolute without being pushy. Forgiving and patient. The Bible called it "long-suffering." Cassie had no doubt suffered much unhappiness at the hands of her community and family, but she didn't seem to harbor ill will for anyone.

Of course, that meant that Zach was far beneath her, both in virtue and in faith. He could live three lifetimes and never deserve her. The thought discouraged him but didn't keep him from wanting her all the same. He *was* a doctor and a star soccer player. Plenty of girls thought he was a good catch. It gave him hope for Cassie.

Even now she voluntarily visited with her mother while they both examined the stitching on one of the quilts up for sale at the auction. Her mom reached up and adjusted the white covering on Cassie's head, and although Zach was too far away to hear their conversation, he could guess that Cassie's mom criticized how Cassie wore it. His mouth drooped into a frown even though Cassie took her mother's criticism with a cheerful, even kindly look on her face. She even gave her mother a kiss on the cheek.

Cassie moved with easy grace as she shifted from quilt to quilt, bestowing that angelic smile on everyone she came in contact with. A woman tending to her quilt dropped an entire tin full of pins as Cassie walked by, and Cassie got down on her hands and knees and helped her pick them up. She helped a fallen toddler back to his feet, kissed every baby she encountered, and found an elderly Englisch woman a chair to rest on.

With every movement and action, she displayed her deep and irresistible goodness. It was an extremely attractive quality, and Zach was extremely attracted. He massaged the back of his neck. She'd already rejected him once. How in the world could he convince her to give him another chance without being annoying?

He also kept a close eye on Cassie to see if the legendary Elmer Lee would appear and sweep her off her feet. Zach, who already knew his limitations when it came to Cassie, envisioned the whole troubling scene in his head. Elmer Lee would march into the barn like David walking into the Valley of Elah to face Goliath. He'd say a few enticing sentences to her in Pennsylvania Dutch, and she'd agree to marry him on the spot. Then he'd take her into his arms, carry her to his buggy, and drive her to the church, where they'd be married immediately and live happily ever after raising a dozen Amish babies.

He clenched his teeth and tried his best to drum that picture out of his head. Cassie had told him she didn't want to be Amish anymore. But what if Elmer Lee was too persuasive and virtuous to resist?

Out of the corner of his eye, he saw three young men stroll into the warehouse. One wore the familiar Amish horseshoe beard. The other two were clean-shaven.

They paused at the door as they peered around the warehouse. A navy-blue streak of lightning bustled over to the three of them. Cassie's mother. She reached out and rested a firm hand on the bearded one's shoulder. They put their heads together as Cassie's mother Esther looked to be talking a mile a minute. She glanced up and her eyes met Zach's from a distance. How did she know right where he was? He looked away, even as he watched them out of the corner of his eye. Esther pointed right at Zach, a gesture that he found appallingly rude. Hadn't her mother ever taught her that it was impolite to point? He thought about that for a second. Anna Helmuth was Esther's mother. Sweet, guileless Anna had most certainly taught her daughter good manners.

The bearded one stared at Zach for a

minute while Esther acknowledged the other two Amish young men, then stormed away in the direction she had come.

Zach's heart flopped around his chest when the three men headed straight in Cassie's direction. Elmer Lee and his two bodyguards? Or his two best men? The one with the beard was of average size, maybe five-eight, five-nine. Zach would have run circles around him on the soccer field. Norman, maybe? The one who had made Titus cry?

The other two could have been weightlifting partners. The shorter looked to be almost six feet with hair the exact color of Cassie's and arms as solid as tree branches. The taller one stood at least Zach's height, about six foot three, but he probably had thirty pounds on Zach. Zach was solid, lithe and muscular, but this one was as thick and as immovable as one of the stone pillars at the Chicago Museum of Science and Industry. He had a square jaw, a cleft chin, and hair so black it glistened under the fluorescent lights of the warehouse.

Cassie's back was turned as they approached. When the one with the beard said something to her, she looked around and her smile wilted like a daisy in the wintertime. Zach took a deep breath. If that was

Elmer Lee, she wasn't happy to see him.

Before her companions had a chance to notice it was gone, she shoved a smile back onto her lips and stiffened her spine as if it were made out of oak.

The one with the beard seemed to be the spokesman. He stretched a smile across his face, almost as painful as Cassie's, and motioned stiffly to his tall, dark, and brooding companion. The Pillar nodded to Cassie, but couldn't have said more than about three words to her. Cassie nodded back, looking as if she wished someone would pull the fire alarm so she could escape.

The one with the beard spoke again. His smile disappeared as he and Cassie exchanged words, and Zach could tell that the bearded one was dishing it out and Cassie was meekly taking it. It looked as if he were giving Cassie a very stern lecture. Like she had with her mother, Cassie lowered her eyes and laced her fingers together.

Instinctively, Zach took a few steps forward. He didn't know much about the Amish culture, but even at the risk of offending everybody, he wouldn't let anyone else bully Cassie. Even her brother.

He decided to get within earshot so he could actually hear what was being said before he rode in on his white horse to rescue the maiden. They might just be talking about the weather. With consternation he gazed at Cassie's expression, pretty sure they weren't talking about the weather. He sidled closer to them and stationed himself behind a large Englisch guy who was intently studying his phone.

"Elmer Lee wants you to go on a ride with him," the bearded one said. "When a boy has gone to that much trouble to arrange a ride, a decent, godly girl should say yes. Have you forgotten your manners as well as your faith, Cassie?"

"We can go to the overlook at the lake," said the tall, dark pillar. His deep bass voice sounded as if he had a ping-pong ball stuck in his throat. Definitely Elmer Lee. As solid as a tank.

"I'm going back to Chicago in a few months, Norman," Cassie murmured, speaking to the one with the beard.

Norman. The one who was supposedly going to make him cry. Zach wasn't intimidated in the least. In his day, he'd flattened soccer forwards twice Norman's size.

"It wouldn't be fair to Elmer Lee to get his hopes up," Cassie said. Apparently Elmer Lee didn't mind that they were talking about him as if he weren't there.

"What is out there for you, Cassie?"

Norman hissed through his teeth. "Do the Englisch boys treat you with respect?"

Zach was about to come out from behind the wide Englischer and intervene when he caught Cassie's soft answer.

"No," she said.

No? The muscles of Zach's jaw tightened. He suddenly wanted to round up all the guys Cassie had ever dated. He'd teach them some respect.

Norman grunted. "The Englisch boys only want one thing from a girl."

"I know," Cassie said, and Zach could hear the real anguish in her voice. "But I will wait for marriage to a man of God."

"Then you'll never marry," Norman said. "Because the only godly men left are the Amish yet."

Cassie's voice was barely audible. "I've made my choice. I'm not coming back."

Zach felt sick to his stomach. Was that what Cassie thought about all Englisch boys? Was that what she thought about him? It made him even sicker to realize that she was not that far from the truth. How many girls had he slept with since high school? Not as many as someone like Finn Mc-Ewan, but still, there had been a few, and Zach had attended enough Sunday School classes to know that his behavior wouldn't meet with God's approval.

"An Amish man would never use a girl the way the Englisch boys do," Norman said. "The only place you are safe is with us."

The other young man spoke up. "We want you to come home. We love you."

Norman definitely wanted to be completely in charge of the conversation. He ignored the other young man altogether. "We fear for your soul. I have a prayer in my heart for you always."

"I'd really like to take you to the lake," the Pillar added.

A man of few words. Why wouldn't he be, with someone like Norman to do his talking for him?

From behind the large cell phone user, Zach saw Norman lay his hands on Cassie's shoulders. "I fear and tremble when I think that my own sister is going to burn in the fires of hell for eternity."

Zach had heard enough. He stepped from behind the fat man and stepped in between Cassie and Norman. "Hey," he said, extending his hand to Norman and trying for a smile. "My name is Zach Reynolds. I'm a friend of Cassie's." No need to be confrontational. Yet.

Norman acted as if Zach were offering a

snake instead of his hand. He frowned persistently as he glued his eyes to Zach's pink shirt. "Are you trying to couple up with Cassie?"

"We're just friends." He moved a few inches closer to Cassie so their pink sleeves were touching, just to goad Norman a little — probably not the most Christian way to behave, but then, Zach wasn't much of a Christian.

It worked. Norman's frown settled into his face like a deep rut in the dirt. "Cassie doesn't want an Englisch boyfriend."

He could hear Cassie's shallow breathing and resisted the nearly overpowering urge to grab her hand and give her something solid to hold on to. He also resisted the urge to lay into Cassie's brother and tell him what was what.

Cassie managed to recover herself enough to speak. "Norman, this is Mammi's foot doctor. Dr. Reynolds, this is my brother Norman."

Norman peered at Zach as if he were sporting a black cape and sinister mustache. Still, he remembered his manners and stuck out his hand. "You did the surgery on my mammi?"

"Yes," Zach said. "She's by far my favorite patient."

Cassie motioned to the shorter of the twin pillars standing beside her. "This is my brother Luke."

Luke looked younger than Norman. Judging from his baby face, probably younger than Cassie, and there was good humor in his eyes. He gave Zach a tentative smile. "Nice to meet you." He had a firm handshake, only to be expected from a guy with arms as thick as loaves of bread. Cassie motioned toward the Pillar, and Zach could see the color creep up her neck. "This is Elmer Lee Kanagy."

Elmer Lee's handshake could have broken the hand of someone who wasn't UChicago's all-conference center back two years in a row. But Zach didn't sense any malice in Elmer Lee's grip. He was a big man, shaking the hand of another big man. Elmer Lee was trying to be neighborly.

Probably.

"You and Cassie match," Elmer Lee said, as if he'd just noticed it.

"She's much prettier than I am." Zach flashed a smile at Cassie, trying to put her at ease. It didn't seem to work, but she did return his smile with a halfhearted curl of her lips.

Another frown layered itself on top of the frown Norman already wore. "Cassie would not be so vain to think she's pretty."

"Elmer Lee thinks her dress is pretty," Luke offered. "Don't you, Elmer Lee."

Elmer Lee nodded.

As if on cue, Cassie lowered her eyes to the ground. Trying to prove her humility or just wishing this conversation would end?

Well, I think she's pretty, Zach wanted to say. *I think she's as exquisite as a ten-carat diamond.* He kept his mouth shut.

Norman folded his arms across his chest. "Mamm says you have your sights set on Cassie. She says you wore the pink shirt on purpose because you want to lead her astray."

"That's not true, Norman," Cassie said.

Norman ignored her. His quick dismissal of his sister made Zach more irritated than anything else Norman had done. "I understand boys like you. You lure girls with your pink shirts and fancy cars for one reason. You want to steal their innocence."

Well, he might be able to lure girls with his pink shirt, but he wouldn't impress anybody with his car. Zach worked very hard not to glare at Norman. The conversation had turned ugly. Titus had warned him not to be overconfident, and Zach understood why. Norman was like one of those bears in the stories they were always reporting about in the news. Some naturalist lives with the bears for months until one day the bears turn on him and eat him alive.

Zach wasn't about to get eaten.

But how to defend himself without making Cassie uncomfortable?

Cassie actually nudged him out of the way and stepped between him and Norman. "Norman, you are embarrassing yourself and our whole family."

"You are the one who embarrasses the family," Norman shot back.

"You can criticize and shout at me all you like," she said, "but I will not let you talk to the doctor this way. He is my guest, and you will treat him with respect or I will walk out of this warehouse, away from Mamm and the family, and never come back."

Zach couldn't have been more astonished if Cassie had laid a big kiss on his lips. The girl who didn't dare stand up for herself against unjustifiable and hurtful attacks was defending him? Not just defending him, but doing it forcefully so that Norman had no other choice but to shut his mouth — that or risk a scene.

Her posture was ramrod straight, her eyes on fire with righteous indignation. She was fierce and beautiful and angelic all at the same time.

He would have defended himself but didn't know if he could have done so without offending the entire Amish community and making Cassie uncomfortable. Meek, gentle Cassie had risked herself for him, even though she surely thought he was like every other guy she'd met in college.

A thread of warmth snaked its way through his veins. She had completely disarmed him. He *had* to convince her to give him another chance.

Norman clapped his mouth shut and glared at Zach. Zach didn't even flinch. Didn't feel one bit like bursting into tears.

"Norman didn't mean to be disrespectful," said Luke. "We're glad you're taking care of our mammi."

Zach tried to focus his attention on Luke when his thoughts were saturated with Cassie. "Anna knitted me a scarf and mittens," he said, grasping for something to keep the conversation light.

This did not make Norman happy. "What is Mammi thinking? You're not even Amish. Doesn't she want someone Amish?"

Zach had no idea what he was talking about. Cassie seemed just as confused. "Mammi hands out scarves like cookies," she said.

Norman looked positively sullen. "But not

mittens too."

"They're very warm," Zach said.

Cassie smiled uncomfortably at Zach. "Dr. Reynolds, would you excuse us for a few minutes?"

He was being dismissed? He'd only come this way to save Cassie from her brothers. Didn't she realize that? Wasn't she grateful?

"Oh . . . okay. I'll go find Felty and we'll get a seat for the auction."

She seemed very happy to get rid of him. "That would be wonderful good."

His heart felt like an anvil as he stuffed his hands into his pockets and strolled away from Cassie, her brothers, and the Pillar.

He was the outsider. Cassie had made that perfectly clear.

He ambled to the furniture up for auction and pretended to be interested in the construction of a rocking chair, all the while keeping an eye on Cassie and the others.

Still standing tall, Cassie said something to Norman, who seemed to brighten immediately. He nudged Luke on the shoulder, and they walked away, leaving Cassie and Elmer Lee staring at each other. Zach ground his teeth together. She had protested that she wasn't interested in Elmer Lee, yet there she was, smiling at him and talking as if he were a long-lost friend.

Oh. Well. Elmer Lee was Cassie's long-lost friend.

Zach had trouble prying his gaze from Cassie's face, but he should give her some measure of privacy with her old boyfriend. If they kissed each other right in the middle of the barn, Zach was pretty sure he didn't want to witness it.

She wasn't going to kiss Elmer Lee, was she?

He turned his back on them, found a bench to sit on, and faced the stack of hay bales that would serve as the auction block. His scalp tingled at the wish that he could grow eyeballs on the back of his head. Nope. He wouldn't look. Cassie's relationship with Elmer Lee was none of his business.

But right now, it was his most profound concern.

He didn't notice Norman until he plopped next to him on the bench. Zach grimaced. He'd hoped to avoid Norman for the rest of the night, but it looked like he was back for round two. Where Zach had restrained himself when Cassie was around, he wouldn't feel obligated to do so when he had Norman alone.

Norman dispensed with any pleasantries and got right to the matter. "What are your intentions with my sister?"

Never a good sign when a guy looked at him like that.

Zach folded his arms across his chest. "You don't like me very much, do you?"

"Nae. I do not."

"Is it because I'm Englisch?"

"I have no respect for a man who hides behind a woman's skirts and is too weak to speak for himself."

"I fight my own battles when I have to, walk away when I can, keep silent when I should." He slid to the bench in front of Norman so they were facing each other, with knees almost touching. "I have no respect for a man who decides he doesn't like somebody before he's really gotten to know him. And I'm certainly not the kind of man who bullies his sister, knowing she won't fight back."

Norman squirmed a little before narrowing his eyes into slits. "I'm not picking on her. I am admonishing her. She must understand the consequences of her actions."

"From what I've seen, you've made the consequences very clear."

"That will be a small consolation if she burns in the fires of hell."

Zach balled his hands into fists. "So you believe that everyone who isn't Amish is going to hell?"

"God placed her in the Amish community. She shouldn't change what God has planned for her life."

"How do you know that she isn't living the life God planned for her? Jesus said not to judge."

"I know that God would not lead her into temptation. I know that men like you do not seek to guard a woman's virtue. You are out to destroy it. I don't want that to be my sister's fate. She is only safe here in the community."

"She knows how to take care of herself."

"But is she happy? Surely you have seen what I have seen in her eyes. She's been disappointed over and over again."

Zach couldn't argue. She'd said as much the other night.

"She knows that she can only find what she is looking for among the Plain people. She wants a man like Elmer Lee."

"There is plenty of virtue among the Englisch," Zach murmured, not altogether convinced himself.

Norman grunted. "Really? What about you? Do you claim that virtue in yourself?"

Zach's confidence slipped, but he didn't take his eyes from Norman's face. "I never claimed to be something I'm not."

"And yet you are interested in Cassie."

Zach didn't even try to protest. He was as interested in Cassie as a starving man was interested in food, but he would never cheapen the feeling by telling Norman about it.

"I can see your desire for her in your eyes."

"It's not like that."

What did he truly want from Cassie? He wasn't sure, but he knew it wasn't a one-night stand. He wanted something deeper, though he was at a loss to define it. But to have any meaningful relationship, he'd have to convince her to trust him.

To do that, he'd have to prove he was different than Finn McEwan and all those other college frat boys.

But he wasn't all that different. He didn't go out looking for girls to hook up with, but wasn't that what he expected after a few dates? He didn't deserve Cassie. Could he ever hope to? Could he be the kind of man she could respect? Or at least feel safe around?

Norman flared his nostrils. "You will not drag Cassie down to hell with you."

"I would never do that to Cassie." Even as he said it, he swore an oath to himself that he never would. Cassie deserved tenderness and love and a man she could trust completely, not only with her virtue but with her heart. Suddenly more than anything in the world, he wanted to be that man. "She is safe with me."

Norman scowled. "Safe? Ha. You aren't man enough for Cassie. You're wearing a pink shirt. What does that tell you?"

Zach thought the shirt said "fashionable." Norman read "idiot."

Norman leaned forward. "It wonders me if you know the first thing about chopping wood or shoeing a horse or raising a barn. Can you fix an air compressor?"

Zach wanted to lie through his teeth. He didn't. "No."

"Do you know how a windmill works or a water pump? What about a water heater?"

"Of course not. I'm from California."

"You can't hitch a horse to a buggy or plow a field. You're ignorant. You'd be like a baby if you tried to live amongst the Amish. Even a five-year-old knows more than you do."

Zach longed to ask Norman if he knew how to set a broken leg or take out an appendix, but something told him that Norman wouldn't be impressed. And he had the depressing thought that Cassie wouldn't be either. Besides, it would sound like he was playing a game of one-upmanship.

186

How had Norman known how to get under Zach's skin? Zach had seen the way Cassie's eyes glowed with pride when she talked about the barn raisings and many things that the Amish did to help each other. And he hated to admit that he didn't know how to milk a cow, probably something the Amish kids did before they even learned how to walk.

Zach was impressed with how resilient the Amish were. At eighty-five Felty Helmuth milked his cow twice a day, but that wasn't all. Every man in the community chopped wood and hefted hay bales. They planted and harvested crops, butchered hogs, felled trees, and raised barns. If the Amish didn't know how to do something, they'd teach themselves — without YouTube, Facebook, or a college education.

Cassie was drawn to the community not only for their faith but for their simple and resourceful way of life. You could take a girl out of the country, but you couldn't take the country out of the girl, or something like that.

Norman turned his eyes to where Cassie and Elmer Lee were engrossed in a very serious conversation. Cassie did the talking and Elmer Lee listened. Zach imagined, with some spite, that Elmer Lee probably only had about a hundred words in his vocabulary.

"Look at them," Norman said. "They belong together. Cassie should be here. If you wrench her from us, she'll be unhappy for the rest of her life."

"Cassie chose to leave. It's the Amish life that made her unhappy."

"She believes that. But a man like you is no good for her. Elmer Lee can give her everything she truly wants."

"I can do anything Elmer Lee can do, and better." He grimaced on the inside the second he said it. It sounded like a playground brag. *My dad can beat up your dad.*

Norman smirked. "Elmer Lee can reduce an entire tree to kindling in a matter of minutes and heft bales faster than a mosquito can bite."

Can he turn a soccer ball on a dead run?

Maybe now was the time to bring up the appendix thing.

Norman had shaken his self-assurance more than he cared to admit.

"You don't belong here," Norman said, "and Cassie does. It's my responsibility to urge her to mend her ways and come home."

Zach glanced at Cassie out of the corner of his eye. She dabbed a finger to her eyes.

He sat up straighter. Had Elmer Lee made her cry? Elmer Lee bowed his head and walked away from her as if he had nowhere in particular to go.

Zach shot to his feet. He'd had enough of Norman, and he needed to see if Cassie was all right. He stared Norman down. "You think I'm too weak to speak for myself? Just try picking on Cassie again, and we'll just see who's weak."

"Is that a threat?"

Zach frowned. "Next time, I won't stand silently by and let you or anyone else bring your sister to tears."

"You Englisch are all the same, angry and violent."

Violent? Did Norman actually believe he meant to do him bodily harm? Punch him in the nose or something? Whatever. Let him think what he wanted. "At least I don't profess to be godly and then abuse people in the name of religion."

Norman clamped his mouth shut and peered at Zach resentfully. He was livid, but at least Zach had shut him up.

Shut him up and offended him.

Norman hadn't expected any better, so it was probably just as well.

Would Cassie be furious or grateful?

Not even Cassie's reaction mattered at the

moment. She was visibly upset, and Zach had to know if he needed to challenge Elmer Lee to a duel. Or a fistfight. Or a cutthroat round of Life on the Farm, Titus's favorite game.

If he had anything to say about it, no one would ever make Cassie cry again.

CHAPTER TEN

There weren't a lot of good places to hide in a warehouse. No large posts to conceal oneself behind or secluded corners to sneak into. She couldn't go outside to be alone without freezing to death, and the little alcove that housed the bathrooms was constantly crowded with people. So she slipped over to the wall farthest from the crowds and ducked behind one of the quilt displays where she wouldn't be seen. Mostly.

Cassie really hated disappointing people. She really hated telling boys no and breaking their hearts. Growing up, her mamm had often scolded her for caring too much about what other people thought of her and putting other people's happiness ahead of her own. But Mamm had no reservations about using Cassie's weakness to her advantage when Cassie wasn't inclined to do what her mother wanted.

Telling Elmer Lee *again* that she wasn't

interested had been difficult. Elmer Lee liked her too much to give up easily. It hadn't helped matters that Mamm and Norman encouraged him. They bore some of the responsibility for his disappointment.

She heard muted footsteps and turned to see Dr. Reynolds sidling behind the quilt display with a tissue in his outstretched hand and a deeply concerned look on his face. The doctor could have been a model or a movie star. Good looks like his were as rare as an original Picasso. He had rolled his sleeves to his elbows, and she could see the muscles and veins of his strong forearms.

Who would have ever guessed that pink could be that masculine?

Holding her breath, she willed her pulse to resume a normal pace.

She really needed to stop staring now.

"Are you okay?" he asked.

Ignoring the sculptured biceps lurking beneath his sleeves, she took the tissue from him and dabbed at her eyes even though they were mostly dry.

"What did he say to make you so upset? I volunteer to teach him some manners if you like."

She smiled and expelled a puff of air. "Elmer Lee is harmless. I wanted to give him a chance to move away gracefully without it seeming like I dumped him."

His lips twitched as if he were holding back a full-blown smile. "You dumped him?"

"I guess I didn't really dump him, since we weren't going out in the first place. I told him that he should find a nice Amish girl because I'm not coming back."

Now he did smile, a smile that could have turned back winter in Chicago. He took two giant steps closer, probably so she could smell that irresistible scent of his. "I'm glad to hear it."

For a second, she forgot she had the power of speech.

He cleared his throat and took a step away as if he realized his presence made her giddy. "I'm surprised he wasn't the one who ended up crying."

She sighed. "He'll be fine. My brother shouldn't plant false hope."

"I have to admit, I felt a little nervous. I thought maybe Elmer Lee would talk you into marrying him."

"I don't think so."

"I was jealous too, but as long as you didn't give him your phone number, I guess we're even."

Zach seemed to have an uncanny ability

to make her smile. "Elmer Lee has been baptized. Giving him my phone number would have been pointless."

He pretended to be insulted. "So you would have given it to him and not to me? I wore pink today just for you. Have you no heart?"

"Apparently not, at least according to Norman."

His smile faded. She shouldn't have mentioned her brother. Norman made grown men cry on a regular basis. "Norman picks on you," he said. "How can you find any patience for him?"

"If I don't argue, he eventually winds down."

He furrowed his brow. "But your silence gives him permission to keep bullying you."

"I'd rather not create more bad feelings by fighting back."

"Norman doesn't have the same consideration for your feelings."

"My feelings don't matter. I'd rather do just about anything than argue."

Zach's eyebrows inched closer together. "If you don't want to upset anyone by defending yourself, why did you defend me?"

"I . . . well, Norman knows better than to treat a stranger so rudely. I'm sorry he attacked you."

"I have a thick skin, and I'm far from helpless. Just ask Taylor Olsen. He took a swing at me, and I broke his arm."

Cassie's eyes became big, wide circles.

He shook his head vigorously. "Not on purpose. I blocked his punch with my forearm so he wouldn't break my nose. Again. He got a red card and a really big cast."

Cassie cracked a smile.

Zach chuckled. "I'm grateful you defended me. It would have been a little embarrassing to stand there and let Norman yell at me. I wasn't about to yell back. The thing I can't figure out is how you agree with everything Norman accused me of, but you still came to my defense."

Cassie felt the warmth travel up her face. "I never said I agreed with him."

His gaze pierced hers. "But you do. You think I only want one thing from you. It's why you wouldn't give me your phone number."

"I think you're a very nice guy, Dr. Reynolds."

He grimaced. "Nice guy? That's not it. You think I want to get you into bed and nothing more." He glanced around their little space as if making sure no one had heard him. "I'm sorry for being so blunt. But I'm right, aren't I?"

She wished she could shrink to the size of a pebble. "In my experience, it's what all the college guys want."

He frowned and scrubbed his hand down the side of his face. "You have a very low opinion of me, don't you?"

Hadn't she made it clear to him that she didn't like conflict? This was shaping up to be a monster-size conflict. Avoidance was her best option. She balled the tissue in her fist and took two steps toward the benches where the auction would be held. "I don't want to talk about it."

"But I do." His gentle hand on her arm stopped her in her tracks. "Please, Miss Coblenz. I promise I won't argue or get angry. I just want to understand you. I want you to understand me."

The weight of so many years of disillusionment pressed down on her. "You already admitted it. I know you well enough," she whispered.

He looked behind him as they both heard the auctioneer calling out bids on one of the quilts. Holding out his hand, he said, "This is a nice secluded corner where we can sit and talk."

She hesitated. Did she really want to take

his hand? Of course she did. That was why she didn't.

"I just want to talk," he persisted. "I don't want to make out with you or convince you to accept a date. Just talk."

She walked to the far wall and sat in the corner on the floor. With only a ghost of a smile on his face, he followed and sat next to her, leaning back against the metal wall. "Cold," he said.

"Not much insulation between us and the outside."

"If I go get my coat, will you promise not to leave until I get back?"

She curled her lips and nodded.

He got to his feet and took off. He came back with his coat, which he quickly laid over her shoulders. "Oh," she said. "I thought this was for you."

"I like it when you wear my coat." His look sent a spark of electricity down her arms. "Besides, the cold doesn't faze me. I used to study in the Reg at UChicago. It's like a freezer in there."

"You forget that I grew up Amish. In the winter I don't think my one-room school-house got warmer than fifty-five degrees."

He looked genuinely worried. "You don't have to wear it if you don't want to."

She tugged it more tightly around her

shoulders. "I've been out of primary school a very long time."

He sat next to her again, but she noticed that he was careful to keep his distance. No arms nudging up against each other.

He rested his arms on his knees. "So, you're dead set against me because you think I'm a pretty bad guy."

"I never said that."

"But you said you already know what I'm like."

She wanted to disappear into the folds of his coat. "You're all alike."

His eyes held something intense in their depths, but he twitched his mouth into a grin. "I ask you, is it fair to lump me with the likes of Finn McEwan? He doesn't even have good hair."

Seeing his expression, she relaxed a little. Maybe he wouldn't growl at her like Norman would. "You're right. It isn't fair."

"Right. I mean, you make this flash judgment about me and deprive me of the chance to take you out."

She rolled her eyes. "So you never did any of those things the rest of your college buddies did?"

He pressed his lips together as if he were thinking real hard. "I'm not going to lie to you. I've done some things you'd find objectionable, but I'd never use a girl the way Finn did." He massaged his jaw as if he were trying to scour the skin off his face. "But I have slept with a few girls. You already guessed that."

"I wouldn't have expected anything different."

Pain traveled across his face as if she had slapped him. He closed his eyes and rested his head against the wall behind him. "I suppose I deserve that."

"I'm sorry. I shouldn't have said anything."

"Don't apologize. Nothing hurts like the truth."

She felt horrible, like she'd just run over a puppy in her car. This was why she didn't like confrontations. Nobody walked away satisfied. "We should go find Dawdi."

He gazed at her, and she saw a yearning that took her by surprise. "No, we shouldn't, not when you're being so honest."

"So brutal."

He turned his whole body to face her. "I want to hear it."

"Sure, you say that now, but wait until I rip your kidneys out of your chest and stomp on them."

He lowered his head and smiled. "Technically, kidneys do not reside in the chest cavity."

"It would still be painful."

"Bring it on."

He coaxed a smile from her in spite of herself. "I know how I sound, like a judgmental, spiteful prude."

"Not at all."

"I'm not like Norman. I won't tell you how to live your life or decide you're going to hell because you're not Amish, but I also have a right to choose my life. I choose to live the way I think God wants me to live."

"Live and let live," Zach said. "But maybe that means you could reserve judgment on a guy until he takes you out. Maybe give him a try." He gave her an innocent grin, as if he had no particular guy in mind.

The words felt heavy on her tongue. She hated being such a disappointment. "It doesn't matter. It's always the same. Different guy, same story."

"Tell me the story."

She shivered and tucked his coat around her chin. "He's always really charming and fun at first. He takes you out to dinner, maybe a movie or a party where all the couples are making out. He gets annoyed when you won't make out with him, but he's not discouraged yet. Maybe he takes you to the lake. Maybe even pulls out the water skis. He spends all sorts of money on you. But when you refuse to sleep with him, he gets angry. He calls you names and accuses you of leading him on." She turned her face from Dr. Reynolds, unable to meet his eye. He had wanted to hear it. "After a few dates, your charming smiles would vanish and every moment we spent in each other's presence would be awkward and painful. You'd despise me for my resistance, make fun of me when you're with your friends, maybe even call me a hypocrite, because, let's face it, nobody could be that *virginal.*"

She didn't realize a tear trickled down her cheek until he reached out and gently wiped it away.

She sniffed hard and shook her head. "This is stupid. I should be numb to the memories by now."

He stared at her as if he might like to shed a few tears himself. "How many stories have you got like this?"

"Three or four guys my freshman year. Two or three as a sophomore. After that I turned down a lot of dates."

The lines deepened around his eyes. "They shouldn't have treated you that way."

"But it's how everybody behaves. At least

in college."

He tilted his head and dug his fingers into the muscles of his neck. "No wonder you hate me."

"I don't hate you." Her gut clenched. "I just don't want to go out with you."

He studied her with a piercing gaze. "What can I do to make it up to you?"

"You don't have to make anything up to me."

"Maybe I'm not what you want now, but what if I try to be the kind of guy you can trust? The kind of guy you would date. What would I have to do?"

"I . . . I don't know."

"Maybe people can change. Maybe just being around you makes men want to be better."

Her heart did somersaults in her chest. He didn't mean it. No guy would want to change for her.

He frowned. "Am I a lost cause?"

"No one is a lost cause, but only God can change your heart."

A shadow darkened his features. "Maybe so."

The look troubled her. What was his relationship with God? "You don't think God can change you?"

"God and I aren't on speaking terms."

He seemed so dark, so profoundly unhappy about it. Dare she ask? "Why not?"

"He took my dad. One day he was fine and the next day he dropped dead from a heart attack." He lowered his head. "I was seventeen. God knew how bad me and my mom needed him. Why would He do that to us? Mom couldn't hardly eat for weeks. Why did God put us through that pain if He loves us?"

"I don't know," Cassie whispered.

"Because He doesn't love us, that's why."

After a moment of hesitation, she placed her hand on his arm. His gaze intensified. "You probably don't want to hear this, but one thing I can promise you is that God loves you. He loves all of us. We're His children."

"Then why does He make bad things happen?"

"I don't think God makes bad things happen," Cassie said. "We live in a hard world. Things happen because we are mortal and frail. We're all going to die, and life is very unfair, but God sent Jesus to make everything right again."

"How does He do that?"

"I don't know, except I know He *can* do it. The Apostle John said that God will wipe away all tears from our eyes. When we get to heaven, everything will be made right, and we won't be sad anymore."

He shook his head. "Maybe."

"Do you think your dad would want you to be angry that he's dead?"

Dr. Reynolds pressed his palm against his forehead. "It doesn't matter if he would want it or not. I'm angry, with or without his permission."

"I'll bet your dad's in heaven growing cherries or farming or whatever it was that made him the happiest," Cassie said.

Dr. Reynolds smiled in resignation. "He liked collecting old stuff like Indian arrowheads and fossils. One time he found an ancient shark's tooth while he tilled the dirt in the orchard. You would have thought he'd discovered gold."

"Heaven is the place where every dream comes true and every moment is filled with happiness. Your dad's there. He's happy. He wants you to be happy."

Dr. Reynolds studied his hands. "Could be. But I rather that he was still here."

"Hopefully, knowing he's in a better place gives you comfort."

"That's the problem. I don't know he's in a better place. I'm not really sure if God even exists."

"Maybe you should give God another

chance." She flashed him an encouraging smile. "You may not believe this after what I just told you, but I know you can find your faith again."

"You do?" In an instant he seemed to shake off his dark mood. He raised his eyebrows like he always did when he teased her. "I'm glad you don't think I'm a lost cause. And you said you liked me well enough."

Her lips curved into a slow smile. "Well enough."

"But what would I have to do to impress you? Dress Amish and chop wood? If a guy like me tried to be a better guy, would you ever give him another chance?"

Cassie wanted to say yes with every cell in her body. She wanted to yell it from the roof. But he was just saying words, and words meant nothing.

He eyed her with so much determination in his expression that she had to lower her eyes. She liked him. How could she bear to refuse him again? She shivered just a little.

"You're cold." He stood and offered his hand and pulled her to her feet. "I've been rude keeping you all to myself." He wrapped an arm around her shoulder as he nudged her around the quilts draped over easels and in the direction of the benches. "Let's get you by one of those heaters."

"Thank you," she said, grateful that the conversation was over.

"This conversation isn't over," he said, grinning as if he'd won an argument, even though they hadn't been quarreling.

Her heart felt as light as a feather when she saw he wasn't inclined to hold a grudge. "There is nothing more annoying than a man who doesn't know when to give up."

"Give up? Miss Coblenz, to keep from annoying you, I might back off. But give up? Nope. I'm not going to give up."

CHAPTER ELEVEN

"Hey, Z, it's Blair. I know you're busy, but really? It would take about thirty seconds to pull your phone out of your pocket and call me. I'll be there in five weeks, and I want to make plans. It's only an hour from Stevens Point to Shawano. It wouldn't kill you to go out to dinner with me, would it?"

Zach blew a puff of air from between his lips and erased Blair's message. He really couldn't avoid this, no matter how badly he wanted to. He'd told Blair they could still be friends, but he hadn't really meant it. He'd be forced to revisit their breakup conversation, and he didn't especially look forward to it.

He put down his phone and resumed typing his report on the hospital computer. Maybe he'd avoid the conversation for another couple of days in hopes it would just go away.

He heard the yelling from all the way

down the hall.

Cringing, he tried to ignore it as he sat at his desk and stared at the notes on the chart in front of him. The child's doctor could handle the problem. Zach couldn't barge in on another physician's patient, no matter how bad it sounded down there. Besides, the child was probably just getting a booster shot. Lots of kids went ballistic at the thought of getting stuck with a needle.

Another full minute of hollering down the hall. Zach heard Marla call for another nurse. The kid must be putting up a pretty good fight. Zach snapped his head up as he heard a metal tray crash to the floor. Something about the sound of a little kid in distress made his gut clench and his protective instincts take over. The little guy must have been terrified out of his mind. Maybe he should see if he could help.

He strode down the hall in the direction of the sound. A little boy who couldn't have been more than six or seven sat on a hospital bed doing everything in his power to keep Marla from sticking an IV line into his arm. Marla was about the age of Zach's mother, and a big woman, but she still couldn't manage to restrain the boy well enough to get a needle in. A woman, no doubt the boy's mother, sat on the bed behind him with her arms around his chest, trying to immobilize him. Alice, the other nurse, held his arm and pressed the boy's thigh with her other hand, attempting to get him to hold still while Marla did her best to find a vein for her needle.

The boy struggled and slapped at the nurses, his eyes red and his face soaked with tears. His pale skin and sunken eyes also told Zach that he was terribly ill.

For being as skinny as he was, he put up an impressive fight.

"Austin, you've got to hold still," his mother said, trying to sound calm while obviously at the end of her rope.

"It's only a little poke," Marla said. "Then it won't hurt so bad."

Zach noticed a small coat and a blue and red striped scarf with a familiar coat of arms hanging on the hook inside the door. He didn't really believe in miracles, but this had to be more than a coincidence. He'd have to consider thanking God or karma or the universe for that beautiful scarf. He stepped into the room and placed a hand on Marla's shoulder. "Can I help?"

The sweat beaded on Marla's forehead, and she huffed the air out of her lungs. "He needs antibiotics, Doctor, but he won't let me put the IV line in."

"Let's put this down for just a minute," Zach said, taking the needle from Marla and smiling reassuringly. She nodded and took a few steps away from the bed. Alice also stepped away. Maybe the little boy would relax if he weren't poised for a struggle. Zach placed the needle on Marla's rolling tray and pushed it a good three feet from the bed.

The boy's mother slid her arms from around him as Zach pulled up the rolling stool and sat next to the bed. He held out his hand. "I'm Zach."

The boy eyed Zach's hand suspiciously and slid his right arm behind his back.

"What's your name?"

The boy sniffed as if he couldn't care less.

His mother bit her bottom lip. "This is Austin."

Zach glanced at Austin's mother. She looked exhausted, with dark circles under her eyes just like her son. "I'm Dr. Reynolds. Nice to meet you."

"I'm Jamie Stetson."

Zach grinned. "Like the hat?"

She returned his smile. "Yep. Like the hat."

Zach turned all his attention to the little boy. "Do you play soccer, Austin?"

Austin furrowed his brow and nodded. He

probably wondered if Zach could read minds.

Zach pointed to the scarf hanging on the hook. "Can I take a look at that scarf?"

Austin still didn't speak, but a wisp of a smile crossed his face as he nodded.

Zach lifted the scarf from the hook and sat down again, spreading it on the bed next to Austin. He widened his eyes as if the scarf were the coolest thing he'd ever seen. "Is this an official FC Barcelona scarf?"

"My dad bought it for me in Spain."

"Sick."

Austin nodded earnestly while still keeping his hands safely behind his back. "Totally sick. It's got the coat of arms on both sides."

"Is Messi your favorite player?"

"Yeah. Everybody said he was too little to play soccer. Like me. All the guys say I'm too little."

"I like Messi, but my favorite Barca player is Jeremy Mathieu."

"Who's that?"

"He plays center back, like me," Zach said. "I used to play soccer."

Austin folded his skinny arms across his chest. "Were you any good?"

"I was pretty good. I played for UChicago."

"I want to play for Barcelona."

Zach propped his thumb under his chin and tapped his index finger on his jawline. "You have to be pretty tough to play for Barcelona."

"I fell off my bike last week and didn't even cry." Austin lifted the hem of his hospital gown to reveal an impressive scab on his knee.

"Then you're tough enough to get a needle poked in your arm, I think."

Austin immediately shoved his hands behind his back and scrunched his face as if he were going to cry. "But it's going to really hurt."

Zach patted Austin on the knee. "One time our soccer team was up one-nil in a game against our biggest rival. In the last minute of the game, the other keeper played the ball over the top, and the forward caught it on a dead run. There was nothing between him and a goal but me."

"What did you do?"

"He came fast with the ball, but I knew if I knocked him over, I'd get called for a foul and he'd get a penalty kick. So I stood my ground and let him run into me."

"Did it hurt?"

Zach winced. "Like being run over by a truck. Knocked the wind out of me too. I thought I was going to die."

Austin bloomed into a smile. "But you stopped him?"

"Dead in his tracks."

He fingered the stitching on his Barcelona scarf. "Mom says something's wrong with my heart."

"Is it?"

"What if they stick a needle in me, and I don't wake up?"

Zach felt heartsick. The biggest thing any little boy should have to worry about was if his mom forced him to eat broccoli for dinner. "Being brave doesn't mean you're not scared. Being brave means that you're scared, and you do it anyway."

Austin rubbed his eyes as if to push back the tears. "But they've already taken a lot of blood, and it hurts."

Zach pressed his lips together and nodded. "Yeah, it hurts, but not as bad as when you scraped your knee. If you want, I'll let Alice give me an IV first so you can see what it's like."

Austin looked surprised. "You don't need one."

"That doesn't matter. Alice could give me an IV while Marla gives you one. Would that make you feel better?"

"Okay," Austin said, sounding not altogether convinced.

Zach turned and nodded at Marla. With her hands on her hips, she curled one side of her mouth and sidled out of the room to fetch another IV tray. She probably thought he was crazy.

Zach rolled up his sleeve and sat next to Austin on the bed. "Will you let me wear your scarf while Alice pokes me, or would you rather wear it?"

"I think . . . I want to wear it," Austin said.

"Okay," Zach said. "If you think it will help."

"Yeah. I think it will."

Zach unrolled his sleeve as he hurried down the hall. He'd left his next patient waiting for over fifteen minutes. Not good. Patients tended to get grumpy when they had to wait. He'd have to apologize profusely and give them an extra dose of Reynolds charm. That usually worked on people. Except for Cassie Coblenz. She was immune to his charm. The very thought made him slouch.

"Dr. Reynolds," Marla called. He turned to see her running down the hall to catch up to him. She placed a hand on his arm. "I don't think we ever would have gotten an IV into that boy. Thank you."

"No thanks necessary. I got a SpongeBob

Band-Aid out of it. I consider it a fair trade."

"You deserve a whole box of SpongeBob Band-Aids. You are an angel sent from God." She winked at him and walked back the way she had come.

Zach shook his head and watched her disappear down the hall. He was only aware of one angel on earth, and he was going to visit her tonight. Of course, the angel thought he was coming to change the dressing on her grandmother's foot, but his real purpose was to show the angel he wasn't such a bad guy and maybe convince her to go out with him.

But Cassie must never suspect he had ulterior motives. He had a plan to sneak up on her.

His heart raced. Trying to win her approval was scarier than getting an IV.

CHAPTER TWELVE

"You're all set, Anna," said Dr. Reynolds, snapping the latex gloves off his hands and stuffing them into his bag.

Mammi rotated her ankle and examined the new dressing the doctor had given her foot. "Your wrappings just get better and better, Dr. Reynolds."

"Why, thank you. It never hurts to get extra practice." Zach finished replacing supplies in the bag that the home health nurse had let him borrow.

Mammi reached over and patted the doctor's shoulder as he knelt beside her recliner. "It's always such a thrill when you come. Don't you agree, Cassie?"

Cassie stood at the sink, trying hard to ignore the thrill of having Dr. Zach Reynolds in their home. He was too good-looking by half, and that smile sent her to the moon every time he flashed it, almost as if he were smiling at her on purpose just to see if he could make her heart race about a thousand miles an hour.

She swirled the dishrag in the water, not doing a very good job of cleaning the dishes, but at least looking busy enough that the doctor wouldn't suspect how sidetracked she got when he came over. He was becoming a major distraction. How could a girl get serious about studying for the GRE when all she did was sit at her laptop and daydream about the attractive doctor?

She looked up from her sink of dishes to see Mammi and Dawdi eyeing her expectantly, and Zach gazing at her with a sheepish grin on his face. Was there a question hanging in the air she should have answered? She picked up a plate and swiped the rag across it, giving her memory a chance to retrieve Mammi's question. "Oh, yes, we love having you come over, Doctor." The answer was sincere, but should she be encouraging him with so much enthusiasm?

Zach's face relaxed into a casual smile. "I'm not sure why. All I do when I come over is eat."

"You're a growing boy," Mammi said. "You need good food in your belly for your circles tonight."

"You mean his rounds, Mammi," Cassie said.

"I know it's not politically correct to compliment a woman's cooking," Zach said, "but, Cassie, you are an amazing cook."

Cassie blushed. "I'm not horrible."

"Not horrible? Those rolls you made on Thursday melted in my mouth like warm butter. And your huckleberry pie could be served at the White House."

"She learned how to cook from her mammi," Dawdi said. "Annie Banannie is the best cook I've ever seen."

"Now, Felty," Mammi scolded. "We're talking about Cassie. Don't divert the doctor's attention."

"I have to run an extra five miles every day just to keep from getting fat."

"Well," Mammi said, "it's the least we can do for all the help you've given my foot."

"And all the help you've given my farm," Dawdi said. He sat on the sofa next to Mammi's recliner rolling skeins of yarn into balls.

Zach checked to make sure Mammi's wound vacuum worked properly. "I haven't been that much help."

"Of course you have," Mammi insisted. "Our buggy has never been so oily."

Cassie smiled to herself. Dr. Reynolds had been coming around for almost two weeks to change the dressing on Mammi's foot, and every time he had come, he'd asked Cassie or Dawdi to teach him how to do something on the farm. Even with his impossible schedule at the hospital, he was eager to learn some useful Amish skills, but she had no idea why he'd ever need useful Amish skills as a doctor.

Cassie had taught him how to milk the cow, which he turned out to be very good at. He had strong arms and hands, so all she really had to teach him was the proper downward pulling motion as well as how to keep the cow from kicking the bucket over or giving him a good whack in the shins.

Dawdi had taught him how to care for the buggy, how to hitch the horse to it, and how to drive it. The driving had been a short lesson because they'd done it in the dark, and Dawdi hadn't wanted to take it down the hill on the ice.

Zach had proved a fast learner, but Cassie hadn't expected anything less. A guy didn't get into medical school by being thick in the head. But why was he so determined? What benefit could he get from knowing how to drive a buggy or fill propane lanterns?

Zach came to the kitchen sink where Cassie kept vigil over the plates. Her heart pitter-pattered like rain on the roof when he sidled next to her and washed in the second sink. He scrubbed his hands like a doctor, thoroughly and clear up to his elbows. She pulled a towel from the drawer and handed it to him before he had to search for one. His smile looked like sunshine.

"Denki," he said. "Did I say that right?"

She smiled at his attempt to learn Deitsch. "Jah. Very good."

He raised an eyebrow. "Now you're just being nice. My accent is atrocious."

"You're making a good try at it."

Grimacing, he picked up the dish towel and started drying Cassie's clean dishes. "When my piano teacher said 'Good try,' it was secret code for 'you might be better suited for the harmonica.' "

Cassie's face got pleasantly warm when he looked at her like that. "I would never say any such thing about your language skills."

"Only because you're too nice to say anything bad about anybody, but what you're really thinking is that the only language I'm ever going to be good at is pig latin."

"What's pig latin?" Dawdi asked.

Cassie giggled. "A language so hard that only the pigs can speak it." She handed him a plate. "This is the last one, Doctor.

Thanks for your help."

"What else can I do before I go? My shift doesn't start until eleven. I know I'm not much help around here, but I'd like to learn."

Mammi picked up her knitting needles. "Do you know how to chop wood, Doctor?"

Zach folded his towel neatly and set it on the cupboard. "Chopping wood is one Amish thing I'm actually good at. I chopped a lot of cherrywood growing up."

Mammi glanced at Dawdi. "He could chop wood for the you-know-what on Saturday."

Dawdi leaned back, frowned, and folded his arms. "I don't want to know anything about that."

"What's the you-know-what?" Zach asked.

Cassie caught his eye and shook her head slightly. Puzzlement traveled across his face, but he knew enough not to ask. "He doesn't need to chop any wood, Mammi. Luke is planning on coming early Saturday morning to chop as much wood as we'll need."

The doctor stiffened at the sound of Luke's name. "Why leave it for Luke when I can do it?"

"It's dark," Cassie said.

"I can take a lantern."

"It's cold."

"I'll wear a coat."

Cassie pushed her lips to one side of her face. "Then I'll hold the lantern for you."

"It's cold," he said.

"I'll wear my coat."

He nodded as if deep in thought. "If you come out, it will give me a chance to show off my muscles by the light of the moon."

Could he read her mind? She pretended to be unimpressed. "You've seen one bulging bicep, you've seen them all."

He flexed both arms. "Not mine. These babies have been known to strike fear in the hearts of soccer players."

She grinned. "I don't see that well in the dark."

Zach smiled mischievously and growled from deep in his throat. "What do I have to do to impress you, Amish girl?"

"For one thing, quit calling me Amish girl."

They both laughed, and Zach went to the hook to retrieve their coats and scarves. Cassie put on the mittens that she had stuffed into her coat pocket, and Zach donned the beanie that Mammi had made him. "Okay, Mammi and Dawdi," Cassie said. "We're going out to chop wood."

Mammi nodded. "Have fun."

They shut the door behind them, and

Cassie lifted the lantern from the hook on the porch.

Zach zipped up his coat. "So what is the you-know-what your dawdi doesn't want to talk about?"

"We're butchering his hog on Saturday, and we need lots of wood for the scalding fire. Every spring he buys a hog to raise, and every winter the family butchers it for him. Killing animals makes him very upset. For his sake, we try to pretend it's not happening."

"But that's why he buys a hog every year, isn't it?"

"Yes, but he doesn't even want to know when we're doing it. We've put it off an extra month already. The family butchers his pig while he stays in the house and reads *Where the Red Fern Grows* or some other very sad book."

Zach furrowed his brow. "Maybe he would feel better if he didn't raise a hog every year."

"Mammi likes the bacon."

Cassie pointed the way to the toolshed, even though Zach already knew where it was. He found the axe and also a whetstone just in case. Dawdi's substantial woodpile stood on one side of the shed complete with a thick chopping block.

Cassie held up the lantern as Zach stood the first log on the chopping block. He winked at her and swung the axe with such force that one swing cleaved the log in two. Maybe it wasn't too dark to admire his muscles. "You know how to chop wood."

"Did you think I was exaggerating?"

"I'm glad you won't be losing any limbs for the sake of Dawdi's woodpile."

She watched as he placed another log on the chopping block and reduced it to kindling in a matter of seconds. He swung the axe as if he were born with one in his hand. With the sweat beading off his forehead, he took off his coat, giving her a better view of those muscles. This activity was as entertaining as anything she'd done for a very long time.

"You're going to wear yourself out for the hospital tonight," she said, as he paused to wipe the sweat from his brow.

"I've got to work off that *yummasetti* you made. What is it, about a thousand calories a bite?"

"Too rich?"

"Like liquid gold." He smiled at her so she knew that was a good thing and swung the axe down on a thick piece of hardwood. "It's kind of amazing that all Amish men aren't several hundred pounds overweight."

"They work hard. Dishes like yummasetti are meant to stick to your ribs for a long day in the fields."

Zach concentrated hard on the next piece of firewood. "I've seen enough of the Amish to know that hard work is a way of life."

"Especially on a farm in the summertime. We'd milk cows and gather eggs, plow fields, weed gardens, care for the horses, all before lunchtime. I had chores inside too."

His lips twisted wryly. "No wonder you left."

She shook her head. "Plain life is almost easier. We only go to school until eighth grade. When I got to the junior college, I was so far behind everyone else I had to take two years of remedial classes after I got my GED."

"But you did well enough to get into UChicago."

"I studied hard," Cassie said.

"How did you afford it? School and living on your own?"

"I didn't need much. I shared an apartment with five other girls." Her lips quirked upward at the thought of that dilapidated box that passed for an apartment. Three space heaters and four blankets and she had still been afraid of freezing to death every night. "I worked part-time during school.

225

Full-time in the summers. I took a year off between sophomore and junior years to work two jobs and save enough to go back, and I patched together several grants and student loans."

He had stopped chopping altogether to stare at her.

Self-consciously, she played with a strand of her hair. "Senior year I got a partial scholarship."

He rested the axe on the ground like a cane and leaned on it. "I had it easy. My dad's life insurance paid for everything."

"I wouldn't say you had it easy. You went to medical school. Most people can't even dream of being that smart."

His lips curled. "Dumb luck."

"I don't think so. You're making the most of the talents God gave you."

He lowered his head, as if he didn't want to talk about the impressive fact that he was a doctor, picked up another good-sized log, and stood it on the chopping block. He took a swing. "Something happened at the hospital this morning. It made me wonder."

"About what?"

"They were having trouble getting an IV into this little kid. He was pretty scared. I went in to try to help. He had a soccer scarf."

"A soccer scarf?"

"Soccer fans love team scarves. This kid had an FC Barcelona scarf, which isn't cheap and isn't easy to come by, so I knew he must be a soccer fan. It gave us an instant connection. He calmed down enough that the nurses could give him the IV."

Cassie's heart swelled. "You were his superhero."

He shook his head. "If he hadn't worn his scarf to the hospital, I wouldn't have known. How many doctors in Shawano played collegiate soccer? And who around here knows who Messi is?"

"Messi?"

"The greatest soccer player in the world."

She studied his face. "You don't think it was a coincidence."

"I don't know what to think. You know more about this stuff than I do. I used to think I knew, but simple faith doesn't cut it when life gets complicated." He buried the edge of the axe into the chopping block and rubbed his hand down the side of his face. "Does God really care that much about a frightened little boy in Shawano, Wisconsin?"

"You mean, does He care enough to send you to save the day? I know He does."

Zach gazed at her before picking up the wood he'd chopped and tossing it into the woodpile. "Then why didn't He care enough to save my dad?"

Cassie's heart thudded for fear of saying the wrong thing. Why did he think she knew the answers to such questions?

Because he trusted that her faith was strong while his was not. He yearned for her to understand, to give him an answer that would help him make sense of his father's death. She wanted to help him so badly, but she didn't know if she would say what he needed to hear.

She clutched the lantern more tightly in her hand. She wasn't up to it, but God was. She just had to open her mouth. God would fill it with words. He was the only one who could change Zach's heart.

She stepped closer to him and ran her mitten down the handle of the axe. "I'm sorry about your dad. I don't know why God didn't save your dad or mine, but I know beyond seeing that God loves us more deeply than we can begin to imagine. 'Why' is a question we can't answer. He said, 'Be still and know that I am God.' "

Zach looked truly stricken, as if he wanted to understand but found it impossible to actually do so. "But what does that mean?"

"I think it means that we must let Him be God, trust in His plan, and do our best to love each other and keep his commandments."

Zach expelled a long, tortured breath. "I can't trust in a plan that brings so much sadness."

"Do you remember the Bible story of Jesus's friend Lazarus?"

"Yeah."

"The Bible says that Jesus wept at Lazarus's death because He loved Lazarus. Mary and Martha were heartbroken. Jesus wept because of their sorrow."

"And then He brought Lazarus back to life," Zach said.

"I'm sure God wept to see you so sad about your dad, but He had a bigger plan for you and your mom and even your dad. Nothing is by accident, and not even a sparrow falls to the ground without God knowing."

To her surprise, she saw tears pool in his eyes in the dim light of the lantern. "Why did I curse God when my dad died and you didn't?"

"I was only ten. Too young to be angry, maybe."

"It's because you're an angel." He yanked the axe from the wood. "And I'm no angel."

229

"Your anger is as much a part of you as your kind heart. God wants your whole heart, the parts that are easy to give and the parts that are hard. Maybe your struggle is a piece of His plan, especially if the struggle makes you stronger in the end." She took the axe from him and, nearly tipping over, dragged it toward the toolshed. "Like if I hefted this axe enough times every day, I'd get bulging muscles like yours."

He held up a hand to stop her, took the axe, and lifted it as if it weighed three pounds. "I'd rather not have to explain to your grandparents why you got a hernia."

"They like you. They'd blame it on me."

They trudged together to the toolshed, where Zach hung up the axe and zipped his coat. "Can I help with the butchering on Saturday? I don't have to be to the hospital until noon."

Cassie made a face. "You want to help with the butchering? It's kind of gross."

"I'm a doctor. Believe me, I've seen gross."

She giggled. "Yep. Feet. Feet are gross."

"Ripping out an ingrown toenail is kind of cool." He motioned for her to go ahead of him as they walked to his car.

She shivered with the cold, but she didn't necessarily want to go inside just yet, not with Dr. Reynolds smiling at her like that.

He slowly pulled out his car keys and unlocked his car.

She shook her head in mock surprise. "You locked your car again?"

He chuckled. "Old habit." He stood next to his car as if he were reluctant to get in. "So, can I help with the butchering?"

"If you really want to. They're starting at six."

"Will I get to meet some of your cousins?"

She winced. "Norman and Luke are doing it this year. And Titus. Titus doesn't have a girlfriend, so the family recruits him for everything."

"Does Titus know Norman is coming?"

"He's a glutton for punishment."

The doctor gave Cassie a wry smile. "So am I."

CHAPTER THIRTEEN

Getting up the hill in Fifi got easier every time he did it. Maybe he'd finally figured out how to drive uphill in the snow. Maybe it was the three bags of snow melt he'd sprinkled all the way down the hill after the second time he'd come up here. Three large bags was a small investment in the grand scheme of things. If he wanted to see Cassie, he had to be able to make it up her hill without plowing his car into a snowdrift.

By the muted light of early dawn, he could see a ribbon of smoke curling from behind the barn. Norman and Luke must have already gotten here.

Zach parked his car next to Cassie's. He couldn't help but smile every time he saw their matching sets of wheels. In his mind, having the same car gave them a connection, a bond. He'd take any advantage he could get.

Wrapping his red scarf around his neck,

he crunched through the snow to the porch. It might have been in the upper thirties today. Cassie opened the door before Zach could knock. She wore a threadbare black coat and a pair of jeans with holes in the knees. She'd tied her hair up in a red bandanna, but some of her unruly curls tumbled around her face like curly ribbons on a birthday gift. He held his breath as a shard of glass seemed to lodge in his chest. He thought he might go mad with the ache to stroke one of those silky tendrils. She got prettier every time he saw her.

With two aprons and a coat draped over one arm, she put her finger to her lips before he had a chance to speak, tiptoed onto the porch, and shut the door quietly behind her.

"Is everything all right?" he whispered, shoving his hands behind his back to better resist the temptation of her curls.

"Dawdi is not to be disturbed. He woke up at four this morning, milked the cow, and then sat down to read *Charlotte's Web*. I don't think it's going to be a very good day for him."

"Hopefully *Charlotte's Web* will put him in a better mood."

Cassie handed him one of the thick canvas aprons she had hanging over her arm. "Are

233

you sure you want to do this? Butchering a pig isn't the most pleasant job in the world."

He didn't really want to spend his morning butchering a pig, but he did want to learn how to butcher a pig, because it was one of the many things Amish men knew how to do that he did not, and he wanted to show Cassie that he was up for anything. It was a stupid thing to do just to impress a girl, but he was desperate and she wasn't just any girl.

"I dissected plenty of stuff in college. I think I'll be pretty good at it. Besides, I have to prove my manhood to Norman and Luke."

She giggled. "I don't think your manhood was ever in question."

"I made the mistake of wearing that pink shirt. Your brothers will need proof before they give me their respect."

"You're almost half Amish already with all the stuff you've learned."

He smiled. She'd noticed how good he was at Amish stuff. Maybe he'd made an impression.

Since the haystack supper, he'd been to Huckleberry Hill six times to change the bandage on Anna's foot. He usually came in the evenings after he finished up at the hospital or in the mornings before he did an afternoon shift, and they usually fed him some mouthwatering Amish dish before he left.

Cassie had taught him how to milk a cow. It left his hands almost too stiff to go to work the next morning, but he saw the advantage of it. Milking made his fingers stronger for surgery and eased Felty's burden at the same time.

"The real test will be a barn raising," Zach said. "That's when I'll know I've really assimilated into the culture."

Her eyes danced. "Luckily, you have several weeks to prepare for that. We don't usually raise a barn in the dead of winter."

"But you butcher hogs."

"The carcass has to cool before we section and cure it. Cold days are the best."

"Let's get to it, then."

"Here," she said, handing him a coat she held with the other apron. "I brought this for you too. It gets messy."

He took off his ski jacket and draped it and his scarf over the porch railing. Then he put on the old coat and buttoned it up. It smelled like manure. He looped the apron strap over his head and tied the strings around his waist. Cassie did the same with her apron. She looked adorable, like an old-time farmer's wife.

"We've got matching aprons," he said.

She looked down at her apron as if seeing it for the first time and grinned. "These are two of Mammi's old ones. She stitched the little hearts at the top years ago. Norman and Luke already commandeered the manly ones."

"Your brothers are going to give me a hard time about the hearts."

She nodded. "I might have to give Norman the evil eye."

"Don't worry about it. I can take care of myself."

"I'm sure you can." The way she looked at him stole his breath. "But I've got plenty of Kleenex just in case he makes you cry." She pulled a wad of tissue from her coat pocket.

"You might want to hold on to it in case I make *him* cry."

Laughter tripped from her lips. "Norman should be shaking in his boots."

"Yes, he should."

They cut across the front yard through the snow and trekked behind the barn where Norman and Luke had set up the butchering operation. The pig, who had no idea what was about to befall him, lounged in a temporary pen near the toolshed. A hot fire danced in a fire pit made of cinder blocks and large stones. A sturdy metal grate rested atop the cinder blocks, and a large vat of water, big enough to hold a pig, sat on top of the metal grate. The water inside was already steaming.

Two sturdy beams were anchored into the ground and angled to meet together at the top like two poles of a teepee. One end of a long, thick board rested on the V where the poles met. The other end of the board had been wedged between the meeting point of two branches of an oak tree. Ropes connected to two pulleys dangled from the board.

They had positioned the fire pit alongside the poles and ropes. Almost directly below the ropes sat a makeshift table made from a long plywood plank and two old doors.

Neither of Cassie's brothers glanced up when Zach and Cassie came around to the back. Luke tended to the fire. Norman sharpened a deadly looking knife. They were all business.

Zach's heart fell like a skydiver without a parachute when he saw Cassie's mother standing near the fire, bouncing a baby in her arms. Once she caught sight of Zach, it didn't take her long to fasten a sneer onto her face. At least she was predictable.

Another woman lumbered toward the fire with a load of firewood in her arms while two small children made circles around her like a Maypole. She was young, maybe a few years older than Cassie, with mousy brown hair and a slight limp when she walked.

Zach rushed to her side and took the surprisingly heavy load from her arms. Amish women were probably as sturdy as the men.

"Thank you," she said, brushing off her hands and giving him a smile. The kindness in her eyes and good sense in her face overshadowed the thin, severe lines of her mouth. "You must be the doctor I've been hearing so much about."

"What have you heard?"

Her eyes twinkled with amusement. "Only good things, to be sure. Norman says you have a very strong will." She leaned closer to him and whispered, "That's not exactly how Norman described you, but I drew my own conclusions."

Zach cocked an eyebrow. "That's very kind of you."

She kept her voice low. "It doesn't hurt Norman to be put in his place now and then. Keeps him humble."

"Are you his sister?"

"His wife. And mind you, I love him to death."

Zach laid the wood on the already tall pile. He never had learned if it was culturally acceptable to shake an Amish woman's hand, but he offered it anyway. "Call me Zach."

She had a firm handshake. "I'm Linda Coblenz. Nice to meet you. This is my daughter Priscilla and my son Jacob." She managed to catch both of her squirmy children so that Zach could shake their hands.

Both children stared at Zach as if he were a frightening beast. To a child whose head barely reached the top of his kneecap, he must have looked very tall. He knelt down in the slushy snow and shook both their hands. "Hello," he said. "How old are you?"

Their mother said something to them in Deitsch. Jacob squeezed his lips together as if no one would ever get a word out of him. Priscilla held up four fingers.

"They don't speak English real good yet," Linda said. "Priscilla is four and Jacob is three, and Mammi Esther is holding Paul. He is thirteen months."

Zach turned and waved to Cassie's mamm, flashing his friendliest smile, hoping maybe she'd come to like him if she saw enough of his teeth. She didn't smile, but she flipped her wrist in his direction in a token wave. That was something, wasn't it?

Or maybe she was trying to flick him away like a pesky fly.

Norman didn't look up from his whetstone. "It's about time you got here. We were afraid you'd chicken out yet."

"He's a doctor," Luke said, reaching across the fire to shake Zach's hand. "He's not afraid of blood."

"He made a very skillful incision in Mammi's foot," Cassie said.

Norman examined the edge of his knife. "Elmer Lee would have come, but he had to fix his sister's leaky roof." He glanced at Zach. "Do you know how to fix a roof, Dr. Reynolds?"

How had Norman managed to tick him off in a few short seconds? "Not a clue."

Cassie immediately went to work stoking the fire.

"Cassie, haven't you even got time to sew patches over those knee holes?" her mamm asked.

Zach clenched his teeth so hard he thought they might crack. Did Cassie's mother do anything but find fault with her?

"These are my hog-butchering jeans," Cassie said. "The holes are part of the fun."

"They look old and ratty. A Plain dress with long stockings would have been warmer."

Zach was amazed at Cassie's forbearance. She smiled at her mother. "I'll be warm enough."

Cassie's cousin Titus loped around the corner of the barn with a straw hat sitting crookedly on his head, a black apron already secured around his waist, and a toothpick perched between his lips. "Did I miss it?" he said.

He slowed his pace significantly when Norman looked up and frowned at him. "While you slept in, it took us an hour to fill the water barrel yet."

Slept in. Only in Amish country would sleeping past six o'clock be considered sleeping in.

Titus's Adam's apple bobbed up and down, and he pressed his lips together. "I'm real sorry I'm late, Norman. I had to milk."

Norman didn't seem to be all that impressed at Titus's excuse. "Did you bring your scraper?"

Titus's lips stuttered into a doubtful smile as he pulled a strange tool from his apron pocket. It looked like a short-handled metal toilet plunger. "Jah, and Mamm's wire brush."

Zach didn't want to broadcast his ignorance, but he did want to know what that tool was. He mentally smacked himself for not doing a little research on the Internet last night. "What is that?"

Kneeling next to the fire, Cassie smiled at him. Was she amused or embarrassed by his ignorance? "It's a bell scraper. We use it to scrape the bristles off the hog once it's scalded."

When he saw the way Cassie's skin glowed from the heat of the fire and the reflection of the flames dancing in her eyes, he found himself wishing that every day were hog-butchering day.

Titus set his bristle scraper on the make-shift table and immediately found little Jacob. Jacob lifted his hands and let Titus swing him around with his legs flying in a circle.

Norman wiped the blade of the knife on his trousers and peered at Zach. "We want you to kill it."

Zach's gaze darted from Cassie to Norman. "You want me to kill the pig?"

"Jah," Norman said. "Have you got the stomach for it?"

"I wouldn't want to mess up." He frowned and studied Cassie's expression. Elmer Lee would certainly know how to do it right. Cassie probably watched Elmer Lee butcher hogs all the time.

"Luke will stun it with a rifle, then you

stick the knife into its throat and slice the main blood vessel. Then we bleed it."

Zach gritted his teeth. Much as it galled him, he'd have to ask Norman for help, which was probably exactly what Norman counted on.

"Show me where to cut," Zach said. "I don't want to do it wrong."

Norman smiled or, rather, gloated. Elmer Lee looked like better boyfriend material all the time. "Come on, Luke. Let's show him."

They walked together to the pen to take a look at the pig. A nice pink porker, probably two hundred and fifty pounds of meat. "You've got hearts on your apron," Norman said.

"They're nice, aren't they?" Zach said. Did Norman really want to tease him about hearts right now?

Luke followed behind with a hunting rifle. That surprised Zach a little. He didn't think the Amish used guns.

"Luke is going to shoot the pig in the head. That won't kill it, but it will stun it enough so it won't feel a thing. Then we'll roll it onto its back, and I'll show you where to stick the knife so you get it right the first time."

Didn't sound too bad, at least in theory.

Zach nodded. "Okay. I'm ready."

Luke checked his rifle. "*Ach.* I don't have a bullet."

"Luke," Norman growled, "you're as empty-headed as Titus."

Cassie threw two more logs into the fire. "Norman, quit picking on Titus. He's a wonderful-gute boy to come and help us butcher the hog."

Luke went inside the barn. Norman set the sharp knife on the table and checked the loop in one of the ropes. Zach couldn't resist getting closer to Cassie, just for a minute while they waited for Luke. He squatted beside her next to the fire pit and warmed his hands. Her smile was encouraging.

"It's not too late to back out," she said. "I won't think any less of your manhood."

The thrill of being close to her warmed him to the bone. "I'll stick it out so your brothers have no reason to make fun of me."

"Except the pink shirt," she said.

"Except the pink shirt."

"And the hearts."

Titus chased Jacob and Priscilla around the lumpy patch of ground that probably served as a vegetable garden in the summer. The children giggled with glee as Titus pretended to be a snarling bear. Without looking where she stepped, Priscilla darted away from Titus's claws and tripped over a mound of dirt. Her momentum sent her sprawling onto the grate over the fire.

She screamed in agony as her bare hands met with the white-hot metal.

"Titus, you *dumkoff*," Norman yelled.

Norman, Linda, Esther, and Cassie all converged to Priscilla at once. Zach bolted to his feet and reached her first. Hooking his elbow around her waist, he snatched her off the grate and pulled her away from the fire pit. He nearly dropped her when he saw the flames crawling up the hem of her dress.

Linda screamed.

"Scilla!" Norman shouted.

If Zach swatted at the flames, Priscilla's legs would have been badly burned. He quickly set Priscilla on her feet and grabbed the burning hem in both his fists. He hissed as a searing pain almost compelled him to let go, but he kept his fists closed until he was sure he'd smothered the flames.

Linda and Cassie both knelt beside Priscilla, who screamed her lungs out. Linda studied one of Priscilla's burned hands while Cassie spoke words of comfort, even though her voice was tinged with panic. Zach's hands felt as if they were on fire, but he nudged Linda aside. "I need to look," he said.

Linda nodded and pulled her hand away.

Four long, thin blisters were already beginning to form where Priscilla's tender skin had made contact with the hot grate, but thank the Lord, they didn't look to be worse than second-degree burns and the grate hadn't touched her face.

Norman suddenly stood over Zach, taking stock of Priscilla's hands. "Stick them in the snow."

"No," Zach said, more forcefully than he meant to. "It's too cold for a burn."

"Too cold for a burn?" Norman said. "It's the best thing for a burn."

Zach didn't have time to argue. Without another word, he gathered the wailing Priscilla into his arms and ran for the house. They both needed cool running water. Cassie and Linda followed, but he soon outpaced them. It was hard to outrun a soccer player, even with a child in his arms.

"Norman, watch Jacob," Linda yelled over her shoulder as she ran.

Priscilla wasn't about to stop crying, not while her hands hurt so badly and a big Englisch stranger seemed to be kidnapping her. "We're going to get some nice, cool water on these hands," he said, in his most comforting doctor voice. She might not have been able to understand the words, but hopefully his tone would have a calming effect.

She eyed him as if he were Frankenstein's monster and bawled even harder.

"It's okay, Priscilla," he heard Cassie call behind him.

Linda said something to her in Deitsch. It didn't help.

Zach burst into Anna and Felty's house as if he belonged there. Felty sat on the sofa under the light of a propane lantern reading a book.

Zach set Priscilla on the counter next to the sink. She tried to struggle away from him. "Miss Coblenz, can you help?"

Cassie came around to his side of the counter and placed a hand on Priscilla's thigh. Linda reached across the counter and held Priscilla's shoulders. They both started speaking Deitsch at the same time, no doubt trying to persuade Priscilla to sit still.

She'd cooperate if she knew how much better it would feel under the water. Zach turned on the water and made sure of the temperature. Then taking a gentle hold of her wrists, he tugged her hands under the stream of cool water. She resisted until the water met her skin. They seemed to sigh in relief in unison. It always amazed him that simple cool water could significantly lessen the pain so quickly.

"What happened?" Felty asked.

"She burned herself on the fire pit," Linda said. "It is a blessed day that the doctor was so quick."

Cassie's smile glowed like a campfire on a frosty evening. "Thank you a million times, Doctor."

Zach fixed his eyes on Priscilla's hands. "I'm glad I was nearby."

Felty closed his book. "I always say that no good can come out of the you-know-what."

Priscilla's crying soon subsided to a whimper as the water washed over her burns. Zach still held her hands in his, so he hadn't gotten a good look at his own burns, but they felt better under the water. With any luck, he'd still be able to wield a scalpel. Or a stethoscope.

He turned to Cassie. "Will you check her legs for burns?"

Cassie lifted Priscilla's dress to reveal a hole in Priscilla's stocking where she had scraped her knee. "No burns," Cassie said. "Just a little scrape."

"I'll get a Band-Aid," Linda said. She marched down the hall to the bathroom.

"And some gauze pads," Zach called.

"And some gauze," Linda repeated.

Felty followed Linda down the hall. "I'll go get your mammi up so she can be part of all the goings-on."

In spite of the pain, Zach couldn't help but smile at Cassie. The bandanna had fallen off her head somewhere between the fire pit and the house, leaving her curls free to frolic like so many golden sunbeams on her head. What he wouldn't give to walk his fingers through those curls.

She eyed Priscilla with deep concern.

"Will you ask her if it's feeling better?" he said.

She said the words to Priscilla in Deitsch. Priscilla nodded. She pulled her hands from Zach's grasp and held them up for Cassie to see.

"Ouchie," Cassie said. Wrapping her fingers around Priscilla's wrists, Cassie turned Priscilla's hands over and kissed the back of each. "We should get these back under the water."

Zach held out his hands to take Priscilla's again. Cassie gasped. "Doctor, what happened?"

He flexed his hands gingerly. Angry red welts crossed both his palms, and blisters marred six of his fingers. "I got off pretty easy."

In alarm, Cassie grabbed one of his wrists

and pulled his hand closer for a better look. If he fastened a pathetic expression on his face, would she kiss him too?

Probably too much to hope for.

"They look terrible. I didn't even notice. Did you accidentally touch the grate when you pulled Priscilla away?"

"Her dress was on fire," Linda said, as she came back into the great room with Felty. "The doctor put it out with his hands."

"You did?" Cassie said.

He shrugged. "I thought stop, drop, and roll might hurt more than it helped."

Cassie looked at him as if she'd just discovered that his secret identity was Spider-Man. "Thank you."

"I'm only glad Priscilla didn't get hurt worse."

She laid a hand on his wrist, sending a pleasantly warm sensation all the way up his arm. "You sacrificed your hands to save my niece."

"It's not that bad."

"You didn't know that it wouldn't be." She studied the welt across his palm. "No more hog butchering for you. The pain must be something awful."

He couldn't stifle a slow smile. "You're making it feel better and better all the time."

Her lips twitched, and she blushed. He

probably shouldn't tease her, but sometimes the temptation was beyond his power to resist.

As much as he wanted to get lost in those blue eyes of hers, his hands were on fire, and Priscilla started fussing. He took Priscilla's hands in his and put them under the running water.

Linda put some soap on a paper towel and dabbed the small amount of blood from Priscilla's knee while Priscilla and Zach soaked. "How long does Priscilla need to keep her hands under the water?"

"As long as she wants. Then she needs something cool like aloe vera. Do you know what that is?"

"We have a gallon of it," Felty said, already making a beeline down the hall again. "I'll be back."

"But no petroleum jelly. There is a prescription burn cream I can get at the hospital if she's in a lot of pain, and she should take some acetaminophen right away."

When Felty came back with the aloe vera, which did turn out to be a whole gallon, Zach pulled his and Priscilla's hands from the water and dried them gently. Linda poured some aloe vera into Zach's open hands and then carried Priscilla to the table to tend to her.

Cassie led Zach to the sofa and sat him down to do a little doctoring herself. He spread the aloe vera over his hands and fingers while Cassie opened a pack of gauze pads.

"Are you going to be okay at the hospital?" she asked.

"I'll be able to get through my shift. It might be a little painful." Okay, extremely painful, but he wouldn't freak her out with the details. "The good news is that it doesn't look like there's permanent damage."

She secured the gauze to his palms with a copious amount of tape. The grace of her gentle hands mesmerized him. Oh, how he wanted to touch his lips to those hands and feel her soft skin against his mouth.

Holding his breath, he shoved his thoughts away from Cassie Coblenz and toward the Green Bay Packers. If he had any chance of self-control, he couldn't let his mind wander into forbidden territory.

The Green Bay Packers had a pretty good team this year, didn't they? For the life of him, he couldn't recall who actually played on the team, not while Cassie sat so close.

He cleared his throat. "We'll have to watch Priscilla for infection, but all things considered, we were both lucky."

Linda had finished with Priscilla's hands.

They sat at the kitchen table looking at a picture book together. "The Amish don't believe in luck," she said.

Cassie nodded. "It wasn't luck. God watched over us today."

It was the same conversation they'd had before, and Zach felt more confused than ever. "But if He watched over us, why didn't He stop Priscilla from falling into the fire in the first place?" He smiled sadly at her. "I'm not trying to be difficult. I really want to understand."

"I know you do," she said. "Bad things happen. People get sick and die. But God still watches out for us, guides and directs us when we'll listen. Luck didn't bring you here today. It was a series of choices and events and coincidences that weren't really coincidences."

"Priscilla could have been seriously hurt if you hadn't snatched her up like that," Linda said.

Cassie smiled that irresistible smile. "I like to think God had a hand in it."

Linda coaxed Priscilla off her lap, and the two of them left their book and sat next to Zach on the sofa. Linda laid a hand on Zach's arm. "I praise the Lord for you today." She turned to Cassie. "Will you give thanks to the Lord for us?"

Cassie looked mildly surprised. "Now?"

"Jah."

Cassie glanced at Zach as if she expected him to protest. He didn't know if he wanted to protest or not.

"Is that okay, Dr. Reynolds?" she asked.

"I don't mind," he said.

Linda kept one hand on Zach's arm and wrapped the other around Priscilla's shoulders. Cassie, on his right side, laid a hand on his other arm. He didn't know if he felt encircled or surrounded.

They bowed their heads.

"Heavenly Father," Cassie began. "We praise You for bringing Dr. Reynolds to us. We are grateful for him and his skills. We are grateful that he has come into our lives to help Mammi and Priscilla. Please take the pain from him today so that he may help the sick at the hospital. Please heal Priscilla so she doesn't hurt. And is it all right if we ask a blessing on the doctor's mother? Her arm is broken. Make life easier for her as she heals."

Even though they were closed, Zach's eyes stung with unshed tears. How long had it been since he'd heard someone thank God for him? And she had prayed for his mother as well. He didn't know exactly what was happening, but something stirred deep within his chest, something he hadn't felt in a very long time. Maybe he'd forgotten what grace felt like.

After his dad died, he had wanted to forget.

They said "Amen" together. Without a word, Linda patted Zach on the cheek, and then she and Priscilla went back to the table and their book.

Cassie's eyes glowed as she studied his face. "That wasn't too bad, was it?"

"No. Not too bad." He fingered the tape around his palm. "Thank you for saying those nice things, especially since you're not all that fond of me."

She cocked an eyebrow. "You're growing on me."

His heart did jumping jacks. "Growing on you? What does that mean?"

"Like a wart."

He chuckled. "Or a tumor?"

"Yes."

He felt his phone buzz in his back pants pocket. It would be a trick getting it out with gauze wrapped around both hands. He scooted to the edge of the sofa so he could reach better. With two fingers, he slid the phone from his pocket and held it carefully in his hand so as not to aggravate the pain. "It's my mom," he said, furrowing his brow.

"Do you mind if I take this? She doesn't usually call unless it's important."

"Of course. You want to be sure she's okay." Cassie ambled to the table and sat down to read with Linda and Priscilla.

"Hey, Mom," he answered.

"Hey, Zach. Is it too early to call?"

"Mom, it's four a.m. California time. I should be asking you that question."

"I couldn't sleep," Mom said.

At four a.m., Mom hadn't called to shoot the breeze. "Is something wrong?"

"Nothing's wrong, but I think I'm going to cry. I got the most wonderful package yesterday, and I just had to call and thank you. You are the best son a mother could ask for. But don't tell Jeff and Drew I said that. They'd be jealous."

"What package?"

"The paper roses are much prettier than I could have made, even with two hands. You have an incredible list of hidden talents, young man."

Zach furrowed his brow. "Mom, I have no idea what you're talking about."

"FedEx delivered a huge box of perfect tissue paper roses yesterday. There's got to be a thousand of them. Just in time for the auxiliary bazaar. A little smashed, but that will be easy to fix. The return address says they were sent from Wisconsin. I thought they were from you."

"Believe me, Mom, no matter how bad I want to help, paper roses are beyond my ability."

"Well, who in the world sent them?" Zach could hear rustling as if Mom were rummaging through her box of paper roses for a clue. "There was also a knitted thing at the bottom of the box. It looks like a sleeve to a fuzzy pink sweater."

Zach felt as if someone smacked him upside the head with a snowball.

"Zach? Are you still there?"

"It's a cast cover."

"A what?"

"The pink thing is a cast cover, Mom. For your arm."

"Oh. How cute. Regina and the other ladies will love this."

He kept his voice low and glanced at Cassie but quickly looked away so she wouldn't know he was talking about her. "I know who sent it."

"Who was it?"

"Can I call you back?"

Mom never needed an explanation for strange behavior. "Okay. In the meantime, could you get an address for me to send a thank-you note?"

"I love you, Mom."

"Love you."

The line clicked dead, but Zach held the phone to his ear as if he were still talking. It gave him a chance to stare at Cassie without needing an excuse to say anything.

Anna had told him she was going to knit a cast cover, but no doubt Cassie, the art history major, was very good at making tissue paper roses. He'd mentioned that his mom needed tissue paper roses. It would have only taken Cassie a few phone calls to figure out exactly what to do.

An invisible hand reached inside his chest and clamped onto his heart. He'd never wanted anything like he wanted Cassie at this very moment — this beautiful, angelic woman who prayed for him and baked yummasetti and made a thousand paper roses for a person she didn't even know.

He wanted her. Ached for her. And not in the lustful way a guy usually wanted a pretty girl — though the physical attraction was certainly there. He wanted to sit next to her in the quiet of the evening and watch the sun dip below the trees. He wanted to share a laugh and a bowl of popcorn and grow old with her.

He yearned to be the kind of man she wanted. The kind of man who loved her with a pure heart.

She must have felt his gaze on her because she lifted her eyes to him. He felt like a blind man seeing a sunrise for the first time. The sensation pulsed into his veins with every heartbeat until his whole being flooded with love so profound he thought he might suffocate.

She smiled at him and turned away, trying to give him some privacy for the phone call he wasn't on anymore.

How long had he been holding his breath? Did he even remember how to breathe?

This was what love was supposed to feel like. The desire to give himself completely to another person, to live and die for her whether or not she returned his love.

He'd shared mutual attraction with the girls he'd dated, a cheap imitation of the real thing, like the difference between rhinestones and diamonds.

He loved Cassie Coblenz. The thought made him feel so light, he could have scored a dozen goals without breaking a sweat. No one would have been able to stop him, not even a bulked-up keeper with a death wish.

Could she ever love him?

His resolve to win her trust took on complete urgency. The goal wasn't just to convince her to go out with him. Now he had to convince her to love him, convince her that he was worthy of her love.

But he wasn't worthy. The list of his flaws would fill a nice-sized bookshelf at the Reg.

The thought only strengthened his resolve. He wasn't worthy *yet*.

If he'd learned anything from medical school, he'd learned that the impossible became possible with grueling hard work and the will to accomplish it.

He'd convince Cassie to love him or break his heart trying.

A knife twisted in his gut when he contemplated what might be at the end of this. Was he fooling himself to think he'd ever be good enough? Or that there weren't a dozen guys right here in Bonduel more virtuous?

It didn't matter. Cassie was worth fighting for, even if he ended up a casualty on the cruel battlefield.

He'd fight for her with every last breath he had.

Anna came rolling down the hall on her handy knee scooter she had borrowed from her grandson Moses. She might as well have been on a skateboard for as fast as she moved. For a woman of eighty-four years, she wasn't very cautious.

Felty came behind her, carrying her latest knitting project and a blanket.

"What happened to my little pumpkin?" Anna said as she rolled all the way to the kitchen. Zach cringed as she nearly crashed into the table before she squeezed the hand brake.

Priscilla held up her bandaged hands for Anna to see and was rewarded with the reaction that every grandchild wishes for. Anna oohed and aahed and clucked her tongue sympathetically, inspiring Priscilla to make little whimpers in proof of how much she suffered.

Anna cupped Priscilla's chin in her hand. "A brave girl like you deserves a cookie and a big glass of chocolate milk. Three cookies. And some graham crackers with frosting. Felty dear, will you bring the cookie jar to the table?"

"If Dr. Reynolds hadn't been here, it would have been much worse," Cassie said, smiling at Zach from across the room. His pulse had never raced so fast.

Anna turned her twinkly eyes to Zach. "Doctor, this is working out better than even I could have seen. You deserve a cookie too. Cassie made snickerdoodles."

"I love snickerdoodles," he said. And Cassie. He loved Cassie.

"You can have four," Anna said.

"Mammi, you really should be off your

feet," Cassie said. "I'll hand out cookies."

Anna made a wide turn with her scooter and rolled in the direction of the recliner. "Be sure the doctor gets as many as he wants."

Even though she could have probably done a dozen pull-ups, Zach reached out and helped Anna settle into the recliner. Felty handed her the knitting and laid the blanket over her legs. "Snug as a bug in a rug," she said, giving Zach's wrapped hand a squeeze. He tried not to wince. "Doctor, you are a gift straight from heaven."

Titus opened the door, stamped the snow off his boots, and came into the house. He immediately went to the table and laid a hand on Priscilla's shoulder. "How is she?"

Linda gave Priscilla a pat in the cheek. "The doctor says she is going to be okay."

Titus knelt down to be eye level with Priscilla. He patted her on the head and said something to her in Deitsch.

Linda frowned. "It's not your fault, Titus. She knows to stay away from the fire."

"I shouldn't have pretended to be a bear. If I'd known how terrifying I was, I would have been a bunny. Priscilla wouldn't have run from a bunny."

"Accidents happen," Felty said, as he picked up his book from the end table and sat down to read. "Especially when you're doing you-know-what."

Titus shifted the toothpick from one side of his mouth to the other. "Norman says I'm a walking accident. But he didn't make me cry this time."

Cassie handed Titus a snickerdoodle. "You're the kindest, best cousin anyone could ever ask for. Most boys your age completely ignore the *kinner.* You play with them. You're everybody's favorite."

Linda put her hands over Priscilla's ears. "Norman needs to mind his manners."

Zach would have liked to teach him some manners right now.

Titus's toothpick drooped until Zach was sure it would fall out of his mouth. "Norman never did like me much. I think *Aendi* Esther agrees with him."

Felty stared at his book as if he could read and talk at the same time. "Esther's had a bee in her bonnet ever since she was little. Don't pay her any mind, Titus. She has a heart of gold."

"But she likes Elmer Lee," Titus said. "She smiled real wide at him when he got here. Did you know she's missing a tooth in the back?"

Cassie seemed to snap to attention. "Elmer Lee is here?"

Zach tensed. Cassie claimed to have no interest in Elmer Lee, but Elmer Lee was an Amish guy, and whether she wanted to admit it or not, Cassie found Amish guys fascinating. She thought they were the only "good" men in the entire world. Who knew what other powers of persuasion Elmer Lee had? He could probably lift tree trunks and anvils with his bare hands and climb wind-mills in a single bound.

"Elmer Lee stuck the pig since the doctor wasn't there to do it."

"I don't need to hear that," Felty said.

Great.

Elmer Lee had come just in time to save the day. Zach could hear Norman already. *Finally, somebody who knows how to do something useful. Someone worthy of my sister. Somebody who knows how to stick pigs and fixes roofs for widows and orphans.*

Zach kind of wanted to throw up. He was completely out of his element.

Titus took a bite of his cookie with the toothpick still at the corner of his lips. His chewing didn't seem to disturb the tooth-pick at all. Had Titus ever swallowed one of his beloved toothpicks? "Aunt Esther is keeping a tight hold of the baby and won't let Jacob near the fire. They sent me to check on Priscilla and fetch the rest of you out to scrape the hog carcass."

Cassie scooted her chair from under the table. "Linda should stay with Priscilla, and Dr. Reynolds's hands are injured, but I'll come out."

Zach studied Cassie's face. Was she eager to see Elmer Lee or just eager to help?

Zach heard a faint crack as Titus's toothpick snapped in two. A deep line appeared between his eyebrows. "Norman says not to come until you're dressed Plain. He says as long as you're staying with Mammi and Dawdi, you should show them respect by honoring our ways."

Cassie seemed to freeze in her tracks. "Oh. I see."

Linda heaved a sigh but didn't say anything.

Titus laced his fingers together and bowed his head sheepishly. "Aunt Esther says to wear the dress she made you, and Elmer Lee says he'd really like to see you in pink."

Zach couldn't help himself. He muttered between his teeth. "Did Luke have anything to say on the matter?"

"He needs a Band-Aid," Titus said.

At least one of Cassie's brothers was staying out of it.

Titus pulled the toothpick from his mouth. Zach got the feeling that he only did that when something was particularly important. "I apologize, Cassie. I promised I'd deliver the message."

Anna pointed a knitting needle at Titus as if she wanted to skewer him. "For goodness' sake, Titus, go tell Norman to get off his high horse."

Titus seemed momentarily confused. "He's not on a horse. He's got his boots ankle-deep in mud."

Linda lifted Priscilla off her lap and stood up. "I'll go help, Cassie. You can read Priscilla another book."

Cassie held up her hand. "It's okay, Linda. Priscilla needs you, and it won't be long before the baby will want to eat. I'll change into the pink."

The muscles in Zach's neck tightened until he thought he might pop an important blood vessel. Cassie had to walk by him to go to her room to dress. It was all he could do to keep from stopping her, to keep from telling her that she didn't have to give in to Norman's demands. Norman was a bully, and Cassie willingly handed control over to him.

But if he stopped her from going, wouldn't that make him just like Norman? He had as little right to boss Cassie around as Norman did.

Zach pressed his lips together and watched Cassie walk down the hall and into her room and shut the door behind her. He wanted to growl. Or pop Norman in the mouth with his fist.

Standing there staring at Cassie's bedroom door, he resolved to do two things: Win Cassie's heart and put Norman in his place.

He'd look forward to both tasks.

CHAPTER FOURTEEN

"Well, I'm glad you're not dead."

"Sorry I didn't call sooner, Mom. It was a sixteen-hour shift and then I came home and crashed."

"I'm relieved to know you didn't die."

Zach flexed the hand where the worst burns were. He wouldn't have believed it if he hadn't experienced it personally, but he'd barely noticed the pain during his shift. He hadn't been able to do much with the awkward gauze pads getting in the way while he treated patients, so he'd taken them off and used his hands as much as ever. He'd wrapped up the blisters on his fingers so they wouldn't burst, but he had needed his hands free. It had been almost as if he hadn't burned himself at all. Had it been due to Cassie's prayer?

Whatever the reason, he was grateful for the sixteen-hour reprieve, because the red welts across his palms were starting to sting as if someone had swiped a barbed whip across them.

"Zach? You okay?"

"Kind of. I burned my hands yesterday."

"How bad?" Mom said, switching into her concerned mother voice.

"Second-degree. Nothing serious, but it really hurts."

"Have you got some aloe vera? Or lavender oil is even better. Should I send you some?" That was his mom. Tell her your problem, she'd tried to solve it for you, even from two thousand miles away.

"I'll see what I can find at the health food store."

"Is there a health food store in Shawano?"

"I don't know."

She grunted. "Now you're just humoring me."

"Mom, can I ask you a question?"

She must have sensed the subtle change in his voice. "Anything, sweetheart. What is it?"

"Do you remember when you dragged me to that musical when I was in high school?"

"Which one? As I recall, I dragged you to several musicals as my date."

Zach sat on the sofa and concentrated on what he wanted to say. Was it weird to talk to his mom about this? "The one about Don

Quixote?"

"Man of La Mancha?"

"That sounds right," Zach said. "I don't know why I remember this, but in one of the songs he talks about reaching the un-reachable star, or something like that. Does that sound familiar at all?"

"Zach, it's only one of the most famous songs in all of musical theater history."

"Whatever."

Mom squeaked as if she'd been stuck by a pin. "Whatever? I've failed as a mother."

Zach smiled. "You paid for braces and made tacos every Sunday night. You did okay."

"The name of the song is 'The Impossible Dream.' " She started humming it over the phone.

He let her finish the whole song. "Lovely, Mom."

"Thank you."

"So there's a part in that song that says, *'This is my quest, to love pure and chaste from afar.'* "

"Yes."

"Do you think it's possible to do that? For someone like me, I mean?"

Silence on the other end. Had she stepped away from the phone to have a heart attack?

"Mom?"

"You've met somebody." Did he detect a tinge of eagerness in her voice?

"I love her, Mom."

Again with the silence. Was his being in love some sort of earth-shattering event?

Yeah.

"Mom?"

"I'm trying not to overreact," she said.

"You're afraid if you act too happy, you'll spook me?"

She laughed. "I don't want you to get the impression that I've been praying for this for months and months."

"Why would I ever suspect that?"

"What's her name?" Mom said. "Give me all the details."

"She's the one who made you all those flowers."

"I love her already."

He heard the grinding sound of the old pencil sharpener. "Mom, you're not taking notes, are you?"

"Of course. To tell the ladies at the auxiliary."

"Not a word, Mom."

"I'm teasing, Zach. I wouldn't gossip about something this important. But I am taking notes. I don't want to forget anything. What's her name, and do you know how to spell it?"

Zach chuckled. "Her name is Cassie."

"Is it short for anything, like Cassandra?"

Zach brushed the back of his hand back and forth across the whiskers on his chin. "Cassandra doesn't seem like an Amish name."

More silence. She was probably choking.

"She isn't Amish anymore," Zach interjected, before Mom suffocated. "But her whole family's Amish. And she's very religious and, okay, virtuous, and okay, Mom, I might as well come out and say it. I'm wondering if a guy like me could ever hope to deserve her, especially since she's a virgin and I'm not."

Zach could almost see Mom's eyebrows fly off her face in the silence on the other end of the line. "Did you strain any muscles trying to get all that out?" she said.

"Come on. It's a little awkward confessing my sins to my mom."

"You think I didn't already know?" Mom said.

"Well, yeah. I knew you knew, but saying it is kind of embarrassing. It doesn't matter. I need your advice."

"Your dad was always better at stuff like this."

The scorching memory at the mere mention of Dad usually had Zach panting for air in a matter of seconds. But tonight, he thought of long talks in the garage working on the Honda and dark nights under the stars solving the world's problems with his dad and a jumbo package of hot dogs. The hundred-percent-beef kind.

They were good memories. Cassie said Dad wanted him to be happy and God did too. For some reason, he almost believed it.

"I'm not very good at dispensing advice," Mom said. "Do I understand you right? You want to prove yourself to this girl, show her a pure and chaste heart, like in the song?"

"Yeah, and she thinks that the only thing I want from her is to get her into bed." His head felt heavy just thinking about it.

"You didn't try that, did you?"

"Give me some credit, Mom." His confidence plummeted. If his own mother assumed the worst, what chance did he have with Cassie?

"I give you all the credit in the world," she said. "You're my son. The fact that we're having this conversation is a sign of your good heart."

Zach leaned back against the sofa cushion. "I don't know how to make her love me."

"You can be your own wonderful self."

"It's not enough. She knew me in college."

"You can't do anything about your past

273

except learn from it. If she's truly a Christian, then she knows people can change. And you know it too. I took you to church for seventeen years. Something should have sunk in."

"Should I tell her?"

"Tell her what?"

"That there will be no touching, no hand-holding, and no kissing until I've won her heart. Like, 'Hey, Cassie, have you noticed how I'm trying to love you pure and chaste from afar?' "

"It sounds a little odd when you put it like that."

"Okay. I won't tell her. I'll show her. I'm going to prove to her that I love her enough to control my passions, because my greatest desire is to be with her."

Mom sighed. "That is so romantic."

"I don't know if it's romantic, but it's the truth."

"You could sing her that song."

Zach rolled his eyes. "Oh, yeah, because that's not odd."

Her voice got quiet all of a sudden. "Thank you for going to musicals with me. I know it was pure torture."

"I did it because I love you. I don't regret a single one. Except maybe *Oklahoma* — the stupidest play ever written."

274

"You're bordering on sacrilege there, young man," she said.

"As long as you still love me, I don't care."

"I love you forever."

"You too, Mom."

CHAPTER FIFTEEN

Was it an unwritten rule of hospitals that they had to stock the world's most boring magazines in their waiting rooms?

She should have brought her GRE book so she could have gotten a little study time in. Instead she was stuck perusing the AARP magazine and a three-year-old copy of *Car Craft.* Running her fingernails down a chalkboard would have been more pleasant, even if she had just read how to rebuild a carburetor.

Dawdi seemed perfectly content with his issue of *Consumer Reports* with a flip phone on the cover. Cassie glanced at the date. 2004. Surely someone at the hospital should be alerted to the magazine problem immediately.

She glanced at the clock. Zach, Dr. Reynolds, said the surgery would take about half an hour. It should be any minute now.

Dawdi pointed to a picture in his magazine. "These new phones look mighty fancy."

Please, Doctor. Please come before Dawdi starts comparing service plans.

Oh, if she could always conjure him up so easily. He came around the corner just as she wished for him, looking as handsome as ever in his pistachio green scrubs. His head was bare, but she could tell he'd been wearing some sort of surgical hat because his hair was attractively mussed just the way she liked it.

He caught sight of her, and his smile could have lit up a soccer field in the middle of the night. Cassie nudged Dawdi, still engrossed in reading about 911 calls on a cell phone, and they stood together to greet the doctor.

He reached out his hand and shook Dawdi's vigorously, then offered his hand to her. It was probably the most fleeting handshake she'd ever experienced. He released her hand almost before he'd even touched her, as if he'd been burned, even though she knew his hands were better. He'd burned them over a week ago.

"The surgery went very well. Better than expected," he said, still beaming like a lighthouse. "We took some skin from her thigh and grafted it onto her foot. I performed the surgery and Dr. Mann observed. He was pleased with the results."

"Can we see her?" Cassie asked.

"Sure," the doctor said. "They just took her to recovery. I'll show you the way."

They followed him down the hall, through two sets of doors, and into a maze of alcoves and curtains. Dr. Reynolds pointed to a space set apart by a hospital curtain. "She's behind there."

Dawdi nudged aside one end of the curtain and ambled into the room to be with Mammi.

Dr. Reynolds looked at her as if he were about to ask for a lock of her hair. "It will be a few minutes before she comes out of anesthesia. Can I introduce you to someone while you're waiting?"

"Yes. Of course."

His smile only got wider, and he motioned with his clipboard. "This way."

They walked side by side through the two sets of double doors and back into the main hall. "I'm glad surgery went well," Cassie said.

He stopped and turned to her, his eyes sparkling with their own light. "I felt it. I wanted you to know that I actually felt it."

"Felt what?"

"Your prayer. I know it made a difference."

Right before they had taken Mammi, Cassie had quietly suggested that they pray for a successful surgery and Mammi's quick recovery. She hadn't wanted to offend Dr. Reynolds, but she had sensed a change in the last couple of weeks and thought he might be willing. He was. Surely, God was changing his heart. "You think God helped you through the operation?"

He nodded. "I've never done that kind of surgery before. It was almost as if God took hold of my hands and guided me. Dr. Mann said I looked like a veteran."

"I'm so glad." She felt as warm as a potbelly stove. Not only because Dr. Reynolds's faith was growing, but because he had trusted her enough to agree to the prayer. She'd judged Doctor Reynolds harshly in the first place. Instead of the jerk she'd thought him to be, he was kind and thoughtful, unselfish and good-natured.

And she liked him, more than she would ever have thought possible. It amazed her how easily she could talk to him and how comfortable she felt being with him. He bristled every time Norman came to Huckleberry Hill and clenched his teeth whenever anyone mentioned Elmer Lee's name. It was very endearing.

She almost regretted not saying yes when he'd asked her out.

Because he wouldn't ask again.

He called her Miss Coblenz and avoided touching her at all costs, seemingly determined to keep a professional distance. She truly appreciated that. Or rather, she used to appreciate that. Now it frustrated her no end.

Didn't he realize that a girl could change her mind?

"I know you want to get back to your grandma," he said, "but there's someone I've been wanting you to meet. Are you okay if we take the stairs? Some days it's the only exercise I get."

Cassie led the way into the stairwell, a dank and dim space with gray stairs and even grayer walls. Dr. Reynolds followed behind her as if wanting to be near just in case she fell backward. "For as much as health professionals tell people they should use the stairs," he said, "this stairwell is very unfriendly."

"This and the magazines."

"We have unfriendly magazines?" he said.

"Old and boring ones in the waiting rooms. Some of them could probably be worth some money if you sold them as antiques."

He chuckled. "I don't know if I can do anything about the stairwell, but surely the administration could spring for some new magazines. I'll get right on that."

She turned and smiled at him. "Will you please?"

On the second floor, they walked halfway down the hall, and Dr. Reynolds tapped on one of the doors. "Come in," a muffled voice said.

He opened the door for Cassie, and she walked into the brightly lit room. A little boy, so skinny he looked like a pile of bones covered with skin, lay in the bed. Dark circles made half moons under his eyes, and his skin seemed to have been stretched over his face. He watched TV with a woman who sat in a chair next to the bed.

Cassie recognized the woman. She looked to be in her late thirties with light brown highlights in her dark brown hair. Her eyes were dark under long lashes and heavy brows. She was thick around the middle with that motherly figure that came from bearing children.

The little boy exploded into a smile when he saw Dr. Reynolds. "Zach!" he said. "Messi scored two goals yesterday."

Dr. Reynolds smiled back. "I know. And

did you see Mathieu save a goal with his head?"

"Yes. That was so sweet."

The boy with the scarf.

The reason that Dr. Reynolds was willing to talk to God again.

With a boyish grin, Dr. Reynolds held up his hand for a high five. Austin gave him one. Cassie thought the doctor had never, ever looked so attractive.

"Barca's playing Madrid on Saturday," the doctor said. "Are you going to watch?"

"No. The game starts in the middle of the night, and this stupid hospital TV doesn't get any good stations."

Dr. Reynolds nudged Austin's arm. "Austin, this is Cassie Coblenz. She's a friend of mine."

Austin tensed. "Are you going to give me a shot?"

"No," Cassie said. "I'm just here for a visit." She held out her hands to show they were empty.

Austin exhaled in relief.

Dr. Reynolds motioned to the woman who had stood up to greet them. "This is Jamie, Austin's mom."

Cassie reached out her hand. "You look familiar."

"I go to the Bible church near the high

school," Jamie said.

"Of course," Cassie said. "I should have remembered. I've only been in town a few weeks, so I haven't learned everybody's names there yet."

Jamie's eyes seemed alight with amusement. "I know who you are. You made quite a stir among the single men the first day you attended services. There was talk of drawing straws to see who got to ask out the gorgeous blonde first."

Cassie felt the warmth creep up her neck, not as much because of the conversation but because of the way Dr. Reynolds looked at her, as if he were intensely interested in what the single guys at church had decided.

Cassie cleared her throat. "I think Peter Bench won. Or lost, depending on how you look at it."

The doctor's gaze pierced through her skull, and his intensity flared like a forest fire.

Jamie nodded. "I would have expected Peter to get first dibs of the three. He's already asked you out?"

"He took me to a fancy restaurant in Green Bay." She glanced at the doctor, who hadn't moved a muscle. He should really stop looking at her like that.

"That sounds like Peter," Jamie said.

Cassie tried to ignore the doctor. "I was afraid to sit on the chair. It looked like they upholstered it out of silk."

"Peter has lots of disposable income. Though why he would live in Shawano with all that cash is beyond me." Jamie's eyes darted between Cassie and the doctor. She reached over and ruffled Austin's hair. "We have a Bible study on Wednesday nights. You're always invited."

"Thank you," Cassie said, feeling palpable relief. It was very kind of Jamie to move the conversation in another direction. "I'll think about it."

"I've been trying to convince the doctor to join us, but he's always got some lame excuse, like surgery or wart removal."

Dr. Reynolds smiled sheepishly and shrugged. "There's a wart epidemic. We're working day and night to keep it under control."

Jamie glanced sideways at Cassie. "If we both work on him, he's bound to crack."

Cassie eyed Dr. Reynolds. She knew how uncomfortable she felt when someone badgered her into doing something she didn't want to do. She smiled. "It's not my place to work on anybody."

Dr. Reynolds's intense gaze softened like warm tapioca pudding.

Jamie smiled back as if sharing a secret. "Not my place either, I suppose, but I'm going to do it anyway."

Dr. Reynolds seemed to have to pry his eyes from hers to look at Austin. "How are you feeling today?"

Austin let out a great sigh. "I'm okay."

"It looks like they're still feeding you medicine through a tube."

"Yeah."

Dr. Reynolds leaned closer and rested his arm on the bed railing, pinning Austin with a sympathetic gaze. "How are you really feeling?"

Several emotions played on Austin's face. Cassie could tell he wanted to put on a brave front but also wanted what comfort the doctor could give him. The little boy in him won out. His eyes pooled with tears. "I'm not very brave."

"Are you kidding?" Dr. Reynolds said. "You're feeling rotten, lying here in this rotten hospital bed, watching a stupid cartoon. You haven't run away or hit any nurses today. I'd say that's pretty brave."

"I hate it here," Austin said.

Dr. Reynolds nodded. "I hate the smell."

"And the food tastes terrible."

"I'm sick of green Jell-O," said Dr. Reynolds.

Austin made a face. "It's better than lemon."

Cassie loved the rich bass of Dr. Reynolds's laughter. "If your doctor says it's okay, I'll bring you some of Cassie's peanut butter cookies. They are to die for."

Cassie self-consciously played with the hair at the back of her neck. She shouldn't get all tingly just because Dr. Reynolds liked her peanut butter cookies.

"My mom sometimes brings McDonald's cheeseburgers," Austin said.

Dr. Reynolds propped his cheek on his fist. "Remember how I told you I played soccer?"

Austin acted as if the question insulted his intelligence. "I know."

"My friend on the team, one of the best keepers you'll ever see, got really sick one night. I had to take him to the emergency room. They tried to give him a shot, and he screamed like a baby. He had a needle phobia."

"What's a needle phobia?"

"He was scared of needles. I had to hold his arm down so he wouldn't jerk it around when they stuck the needle in. That made it worse, because it hurts a lot less if you relax."

"I know," Austin said. "Marla told me."

"So it's okay to be scared, and it's okay to cry and fuss. Even the big guys freak out sometimes."

Austin rubbed his eye. "But it doesn't do any good to make a fuss about it. That's what my mom says."

"But it doesn't mean you're not brave. It just means it's hard."

"Really hard," Austin said, letting out a long, slow breath.

Dr. Reynolds nudged Austin's shoulder with his fist. "So give yourself a break. I'm here to help. I'll hold your arm down if you need me to."

"Mom says Jesus will help me too."

Dr. Reynolds made only the slightest hesitation. "Yes, He will."

"Will you say a prayer to Jesus?" Austin asked.

Cassie didn't know how Dr. Reynolds could have said no to that trusting face turned up to his.

Dr. Reynolds nodded slowly. "I will."

Austin clasped his hands together and bowed his head.

The doctor raised an eyebrow. "Now?"

"Yes," Austin said with a giggle. "When did you think?"

Dr. Reynolds cleared his throat before bowing his head and closing his eyes. Cas-

287

sie did the same.

"Dear God," he began. The sound of his voice, so deep and heartfelt, gave her goose bumps all the way up her arms. "Hallowed be Thy name. My friend Austin is afraid. Will You comfort him and help him to sleep well tonight? Will You please help him feel better and heal his body so that he can get out of this hospital and play soccer and never eat green Jell-O again?"

Cassie felt a tear roll down her cheek. Dr. Reynolds prayed like someone who knew how but haltingly as if he hadn't done it for a very long time. This was the man who was mad at God? The one who'd lost his faith? She didn't believe it for a minute.

"Amen," they said together.

Cassie wiped the moisture from her face. She looked at Jamie's. Her eyes were glistening with tears too.

Austin beamed. "Now I know I'll get better."

Dr. Reynolds studied Cassie's face and gave her a doubtful smile. "That bad, huh?"

She smiled back. He always said that. "It was beautiful. I'm kind of a baby," Cassie said barely above a whisper. If she tried to talk louder, her voice might crack.

"I reduce women to tears with my sorry attempts to talk to God."

288

Jamie reached over and slugged him lightly on the shoulder. "You did fine."

"Ouch!" he said, rubbing his shoulder as if she'd really hurt him, but it would take a lot more than that to bruise those rock-solid arms.

"Soon you're going to have every patient in this hospital requesting prayers," Jamie said. "Especially the ladies."

A nurse tapped lightly on the door and came into the room carrying Austin's breakfast tray. "Good morning, Austin," she said, in her chipper nurse voice. "Time for breakfast." She gave Dr. Reynolds a playful smile and a wink. "Good morning, Dr. Reynolds."

"Hi, Stacey."

Cassie felt annoyed for no reason whatsoever, except maybe for the fact that the nurse made googly eyes at the doctor. But why should she care about that? It was none of her business how many girls fell at Dr. Reynolds's feet, or what kind of relationship Stacey and the doctor had.

It might not be any of her business, but when Dr. Reynolds smiled back at that nurse, an illogical pang of jealousy stabbed her right in the chest. What had happened to her? She was supposed to be immune to Dr. Reynolds's charms. Wouldn't he still try to jump into bed with her at the first opportunity? Shouldn't his many character flaws keep her safely indifferent to him?

But she wasn't indifferent. Down in the deepest place in her heart, in spite of everything, she liked him, and she rebelled at the thought that he was like the other Englisch guys she'd known in college.

Once she'd refused to go out with him, he'd never pushed her or made her feel guilty for saying no. He hadn't been mad about it either, as if she were an idiot for not wanting to go out with him. She got that a lot from guys.

Rational or not, Cassie found herself seething with jealousy over a wink and a smile. And she didn't like the feeling one little bit.

The nurse pulled the portable table in front of Austin and set the tray on it. "Smells delicious," she said, as she took the lid off the tray.

Dr. Reynolds set his clipboard on the bed and leaned over to get a better look at Austin's breakfast. French toast, eggs, orange juice, and green Jell-O.

Austin and Dr. Reynolds met eyes. In unison they threw up their hands and screamed. Dr. Reynolds squealed like a little girl, which sent Austin into a fit of laughter.

Cassie and Jamie laughed too.

"I'll save you," Dr. Reynolds bellowed.

Cassie practically jumped out of her socks when Dr. Reynolds scooped Austin's Jell-O from the tray with his bare hands and ran around the bed to the trash can, holding the green stuff away from his body as if it were toxic. He flipped the Jell-O into the can with a flick of his wrist.

Austin gave him a round of applause.

"Doctor," Stacey stuttered, "I don't think you're supposed to do that."

Dr. Reynolds rinsed his hands at the sink and draped an arm over Jamie's shoulder. "It had to be done, Stacey," he said. "Don't you agree, Miss Fedora?"

Jamie jabbed her elbow into his ribs. He doubled over in mock pain. "It's Miss Stetson," Jamie said. "And you owe me a dollar. I was going to eat that Jell-O."

"That was awesome," Austin said, still giggling.

Stacey only had eyes for the doctor. She smiled and shook her head. "If you say so. You're the doctor." She gave him one last enticing glance, as if inviting him to follow her, and walked out the door, swinging her hips like a pendulum as she went.

To Cassie's relief, Dr. Reynolds didn't seem to notice. "Call me anytime. I'm not afraid to do battle with evil foods." He picked up his clipboard. "Cassie and I have to go now. Her grandma just got out of surgery, and she needs to be with her." His eyes met hers, and he smiled. The look he gave her was so attractive she thought she might faint.

"Okay." Austin picked up his fork and stabbed at his eggs. "Come back, and we can play FIFA sometime."

"Bye, Austin," Cassie said. "It was nice to meet you."

"I expect to see you in church on Sunday, Doctor," Jamie said as they walked out the door.

The doctor shot a mischievous grin over his shoulder and kept walking.

They ambled down the hall and into the stairwell. "Great kid," Dr. Reynolds said.

"Is he going to be okay?"

His face looked as if it had fallen into shadow. "He's a fighter."

"I can tell."

"I'm worried, though. Even though I'm still mad at God, I've said a lot of prayers for Austin, just in case."

"I'm glad you're not too mad to talk to Him."

He smiled faintly. "This is the first time we've been alone for more than a week."

"Is it?"

"On Wednesday after I changed your mammi's foot dressing, your dawdi showed me how to clean the horse's hooves. On Friday, we fixed the water pump and unclogged the toilet."

"I'm sure you enjoyed that."

"Immensely," he said, making her laugh at his teasing grin. What kind of a man volunteered to unclog the toilet just to be nice?

He suddenly became serious and eyed her as if he had something very important on his mind. Was he going to ask her out again?

Her pulse surged with anticipation.

"Miss Coblenz —"

This was not starting out well. A guy didn't call you "Miss" if he was about to ask you out. "Miss Coblenz sounds like an old lady. Please call me Cassie."

The seriousness vanished, and he seemed like a little kid for a minute. "Are you sure?"

"You come to my house three times a week. You unclogged my toilet. You should call me Cassie. And I didn't mean to interrupt you."

She might have just given him permission to eat all the snickerdoodles in the cookie jar. "Okay, Cassie." She loved the way it sounded when he said it, like someone wrapping a warm blanket around her shoulders. He raised his eyebrows. "Can I call you Cassandra when I'm feeling especially fancy?"

She coughed as the embarrassment lodged in her throat. "My . . . my real name isn't Cassandra."

"Just Cassie, then?"

She coughed again. Was she breaking out in hives? "I'm named after a woman in the Bible, full of good works. She made coats and stuff for people. I think my mamm had hopes I'd be a good quilter when I grew up."

"I don't remember a Cassie in the Bible."

Might as well get her shame out in the open. "My name is Dorcas."

His mouth fell open, and he stammered incoherently for a moment. "Dorcas?"

Her lips twitched upward at the look on his face — a mixture of disbelief, amusement, and sheer panic that he'd have to lie and tell her he liked her name. The laughter bubbled from inside her. "It's okay. I'm as horrified as you are."

He decided it was safe to laugh. Their mirth echoed off the cement walls of the stairwell. "Cassie it is. Or I could call you Dorcassie. It sounds sort of British."

She attempted a stern glare. "Don't you dare. I'll never be able to show my face in public again."

"Dorcas. It's kind of cute."

"Don't try to smooth things over." She tucked a lock of hair behind her ear. "I know how you really feel."

"Do you?" His piercing gaze held her captive for one breathless moment and then disappeared. He looked down and cleared his throat. "If I call you Cassie or Dorcassie, will you call me Zach? It's short for Zacharias."

"Really?"

He grinned. "No. I just wanted to make you feel better."

She made a face at him.

"When you call me Dr. Reynolds, it sounds like you're trying to keep your distance."

That was exactly what she had been trying to do. "I want to show you the respect that a doctor deserves. You've earned the title."

He groaned. "I'd rather have your friendship than your respect. I mean, I like to be respected, but respect seems like something you should give to old people."

"I've seen how good you are to your patients. You have my respect."

His expression radiated something akin to tenderness. "Can we be friends too?"

She felt warm all over. "I'd like that."

He slowly reached toward her, and for a breathless second, she thought he might take her hand. Instead, he dropped his arm to his side and took a step back, but he didn't stop looking at her like a kid looks at the tree on Christmas morning. "Cassie." Saying her first name made him smile. "Cassie, there aren't enough words to tell you how grateful I am for what you did for my mom. She was so worried about those flowers. I can't believe you made a thousand."

The way he looked at her made her feel as if warm honey flowed through her veins. "It wasn't just me. Mammi took a break from her knitting, and my mamm spent the day helping us too."

"Your mom?" He raised both eyebrows in surprise. Mamm hadn't exactly made a good impression on him. "Why would she do that for someone she's never met?"

"I told her how upset you were about it. We all wanted to help."

"How can I repay your kindness?"

"Repay? After all you've done for my mammi? Believe me, the balance is owing to you."

He lowered his head. "I'm a doctor. It's my job."

"No doctor I've ever met would unclog a toilet for one of his patients."

He flashed a self-effacing smile. "It's a bonus service."

"You've got some very useful skills. Any Amish mammi would be impressed."

This seemed to make him disproportionately happy. "You noticed?"

"I've never seen a more eager or faster learner. You could make a go of it as a farmer."

"Even an Amish farmer?"

"Yes. If you weren't such a good doctor."

His eyes shone. "I don't think I'll quit my day job just yet, but it's nice to know you think I could be Amish. Maybe I should grow one of those beards."

She giggled. "Maybe you should."

"Why does Norman have a beard but Luke doesn't? Can't he grow one?"

"Men don't grow beards until they're married," Cassie said.

"That's too bad. I thought I'd grow one just to show Norman I could. He probably doesn't think I'm manly enough."

Cassie shook her head. "Nobody measures up to Norman's standards unless they're Amish and approved by my mother."

Zach deflated slightly. "Maybe we should tell Norman I unclogged the toilet. That might ramp up my manliness."

"It's probably as high as it can go already."

He whipped his head around to look at her. "You think so?"

Cassie's heart skipped a beat as she felt the blush on her cheeks. "You put out fires with your bare hands."

He grinned. "And I'm manly enough to wear pink."

"Norman would never even dare attempt that."

CHAPTER SIXTEEN

Cassie's heart did a double flip-flop when she drove up the hill and saw Zach's matching Honda parked in front of Mammi's house. He was early. Last week after surgery, he told her he'd be by today at ten a.m. She parked her car beside his and checked her phone. Only nine o'clock.

She swiveled the rearview mirror to get a look at herself. *Ach, du lieva.* She looked a mess. She had pulled her hair into a clumsy ponytail, and she wasn't wearing any makeup. Not to mention the fact that her workout clothes were damp with sweat, and she probably smelled like a high school gym locker.

After he saw her sorry state, she had no hope he'd ask her out again. The girls Zach dated would probably never dream of sweating.

There was nothing she could do about it. She couldn't very well sit in the car and wait for him to leave. He'd see her anyway when he came out to his car. Groaning, she opened her Honda door and crunched her way through the snow to the house. She went into the house and waited for the people inside to recoil in disgust.

Zach sat on the edge of the sofa next to Mammi with a ball of red yarn at his feet and a pair of knitting needles in his fists. His tongue stuck partway out of his mouth, and his brows were pulled together in concentration. An unrecognizable tangle of yarn hung from his knitting needles.

"Cassie," Mammi said from her perch on the recliner. "I'm teaching Dr. Reynolds how to knit."

Zach focused all his attention on his disastrous pile of yarn. "I'm making a pot holder in case I ever own a pot."

Mammi beamed as if Zach were her prize pupil. "He's giving it a very good try yet."

Zach held his needles like two tennis rackets and tried to loop the yarn without dropping them. "What she means to say is, 'I'm really bad at this.' It's the piano teacher secret code."

Cassie couldn't hold back a smile. Just when she thought the doctor couldn't get any more endearing, he surprised her. His eagerness was as cute as a pet store full of puppies.

A pleasant ache grew in her chest and throbbed through her veins. She suddenly wanted Dr. Reynolds to drop those knitting needles, march across the room, and kiss her silly.

She didn't even care that she was sweaty.

The knitting needles and that concerned, almost grim look on his face made him that much more attractive.

Oh, sis yuscht. She was in trouble.

"Insert the right needle into the loop on the left needle," Mammi said, using her own pair to show Zach how to do it. "Good. Now wrap it under and over the right needle. You see? Easy."

Zach listened to Mammi's every instruction as if he were getting a tutorial on how to do brain surgery. Cassie sincerely hoped he was better at brain surgery, because the knitting looked hopeless.

Cassie hung her coat on the hook, wondering if she should make a beeline for the shower before Zach got a good look at her. Too late. He glanced up, and his face broke into a smile. "Wow," he said. "You look great."

"A bigger lie never was told in this house," Cassie said.

He pinned her with an earnest gaze. "I'm

not lying. That green goes great with your eyes."

She turned her face slightly so he wouldn't notice the blush. "It's okay, you don't have to —"

"And your hair . . ." He stopped short. "Is it okay to tell you how pretty you are? Some women get offended by that."

Mammi leaned close to his ear. "Whatever you do, don't tell me I'm pretty. The Amish aren't supposed to notice such things. It makes us proud."

Zach grinned and nodded. "Okay."

"But praise my granddaughter all you like. She has lovely hair and nice skin. She gets them from her dawdi."

Zach peered at Mammi. "She definitely gets her good looks from you, Anna. But don't tell any Amish people I said that."

"I've always tried to look pretty for Felty's benefit, but save your praise for Cassie. She's the one who's not married yet."

Zach turned his eyes to Cassie. "I'm just getting started."

"Not if you want to concentrate on your knitting," Mammi said.

Zach lifted his hands to show Mammi. He'd somehow gotten his index finger knitted into his pot holder. "I'm afraid Cassie has distracted me."

Mammi smiled kindly, so as not to discourage him, but even she could see he was a lost cause. "Maybe we should take a break. You can always come back another day and finish. It's going to be a very nice pot holder once you're done with it."

To his credit, Zach acted as if he were disappointed about not finishing his knitting project. He gave Mammi a slight smile before wrestling his finger out of the middle of the yarn and depositing his needles on the table next to Mammi's recliner.

He stood and clapped his hands together. "Now, what else can I do?"

"Cassie's doing laundry today." The way Mammi said it made it sound fun.

Zach's eyes lit up. "By hand?"

"Sort of," Cassie said.

"I'd love to help."

"Are you sure?" Cassie said. "You've already burned yourself. I'd hate it if you smashed a finger."

"Sounds exciting. I didn't even know that was possible doing laundry." Cassie took him to the washroom, a small space next to the bathroom.

"It's better not to let Norman catch me knitting. There'd be no recovering from that," Zach said as he followed close behind.

"I don't know which is worse to Norman,

303

knitting or laundry. If you're trying to establish your manhood, you'd better not come within ten feet of the washroom."

"In my world, a real man does laundry, no matter what Norman thinks." He rolled up his sleeves. "How is it done?"

The washer was little more than a square tub with an agitator in the bottom and a wringer propped on the side. While Zach watched, she turned on the hose that Mammi kept there and started to fill the laundry sink and tub. Once she filled the tub, she measured a capful of soap and let Zach pour it into the water.

He pointed to the gas-powered motor next to the washer. "Is this a lawn mower engine?"

She smiled. "Something like that. The exhaust pipe runs out the window but the motor is very loud. Do you want to start it?"

"It's because I have muscles, isn't it?"

"Yes. That's why I wanted your help with the laundry. I don't know how I will be able to do it without you."

Zach pulled the starter cord, and the engine roared to life.

"It's noisy," Cassie said, raising her voice to be heard over the hum of machine.

"Do you see that knob at the front of the

washer?" she asked.

"Yep."

"Pull it out, and the agitator will start."

He bent over and pulled the knob. The agitator swished the water around and bubbles began to form on the surface. "It's like my washing machine at the apartment," he said, "except smaller and noisier."

"I'm glad to know you do laundry."

He curled one side of his mouth. "Only when I run out of underwear."

She picked up the laundry basket and propped it on her hip. "The clothes go in one at a time. And be careful not to get your hand caught in some moving part. I'd hate to be responsible for ruining your promising medical career."

He grinned. "I think I could practice pediatrics with a hook."

She shook her head. "Kids are scared enough of the doctor as it is."

Cassie had been very selective about what she'd put in the laundry basket. None of her clothes and positively no underwear, to spare both her and Zach the embarrassment. They put in Mammi's dresses and Dawdi's trousers. The agitator pulled each article under the water as it rotated back and forth.

Cassie placed the lid on the tub. "We have

to let it wash for a few minutes."

"That's a pretty cool invention," Zach said, then laughed. "I guess they got cooler and cooler through the years."

"I think this one is older than me."

"You're nice to let me tag along."

Cassie ignored the way the butterflies in her stomach fluttered wildly. She'd like to have him tag along more often. "You won't think I'm so nice when we hang these on the line."

He winced. "Outside?"

"You might get frostbite. It's not too late to back out."

He gave her a wide grin. "Bring it on."

"The clothes don't really dry. They freeze. Sometimes you see icicles hanging off pant legs or frost forming on dresses. Once they're frozen solid, we bring them in and hang them to finish drying inside. Unmentionables dry inside all year round."

"I'm glad you mentioned the unmentionables. I was wondering."

They gave the washer about ten minutes before removing the lid and examining the clothes. "Okay," Cassie said, "this is the fun part. But also very perilous."

"More dangerous than frostbite?"

"Yes. If you get your fingers caught in the wringer, they'll be squished and you'll definitely be wearing a hook."

He nodded cheerfully. "No fingers in the wringer. Got it."

She turned off the agitator and turned on the wringer. The two rollers rotated in opposite directions to pull the clothes between them and wring out the water.

"Put clothes the long way in." Cassie showed him how to feed clothes into the wringer.

"Cool," Zach said. "I can do that."

He carefully fed the clothes in one side, while Cassie caught them coming out the other side and dropped them in the laundry sink for a rinse.

Once everything was rinsed, she fed them back the other way through the wringer and Zach caught them on the other side and piled them in the basket.

He insisted on carrying the basket outside to the clothesline. They both bundled in their winter coats, boots, and bright red scarves. She put his beanie on his head and tied the scarf around his neck while he held the basket at the ready. When they walked outside, the sun peeked from behind the clouds and the thermometer on the porch read thirty-two degrees. Nice and warm for a February day.

"It feels like it's almost maple sugaring

time," Cassie said as she gave Zach a handful of clothespins.

"You mean when you collect the sap?"

"It needs to get a little warmer. We usually start at the end of February, first part of March." The cold stung her fingers as she hung a pair of trousers on the line. "Dawdi gathers the family together and announces that the sap is running. It's very exciting, especially for the children. We do maple syrup and huckleberry jam every year."

He took another pair of trousers from the basket. "I'd like to see that."

She glued her gaze to the clothespins but watched him out of the corner of her eye. "I'd like you to be there."

He smiled so wide she thought his lips might fly off his face. She contained a smile, but couldn't keep her heart from skipping around in her chest.

She showed him how to pull the line and hoist the clothes higher into the air. The clothesline ran through a pulley hanging from the eaves of the house. Many clothes could be hung on the line at once.

"Have you seen Austin this week?" she asked.

"Every day."

"How's he doing?"

"He's a brave little kid. I think I would have cried uncle a long time ago. The problem now is that Dr. Perez says the antibiotics aren't working. He's got heart valve damage. He'll probably have to have surgery." He fumbled with one of the clothespins before using it to pin one of Mammi's aprons to the line. "I almost went to church last Sunday, but then I had to admit a patient to the hospital."

"Jamie finally got to you?"

"Nah. I wanted to check on the three guys who were so eager to ask you out. See if they deserve you or not."

Even though she could tell he was teasing, Cassie's mouth suddenly felt as dry as one of her aging art professor's lectures. "I'm not . . . they're not . . . You don't need to worry."

"I guess I feel a little protective of the girl I milk cows with."

She liked the thought of Zach watching over her, even if he didn't really mean it.

He studied her face. "Is it politically incorrect to say that? Because I'm not implying you can't take care of yourself. I know how guys have treated you before."

She lowered her eyes. "Church guys are safe."

"Oh." For whatever reason, he suddenly

seemed to shut down, as if he didn't want to talk to her anymore.

What had she said, and how could she get him to smile at her again? "You . . . you don't need to worry," she stammered, "because I've already been out with them."

He looked uncertain and a little ill. "All of them?"

She stretched her lips across her teeth. "After I told Peter I wasn't interested, Brandon kind of swooped in. Then Greg didn't waste any time once I let Brandon down."

She could tell he tried hard not to smile. He wiped his hand across his mouth and picked up one of Dawdi's shirts. "Well, okay. Good. I guess I don't have to come to church, after all."

"There was a new guy there last week who hasn't asked me out yet."

He peered at her suspiciously and narrowed his eyes. "You're making that up."

"He's from Florida, and he's got the most attractive tan. And really white teeth, like Brad Pitt. And a red Mustang. He just graduated from Florida State. That isn't a party school, is it?" she said, batting her eyelashes and trying to look as blissfully innocent as possible.

"I have a hunch this guy from Florida

doesn't exist."

"But can you be sure?"

He huffed and puffed. "Fine. I'll be at church next week to check out Mr. Florida State. But I guarantee he doesn't know how to do laundry the Amish way."

"He might not even be there."

"He'll hear I'm coming and run squealing all the way back to Florida."

She giggled. "Probably."

From that side of the house, they could see a single horse and buggy clomping and crunching up the snow-covered lane.

Cassie groaned inwardly. Norman had promised to come today with Luke and Elmer Lee under the pretense of readying supplies for maple syrup time. But he'd also instructed Cassie to have a batch of bread pudding hot and ready in the oven. Elmer Lee loved bread pudding with raisins and dried cranberries, and Norman expected Cassie to feed the three of them supper with bread pudding for dessert.

And to wear the pink dress Mamm had given her.

Norman would be indignant when he found her in workout clothes hanging laundry with Zach Reynolds instead of baking in the kitchen in her charming pink dress. Well, it wasn't her fault Norman was three hours early.

Zach stiffened. Norman was surely the last person he wanted to see, even including the imaginary Mr. Florida State.

Norman stopped the buggy alongside the two identical cars. Luke jumped out and unhitched the horse with the skill and swiftness of someone who had done it hundreds of times. Unhitching the horse meant they were planning on staying for a while. She hadn't expected anything less, but her stomach still felt as if she'd swallowed a bag of lead pellets.

Luke waved to them as he led the horse to the barn. Norman stepped out of the buggy. Elmer Lee unfolded himself. Buggies weren't all that accommodating to long legs.

Norman marched in Cassie's direction with Elmer tagging along behind. Norman came close to Cassie and leaned his head until their foreheads were almost touching. "I told you to wear the pink dress," he hissed so Elmer Lee, still a few steps behind, wouldn't hear him. "Those pants you are wearing are indecent. Too tight."

Cassie's stomach felt as if it would sink to her toes. "I came from the gym and haven't had time to change."

Out of the corner of her eye, she saw Zach

standing ramrod straight with his fists clenched at his sides and the muscles of his jaw twitching slightly.

"I told you I'd be here at nine. I made sure to be late so you'd be ready," Norman said.

"You said noon."

Elmer Lee finally caught up to Norman. Her brother took a step back and pulled Elmer Lee forward. Elmer Lee looked her up and down as if he were inspecting a horse. "Hello, Cassie."

"I'm sorry she's not wearing her Plain dress today," Norman said. "I know you don't like it when she wears pants."

"I like the pink dress," Elmer Lee said. "And a kapp would show me that you are devoted to God."

Cassie held her breath. She could endure the humiliation, but Zach looked as if he were about to explode. He had told her that he thought Norman was a bully. But she could handle him. The last thing she wanted was for Zach to make a scene.

Zach crossed his arms over his chest and spread his feet into a wide stance. "Cassie goes to church every week. That seems pretty devoted to me."

Norman glared at Zach. "Devotion to a false creed is damnation."

"Browbeating in the name of devotion is hypocrisy."

"What do you know?" Norman said. "My sister doesn't even care that she has broken our *mater*'s heart and hurt our entire family. Jesus would have us go after the lost sheep. It's our duty as Christians and my duty as a brother."

Cassie was on the verge of tears. The arguing was worse than Norman's sharp words. She knew how to absorb the hurt that Norman inflicted on her. She didn't know how to make peace between two angry men, especially when she had been the cause of the contention.

As Zach opened his mouth to reply, he glanced in Cassie's direction. Whatever he was going to say died on his lips. Holding up his hands as if stopping traffic, he took two steps backward. "I'm not here to argue. I'm just here to hang clothes, and the sooner I get done, the less chance there is for my fingers to freeze."

He dragged the laundry basket to within easy reach, turned his back on the rest of them, and began hanging clothes as if trying to beat a storm.

Cassie couldn't relax, but her heart swelled with gratitude for that show of meekness. He had truly turned the other cheek. Norman never did.

"You best go change, Cassie," Norman muttered.

Cassie did as she was told even though it was the cowardly way out, even though Zach probably despised her for her weakness. Even though it meant Norman had won.

Let him have his little victory. It would be little comfort if his harshness compelled her to turn her back on her family forever.

CHAPTER SEVENTEEN

Even with the temperature hovering near freezing and his fingers feeling like they were going to fall off, the heat rose off Zach's body as if he were boiling from the inside out.

He'd be horsewhipped before he let Norman Coblenz and Elmer Lee bully Cassie. No one, not even her own brother, would be allowed to hurt her as long as Zach had something to say about it. And he had an awful lot to say about it.

He loved her too much to provoke Norman when she stood there pleading with her eyes for him to stop. He could pretend to be contrite if it made her happy but only until she disappeared safely into the house. With his back turned and his laundry basket empty, he heard her walk up the porch steps and close the front door.

He slowly turned to face Norman and Elmer Lee and Luke, who had just come from the barn. He felt sorry for Luke, who was going to get his share of Zach's wrath when he had no clue what had happened. Or maybe he did know. Maybe they'd all come to Huckleberry Hill today to browbeat Cassie into submission.

Zach put on the face he showed to hostile soccer opponents, the expression that said, "If you mess with me, I'll rip your head off."

"Norman," he said, because Norman was clearly the ringleader of the gang, "I'm only going to tell you nicely one more time. I won't put up with you talking to Cassie like that. If you want to yell at somebody, yell at me, but leave Cassie alone or you'll have to deal with someone who's not afraid to fight back."

Norman's face turned to stone. Elmer Lee looked only slightly less imposing, mostly because there remained a spark of confusion in his eyes. Luke turned pale. He'd just walked in on something he clearly didn't want to be part of.

"It's okay," Luke said. "Whatever Norman did, he didn't mean to hurt Cassie's feelings. He —"

Completely ignoring Luke, Norman took a step forward and folded his arms across his chest. Zach folded his arms in return. They must have looked like two sea lions

317

on the Discovery Channel about to do battle.

"Not afraid to fight back?" Norman said. "This is the second time you've hid behind Cassie's skirts."

"I'm not hiding now."

"I'm not afraid of you, Dr. Reynolds." Norman motioned to the laundry basket at Zach's feet. "Is this all you know how to do? Woman's work? I noticed how you turned tail and ran into the house the first chance you got when we butchered that hog."

Zach almost plowed his fist into Norman's pointy nose. He'd saved Norman's own daughter from a terrible accident and gotten injured in the process, and Norman accused him of not being man enough to stick a pig? His gut clenched with the impulse to flatten Norman with a swift right hook to the jaw. But he didn't move. He wasn't a brute, and Norman wouldn't appreciate his reasons for giving him a bloody nose.

Norman pointed his thumb at Elmer Lee. "He's not afraid to stick a pig."

Luke seemed to have a little more sense than Norman. "The doctor pulled Priscilla out of the fire. Don't you remember?"

Zach nodded a thank-you to Luke before turning his attention to Norman again. "I

318

don't care what you think of me, but you will leave Cassie alone or I will make you."

Norman's scowl cut deep lines into his face. "I am a man of peace. If you strike me, I will turn the other cheek. Your threats have no power over me."

"Cassie likes godly men," Elmer Lee said.

Zach scrubbed his hand down his face. "Get off your high horse. I would never hit you. I'm not that stupid or that volatile. You've had free rein to pick on Cassie because she doesn't fight back. You make her feel guilty and small. Just remember that the next time you try it, I will fight back for her."

"Cassie doesn't argue with me because her own guilty conscience whispers to her that I am right. She will come back to our way of thinking if we show her the way. If we remind her of her wicked ways and keep the memory of her sins before her eyes, she will yearn for forgiveness."

Luke's eyes darted between Norman and Zach. "Cassie doesn't —"

"Keep quiet, Luke," Norman snapped. "You don't know anything."

Norman didn't realize that he pushed Cassie further away from the church and her family with every harsh word he uttered. "Cassie is not wicked," Zach said through clenched teeth.

Norman lifted his chin. "The Englisch know nothing about the ways of God. You like her, but what can you offer her? If you truly cared about her soul, you would stay away from her."

Zach stood his ground. He wouldn't let Norman weaken his resolve to be the kind of man Cassie could love. The kind of man Cassie deserved. "Your mistake is underestimating me."

Norman turned his face away from Zach. "I have said what I have said." He turned toward the house. Elmer Lee followed close on his heels. Luke was a little slower to go along.

"Wait," Zach said.

Norman and his wingmen turned back.

"I want your promise that you'll leave Cassie alone," Zach said, knowing he wouldn't get any such promise.

Norman grunted his disapproval. "I'll not stop trying to save my sister."

"Then we haven't solved anything."

"Stay away from Cassie," Norman said. "That will solve everything."

"You're stubborn and self-righteous."

"And you want to pick a fight."

A crazy idea popped into his head. "What about a friendly contest?"

"What do you mean?"

"A wrestling match." Zach didn't technically know how to wrestle, but he'd had it out with a few center midfielders before, and Norman wasn't near as intimidating as that. "We draw a circle in the snow. If I throw you out of the circle, you promise to quit pestering Cassie about coming back to the church. You never mention that pink dress or white kapp or question her faith again."

Norman glanced at Elmer Lee. "And if I win?"

Zach swallowed the boulder-sized lump in his throat. The stakes had to be high to gain Norman's cooperation. "Then I promise not to set foot on Huckleberry Hill again."

"What about my mammi?"

"I will still see her at the hospital like all my other patients." And Cassie too. Hopefully Norman wouldn't think about the other places he and Cassie could run into each other. But how would he win her heart if he couldn't come to Huckleberry Hill?

Zach glanced toward the house. What would Cassie say if she knew what they were plotting? She'd probably hate him for life. "Cassie can't know."

Norman stuffed his hands in his coat pockets and mulled it over. "Elmer Lee will be Cassie's husband someday. He should wrestle you."

Zach should have anticipated that. He had several inches on Norman. Cassie's brother would never agree to a wrestling match he couldn't win.

Elmer Lee didn't even flinch. He was big and powerful, and Zach did laundry and wore pink shirts. No doubt he thought he could clear Zach out of any circle with a flick of his wrist.

Zach would have smacked himself upside the head if he had an extra hand. Wrestling Norman or even Luke was one thing, but Elmer Lee looked as if he ate nails for breakfast. He eyed Elmer Lee's thick arms and solid frame. It wasn't too late to back out.

Zach took a deep breath and squared his shoulders. Nothing mattered but Cassie's happiness, and he wouldn't gain Norman's cooperation easily. He'd have to do it the hard way. His gaze traveled the length of Elmer Lee's large frame. He'd have to do it the really hard way. He didn't have any wrestling experience, except with his older brothers, who had never been gentle. He suddenly felt grateful for all the times they'd ground his face into the dirt. He'd learned a few things.

Besides, he'd been able to hold his ground when he had gotten older. A lot of what happened on the soccer pitch felt like wrestling. He was a brick wall. If he was smart about it, he could take Elmer Lee down.

Zach nodded. "Do you agree, Elmer Lee?"

Elmer Lee flared his nostrils like a horse before a race. "A friendly match."

They shook on it.

"The bishop wouldn't approve," Luke said. "We believe in nonviolence."

"It will be friendly," Norman said. Nobody argued with him, but nobody believed it either, not even Luke.

"We can't do it here," Zach said. "I don't want Cassie to see."

Norman smirked. "You don't want her to see you get beat."

"I know a place," said Elmer Lee. "Flat ground, lots of snow."

Zach held up his car keys and jangled them. "I'll drive."

Cassie took the fastest shower of her life. Hopefully Zach had gone back to the hospital, and Elmer Lee and her brothers were in the barn hunting for sap buckets. She had been reluctant to leave them outside alone together, but she thought the best way to avoid conflict was to remove the source of conflict itself. Her. Maybe Zach would stop glaring at Norman if Cassie weren't there for Norman to admonish. She could only hope.

The pink dress went over her head. After securing the front with straight pins, she tied a half apron around her waist. She towel-dried her hair and put it into a stumpy little bun before pulling the prayer covering over it and pinning it in place. She'd done it so many times, it barely took her five minutes.

She pulled on her stockings and went to the great room. Dawdi perused a seed catalog, and Mammi was attempting to fix Zach's knitting project. It wasn't going well. She'd surely have to throw it away and start over.

Cassie went to the front door and slipped her feet into her snow boots, then donned her coat and rushed outside. She half expected to see Zach and Norman engaged in a fistfight. Instead, she saw lots of footprints and no men. The buggy stood where they'd left it, but when she looked in the barn, her brothers were nowhere to be seen. She came back outside scratching her head.

Zach's car was missing. Where had they all gone?

CHAPTER EIGHTEEN

Elmer Lee had picked a good spot. A pasture somewhere on the outskirts of Bonduel with flat ground, lots of space, and no one in sight for miles. A good place to dispose of his body if they wanted to. Not that Norman would do that. Zach had watched too many TV movies.

Zach parked his car on the hard ice alongside the dirt road. They got out and trudged through the deep snow to the middle of the field. Norman found a long stick and drew a circle in the snow, maybe ten feet in diameter.

Zach hadn't been able to formulate any sort of strategy on the ride over. The scarf had come off in the car, but should he take off his coat, or would that just make it easier for Elmer Lee to wrap his arms around him? What about gloves? He didn't feel sure about anything except that Elmer Lee wasn't going to budge him out of that circle.

He refused to lose Cassie.

He stepped into the circle and took off his coat. He'd move more quickly without it, and if there was anything he'd learned in soccer, it was that quickness trumped brute force. Usually.

The cold sliced through his skin like sharp pieces of glass, but he ignored it. He'd be sweating soon enough.

With his coat still on, Elmer Lee stood on the opposite side of the circle facing Zach.

"We shouldn't do this," Luke said.

Zach gave him a quick smile. "It's okay. No one's going to get hurt. Isn't that right, Elmer Lee?"

Elmer Lee nodded. He didn't seem like the vindictive type, just someone easily led by a bully like Norman.

It went without saying that they were really fighting for Cassie, and she was worth every drop of blood. Elmer Lee wouldn't go down easy.

And Zach really hoped there wouldn't be blood.

"The first person with any part of their body out of the circle wins," Norman said, almost cheerfully. Of course he was cheerful. Elmer Lee would be doing all the work.

Zach didn't waste any time. Trying to push him out of the circle with sheer momentum, he ran at Elmer Lee and clapped his arms around him in a bear hug. Elmer Lee stumbled backward but didn't step anywhere near the edge of the circle. He hooked an elbow under Zach's armpit and tried to wrench Zach's arm from around him. Zach countered with a quick twist so he still had his arms around Elmer Lee but was now behind him.

Planting his foot, he kicked his leg and swiped Elmer Lee's feet out from under him. Norman shouted as both Zach and Elmer Lee tumbled to the ground with Zach on top. In an amazing show of strength, Elmer Lee reached behind him, grabbed onto Zach's T-shirt, and pulled Zach off his back. Zach rolled away from Elmer Lee in the snow as Elmer Lee stood up and came barreling toward him, trying Zach's first strategy.

At the last second, Zach crouched low and took Elmer Lee's legs out from under him. Elmer Lee landed on his stomach, and Zach flopped on top of him. Zach made the mistake of not keeping his head low. In an attempt to escape, Elmer Lee elbowed him in the face.

He heard a sickening crack as pain shot through his head. His vision blurred, and he held on tight until the dizziness subsided and he could see straight again. The pain knocked the wind out of him, and he gasped for air. The Amish guy had broken his nose.

Blood poured from his nose and dripped onto Elmer Lee's coat and face. Elmer Lee must have felt the warm moisture on his cheek, because his resistance slackened. His hesitation proved his downfall because Zach was going to take any advantage he could get. By shoving his hands into the snow and curling them beneath Elmer Lee, Zach was able to wrap his arms all the way around the wide span of Elmer Lee's chest. Digging his boots into the frozen ground, he lifted Elmer Lee just enough to shove his head and one of his shoulders out of the circle.

He thought he heard Norman groan behind him, but his ears were ringing too loudly to be sure.

Good enough, as far as Zach was concerned. The adrenaline pulsed through his veins as he struggled to his feet and staggered away from Elmer Lee. Elmer Lee rose to his hands and knees first and then stood. He swayed a bit, but he didn't look worse for wear. A light red scrape marred the side of his face, but it probably wouldn't even show in a couple of hours. Nothing like the blood pouring from Zach's nose or the double shiners that were bound to follow.

Could you bleed to death with a bloody nose?

Not without a lot of effort.

Norman patted Elmer Lee on the arm, mumbling something Zach couldn't hear. He didn't care what they were talking about. He had won, and Norman had lost. Cassie would get some peace.

Zach bent over so the blood from his nose could drip into the snow. Blood looked extra red against a sparkly white background. He certainly hoped it stopped bleeding by the time his shift started at five. He reached down, scooped up a handful of snow, and placed it over his nose. He hissed at the icy coldness. Nothing stung like a broken nose. Would his nose be more crooked than it already was? Maybe Elmer Lee's elbow had straightened it out for him. Would Cassie like him with a normal nose? Did she even like him now?

Luke handed him his coat, with only the faintest of smiles on his face. Zach opted not to put it back on. He was soaking wet. It would only make him colder when he got in the car.

Elmer Lee shuffled through the snow and handed Zach a handkerchief.

"Denki," Zach said, with as flawless an

accent as he could muster with a handful of ice pressed against his nose.

"Is it broken?" Elmer Lee asked.

"Yeah."

"*Ach, du lieva.* I'm sorry. I didn't try to."

Zach held the handkerchief at his chin to catch the blood and melting snow that dribbled down his face. "I know. I put my face in the wrong place."

Elmer Lee gazed down at the red snow. "No hard feelings?"

"No hard feelings."

Norman frowned. "This doesn't mean that Elmer Lee won't still try to convince Cassie to marry him."

Zach pulled his hand from his nose. "As long as you don't say one more word to Cassie about the church or her soul or how she's destroying your family, Elmer Lee can do all the courting he wants."

If Zach had anything to say about it, Cassie would soon forget all about Elmer Lee.

CHAPTER NINETEEN

Zach flexed his arm and rotated his shoulder. A little sore, but nothing he couldn't handle. More than one soccer collision had left him worse off than this.

His nose was the big problem. The swelling would eventually go down, but the two black eyes would linger for days. There would be no hiding them from Cassie unless he wore a pair of sunglasses everywhere he went. She'd get suspicious.

What was he going to tell her?

Just thinking of Cassie got his heart racing as if he'd just run the hundred-meter sprint. Had he ever truly loved a girl before her?

He strolled down the dim hall of the hospital with a cup of coffee in one hand and checked his phone for the third time. Three a.m. Only two more hours to go on his shift. Then he could go home and sleep off this throbbing broken-nose headache.

He paused at Austin Stetson's door. Austin's mom often slept on a cot in Austin's room, but she was working the night shift and Austin was alone tonight. Zach felt bad for anybody who had to sleep overnight at the hospital, but especially a little kid. Austin had been here for weeks, and Zach had promised his mom that he'd check on him when she couldn't be around.

Zach put his ear to the door. He heard the normal hisses and beeps of the machines in Austin's room, but he also might have heard something else. Soft whimpering or the faint voices coming from the nurses' station?

As silently as possible, Zach opened the door and tiptoed into Austin's room. He'd hate himself if he woke the poor kid.

Austin lay on his back with his head propped against his pillow. His hand covered his face, but Zach could still see the tears that slid down his cheeks and found a path down his neck to where they soaked into the collar of his Manchester City pajamas.

"Hey, bud," Zach whispered. "Having a bad night?"

Austin swiped his hand across his face, erasing most of the evidence. He didn't like to cry in front of Zach. "I'm okay," he said in a small, quivering voice. He squinted at

Zach in the dim light. "What happened to your nose? It's big and red."

"A wrestling match. The guy accidentally caught me in the face with his elbow."

"Did you win?"

"Always."

Austin cracked a smile.

Zach set his coffee cup on Austin's tray and lowered himself into the chair next to his bed. "You know you have my permission to cry your eyes out whenever you want."

"I know, but Parker Plotsky says only babies cry."

Zach leaned his elbow on Austin's bed. "What does Parker Plotsky know? Has he ever been in the hospital?"

"I don't know."

"Has Parker Plotsky ever had four needles stuck in him in one day or had to pee in a cup?"

"No."

"Then tell Parker Plotsky to shut his mouth."

"He's my best friend."

"You can be nice when you tell him to shut up."

One corner of Austin's mouth curled upward. "Are you on the night shift?"

"Yeah. Pretty boring. What about you?"

He shrugged. "Sometimes I don't want to go to sleep because I'm afraid I won't wake up."

Zach's heart broke for about the thousandth time since he'd met Austin. How much could God ask of one little kid? Times like these he wanted to shake his fist at heaven and chew God out for not doing His job. But Cassie had told him to be still, so he usually just bowed his head and prayed for understanding. The funny thing was, he always felt better after he prayed, as if God were giving him the grace and comfort drop by drop. Maybe if he was patient, God would eventually fill him up.

"You don't have to worry, Austin. You'll always wake up."

"How do you know?"

Zach cleared his throat. What had Cassie said about heaven? "Well, you'll either wake up in the hospital, or you'll wake up in Jesus's arms and He'll take you up to heaven where you won't ever be sad or afraid, and they'll never stick a needle in your arm again."

"Mom says there's no pain in heaven."

Zach nodded. "And you can play soccer all day long if you want and never get tired."

"Will I be as good as Messi?"

"Better. Cassie says heaven is where

dreams come true."

Austin was quiet for a minute. "Is that real?"

"Of course it is." Something warm and golden threaded through his veins and suddenly he *did* know that what he told Austin was true. The realization momentarily stole his breath away.

Heaven was real, and God wanted this one little boy to know it.

Austin smiled weakly. "Will you do me a favor?"

"Sure."

"When you pray, will you ask God to make me better?"

"I already do."

Austin tucked his legs up to his chin and rested his arms across his knees. "God will listen to you because you're so nice. Just like Cassie."

"My friend Cassie?"

"Yeah." He pointed to an orange and cream striped beanie hanging from the metal arm that held the TV. "She brought me cookies and a beanie yesterday. She made the cookies, and her grandma made the beanie."

Zach couldn't hide his astonishment. "She came to visit you?" He reached over and pulled the beanie from the TV stand and pressed it to his face hoping to breathe a little of Cassie in with the beanie. He couldn't smell anything, not with a nose the size of a small country, but he imagined the beanie would smell like honey and lemon or vanilla and peanut butter, depending on what cookies she'd made that day. "What kind of cookies were they?"

"Captain America shields."

Zach wasn't sure what Captain America shields smelled like, but on Cassie they no doubt smelled wonderful.

Zach didn't know why it surprised him that Cassie had come to visit Austin. He should have known by now that if there was anything in Cassie's power to do, she'd do it.

His longing for her swelled until he didn't think he could stand it. Just when he was sure he couldn't be any more in love with her, she did something like this.

His heart tied itself into a knot.

Austin snatched the beanie from him and stretched it onto his head. "Sick, huh? Netherlands colors."

"Totally sick. And it'll help keep your toes warm."

"You mean my ears," Austin said.

Zach laid a hand on Austin's head. "Covering your head makes your feet warm. I used to do it at soccer practice all the time."

"Really? Sick."

Zach pulled his phone from his pocket. "Hey, there's a Man City game on right now, and I can get it on my phone. Do you want to watch it while I finish my rounds?"

Austin tried not to look too eager. "You probably need your phone."

"I've got a pager."

Austin grinned from ear to ear. "Okay."

"But you have to promise me to go right to sleep as soon as it's over."

"Sick."

"And don't break my phone." Zach found the game on his phone and handed it to Austin.

With his eyes glued to the screen, Austin settled deeper into his pillow. "That Cassie girl likes you."

That got Zach's attention. "How do you know?"

"She smiles and her eyes get weird when she says your name. Like Emily Loftus. She chases me around the playground at recess."

Austin didn't seem inclined to say more as the game commanded his attention. Zach waved good-bye and tiptoed out of the room.

If he were still in elementary school, he'd be chasing Cassie around the playground.

Wouldn't it have been cool if Cassie chased him back?

CHAPTER TWENTY

"A few more weeks in this recliner, Anna, and you'll be up and running around this place like a track star," Zach said as he snapped the gloves off his hands and threw them in his bag.

Mammi's eyes twinkled. Zach's visits were her favorite part of the day. They were becoming Cassie's favorite part of the day too. "I never was a gute runner. My legs are too stubby yet. But I'm also closer to the ground so I don't fall as easy as the tall people. You're tall, Doctor. You probably fall down all the time."

Zach nodded. "It hurts worse because it's such a long way down."

Cassie stood at the counter rolling her cookies in cinnamon and sugar before popping them into the oven. Zach liked cinnamon, and she wanted him to have some cookies to take to the hospital with him tonight. He came to the sink and washed his hands, smiling as if just standing near her were a treat. Why did that smile make her blush through seven layers of skin?

Dawdi came shuffling down the hall, singing the wrong words to one of his favorite songs like he often did. Dawdi had thousands of tunes stored in his memory, but when he didn't remember the words, he simply made up his own. *"God, make my life a little flower, that bringeth smiles to all, I'm happy blooming in the bower, although the garden's small."* He carried his snow boots in one hand and two long, polished sticks in the other. "How does Anna's foot look, Doctor?"

"The skin graft is taking well," Zach said.

"It's because I had a handsome surgeon," Mammi said. "Don't you agree, Cassie?"

"I don't know that Dr. Reynolds's good looks had much to do with your surgery, Mammi."

Zach raised an eyebrow. "You think I'm good-looking?"

How many more layers of skin were there to blush down to? "I never said that."

Zach chuckled at Cassie's discomfort before turning to Mammi. "Your foot is looking better and better all the time."

After propping the sticks against the wall, Dawdi sat on the sofa to put on his boots.

340

"And you're looking worse and worse, Doctor. I thought you was wearing a mask when you first came in."

"I get lots of attention at the hospital, mostly from horrified patients."

"And you say your friend elbowed you in the face?" Dawdi said in amused disbelief.

"We had a wrestling match. It was an accident."

Cassie would never understand the male need to get down on the ground for a friendly game of Shove Your Opponent's Face into the Dirt, even though her brothers used to wrestle all the time when they were younger. Zach acted as if he didn't mind the two black eyes, but she felt sorry for him all the same. His nose was still a bit swollen, and it looked like it really hurt.

Dawdi finished lacing up his snow boots. "I'll be back," he said, grabbed his sticks, and then bent over and kissed Mammi on the cheek.

"Where are you going, Dawdi?"

"I'm going out among the maples to see if the air is right for the sap to start running."

"Felty dear, it's nearly dark," Mammi scolded. "Even using those canes, you'll trip over a rock and die in the woods, and I won't be able to come look for you because the doctor says I should stay off my foot."

"These aren't canes. Canes are for old people," Dawdi said. "These are walking sticks."

How old would Dawdi have to get before he considered himself an old person?

"I ain't never tripped yet with my walking sticks. But if I die, you can send Cassie out to find my body. I want to be dressed in the blue shirt for my funeral."

"I'll go with you and bring your body back if necessary," Zach said, flashing that playful grin. "I want to learn how to tell if the air is right for maple syrup."

Dawdi pulled his coat from the hook. "It's tricky, especially for someone like me who doesn't have much of a sense of smell. You can tell the sap is running by the faint scent of spring in the air."

"What does spring smell like?" Zach asked.

"I can't describe it, but you'll know it when you smell it. I've learned to feel it in my bones."

Cassie smiled. Dawdi's extra sense worked better than a thermometer.

Mammi shifted in her recliner to get a better look at Dawdi. "You'd better take Cassie with you. Dr. Reynolds has nice hair and looks very strong, but if you die, he'll need

342

Cassie to keep him from getting lost in the woods."

Zach seemed to think it was a very good idea. "I'd totally get lost."

"What about my cookies?" Cassie said, wanting someone to talk her into going. A moonlight stroll in the crunchy snow with Zach Reynolds sounded like a wonderful scheme.

And when had she become this captivated by the doctor?

Mammi picked up her knitting. "You can bake them when you get back. They'll keep."

That was all the persuasion Cassie needed. She rinsed her hands and practically lunged for her coat on the hook. She stepped out of her shoes and into her boots that sat next to the door. Zach donned his coat and laced up his snow boots. He needed them so often here that he had made it a habit of bringing them just in case.

Cassie and Zach put on their matching scarves, and Zach slid his homemade beanie onto his head. Cassie loved that he loved that beanie. It made Mammi so happy to see him wear it.

They trudged out into the snow, which was thinning at the edges of the lawn like a receding hairline. Dawdi led the way down the snow-covered path that took them deeper into the woods. Zach gave Cassie the flashlight and motioned for her to go ahead of him. "I'll watch for bears and mountain lions and catch you in case you fall backward."

A smile tugged at Cassie's lips. Who said chivalry was dead? Should she take so much pleasure in the fact that Zach wanted to watch out for her? "You think I'm going to fall?" she asked, glancing back at him as if he'd insulted her entire family.

He chuckled. "I'm the novice with this whole Amish thing. Maybe it's *my* body you'll have to drag out of the woods."

"You're pretty heavy. I'd have to call that new Florida guy at church to come help me."

She heard him growl behind her. "The guy who doesn't exist."

"He's strong enough to carry you all by himself."

"Over my dead body." Zach stomped his feet extra hard behind her.

"Yes, that's the idea," Cassie said.

"I want to be buried in my pink shirt."

Cassie giggled. "If I die, whatever you do, do not let Mamm bury me in that pink dress."

"I love that pink dress."

"Don't you dare." Cassie tried to point

the flashlight so that Dawdi could see by its light. He didn't seem to need it. He must have known exactly where he wanted to go. "How far are we going, Dawdi?" she asked. Surely the air five minutes from the house was just as suitable as the air three miles from the house.

Dawdi turned to look at Cassie and Zach. "I think we need a little more time and a little more moonlight."

Cassie tried to find the moon through the bare trees. It peeked over the horizon to the east.

"We could try the clearing by the big boulder."

"Jah, we might do that," Dawdi said, poking the snow with one of his walking sticks. "It has to be the perfect spot." Dawdi smiled at Cassie as if he knew something she didn't and plunged headlong into the woods. Cassie had to take long strides to keep up. With those walking sticks, Dawdi could have given a few soccer players a run for their money.

She turned back and gave Zach an apologetic look. He probably hadn't bargained for an all-night trek through the woods. He smiled at her as if he were having the best time of his life. Was there ever a moment when he wasn't having the best time of his life?

"This cold air is really clearing out my sinuses," he said. "Maybe I'll be able to smell whatever it is I'm supposed to smell."

"Dawdi might lead us into Canada before he's satisfied."

"Is my nose still okay?" he asked.

"What do you mean?"

"Does it look more or less crooked than before I broke it this time?"

Cassie pointed the flashlight in Zach's face. He spread his hands in front of his eyes and shrieked. "I can't see. Help me, help me. I'm blind."

She rolled her eyes and lowered her flashlight so it pointed at his chest. "Those black eyes truly are nasty."

"But what about my nose?"

"It's a little swollen and has some discoloration, but it looks about the same level of crookedness to me."

He furrowed his brow. "Are you sure? Because girls really like my crooked nose."

She laughed and started walking again. "Do they?"

He jogged to keep up with her. "Do you think my crooked nose is attractive?"

Very attractive, like the rest of him. "You look like you've been in a fight or two."

"But do you like it?"

"You should never be ashamed of your deformities," she said, flashing him a playful grin.

He threw back his head and laughed. "My deformities? How many do I have?"

"It doesn't matter. What matters is that you love yourself and never let someone like Norman destroy your self-esteem."

"Too late," he said. "You've completely destroyed it." He stepped in front of her and walked backward, grinning like a cat. "Then again, in the house you said I was good-looking."

She kept on walking as she felt the blush travel up her face. "I must have been delirious."

She tried to walk past him, but he stepped in her way so she couldn't get around. "But seriously, what do you think about the nose?"

She stopped walking again and smiled at him in surrender. "It's the same level of crookedness, and it looks very handsome on your face, as you well know."

His grin couldn't have gotten any wider. "I'm glad it's not more crooked. The girls would have been falling at my feet."

Cassie laughed at his mock relief. "How horrible for you." She glanced down the path. Dawdi was far ahead. "Dawdi, wait for us."

Her clunky boots made it hard to match Dawdi's quick pace. Had he forgotten they were behind him? Even though she held the flashlight, she stubbed her toe on something dark and large in her path and tripped spectacularly. More quickly than she would have thought possible, Zach snaked his arm around her waist and pulled her up before her face met the snow.

"Are you okay?" he said as he pressed her close to him, making sure she landed securely on her feet.

Firmly in his grasp, she turned to look at him and found his face within inches of hers. She felt his warm breath on her cheek and his muscled, tensed arm against her back. In the dim light cast by the flashlight, she could see a look of pure shock overspread his features, as if saving her from a mouthful of snow was not at all what he had expected.

Almost immediately, the shock gave way to some deeper emotion. He held his breath and stared at her lips as if he were starving. She could feel the tension in his arm, see it in the muscles of his neck, and sense it in the beating of his heart so close to hers. Her own heart thudded against her chest like a bass drum, and the forest seemed to stand still. She would have been perfectly happy if they had been the only two people in the whole world.

"You smell like cinnamon," he whispered.

"You smell like . . ." That was all she could manage from her muddled brain.

He leaned closer. Was he going to kiss her? *Oh sis yuscht.* Her heart raced so fast, it could have won the Kentucky Derby.

Just as she thought she might be prepared for a kiss, a soft groan came from deep in his throat, and without warning, he released her. He took a giant step backward. "Your dawdi is a fast walker," he said, taking a deep breath.

The forest seemed to spin briefly before everything righted itself. She let out the air that had been imprisoned in her lungs, and a profound ache grew in a forgotten corner of her heart at the realization that for the hundredth time since she'd been in Bonduel, he had avoided her very touch. She thought about the day of Mammi's surgery. He had shaken her hand as if he'd been forced to pet a snake. He must have found her repulsive indeed if a mere handshake made him cringe.

The blood in her veins thickened into molasses, and her heartbeat felt more like the dull thud of a sledgehammer than the drumbeat of a love song. "Thank . . . thank you. I didn't think I would trip."

"You're okay now."

"Jah. Yes, I'm okay now," she lied. When he had let go of her, she felt as if he had taken the sun with him. She craved the warmth of his embrace and the comfort she knew she would find in his arms.

A shiver of longing trickled down her spine. What was she thinking? Zach Reynolds had been the star of the university soccer team. He was a doctor with a degree from a prestigious medical school, and one of the funniest, kindest guys she'd ever met.

He'd asked her out once, but he'd never consider asking her out again. She was a mousy art history major, easily overlooked in a roomful of women. Her heart sank. He might have been her friend because of Mammi, but she was the last person Zach Reynolds would ever want to date.

They had long since lost Dawdi. They stood alone and separate as if they'd become strangers in a matter of seconds. Their breath hung in the crisp February air, and with the trees stripped of leaves, the forest seemed empty, barren like a cold desert crammed with stone pillars that stretched in homage to the sky. Zach seemed dazed, as if someone had conked him in the head with a two-by-four.

The sound of Dawdi's footfalls in the snow broke the silence. Cassie shined the flashlight in his direction as he trudged toward them. "I lost you," he said.

"Sorry, Dawdi. I almost fell."

"You should find some good walking sticks. You don't fall when you have walking sticks." He pointed to the north. "I found a place for smelling, just up ahead."

Zach shook his head as if to clear it and glanced at Cassie. His expression made her want to cry. "I'm sorry, Felty. I made a big deal about coming with you, but I just realized I need to get back to feed my turtle."

Feed his turtle? That was a lamer excuse than having to wash his hair.

Dawdi nodded. "No turtle should go hungry. Do you want us to walk you back to your car?"

"No," Zach said, more forcefully than he needed to. "I don't want to interrupt your smelling. I can find the way back." He didn't wait for a reply, just started walking backward the way they'd come. "Thanks for a great dinner, Cassie. I'll see you in a couple of days."

Cassie tried to look anywhere but in the direction Zach walked. She might be able to maintain her composure if she pretended he was already gone. A weary sigh escaped her lips. In his mind, he was long gone.

"Come on, Dawdi," she said, pointing the flashlight down the path. "Show me the place you found."

"No need," Dawdi said. "My bones don't lie. The sap will be running in ten days. We'll start two Mondays from now."

"You already know?"

"You and the doctor were lollygagging, and I thought you might want to be alone. *Die youngie* prefer to do their sparking without the grandparents hovering about."

Dawdi's words only compounded the heaviness she felt. Zach would never want to "spark" with her.

"Nothing spoils the romantic mood like an old man with two walking sticks," he said cheerfully, not sensing the unhappiness behind Cassie's silence. "Not that I'm an old man. Older than you and Dr. Reynolds, anyway. I had to do something to pass the time."

With both of his sticks in one hand, he put his arm around Cassie and nudged her down the path toward home. "Your mammi will be pleased to know that things are coming along nicely yet." He cleared his throat. "With the sap, I mean. Maple sugaring is one of her favorite times of the year. So much wonderful can happen that we don't even expect."

"I can't do this, Mom," Zach said, dragging his fingers through his hair.

"Can't do what? You've been to medical school. I think everything would be downhill from here."

"I can't do the 'Impossible Dream' thing. You know. Love pure and chaste from afar."

"This girl must be amazing."

"She's everything, Mom. And I almost screwed it up." Cassie had been so soft and vulnerable in his arms, and he'd nearly lost his senses and kissed her. "When I'm with her, I go crazy just wondering what it would feel like to hold her hand. And, heaven help me, I can't stop staring at her lips. She probably thinks I'm the weirdest guy in the world. What guy goes around staring at lips?"

"You know, Zach, when I was growing up, hardly anybody had sex before marriage. Wow, I sound old, but it doesn't hurt you to learn a little self-control. It's not an altogether foreign concept. Lots of people wait until they're married."

Zach ran his hand across the back of his neck. "Those are the virtuous people. I am not virtuous. You should have heard the thoughts racing through my head tonight."

"Do you remember your dad's definition of courage?"

"Sure. I used it on a patient the other day. Courage is being scared and doing it anyway."

"Right. It wouldn't be virtue if you weren't tempted. Virtue is facing the temptation and choosing the harder way."

Mom always made such good sense. He had wanted to kiss Cassie in the worst way tonight, but he had controlled himself. It was a small victory. "It never hurts to learn a little self-control."

He could almost hear Mom smiling over the phone. "It's nothing you didn't hear a hundred times growing up."

"I wasn't listening."

"You were listening while pretending not to listen." She paused for a minute. "Whatever you do, don't break this girl's heart. You'll never forgive yourself."

"It's a thousand times more likely that she'll break mine. I can't even convince her to go out with me."

"She needs to learn to trust you."

Zach nodded. "That's why I'm going all out on this virtue thing."

"I love how you call it 'this virtue thing.' "

Zach, not quite so annoyed with himself, sat down on his ancient sofa. "How's your arm?"

"Two more weeks in a cast, but the auxiliary bazaar went off without a hitch. The roses were beautiful. Tell Cassandra thanks again."

"It's not Cassandra. It's Dorcas."

He heard her jaw drop from California. "What are some parents thinking when they name their poor children?"

Zach chuckled. Mom was always so practical. There was no time for absurdity in her world. "By the way, some Amish guy broke my nose."

"Were you fighting over Cassie?"

"Something like that."

"Well, young man, you know I don't like fighting, but if it happens again, protect your face. I don't want you scarred for life."

"It's not bad. She likes my crooked nose."

"Don't we all."

Almost immediately after Zach hung up the phone with his mom, it rang again. He didn't even glance at the number, assuming Mom had forgotten to tell him something.

"Z? It's about time you actually picked up. You said we could still be friends."

Blair. He cussed himself out for not checking the caller ID. "Hi, Blair. Of course we're still friends. I've been busy."

"Did you get my message? About being in Stevens Point next week?"

"Yeah. I got it. I've been busy."

"I closed a two-hundred-thousand-dollar deal in November. It's not the hugest thing the company's ever seen, but it earned me a nice commission."

"That's great, Blair." *I don't really care, but good for you.* He wished her well, he really did, but his interest in Blair had waned like a spent candle.

"So, I bought a Lexus, and you've got to see it."

"I don't know if I can handle the envy. Once I see your car, I'll probably cry every time I climb into my old Honda."

Blair squeaked with glee. "You will. It's that chrome blue color you like so much. With a sunroof. I figured, hey, it's not every day I buy a new car. I might as well go all out."

"With premium sound?"

"Fully loaded."

He groaned. "I'm turning green."

"So, do you want to see it? Stevens Point is like super-close to Shawano. We could meet for dinner."

He massaged a spot just above his eyebrow. "I don't know, Blair. My schedule is unpredictable, and it seems like I'm at the hospital twenty-four seven." *When I'm not on Huckleberry Hill.*

"Come on, Z. I only want to meet for dinner."

"I'm very busy." It was the cowardly way out, and he knew it. But today, the last thing he wanted was another heart-to-heart with Blair about why he didn't want to date her anymore.

"You keep saying that. It's a lame excuse," she said, with just a hint of petulance to her tone.

"Yeah. It's lame. I'm sorry."

She tried too hard when she sensed he wouldn't budge. "Let's do this. I'll call you when I get into town. If you happen to have a free night, we can get together. The car really is worth taking a look at."

Good plan. He could ignore her calls, and she could come and go from Stevens Point without creating any sort of ripple in his life. Maybe she'd take the hint and quit trying for a relationship. "That sounds great. I'll wait for your call."

"I'd rather not have to track you down." She laced her laughter with sarcasm. "Answer your phone."

Hopefully he'd be smart enough to check

caller ID before he did anything as foolish as that.

CHAPTER TWENTY-ONE

The snow and ice were mostly melted as Zach made his way up the lane to Huckleberry Hill. His car didn't sputter once. Fifi seemed to be getting used to the brisk Wisconsin weather.

His heartbeat surged when he caught sight of her. She looked like a vision in a puffy white coat and red scarf. She wore a bright white beanie, and wisps of yellow hair escaped from under her hat. He gripped the steering wheel tighter. Oh, how he wanted to stroke his fingers through that hair!

From what he could tell, under the coat she wore a plain gray dress and a pair of black boots. Had her mamm talked her into that dress? He clenched his teeth. Maybe Cassie had worn it to avoid trouble before it even started.

It didn't matter the reason. It made Zach want to challenge every Amish person in Bonduel to a wrestling match.

He gazed at Cassie from behind his windshield, and the familiar longing came to life inside him. Cassie hadn't been exactly cold to him this week, but she hadn't been warm either. She'd stopped smiling spontaneously at him after he'd been forced to flee the forest to avoid kissing her. Maybe she had realized how close his resolve had come to crumbling. Maybe she didn't want anything to do with such a weak and untrustworthy man.

He swallowed the lump in his throat and resolved to show her that he could be what she wanted. He would always maintain his control, and maybe she'd learn to trust him.

She stood on the edge of Anna and Felty's yard holding a galvanized metal bucket in each hand, looking down the lane as if she were waiting for him. She bloomed into an unexpected smile when he waved at her. Maybe she was happy to see him, after all.

But his heart tripped over itself and thudded onto the pavement as Elmer Lee, Luke, and Norman came out of the house and converged on Cassie. It was lucky he was sitting in the car with the windows rolled up. It wouldn't be good if Cassie heard the growl that came out of his mouth.

Cassie had said that a lot of the family were coming. Zach had been hoping that it was different family. And indeed, he had never seen most of the handful of Amish men and women congregating in the yard. Lots of new relatives to meet. He hoped they weren't all as abrasive as Norman. Enduring Norman was taxing enough.

Norman and Cassie's bossy, prickly Amish mother.

Hopefully, Esther had better things to do in her spare time this afternoon than to tap maple trees with the family. At least he could hope that Norman would honor his promise and quit bullying Cassie about being baptized. Then Zach could focus on being close to Cassie instead of thinking about rearranging Norman's face.

He felt like the marshmallow man as he climbed out of the car and headed in Cassie's direction. He hadn't known quite what to expect of sap collecting, so he had worn a pair of thermal underwear, a long-sleeved T-shirt, sturdy winter boots, snow pants, and his coat with a faux-fur lined hood and that special thin insulation. And of course, Anna's red scarf, the mittens, and the beanie she had knitted. When he got out, he realized the afternoon temperature was a lot higher than he'd anticipated — several degrees above freezing anyway.

Norman took one look at Zach and busted

out laughing. "You're going to sweat something wonderful, Doctor."

Zach pressed his lips into a line. He hated to admit Norman was right, but it had to be at least forty degrees out here. There wasn't a cloud in the sky. It had turned out to be a sunny day, and the sweat already trickled down his back. Was there a graceful way to shed his layers without attracting Norman's ridicule? Unfortunately, Norman had only promised to stop bothering Cassie. He apparently had no reservations about mocking Zach.

"There's no reason to make fun of him," Cassie said. "How could he know how cold it was going to be this afternoon?"

Elmer Lee riveted his gaze to Zach's face. The black eyes looked much better after nearly two weeks. There was still a lot of purple and light blue around both eyes, with hints of yellow and green for variety, but compared to what it had been last week, he didn't look too bad. Still, if Elmer Lee felt a little guilty about breaking Zach's nose, it served him right.

Zach unwound his scarf and let it hang loosely around his neck. The minute Norman was out of sight, the coat was coming off. *"Gute maiya,"* he said, doing his best with the accent.

Norman and Elmer Lee eyed him as if he'd said "good day" in Chinese instead of Deitsch.

What a stupid idea to attempt to impress anybody with his nonexistent language skills.

Cassie gave him a courtesy smile as if to say, "Oh, you're so cute to try to attempt the language, but maybe you shouldn't ever do that again in front of my brother."

Luke proved more polite than either of his companions. He extended his hand and smiled warmly. "*Gute maiya,* Dr. Reynolds."

"What happened to your face?" Norman asked, almost pulling off wide-eyed innocence in his expression.

"An accident," Zach said, waving Norman's question away as if the colorful bruises around his eyes were no big deal. He didn't want Cassie to suspect that Norman had anything to do with the condition of his face, and he kind of felt sorry for Elmer Lee. Even though Elmer Lee had broken Zach's nose, Norman was the one who had volunteered him for the wrestling match, and Elmer Lee really had felt bad about breaking Zach's nose.

"He was wrestling with a friend," Cassie volunteered.

Norman smirked. "Looks like you got the

worse end of that fight."

Zach gave Norman a wide smile. "You should see the other guy."

Cassie grinned and shook her head indulgently. "I'll never understand why boys think pummeling each other is fun."

"It's not fun," Elmer Lee said, shifting his weight and looking positively sullen. "He didn't mean to break your nose."

Zach glanced at Cassie as his mind raced for another topic of conversation. Cassie didn't seem to notice anything strange, but if they kept talking about it, someone was bound to let something slip. "Are the Brewers going to be any good this year?" The blank stares he got from his companions told him he'd said the wrong thing. He mentally conked himself on the head. What did the Amish know about baseball? He didn't even like baseball. It was just the first thing that had popped into his head.

Someone tapped Zach on the shoulder. At least he thought someone tapped him on the shoulder. He was wearing about six layers. He couldn't be sure. He turned to see Titus with the ubiquitous toothpick in his mouth and two other Amish men. "Hullo, Dr. Reynolds."

Zach smiled and shook Titus's hand. It was nice to see a friendly face.

Titus pointed to the blond man who was almost as tall as Zach. "This is my brother Ben, and this is Cassie's nephew-in-law Tyler Yoder."

Zach smiled and raised an eyebrow. "How does that work?"

"He married my niece," Cassie said as if that cleared up all confusion.

Tyler Yoder had dark hair and dark features, and the makings of a thick beard grew on his chin the same as Ben, except that Ben's beard was blondish brown and barely visible on his face. They had both probably been married less than a year.

Tyler had good humor in his face even though his lips didn't even hint at a smile. "I married Beth, who is Sarah Beachy's daughter. Sarah is Cassie's oldest sister. Cassie is Beth's aunt. That makes me Cassie's nephew-in-law."

Ben seemed even less inclined to smile than Tyler, but neither of them acted hostile, at least at the moment. Norman, on the other hand, glared at Zach as if he were going to pounce on him at any moment. Probably nothing would make Norman happier than Zach's immediate departure.

"Thank you for helping our mammi with her foot," Ben said. "Titus and Cassie tell me you have been very kind to her."

365

Zach relaxed slightly. Neither of them seemed concerned that Zach might drag Cassie into a life of wickedness and depravity. "Anna is my favorite patient."

A pretty young woman in a black coat and dark blue dress walked their way as if to join in their conversation. Her foot caught on a chunk of snow, and she tripped. Ben shot out a hand and caught her arm before she ended up on the ground. Gazing at her as if she were the sun, moon, and stars, he secured an arm around her waist to make sure she was stable and pulled her into their circle.

She grinned as if this sort of thing happened all the time. "Sorry. I don't do very well in snow."

"Dr. Reynolds," Ben said, smiling for the first time, "this is my wife Emma."

Zach's gut clenched. Ben's obvious affection for his wife mirrored what he felt for Cassie. Would he ever get to show her how much he loved her? Would he have a chance someday to wrap his arms around her, whisper deliciously sweet words into her ear, and plant kisses on those petal-soft lips?

He took a deep breath. It would be better if he didn't drive himself crazy today.

"This is Mammi's foot doctor," Ben said. "The one your mammi talks so much about? The one who broke his nose?"

Ben nodded.

Emma smiled at Zach like a dear friend. Maybe Norman's resentment hadn't infected the rest of the family. "You and Cassie have matching scarves."

Cassie fingered the scarf around her neck. Was she happy about the matching scarves or afraid they'd make trouble? "Mammi made them for us."

"Mammi Anna is quite fascinated with you, Doctor," Emma said. Her lively eyes twinkled as if she knew more than she was letting on.

"But how was she able to convince you to make a house call three times a week?" Tyler asked.

Emma nudged her cousin-nephew-relative-in-law in the arm. "Look at Cassie, Tyler. Do you think it would take much to convince the doctor to come around?"

Cassie lowered her eyes and turned pink with that attractive blush that Zach loved so much. It hadn't even taken a puff of air to convince Zach to come to Huckleberry Hill. He'd follow Cassie to the Amazon jungle if he had to.

Ben's lips curved upward slightly. "Mammi can be very persuasive when she wants to be."

"The doctor cares for Mammi's foot," Norman said too loudly. "But Elmer Lee helped us butcher the hog yet."

Titus pulled the toothpick from his mouth. "The doctor saved Priscilla from catching fire."

Norman's frown settled deeper into his face. "It wouldn't have happened if you hadn't been chasing her."

"It wasn't Titus's fault," Cassie said.

Zach nodded. If she hadn't said it, he would have.

Titus grimaced and stuck the toothpick back in his mouth. "I should have been a bunny."

Emma laid a hand on Titus's shoulder. "You would have made a wonderful-gute bunny." She turned to Zach. "Cassie says you put out the fire with your hands and got burned yourself."

"Anyone would have done the same," Zach said. "Titus would have, but he was too far when it happened."

"Elmer Lee fixed his sister's roof during a snowstorm," Norman said.

Zach almost laughed out loud. Cassie tried valiantly to suppress a grin. Norman couldn't bear to surrender bragging rights. It was becoming a little comical.

Ben folded his arms across his chest and

stared at Zach. "I like you. You'll do just fine."

What did he mean by "do just fine"? Do just fine with the sap collecting?

Zach's smile faded as Cassie's mother sauntered out of the house and down the porch steps with a battery-operated drill in each hand. She looked like a gunfighter from the Old West complete with scowl and menacing look in her eye. She zeroed in on Zach, and he could almost hear her hiss like a cat. What possible threat could he be? He was surrounded by Amish people, some of them as tall and muscular as he was.

Was there anything he could do to soften her up a bit?

"Gute . . ." Wait. Probably shouldn't try that. His Deitsch seemed to raise a lot of hackles. "Good afternoon, Esther," he said flashing the smile he only used for special occasions.

"Afternoon, Doctor," she said with little enthusiasm. At least she didn't snarl. "Good to see you, Ben and Emma, Tyler. How is Beth?"

"She is feeling a little better. She thinks the worst of the morning sickness has passed." Tyler motioned to a little boy running circles in the snow. "I brought Toby. Neither of us have tapped maples before."

"Neither have I," Zach said.

Tyler nodded solemnly, which seemed to be his normal state of emotion. "We can learn together."

"Elmer Lee has been tapping maples ever since he could walk," Norman said.

"We have trees on our property," Elmer Lee said. "There's enough land to build two or three more houses."

Zach pressed his lips together. Elmer Lee had land, and a girl like Cassie would want her man to build her a house.

He should buy some land.

"You've got to drill the holes just so or you'll damage the tree," Esther said. She handed a drill to Elmer Lee and one to Norman. "Norman, take the doctor with you and show him how it's done. Doctor, you'll have to carry the buckets and the taps. Cassie will go with Elmer Lee. No trees less than eighteen inches."

Zach nearly bit through his tongue. The thought of spending the afternoon with Norman instead of Cassie was worse than the prospect of tooth decay.

"But, Mamm," Cassie said. "Dr. Reynolds —"

"Won't do us much good if he doesn't know what he's doing," Esther said.

His hands were tied. If he put up any sort

of a fuss about being with Cassie, he'd come across as selfish and disrespectful. Cassie hated conflict. If he wanted to make her happy, he'd try to please her mother.

Besides, Elmer Lee had been tapping maple trees for years. Zach needed to keep up.

He stole a glance at Cassie and smiled reassuringly. "I know I can learn a lot from Norman."

With his gaze still fixed on Zach, Ben frowned and rubbed his fingers back and forth across the whiskers on his jaw. "Emma and I will take Titus and Tyler."

"I have a drill," Titus said as he, Ben, Emma, and Tyler headed toward the stack of metal buckets near the barn.

"Can I try the drill?" Emma said.

Ben furrowed his brow. "Uh, do you want to have all your fingers at the end of the day?" he asked as they walked away.

Esther pursed her lips. "Emma is a little accident-prone," she whispered. She pulled two pieces of fabric from her pocket, one white and one black. It took Zach a minute to realize what they were. "I don't know why your mammi made that hat when she knows I disapprove of them."

"I'll grab some buckets yet," Luke said, sprinting away from them as if he couldn't remove himself from the conversation fast enough.

Esther shoved the two head coverings into Cassie's hand. "Put on a proper kapp and bonnet so I don't have to be embarrassed for my daughter. And remember the devotion you owe to God."

Cassie's cheeks flushed bright red as she glanced at Zach, almost as if she were more concerned he'd say something than she was about her mother's offensive behavior.

Zach clamped his teeth together so hard, Elmer Lee could probably hear them grinding together inside his mouth. But he didn't speak. He didn't lash out at Cassie's mother like he ached to. Cassie wanted him to stay quiet even though she was the one hurt by her mother's harshness.

He might have shut Norman up, but Esther was still around and she was worse than Norman. But how to get Esther to leave Cassie alone?

He couldn't very well challenge Esther to a wrestling match. What about an old-fashioned gunfight with drills? Or a cut-throat round of Scrabble?

Cassie slid the beanie off her head. Wisps of her hair floated in the air, suspended by static electricity. Her hair was already pulled into a ponytail. Esther handed her some bobby pins, and she fashioned a bun at the back of her head before taking a breath and managing a weak smile. "You and Norman go on ahead. I'll see you in the forest."

Zach turned his back and walked in the direction of the buckets. He couldn't watch Cassie's humiliation without lashing out at Esther. But no matter how much Cassie appreciated it, it just about killed him to walk away. No need for a coat or long underwear or a scarf. He was steaming. He unzipped his coat and pulled the beanie off his head.

Ben and Emma stood with their heads together near the barn, deep in conversation. They turned and looked at Zach, and he knew without a doubt they were talking about him. Emma nodded and walked into the barn. Ben motioned for Zach to come near. Zach did so reluctantly. No matter how nice Ben seemed, Zach was kind of fed up with Amish people right now.

Ben glanced in Esther's direction and put a hand on Zach's shoulder. "Aunt Esther means well."

Zach tried to temper his resentment. Ben didn't deserve it. "Does she?"

"My aunt thinks she'll be happy if she forces Cassie to be baptized. But that won't make her happy. It will only make Cassie miserable."

"Yeah. It will."

"If she can convince Cassie to fall in love with Elmer Lee, she thinks all her troubles will be over. And you, Dr. Reynolds, are trouble."

Zach snapped his head up to study Ben's expression. He was grinning.

"Elmer Lee won't stop trying as long as Norman keeps filling his head full of hope." Ben fingered the whiskers on his chin like someone unused to them being there. "Emma and I are guessing that you don't want to spend the day with Norman."

"Esther wants me to spend the day with Norman."

Ben's mouth curled upward. "Don't worry. Pretend to cooperate with Aunt Esther, and we'll fix everything."

"Who is 'we'?"

"My wife is smart. We like you. And Cassie deserves a good man."

Zach's heart swelled inside his chest. "You think I'm a good man?"

"Don't break her heart, okay?"

"Never."

Ben twisted his lips into a wry smile. "That's a piecrust promise, Doctor. Be careful how you make it."

Ben grabbed four buckets from the stack. There were galvanized metal buckets and the plastic five-gallon kind. It probably didn't matter what they used to catch the sap. Zach grabbed four as well and went to join Norman on the path deeper into the woods.

Felty came out of the house carrying a bucketful of metal pieces that looked like waterspouts. He waved to Zach. "Hullo, Doctor. It's a perfect day for maple sugaring." Zach rushed to his side and took the bucket from him.

It was heavy. Felty shouldn't have been carrying it. He never behaved like an old man. "These must be the taps for the trees."

"Jah. They're called spiels. Cassie washed them last night. I need to hand them out."

Felty followed behind as Zach took the bucket of spiels and set them on the ground near the trailhead. Cassie's relatives gathered around Felty with their buckets and drills, three or four power drills and a couple of hand-operated ones. Zach stood next to Felty, envying Elmer Lee and Luke, who stood next to Cassie. Their eyes met, and she smiled at him. His heart thumped wildly. She looked beautiful in everything she wore, even the black bonnet, but the very sight of it made Zach clench his fists involuntarily.

"Everybody take some taps," Felty said,

"and don't drill too deep into the trees. The birds need a home this summer."

Cassie grabbed several taps from the bucket. Zach caught a whiff of her as she came close. Vanilla and roses. Was she deliberately trying to make him go nuts?

She leaned in close. "Thank you for not being mad about my mamm."

Not mad? He was livid. He must have been a better actor than he thought. He proved it by smiling at her as if her mamm's unacceptable behavior hadn't even crossed his mind. "You look cute in that bonnet."

She rolled her eyes. "Maybe. But I'm wearing lip gloss in protest."

She shouldn't have said that because his gaze immediately traveled to her supple and well-glossed lips. He knew without even asking that they'd taste like vanilla. Vanilla was one of his favorite flavors. He pressed his hand to the side of his face. He'd be practically useless for the rest of the day.

"Norman is good with the tapping, and he's really very nice once you get to know him. It might be fun." She studied his face. "Please don't be mad."

He gave her the smile she needed to see. "I want to learn how to make maple syrup. What better teacher than Norman?"

She flashed a half smile. "He's really been

trying hard to get along. He hasn't said a word about my joining the church for days. I think he finally understands me and respects my decision."

Zach pressed his lips together and nodded. Respect had nothing to do with it. He would never again underestimate the power of a friendly wrestling match. Norman had honored his promise.

Elmer Lee came up behind Cassie. "I'll carry your buckets. And the taps."

A twinge of jealousy sliced into Zach's chest as Cassie smiled at Elmer with her shiny lips. Darn that Elmer Lee for being a gentleman. Zach should have been the one to be a gentleman, but thanks to Esther, he'd be stuck with Norman, which was going to be just about as much fun as yanking out his own ingrown toenail.

Norman was the last to get taps from Felty's bucket. He loaded his pockets while taking breaks to glare at Zach. *As fun as ten ingrown toenails at once.* "Can you carry the lids?" he said as if he thought Zach wasn't capable of doing anything.

Norman carried the drill, a hammer, and the buckets. Zach carried the bucket lids and a pocketful of taps. He fell in step behind Norman as they hiked into the woods. Cassie and Elmer Lee were already a hundred feet ahead of them, Cassie with a hammer and her black bonnet, Elmer Lee with the buckets and a satisfied look on his face.

Zach took the crisp, clean afternoon air into his lungs. Patches of snow still covered most of the ground, but here and there the muddy forest floor was visible where the snow had begun to melt. The trees lifted their bare branches to the sky as if they were praying for spring. Not a cloud, and the sky was so blue, it hurt Zach's eyes to look at.

Their small group spread out among the trees in what Norman called a sugar bush, which as far as Zach could tell was the name for the grove of bare maple trees where they were going to tap. He'd lost sight of Cassie already. Hopefully she and Elmer were having a miserable time.

Norman picked a tree, set the buckets on the ground, and immediately started drilling a hole in the bark.

"Do you have to go a certain height on the tree?" Zach asked. "How deep does the hole have to be?"

"I'll do all the figuring," Norman said, snapping at Zach as if he were a teenager who'd forgotten to take out the garbage. "Just hand me a tap when I need it and don't get in the way."

Zach had the sudden urge to kick Norman's buckets and scatter them around the snowy forest floor. He didn't. "Look," he said, folding his arms across his chest. "You don't like me, and that's fine. I get it. I don't like you either. In fact, I think you are the rudest, most arrogant, self-righteous person I've ever met."

Norman's nostrils flared, and he scowled.

"I could have refused to come, and I could walk away right now and take Cassie with me. So maybe you should keep your mouth shut."

"Maybe you should leave our family alone, Doctor."

Zach wouldn't be defeated that easily. "I'm not going anywhere. Teach me what to do."

Norman seemed to chew on his words like a piece of gristle. Zach could see the indecision in his eyes. Would he put up a fight or give in?

Norman relaxed his shoulders slightly. "Okay. I will teach you how we do it. But don't expect me to let you use the drill. I don't trust you that far."

Zach pursed his lips. It was probably as much of a concession as he'd ever get from Norman. He nodded curtly. "Show me."

Norman pointed the drill at the tree. "A

tree this big can take two or three taps. You want to drill on the southern-facing side because the sap runs better on the warmer side of the trunk." He traced his finger along the bark about shoulder height. "This tree has been tapped before. Do you see the old holes?"

"Yes."

"Don't drill a new hole vertical to an old hole. They have to be staggered or the sap won't run."

Norman showed him how to point the drill slightly upward and drill only an inch and a half into the tree. Once he made the hole, Zach fit the spiel and Norman hammered it in. "Hammer only until you hear the tap slip into place. If you hammer too hard, you'll split the wood."

Zach watched in amazement as the sap, which looked like water, began to drip from the spiel almost as soon as it was in place. The spiel had a little hook beneath the spout where Norman attached the bucket. Then Zach put a lid on top.

They repeated the process on the same tree about a third of the way around from the first tap. Norman let Zach hammer the spiel and hook the bucket onto the bottom of it. "Someone empties the buckets every day," Norman said. "We can get ten to twenty gallons of sap from one tree."

"That's a lot of syrup."

Zach could see a snide reply forming on Norman's lips. Instead, he took a deep breath and gave Zach a half smile. "It takes forty gallons of sap to make a gallon of syrup."

"No wonder it's so expensive."

"The syrup money gives Mammi and Dawdi a little bit of extra income."

"You're kind to help your grandparents out."

Norman looked at him as if he were crazy. "It's what we do. We help each other. That's why I try to help Cassie see the right way. I would be heartbroken if she sinned herself out of heaven."

Zach took a deep breath and counted to ten. Mom said it always worked for her. It didn't seem to work for him. "We're never going to see eye to eye, so maybe you should save your breath."

"Fine," Norman said. "You won't see what you won't see."

Whatever.

Titus ran toward Zach and Norman's tree as if the forest were on fire. Zach immediately scanned the area for Cassie. Had there been an accident?

Titus yanked the toothpick from his

mouth and hurled it to the ground. "Norman, you've got to come help Emma with her tree. She's trying to drill a hole, but she's holding the drill upside down and it's making a funny noise."

Someone plowed a furrow into Norman's forehead. "Where's Ben?"

Titus seemed almost too breathless to reply. "He's helping Cassie."

The furrow got deeper. "Where's Elmer Lee?"

"He's helping Tyler Yoder."

Norman's voice pitched higher with each question. "What happened to Luke?"

Titus squinted at Norman in frustration. "Will you come and help Emma or not?"

"Why can't you help Emma?"

Titus stared at Norman as if the answer were obvious. "I'm her brother-in-law. She won't listen to me."

Norman threw up his hands. "That doesn't make any sense, Titus."

Titus held out his hand. "I'll take your drill and work this tree with Dr. Reynolds."

"Why am I the only one who knows how to do anything around here?" Norman huffed. He shoved the drill into Titus's hand. "Don't break my bit. And don't let the doctor use it."

Titus nodded eagerly. "Okay. Thanks for

helping Emma. I wouldn't want her arm to fall off or something."

Norman stormed off in the direction Titus pointed. For him, the world in general must have been one big nuisance.

"I know how to use a drill," Zach said as soon as Norman was out of earshot.

Titus grinned. "Of course you do. You drill into people's teeth every day."

Zach curled his lips and raised his eyebrows. "I'm a doctor, Titus, not a dentist."

This news seemed to make Titus excessively worried. "Oh. I was going to have you look at this filling that's been bothering me."

Zach chuckled. "I can't help you. But if you ever need a mole removed, I'm your guy."

"Maybe I shouldn't let you use the drill."

"You'd be amazed at how good I am with a drill." He clapped Titus on the shoulder. "This tree is tapped. Should we go find another one?"

"No," Titus said. He leaned very close to Zach and whispered, "We need to stay right here. Ben and Emma have a plan. We're playing musical trees."

"Sounds like a fun game."

"Ben went to Cassie's tree and sent Elmer Lee to Tyler Yoder's tree. Then they told Luke to go find Emma's tree, but Emma is hiding. So now Ben is going to send Cassie to your tree, and I will go back to Cassie's tree and make sure Elmer Lee is too busy to go looking for Cassie."

Zach cracked a smile. "What about Cassie's mamm?"

"Do you really think Aunt Esther is going to be able to untie this knot? We'll be done before she knows she's been *ferhoodled.*"

Zach had the feeling he'd been ferhoodled. Titus's game of musical trees was a little difficult to follow.

All confusion cleared like the sky after a storm when Cassie appeared from among the trees and walked toward them. She glanced tentatively at Zach and Titus. "Ben said you needed me?"

Yep, he needed her. The need was an ache in his gut the size of the Grand Canyon. The need was a hole in his heart big enough to park a truck in. He cleared his throat. "Uh, yes. I thought you could help me tap the next tree. Titus was just leaving."

Titus glanced at him sideways. "I was?"

"Weren't you going to help Elmer Lee?"

Titus brightened. "Oh, jah. Step seven of the plan." He slid his hand in his pocket, pulled out another toothpick, and stuck it between his lips. "I'll go see if Elmer Lee needs me." He leaned his head close to

Zach's. "Um, just to be cautious, hide behind a tree if Aunt Esther comes by." He took three steps, turned back, and pointed his toothpick at Cassie. "Don't let the doctor use the drill."

He trudged east even though Cassie had come from the west. Titus might never find Elmer Lee's tree.

Cassie laid her palm against the tree. "I have a feeling there's some sort of scheme going on."

Zach tried to look innocent. "I have that feeling too."

Cassie eyed him suspiciously. "What have you been up to?"

"Me? I've been patiently enduring Norman's dirty looks and daydreaming about you."

Her lips twitched skeptically.

He took off his coat and hung it on the branch of the tree. "Ben and Emma took pity on me and decided that I shouldn't have to spend the day with Norman when I'd much rather spend it with you."

Her mouth kept twitching, but a grin grew behind it.

"But I'm being selfish. If you'd rather tap trees with Elmer Lee, I understand. I'll probably die of a broken heart, but I'll understand."

The slight grin bloomed into a smile. "I'm confident you won't die of a broken heart."

"You want to go running back to Elmer Lee?"

A giggle tripped from her lips. "Elmer Lee is a very nice boy, but he doesn't have a matching scarf or a matching car. And his nose is perfectly straight. What's exciting about that?"

Zach couldn't have been happier if Norman had decided to take a vow of silence. Did the Amish do that? Maybe that was just monks and nuns. "And I'll bet Elmer Lee doesn't look very good in pink."

"Definitely not. I kinda like the pink."

"If Elmer Lee wants any chance with you, I'll have to break his nose in a wrestling match." He picked up his stack of buckets. "Let's go tap another tree. I'm getting good at it."

Cassie stopped as if she had run into a wall. "What do you mean you'll have to break his nose?"

"If . . . if he wants it to be crooked like mine." He held his breath as he saw the wheels turning in her head. He shouldn't have said that.

She looked ill, as if she'd eaten a whole bottle of Anna's canned peaches. "Elmer Lee was talking about broken noses, and he said he hurt his arm in a wrestling match. *Oh sis yuscht.* He's the one who broke your nose." She caught her breath and looked at him in horror. "Did you . . . did you attack him?"

His heart sank to think that was what she thought of him. "That's not how it happened."

Cassie would do anything to avoid conflict, but from her labored breathing he could tell how upset she was. She wrapped her arms around her waist and paced back and forth in a four-foot square next to the tree. "No wonder he turns pale every time he looks at you. He would never purposefully hurt anyone."

"I know, Cassie. Look —"

Her voice shook, but she wouldn't look at him. "Did you provoke him? The Amish are peaceful, Zach. How could you do that?"

"I'm the one with the broken nose."

Her expression was bleak as she backed away from him. "I'll go help Dawdi tap trees. You are fine without me."

He broke his rule not to touch her and laid a hand on her arm. "Will you let me explain before you decide to hate me?"

"I don't need an explanation."

"That's what you thought that night you and Tonya came to Finn's apartment."

She hesitated. He jumped at the opportunity. He took two buckets from his stack, overturned them, and sat down on one, motioning for Cassie to sit beside him.

"It's cold," she said.

"Pretend you're at the Reg."

She sat down on the uncomfortable chair and crossed her arms over her knees, gazing into the distance, looking anywhere but at him.

"You're right. I deserved the broken nose. My temper and my inner soccer player got the better of me, but I didn't attack anybody. Norman upset you. I challenged him to a friendly wrestling match."

She turned her head and stared at him in disbelief. "Norman? You could break his arm just by shaking his hand too hard."

"Elmer Lee took his place. It seemed only fair since I'm a lot bigger than Norman, but Elmer Lee wasn't happy about it. That's when I should have just let it go." He wanted to take her hand in the worst way possible. Instead, he leaned forward and gazed into her eyes. "I know how offensive fighting is to your people. But, Cassie, I couldn't stand by and let Norman treat you like that. He promised to stop bullying you if I won the match."

"And if Elmer Lee won?" she murmured.

"I promised not to come to Huckleberry Hill again."

She lowered her eyes and nodded.

He clenched his fists and folded his arms. He could look, but he mustn't touch. "It just about killed me to make that promise, but I did because I knew it was the only way I'd get him to leave you alone."

She raised her head. There might have been a spark of warmth in her blue eyes.

"Norman agreed to the wrestling match because he wanted to keep me off Huckleberry Hill," Zach said. "How could he know that the possibility of not seeing you was all the motivation I needed?"

It was a very good sign that one side of her lip curled upward as if she were thinking about smiling. "So you won the match, but Elmer Lee doesn't have a mark on him?"

"I didn't want to hurt him, and he didn't want to hurt me. He caught me with an errant elbow. When I started bleeding on him, he stopped fighting back. It was just the diversion I needed to take him down."

She still resisted a smile. "Any advantage you could get, I guess."

"I wasn't about to lose."

"You meant well. Thank you."

"Thank you?" He was definitely making

progress.

"Nobody's ever come to my defense like that before. I am astounded that you got a broken nose for me." She reached over and curled her fingers partway around his upper arm. He tensed, but if she was the one doing the touching, it was probably okay. "But you must let me deal with my family in my own way. It's easier on everyone if I don't make a fuss."

"It's not easier on me. Seeing the way they treat you makes me want to pull out my hair. It's okay for you to defend me, but it's not okay for me to defend you? That doesn't seem fair."

"They're my family."

And you're the girl I love. "But you won't stand up to them."

"I don't want to. It only stirs up trouble and hard feelings."

"No matter what, I will defend you. All you have to do is ask. I'll be there."

She turned a light shade of pink. "That's very kind of you."

"So will you forgive me for being an idiot?" he said.

Her smile finally broke through. "You're not an idiot. Just overzealous."

"Like Sir Galahad, maybe?"

Her eyes danced. "No. Not really."

He groaned in mock defeat. "I'm sure Sir Galahad never wore pink."

"He was more of a chain mail kind of guy."

After letting himself stare at her for a minute too long, he slapped his knees and stood up. "We should get tapping trees or people will begin to suspect that the only reason I came today was to see you, which is true, but we wouldn't want Anna to get her feelings hurt."

Cassie didn't lose her smile. He was definitely making progress.

Her lips formed into an *O*. "I almost forgot," she said, stuffing her hand into her coat pocket. "I have something for you." She pulled out a small gray rock and handed it to him.

"What's this?"

"Luke found a trilobite last fall while he plowed the fields. I mentioned your dad liked fossils, and Luke thought you might want to have it."

Zach turned the small stone over in his hand and examined the bumpy, oval-shaped impression left on the rock thousands of years ago. "My dad would have loved this."

Keeping her eyes on Zach, Cassie walked toward another good tapping tree. "A good memory of him to hold on to."

Zach's heart seemed to expand two sizes.

It still wasn't enough to hold all the love he felt for her. "Denki. I'll think of both of you whenever I look at it."

They found a good thick maple within twenty paces of the first one. Cassie let Zach use the drill, even though Norman and Esther would have given her detention if they found out. He drilled the hole and hammered the spiel into place. Cassie propped the bucket under the spiel as the sap began to dribble out. "Here," she said, sticking her finger under the flow of sap. She popped her finger in her mouth. "Have a taste."

Zach got a little sap on his finger and tried it. It tasted like weak sugar water. "I'm not impressed," he said.

She grinned and cuffed him on the shoulder. "The maple flavor comes out when we boil it down. It's like faith, which without works is dead."

He picked up a lid and set it on top of the bucket. "It works, you know," he said, keeping his gaze squarely on the bucket.

"The drill?"

"Faith. Yesterday a patient came in with a strange rash. It had me baffled. I went into my office, locked the door, and knelt down to pray. The minute I said 'amen,' the answer came to me. Hot tub folliculitis. I don't know that an answer has ever been that sudden before."

Her smile was like the sun reflecting off the lake. "God will always give you an answer. 'Seek and ye shall find.' "

"I'm beginning to believe it."

They both turned their heads when they heard a car honk its horn. The noise came from the lane in front of Anna and Felty's house. "It wonders me who that is," Cassie said.

Zach winked at her. "You haven't got a date with Mr. Florida State, have you? Is he here to pick you up in his red Corvette?"

"It's a Mustang," she said.

He snapped his head around to look at her. Did this Florida guy actually exist?

She laughed at his shocked expression. "Maybe it's somebody for you. You know more people who drive cars than all my relatives combined."

Zach's heart leaped inside his chest. "I turned off my phone because I'm not on call. Maybe they've been trying to get hold of me about Austin. He's going in for surgery tomorrow, and he wasn't doing very well last night. Marla and Jamie know to look for me here."

"Do you have any messages?"

Zach pulled his phone out of his pocket and turned it on. Three voice messages and seven new texts. Someone definitely wanted to get hold of him. Had they come all the way to Huckleberry Hill because they couldn't reach him by phone?

He quickly opened his text messages. They were all from Blair. His heart skidded to a stop.

I'm just outside of Oshkosh. Don't worry, I'm not texting and driving. What is your schedule like? I'll be in Stevens Point for a whole week.

How could he have forgotten that she'd be in town this week? The good news was that Stevens Point was far enough away to give him a good excuse not to see her.

Like he told her, he was pretty busy. Busy trying to get Cassie to fall in love with him.

Cassie stared at him, concern written all over her face. He frowned and shook his head. "False alarm. These texts are from a friend of mine who lives in Chicago." She wasn't in Chicago at the moment, but she lived there.

The next text had been sent an hour later.

I'm at the hotel. Is there anything better than a one-star around here?

A short time later she'd sent another.

Call me when you get a break.

The next text was in all caps.

CALL ME.

Then, I got out of my meeting early. I'm driving up to Shawano right now. We can meet up after your shift.

He felt like a fly that had just met the flat end of a flyswatter. Would Blair really be so bold as to drive up here? When she didn't find him at his apartment, would she stalk him at the hospital? What would she do when she didn't find him at the hospital?

With growing dread, he listened to his messages.

"Z, I'm driving around Shawano looking for decent places to eat. Call me. How long are your shifts at the hospital?"

"I'm going to ask for you at the hospital. Will they let me see you if I tell them I've got poison ivy? I'm not paying for an office visit. Ha ha."

Listening to her last message tied every muscle in his body into knots.

"The nurses here are very nice. Stacey says I might be able to find you at a place called Huckleberry Hill. I hope I don't drive into some redneck backwater and get kidnapped, or worse, lose cell service. Call me as soon as you get this message."

"Is everything okay?" Cassie asked, knitting her brows together.

Zach worked hard to unclench his jaw so he could speak. "Everything's okay. Nothing about Austin. Just that friend trying to reach me." If he ignored Blair, would she go away? He could take Cassie deeper into the woods until Blair gave up and went back to Stevens Point.

Titus, with bright eyes and red cheeks, came crunching through the snow. He'd lost his toothpick. "Dr. Reynolds, there's a girl looking for you. She says she's your girl-friend, but I told her she has the wrong Dr. Reynolds, because our Dr. Reynolds doesn't have a girlfriend. She told me to come get you anyway. What do you think? She acted sort of crazy."

Zach glanced at Cassie. She didn't move a muscle as she stared at his face. "She used to be my girlfriend, Titus." He gazed point-edly at Cassie. "We broke up almost a year ago."

Cassie pursed her lips and nodded.

"If I don't bring you back with me," Titus said, "she might get angry. She's testy, like Norman, and she's got long red fingernails like a cat."

Zach's lips curled upward. Had Titus ever seen red claws on a cat? He kept his eyes on Cassie. "She closed a big deal and bought a new car. She wants to show it to me. Will you come?"

Cassie seemed genuinely surprised by his

invitation. "You want me to come with you?"

"It might be good to have backup in case she uses those fingernails."

"I'll come," Titus said. "I've seen the fingernails. I'm prepared for anything."

They left their buckets in a stack, with the drill and hammer stuffed inside the top one, and trudged through the half-melted snow to the lane in front of Anna and Felty's house. Blair sat in her car, avoiding contact with the natives no doubt, while Felty stood next to the driver's side window and tried to talk to her through the one-inch slit in her window.

As they got closer, Zach realized that Felty was singing. *"And the Death Angel whispers, it's time to come home. Then it's good-bye to everyone I've met in my day. I'll see you soon on that reunion day."*

Through the windshield Zach could see the polite but mortified smile Blair had pasted on her face as if she were debating whether to drive down the hill as fast as her new Lexus would go. She stared straight ahead, probably fearing the Death Angel would swoop down and scoop her out of her car.

Zach, flanked by a suspicious Titus and a wary Cassie, walked around the back of the

397

car to the driver's side door and knocked on the window.

Blair nearly jumped out of her skin. When she saw who had knocked, she unlocked her door, leaped out of the car, and threw her arms around Zach's neck as if he'd rescued her from a burning building. "Z, am I glad to see you. I was starting to wonder if I'd gotten caught in one of those weird made-for-TV movies."

Zach let her cling for a minute without hugging back. He wasn't happy to see her, but Blair was more of a nuisance than anything else.

He looked at his companions. Titus seemed positively terrified by Blair's long fingernails and crimson lipstick. Cassie's face was a mask of indifference, but her arms were clamped tightly around her waist and she seemed to labor slightly for air.

"These are my Amish friends," Zach said, nudging Blair away from him. "Nothing to be afraid of."

Blair swept her long raven hair over her shoulders and tugged her tailored coat over the top of her skintight blue jeans. She looked as if she'd been personally dressed by a designer. "I wasn't afraid, just annoyed that you hadn't returned my calls. Do you even get service up here? Whoa. What happened to your eyes?"

Zach waved away her question. "I broke my nose. Nothing serious. Blair, I'd like you to meet Felty Helmuth and his grandson Titus. They're Amish. Do you know about the Amish?"

Blair batted her eyes. "Of course I know about the Amish. They make those quilts."

Felty leaned close to Zach's ear. "She seemed a little tense. Singing usually calms people right down." He stroked his beard. "Didn't seem to help this one."

Blair gave Titus a fake smile. "I hope I wasn't rude. I felt a little uptight that I couldn't find Zach. I didn't mean to snap at you like that."

"No harm done," said Titus, rocking back and forth on his heels. "I've had lots worse from Norman."

Felty raised his finger in the air. "I've got just the thing for you." He turned around, walked up the steps and into the house.

Cassie seemed to be drifting backward. Zach cupped his fingers around her elbow and nudged her forward. Even though Cassie was dressed in Plain clothes, Zach could practically see alarms going off in Blair's head when she laid eyes on Cassie. Girls seemed to instinctively know when someone threatened their territory. Her eyes turned icy, and that fake smile she'd used on Titus spread across her face as if it had been ironed there.

"This is Cassie Coblenz," Zach said, sidling closer to Cassie so as to leave no doubt in Blair's mind.

"Nice to meet you," Cassie said, in that mousy voice she used whenever Norman picked on her.

"You Amish too?" Blair asked, her voice pitched so high she sounded like a chicken.

"Cassie used to be Amish," Zach said. "She's visiting her family for a few months. She graduated in December."

"Oh, that's nice," Blair said, the apathy evident in her voice. "I thought you were Amish. The bonnet is really sweet."

"Thank you," Cassie said, even though she surely knew it wasn't a compliment.

Blair reached over and fingered the edge of Zach's scarf. "You and Zach have matching scarves. How cute."

Zach flashed Cassie an apologetic smile. She didn't move a muscle.

Blair dismissed everybody with a turn of her head and a swish of her hair. "Well, it was nice meeting you. I hope we see each other again very soon." She'd apparently learned all she wanted to know about one of the most fascinating cultures and peoples in the country. That was Blair. If she didn't see any benefit to her or her career, she didn't bother to make an effort.

"I promised Zach I'd take him for a spin in my new car." She reached out, grabbed Zach's hand, and pulled him toward her. "You wanna drive?"

"No, that's okay." He slipped his hand from her grasp. He'd rather wrestle Elmer Lee and the entire Notre Dame soccer team all at the same time than get in that car with Blair. But as annoyed as he felt, he couldn't embarrass her in front of everybody. A short drive around Shawano wouldn't hurt. The good news was that Shawano wasn't all that big. Even if they drove all the way around the lake, they'd be back within the hour.

That thought cheered him considerably.

Blair made her voice low and sexy. She must have thought that still worked on him. "I know you're dying to drive, Zach."

Zach finally let himself really look at Blair's new car. It was a beauty, with smooth lines and shiny chrome. He could practically feel the steering wheel in his hands and the powerful engine beneath the hood. Of course he wanted to drive it, but if he wanted it that bad, he'd find a dealership where the most obnoxious car salesman wouldn't be near as annoying as Blair at this very minute.

Blair nibbled on the tip of her finger. "Don't you want to see how it handles?"

"You drive, Blair."

Blair seemed disappointed but undeterred. "Okay, then. Get in."

Zach opened the driver's side door for her. His mom had taught him to be a gentleman, no matter how abrasive the lady proved to be. Blair flashed him a flirty smile and slid into her seat.

He closed the door and leaned his head to one side to get Cassie to look at him. She stared faithfully at her feet.

"Cassie," he said.

Her feet couldn't have been that interesting. "Yes?"

"I'll be back soon to help finish the trees."

She finally looked at him and smiled, but the light had gone out of her eyes. "Of course."

"She seems like a real nice girlfriend," Titus said.

"She's not my girlfriend," Zach said. "Just a friend."

Titus nodded. "If you say so. How long will you be gone?"

Blair started the car. The engine purred just like Zach knew it would. She rolled down her window. "I'm taking Zach to dinner," she said. "Any good restaurants in town?"

"I won't have time for dinner," Zach said.

"I don't mind," Blair said. "I drove all this way to see you. The least I can do is take you out." She rolled up the window before he could argue, although she'd get plenty of argument when he got in the car.

Felty came out of the house and bounced down the steps. He knocked on Blair's window. "I have a gift for you," he yelled.

Blair pursed her lips and reluctantly rolled down her window.

Felty pulled a pair of pot holders from his pocket. One lime green and one baby pink. "Anna said there's nothing that comforts a nervous condition like homemade pot holders. She wants you to have these."

"Oh, okay. Thanks," Blair said, more perplexed than grateful. She took them from Felty and stuffed them into her purse.

Zach went around to the passenger side of the car. "I'll see you soon," he said, making sure Cassie made eye contact with him.

"Have fun," she said, smiling as if she'd just been kicked in the shins.

Blair pulled forward and back, making a three-point turn to get the car pointed down the hill. A grin played at her lips until they got all the way down the hill, when the dam seemed to burst and she laughed as if she'd been holding it in for weeks.

"You want to let me in on the joke?" Zach said.

She snatched the two pot holders from her purse. "Pot holders. He gave me pot holders. Have you ever seen anything so bizarre?"

Those pot holders were lovingly knitted by Anna Helmuth, the sweetest little mammi in Wisconsin. She'd given them as a gesture of friendship. If Blair had ever met Anna, she never would have poked fun at her pot holders.

"Where did you find those hayseeds?" Blair said, her voice charged with amused disbelief.

Zach rolled his eyes. "Anna is one of my patients. They're my friends."

"What is it with the beard on the old guy?"

"All married Amish men grow beards. It's part of their tradition."

Her eyes grew wide. "If my husband had to grow one of those, I think I'd kill myself. Of course, if all the wives are as homely as that girl, maybe they don't mind the beard so much."

Zach stiffened. He couldn't let that slight go unchallenged, even though he knew what Blair's reaction would be. "Cassie is the

404

prettiest girl I've ever laid eyes on."

She raised her eyebrows. "Really? That granola is the prettiest girl you've ever laid eyes on? Come on, Zach. I can do better than that in a ponytail and an old sweatshirt. I've seen bag ladies more attractive."

Zach folded his arms and stared out the window at the bare trees and empty pastures. He was done talking about Cassie. It wouldn't change Blair's mind about anything, and her insults only served to make him ferociously angry. No matter what, he would *not* challenge Blair to a wrestling match.

She tucked a lock of hair behind her ear. "What do you think of my car? Do you like the leather seats? They're heated. And a V-6 turbo engine."

"It's really nice, Blair."

"Really nice? I drive all the way up here for 'really nice'? I think you can do better than that. You should drive it. See what it's got."

Driving it wasn't such a bad idea. That way he could control how far they went and how soon he got back to Huckleberry Hill. "Okay," he said. "Pull over."

She flashed a delighted smile. "Whatever you want."

She pulled to the side of the road, and

they traded places. He put it into drive and headed for the highway. The steering was so smooth, it almost felt like they were floating.

Blair reclined her seat slightly and kicked off her pink heels. How did she get around in the snow in those things? She combed her fingers through her hair, a gesture that used to drive Zach wild. He knew what she was trying to do.

"I like it when you drive," she said. "You look so powerful behind the wheel."

He merged onto the highway. The Lexus accelerated like a dream.

She tilted her head and studied the speedometer. "Only sixty-five? Really, Zach?"

"I'm being cautious."

"That's not the Zach I know."

"It's the one you're getting today. I don't want to go far. I've got to go back and get my car."

"There's no hurry. We could go back and get it in the morning." She nibbled on the tip of her index finger and winked at him. "My meetings don't start until after noon tomorrow."

He shook his head and expelled a deep breath. "You know that's not going to happen. It's been over for a long time, Blair."

She stuck her bottom lip out in a pout.

"It's just one night. Don't you want to have a little fun, no strings attached?"

Zach might have bought into that a few months ago, but he was beginning to realize that there were always strings attached — physical, emotional, spiritual strings that didn't untie themselves simply because both people wanted them to. He'd seen the consequences of casual intimacy firsthand with patients who came into his office and in girls who'd been tossed aside by Finn McEwan and the boys in his club. When he looked into Cassie's eyes, he'd seen what he wanted to become and how he wanted to behave.

A one-night stand with Blair Baker was not it.

It only took about ten minutes on the freeway to get from Bonduel to Shawano. He guessed Blair would have been happy to have him drive clear to Chicago. She'd have to settle for a drive by Walmart and the lake.

She smirked when he exited the freeway. "It's not that far to Stevens Point. Or we could go the other way to Green Bay. They've probably got a decent restaurant or two. Probably."

"I want to get back to help the Helmuths with their maple trees."

Blair retrieved a tube of lipstick from her

purse and dabbed a little on her already dark lips. "I think you've been breathing too much of this country air. You're a doctor, Z, not a redneck."

"I'm more of a redneck than you think. I used to be a cherry picker, remember?"

"What? You trying to revisit your childhood? And what is this weird thing you have for that little Amish girl?"

"What weird thing?"

"You like her, but she's definitely not your type. I think I'd die of embarrassment if you left me for that one."

He tightened the muscles of his jaw and took a deep breath. She was being purposefully petulant. He wouldn't take the bait. Cassie's beauty needed no defense. "I've already left you."

She leaned her elbow on her knee and propped her chin in her hand. "Zach, we dated for two years. We had the friendliest breakup in history. We gave each other a lot of support. Can't you even give me two hours out of your busy schedule?"

"I don't know what the point is, Blair. I don't want to get back together."

"We were friends too."

"What's the point?" he said again. Every minute spent with Blair was a minute he could have been spending with Cassie.

408

"The point is to have dinner. Do some catching up." When he didn't respond, she tapped him on the leg and dragged one of her bright red fingernails lightly over the sleeve of his coat. "You're so tense, like you're waiting for me to pounce."

"Are you going to?"

"I'll be honest, Z. I'd love to get back together." She raised her eyebrows. "There's nobody quite so fine in a pair of Levi's. But I'm not going to push the issue, and I'm not one of those creepy stalkers. I like you more than you like me. Get over it, and come to dinner."

Would his agreement get Blair off his back once and for all? Probably not, but it would get her off his back for the time being. He could have a brief dinner with Blair, send her back to Stevens Point, and go to Huckleberry Hill afterward. His shift didn't start until midnight.

"I can do McDonald's," he said.

She frowned but must have realized that was all she was going to get. "I'll buy."

Dinner didn't turn out so bad, probably because he knew it would be short. He could endure a lot if he knew there was an expiration date. Blair was pretty and smart and he mostly enjoyed her company. She was a poor substitute for Cassie, but if eating dinner with Blair tonight meant he'd never have to do it again, he was willing to sacrifice.

In the McDonald's parking lot after dinner, Austin's mom Jamie called and asked if Zach could swing by the hospital and look in on Austin for a couple of minutes. His surgery was tomorrow, early, and Jamie was afraid Zach might not be available right before Austin went in.

Blair wasn't happy about it, but she drove him to the hospital and waited in the car while Zach went in to see Austin. He wasn't keen on taking Blair into the hospital. Blair didn't particularly like children, and she got nauseous around sick people.

Austin looked horrible. He was as skinny as a flagpole and pale as a ghost, and the circles under his eyes were almost as dark as any black eye Zach had ever gotten. The surgery was coming none too soon.

Zach gave Austin a pre-game speech and a pre-game arm wrestle and prayed with him before saying good night.

It would be a rough time yet, but God would not abandon a little kid who needed His healing power so badly. Zach felt it in his bones. Austin was going to be okay. Zach had said another prayer on his way out the door as an extra precaution.

It was nearly seven when Blair pulled alongside the two matching cars sitting in front of Helmuths' house.

She put the car into park and gave him a weary smile. "I'll be here until Saturday. Call me if you want some company."

He wouldn't. Instead, he would be the person Cassie wanted. The man she deserved.

And, as an added bonus, he would learn how to make syrup.

Chapter Twenty-Two

It was already dark when Cassie, Titus, and Dawdi each took a sled to collect sap from the buckets hanging from the trees. The buckets would overflow by morning if they weren't emptied tonight. On warm days it kept two or three of them busy all day emptying sap buckets. Mammi and Dawdi and one other person could usually manage it, but it was a full-time job, and that didn't include boiling down the sap to make syrup. This year, since Mammi was off her feet, they had only tapped sixty trees. That would still give them plenty to do for weeks.

The rest of the family had gone home once they'd completed the tapping. Ben and Emma planned on returning tomorrow to help with the collecting and boiling.

Cassie pulled the sled with both hands and wore a headlamp to see her way in the dark. She, Titus, and Dawdi had separated from each other, she to the west, Titus to the east, and Dawdi to the north in hopes of getting all the buckets and not duplicating each other's steps. The taps spread out over a half a mile of space, and they knew the paths well.

After finding a stand of tapped trees, Cassie unhooked a bucket from one of the spiels, poured the collected sap into her ten-gallon plastic bucket, and replaced the smaller bucket on the tree.

She usually didn't mind collecting sap, even in the dark. It was satisfying to see the full bucket and hear the slap of liquid as she poured the sap into the larger bucket. But tonight her feet felt heavy, as if she were wearing lead-lined boots. She barely had the energy to put one foot in front of the other.

Zach said he'd be right back, but Cassie had taken one look at the beautiful, sophisticated woman behind the steering wheel of the steel blue Lexus and knew he'd be gone for a long time. Maybe forever.

That raven-haired beauty queen with the hot pink stiletto heels was definitely Zach's type, more than Cassie could ever hope to be. It shouldn't have bothered her. She had made peace with her insignificance, but sometimes she wished she were flashier, like a Christmas tree ornament. An ornament that would catch the attention of Dr. Reynolds.

She looked down at the gray dress Mamm had insisted she wear. The thought that she'd never be enough for him cut like a knife into her soul and left her panting for air.

From the seven trees, she filled her ten-gallon bucket to the brim, snapped on the lid, and made sure it sealed tightly. It would be bad if she lost half the sap on the way back to the sugar shack.

She dragged her sled through the snow, doing her best to pull through the tracks she'd already made. It would make the sled easier to pull. Ten gallons of sap was a heavy load.

She emerged from the forest and onto the lane in front of Mammi and Dawdi's house just as a car pulled up the hill. The ex-girlfriend's Lexus. They'd come to retrieve Zach's car. Cassie didn't want to have an accidental encounter with either of them. Let Zach drive down the hill and never come back. She didn't need the heartache.

Stopping at the edge of the path, she turned off her headlamp and sidled close to a tree. In the dark, they'd never notice her.

She heard the car door open. Because of the distance, their voices were muffled, but

Cassie could make out well enough what they said.

"Call me if you need company," Blair said.

"Thanks for letting me drive your car. I hope your meetings go well."

Zach slammed the car door, and the gravel crunched under Blair's tires as she turned her car around and drove down the hill. Cassie expected to hear Zach's key click into the lock on his car door but instead, she heard footsteps as he seemed to be walking in her direction.

A voice to her left almost made her stumble backward. "Are you hiding from me or Blair?"

She caught her breath and gave him a dirty look, although he wouldn't have been able to see her scowl in the dark. She turned on her headlamp. "What do you think you're doing, sneaking up on me like that?"

Zach chuckled. "You were hiding behind a tree, ready for an ambush. I had to make the first move."

"I was not." She didn't especially want him to see her like this, with her hair stuffed into the bonnet and smudges of dirt down her ugly gray dress. It was a sure bet that Zach preferred pink heels to mud-caked boots, and well-manicured nails to hands smeared with dirt. Ignoring the stab of pain in her chest, she grunted and tugged at the sled to get it moving then marched toward the sugar shack as if she had somewhere very important to go.

He dogged her steps. "Can I help?"

"The tapping's all done. The family left. Titus, Dawdi, and I are collecting the first sap."

"I'm sorry I missed it."

Why should he be sorry? Blair had made him a better offer. Cassie picked up her pace, which proved difficult pulling a ten-gallon bucket of sap behind her.

He shuffled next to her and took the towrope from her hand. "Where to?"

"You don't have to."

"I want to help." He smiled hesitantly and gestured to her headlamp. "This is a very convenient light."

Cassie brushed some hair away from her face before remembering how dirty her hands were. She shoved them behind her back. "The sugar shack is in a clearing just beyond the toolshed."

"Will you show me?" he prodded, as if sensing her reluctance.

She walked beside him so that both of them could see the way with her headlight. His closeness only served to further agitate her. She wasn't his type. How stupid of her to dream.

She led him around the barn, past the toolshed, and through a row of sumac bushes to the sugar shack, basically four poles holding up a roof over three fire pits.

He hefted the bucket from the sled as if it were empty. "Where do you want this?"

"Stick it in that bank of snow. It needs to stay cold until we boil it down in the morning."

The snow crunched as Zach shoved the bottom half of the bucket into the drift. He brushed his hands off and smiled at her. "What can I do now? Do we need to collect more sap?"

"Nothing more tonight. Thanks for your help." She turned and hiked back through the sumac bushes. Hopefully he'd take it as a signal that he could go.

He stood rooted to his spot for a second before jogging to catch up with her. "Do you want me to look in on Anna? I haven't seen her today."

Cassie attempted a smile. "She's fine. She finished several pot holders and a blanket this afternoon."

"Does she want me to look at her foot?"

She bowed her head so he wouldn't see anything amiss in her eyes. "You don't have to feel obligated, Doctor." She fiddled with her bonnet strings as an excuse not to look at him. "I'm sure there are other places you'd rather be and other people you'd rather be with."

He stopped dead in his tracks. She kept walking.

"Cassie?" he said.

She would have been very rude to not turn around. She reluctantly stopped and looked at him.

He drew his eyebrows together. "What's wrong?"

"Nothing."

He came closer and tilted his head to one side. "You're upset. That's not nothing."

The headlight gave her an advantage. She could see his features clearly, but when he looked at her, all he would be able to see was the bright light.

"Blair's life is very exciting compared to hog butchering and maple sugaring."

"Not really."

Cassie wished for a glass of water to clear her dusty throat. "She has a nice car."

He shrugged. "You've seen one Lexus, you've seen them all." He raised a hand to shield his eyes. "Cassie, do you think you could turn off the light? I feel like I'm in the middle of a police interrogation."

Reluctantly, she clicked the headlamp off.

At least he wouldn't be able to see much of her face by the light of the stars or the lantern that hung on the peg next to Mammi's front door. She'd rather not compound her humiliation.

"I'm really sorry I left you to drill trees by yourself."

"Elmer Lee and I finished together."

"Oh." He scrubbed his hand down the side of his face. "Blair wanted to show me her car. I thought it would be rude not to let her take me for a ride in it. Are you mad at me?"

"You've been so kind to our family. I could never be mad."

He stepped closer and reached out his hand as if to brush his fingers against her cheek. As usual he thought better of it. He really couldn't stand the thought of touching her, could he? The concern was still evident in his eyes though. "Then what's wrong?"

"Blair is very pretty."

"Okay?"

"You don't have to come here out of a sense of obligation when you'd rather be with her."

He widened his eyes. "I wouldn't rather be with her."

"I'm a nobody. My grandparents, my family, we're nothing."

A storm gathered in his eyes. "That's not true, Cassie," he said, his voice rough and gravelly like thunder rolling in from the east.

"Blair has an important career. She's going places, meeting people, brokering deals, making money. Her life is so exciting, so purposeful."

A reserved smile played at his lips, as if he had hope for something but didn't dare give the hope wings. "Are you jealous of Blair?"

They both turned as Dawdi and Titus appeared from the woods dragging their sleds behind them.

"The tree buckets are emptied," Titus said, tapping the ten-gallon bucket on his sled, "and our buckets are full." The toothpick in his mouth bobbed up and down. "We tried not to listen too hard."

"I don't know about you, Cassie," Dawdi said with a tease in his expression. "But Titus and I aren't nobodies."

How long had they been standing out of sight listening in? "I know, Dawdi. You're right."

"I've been married sixty-four years to the best woman in the world. I've got thirteen children and nearly a hundred sensible grandchildren. Titus is about the best helper a dawdi could ask for."

Titus nodded. "But we weren't listening all that hard."

Dawdi nudged Titus's elbow. "Let's take this sap to the sugar shack and get inside. It's cold enough to freeze my toes off."

Zach studied Cassie's face as Dawdi and Titus pulled their sleds around behind the barn. "Are you cold?"

"Jah."

"Can we go in the barn and talk?"

"I should get inside."

He made puppy dog eyes at her. "Please, Cassie. We need to talk."

We need to talk. Code for "I'm not really interested."

She gave in and led the way to the barn. It wouldn't be much warmer, but at least her cheeks wouldn't turn bright red from the cold.

The pungent odor of manure and hay tickled her nose as she entered. She took the propane lantern from the peg and set it on Dawdi's workbench. By the beam of the headlight, she found matches in one of the drawers and lit the mantel. The lantern hissed to life and sent a bright glow into the dark recesses of the barn. She turned off the headlight, peeled it from her head, and set it on the worktable. Iris the cow and

Dawdi's horse stirred quietly in the shadows.

Cassie leaned back against one of the supporting beams and peered at Zach. He was unbearably handsome. It was going to hurt really bad this time. The warmth of the barn felt stifling. She took off her bonnet and let it dangle from her fingers.

Zach eyed her hair, then stuffed his hands into his pockets as if imprisoning them. "I've got to know, Cassie. Why are you so upset about Blair?"

She took a deep breath. Might as well confess her weaknesses. Zach already knew what they were. It was the reason he kept his distance. The reason he wasn't interested. "It's not Blair. I don't want her life. I never fit in at college because I want a little house with a white picket fence. I want children and a husband and a quiet life full of quilts and church and family." She turned her face from him. "I don't have earnings potential or a stock portfolio. I'm not ambitious or modern. I have old-fashioned values and outdated morals."

"Then why are you jealous?" he whispered.

Her voice cracked in about a thousand different places. "Because she's the kind of girl you want, and I'm not."

There. She'd said it. Let him relish his victory, the fact that she had disliked him so much at first.

His expression melted like butter on a stack of warm pancakes with thick maple syrup on top. "Cassie, do you like me?"

She wrapped her arms tightly around her waist. "Of course I like you."

"But do you *like* like me?"

"*Like* like you?" He wasn't going to make this easy. She sighed from deep within her throat. "Jah. I like like you." She thought maybe she loved him, but he would never get that out of her.

"Do you want to hear something shocking?" His smile put that propane lantern to shame. "I *like* like you too. But it's probably more like seventeen likes." He took a step closer. "You are the girl I want."

She furrowed her brow. "No, I'm not."

"I've never been so sure about anything."

Her heart sprinted down the lane and back. "But how can that be? I'm not smart or ambitious or tough."

"I know enough women who are tough. I want a woman who is tender. I want a woman who is sweet and soft and strong at the same time."

"I'm not strong," she murmured, mesmerized by the intensity she saw in his eyes.

"You had the strength to leave your community. You went to college without even a high school education. You fought off a lot of jerks. You absorb your mother's criticism and return it with kindness." He took another step closer. "Cassie, you are the strongest person I know."

She felt a tear trickle down her cheek. She wanted to believe him so badly. "It doesn't matter how much you like me if you find me repulsive."

He jerked his head back. "Repulsive?"

"I've seen how you avoid touching me, like I've got some contagious disease. You cringe when you have to shake my hand."

He looked stunned. "Oh . . . wow. Is that . . . is that what you think?" With both hands, he kneaded his forehead as if he were trying to sand his eyebrows off. After what seemed like three weeks, he dropped his hands and took another step forward, gazing at her as if she held all his happiness in her eyes. He was so close she could feel his warm breath on her face. "Cassie, sometimes I want to kiss you so bad, my whole body shakes. Sometimes I think I'll go insane."

"You do?" She couldn't keep from sounding breathless as he focused his gaze on her lips. "Then why . . ."

"I want to be your key chain," he said, his voice as soft as a feather pillow.

"My key chain?"

He winced. "Ever since I laid eyes on you, I've been trying to deserve you, trying to be the kind of man you could love. Don't freak out, Cassie, but I love you. I love you so much that I can barely function when I'm not with you."

Warmth pulsed through her veins as her heart hammered an untamed cadence.

"I want to be your Sir Galahad," he said. "To love you with a pure heart, to prove myself worthy."

She couldn't breathe. The emotions swelling in her chest and swirling inside her head were too intense. He loved her! "Really?"

"Really."

"Then I think you'd better kiss me."

Without a second's hesitation, he pulled her into him as if she were his missing piece. His solid arms enveloped her as he pressed his lips to hers and kissed her like a thirsty man in search of water.

All she could do was hold on tight and hope that her legs would still support her when he let go. Who knew so much blissful emotion could be put into one kiss? She was flying. She was dancing. She was wind and light and water, all at the same time.

If she could bottle this feeling like she bottled maple syrup, she'd be a billionaire.

Still keeping his arms firmly around her, he pulled away, breathless and trembling. "Do you know how long I've wanted to do that?" he whispered. He kissed her again, more deliberately this time, but his touch still left her lightheaded.

He traced his thumb along her jawline and brushed a wisp of hair from her cheek. "Have I scared you away yet?"

"I may be timid, but I don't scare easy."

He laughed and tried to squeeze the stuffing out of her. Then he kissed her again until she felt like a quivering pile of jelly. It was the most wonderful, off-kilter feeling in the world.

This time he pulled away quickly and took two giant steps backward. "We should stop now."

Putting a halt to the kissing was the last thing Cassie wanted to do. "Why?"

He ran his fingers through his hair. "It's better to stop while I still have a shred of self-control left."

"I trust you," she said.

He gave her a crooked grin. "That's why we need to stop." He held out his hand to her. "Is this okay?"

She smiled and laced her fingers with his.

"Better than okay." She picked up her head-lamp, doused the lantern, and strolled out of the barn hand in hand with Zach Reynolds. She felt like laughing at the pure joy of it.

They ambled up the porch steps. All Cassie could think about was how much she liked the feel of Zach's hand in hers.

They stood at the front door. "Can I see you tomorrow?" he asked.

"I'll be boiling sap all day," she said.

"Do you need a wood chopper?"

Her heart skipped imagining the sight of Zach hefting an axe. "More than anything."

"I'll be here as soon as my shift is over. If Elmer Lee comes wanting to chop wood, don't let him do it. And don't let him kiss you either."

She giggled. "I promise not to let Elmer Lee near the wood or my lips."

"Good," Zach said. "Because I'm not afraid to break my nose again."

Still keeping hold of her hand, he leaned over and brushed a swift kiss across her lips. "I had no idea this much happiness existed in the entire world."

"Me either."

They both jumped as Dawdi threw open the front door, practically yanking it off its hinges. "Come in, Doctor. It's warmer if you do your kissing indoors."

Zach chuckled. "I better go. My shift starts in a couple of hours and I need to get some sleep. My friend Austin is having surgery in the morning."

Cassie squeezed his hand. "Austin is going to be okay, Zach. God is faithful. He will see that surgery goes well."

The warmth in his eyes made her feel squishy. "I know you're right. You've made me believe in God's goodness again."

Titus and Mammi appeared at the door, Mammi with her scooter and Titus with his toothpick. "Give me your hands," Mammi said, her eyes alight with determination. "Five prayers together will hie straight to heaven."

Zach looked at Mammi as if she'd just offered to donate a kidney. "Thank you," he said. "I'd really appreciate it. How can Austin not get better with all of you praying for him?"

"God will hear us," Cassie said.

"Titus," Dawdi said. "You were a good tree tapper today. Will you pray?"

Titus nodded solemnly, pulled the toothpick from his mouth, and bowed his head.

Holding hands, they stood together in the doorway and prayed for Austin. Cassie slipped in her own little prayer of thanksgiving for Zach, his growing faith, and the happiness she'd found just being with him.

He was an unexpected and essential blessing, and she didn't ever want to live without him.

CHAPTER TWENTY-THREE

Bundled up in her coat and scarf, Cassie sat on an overturned bucket with her GRE study book in her lap watching the maple sap boil. Boiling sap wasn't a hard job, but someone had to be there to make sure the fire didn't burn out and the forest didn't burn down. Under the simple shelter, three large copper kettles sat on tripod stands atop three fire pits made of cinder blocks and bricks. They burned hardwood because it gave the syrup a smoky flavor that customers had come to expect from Huckleberry syrup. It was Cassie's job to tend the fire, haul wood from the woodpile, stir the sap occasionally, and study for the GRE, if she could.

She found any academic pursuit impossible today because Zach kept creeping into her thoughts and taking up residence there. Just remembering his kisses last night and the warmth of his arms tightly around her made her feel giddy and ecstatic and oh, so breathless.

What time did he say he'd be coming? She'd be worthless until he got here. And when he arrived, she'd be even more worthless.

She stood and set her book on the stool. Maybe she should get more wood. The first kettle of sap had been boiling since nine this morning. It had almost boiled down enough to transport inside and finish on the stovetop. Once it came to the right temperature, Cassie and Emma would quickly pour the finished syrup into pint jars. They'd sell a lot of syrup at the May auction.

Emma and Ben had come this morning to help empty buckets, and they would return in about an hour to empty them again and help Cassie bottle the syrup. Titus lingered somewhere, helping Dawdi with the chickens or the milking, ready to do any heavy lifting she needed.

She trudged to the woodpile by the toolshed, filled her arms with logs, and went back to the sugar shack, where she deposited the wood on the ground near the first fire.

"You didn't let Elmer Lee chop that, did you?" Zach's smile was like springtime as he ducked between the sumac bushes and came to her.

Her heart did seven somersaults and a triple backflip. His coat was unzipped, and he wore the pink shirt she liked so much. *My,* but he was handsome. She'd never get enough of that crooked nose.

He stood on the edge of the clearing as if waiting for her to give him permission to approach. She grinned at him and stretched out her hand. He let out a deep breath, and in two long strides he'd closed the distance between them, hooked his arm around her waist, and planted an achingly gentle kiss on her lips.

"Is that okay?" he said. "Because I am capable of keeping my distance. I don't like to, but I can."

"If you keep your distance, I'll be able to keep my wits," she said, wrapping her arms around his neck and pulling him close for another heart-pounding kiss. "But who needs wits?"

Both arms slid around her this time, and he lifted her feet right off the ground in his enthusiasm. After he kissed her again, he set her on her feet and released her. She nearly toppled over. Kissing tended to make her ankles mushy.

He coiled his hand around the back of his neck. "It's a little disconcerting how hard it is to control myself when I'm with you.

432

You're just so beautiful. But I promise your virtue is always safe with me."

She wanted to kiss him for being so noble, but maybe that wasn't such a good idea when her pulse already raced out of control. "I know," she said as she felt a blush warm her cheeks. "Thank you."

"So, I've written down the rules." He pulled a folded piece of paper from his back pocket.

"Rules?"

"They are the kissing rules that my mom made when I was a teenager. I didn't follow them, but I still remember what they were."

Cassie curled one side of her mouth. "Your mom made kissing rules?"

"She and Dad. They had three sons, and she's a very smart lady." He unfolded his paper and read. "Rule number one: No kissing while sitting down." He glanced up at her and flashed those white teeth. "This is so you don't end up making out on the couch in the rec room. Rule number two: No kissing in the car, which if you follow rule number one, you don't really need rule number two unless you have a really tall car that you can stand up in."

"Like a motor home."

"Rule number three: No being alone together in anybody's bedroom. And rule number four: Three kisses max per date."

Cassie dropped her jaw in mock horror. "Only three? We've already reached our limit."

He squinted and studied his list more closely. "Maybe that's a typo. I think it's supposed to say 'thirty.' "

"And maybe it depends on your definition of a date. We're just hanging out at the sugar shack. I don't think you can officially call this a date."

He smiled and breathed a sigh of relief. "Dating is so overrated." He inclined his head and gave her a swift kiss before sliding an arm around her shoulder. "How is the sap coming along?"

"It's almost as exciting as watching paint dry, only colder." She pointed to the first kettle. "This one is almost ready to take to the house."

"You've been busy."

She caught her breath. "How did Austin's surgery go?"

Zach nodded eagerly. "Dr. Perez said it went really well. He's in recovery now. Jamie promised to call as soon as he's lucid enough for visitors."

"Oh, Zach. I've been praying so hard."

The tenderness in his eyes stole her breath. "Thank you. So have I. He was doing well enough that I thought it was okay to sneak out for a minute to come and see you."

"And when do you sleep?"

"I don't need sleep. Not when just thinking of you gives me a boost of pure energy."

Zach's phone rang. Cassie smiled when she heard his ringtone. *"Because I'm happy. Clap along if you feel like a room without a roof . . ."*

He smiled with his whole face. "I changed it last night. You know, 'cuz can't nothing bring me down."

She giggled.

"It's Jamie," he said. "I'll put her on speaker." He swiped his finger across the screen. "Hello, Jamie?"

"Zach?"

"Yeah, I've got you on speaker with Cassie. She's been worried about Austin."

Cassie's heart plunged to the ground when she heard the gut-wrenching sob on the other end. "Zach. Something happened. He went into cardiac arrest."

Zach furrowed his brow. "Okay. I'm coming over right now. Everything's going to be okay."

Another sob that shattered Cassie's hopes. "You can't. You can't help. Austin . . . Austin is gone."

435

Cassie clapped her hands over her mouth as a gaping, gnashing emptiness threatened to consume her. Austin was dead? That poor little boy. That poor sorrowing mother.

Zach gasped and turned as pale as Death himself. His phone slipped from his fingers, and he stumbled backward as if he'd been shot.

"Oh, Zach," Cassie moaned. "I'm so sorry." She reached for him, but he recoiled from her touch as if he wanted to suffer the full weight of exquisite grief all by himself.

Pressing his palms to his eyes, he doubled over and roared in anguish. Cassie had never heard a more primal, heartrending sound.

Stunned by some invisible bolt of lightning, Cassie drew a gulp of air into her lungs. "We've got to get over there. We've got to see what we can do for Jamie."

With a wild look in his eyes, he paced around and around the clearing as if he had to get somewhere quickly but had nowhere to go. "God wasn't supposed to let this happen. We prayed, Cassie. All of us prayed. He wasn't supposed to let this happen." He scrubbed his fingers through his hair. "You told me I just needed to have enough faith. Why did God take him?"

"I don't know."

436

He seemed to turn on her. "You knew all the answers before, and suddenly you don't know anything? You told me . . . you were so sure."

"I'm sure of God, but nothing else."

"You're sure of God? How can you be sure of God? Austin wanted to play soccer." Zach lifted his tearstained face to the sky. "Was that too much to ask? Are You so heartless that You couldn't even let a little boy live long enough to play soccer?"

Cassie's tears flowed down her face. "Zach, it's going to be okay. Austin is with God now. He doesn't have any more pain. He's free."

Zach snapped his head around to glare at Cassie. "You said God would heal him."

"No, Zach. I said that God *could* heal him, but our ways are not God's ways."

"So God wanted Austin to die?"

Cassie didn't know what to say. Zach was inconsolable, and she found it impossible to give him answers she didn't have. If he blamed God for Austin's death, she didn't know how to comfort him. Jesus could not heal him if he wouldn't open his heart to God's love.

Zach seemed to lose all strength. He sank to the overturned bucket, propped his elbows in his knees, and cradled his head in his hands.

Cassie came close and laid a light hand on his shoulder. He didn't move. "I don't know anything, Zach," she said softly, her voice trembling. "I don't know why God chooses death for some and not for others. All I know is that Jesus said, 'I am the resurrection and the life. He that believeth in me, though he were dead, yet shall he live.'"

With his face still buried in his hands, he took great shuddering breaths that seemed to shake his whole body. When he spoke, his words were muffled and heavy, but she heard them clearly enough. "I don't buy into your blind faith anymore, Cassie."

Her mouth went dry. "My blind faith?"

He lifted his head. "What has all your feel-good religion gotten me? What good has it done for anyone? Did Jamie think all her church work would save her son? Did all your praying give him one more minute of life?"

"It was in God's hands. All we could do was pray and leave it in God's hands."

He frowned and pressed his palm to his forehead as if he were trying to erase the pain. "I had faith because you had faith, Cassie. I let down my guard and you led me right into an ambush. I was weak and trusting and naïve. You made me believe."

He laughed softly, bitterly. "You made me believe."

He might as well have slapped her. "I'm sorry" was all she could think to say. She stood in a barren, frozen wasteland where spring would never come again.

"I'm sorry too," he said, spitting the barely audible words out of his mouth.

She shook so violently, she could barely speak. "It doesn't matter what you think of me right now. We've got to get to the hospital to be with Jamie."

He stood and squared his shoulders. "Not *we. Me.*"

She felt the sting of his bitterness all the way to her bones. "Zach, don't do this."

He scooped his phone off the ground and marched out of the clearing. "Keep away from me with your blind faith and your meaningless platitudes," he snapped. "I'm not listening anymore."

And then he was gone, taking her heart with him. Numb with grief, she sat down on her bucket and cried until Titus found her and took her into the house.

Zach eased his body onto the sofa. He felt like an old war vet with a dozen battle scars and a thousand aches and pains. He'd been at the hospital for over two hours, helping

Jamie make arrangements for the body, closing the loop with Austin's doctors, keeping Jamie's cup refilled with hot black coffee. Two sugars, no cream.

An hour after he'd arrived, Cassie had shown her face at the hospital, along with several friends from church and Jamie's parents and brother. Jamie's ex-husband was also there, looking like one of the walking dead from one of those dark and disturbing television shows.

Most patients with subacute bacterial endocarditis did well with heart surgery. Austin was just too sick. His little body couldn't take the stress.

Zach had set aside his own grief so that he could help everybody else deal with theirs. Wasn't that what doctors were supposed to do? Be a comfort to their patients even when they were barely surviving themselves?

He should probably call Mom. She had been thrilled when he'd asked her and her Bible study group to pray for Austin. Not thrilled that Austin was sick, but thrilled that her son even considered prayer as a solution to anything.

Yeah. Well. He wouldn't try that again.

He pulled out his phone. He hadn't looked at it for hours. There was a text from Cassie that he didn't want to read. She had served him a heaping plate of hope, but now it tasted like poison.

She'd probably sent some Bible verse or some well-meaning cliché like He was too good for this world or God must have needed another angel in heaven. God didn't need another angel. God had millions of angels. Surely He could spare the life of one little boy and still have a pretty good choir.

He reluctantly opened Cassie's text, just in case she'd sent something crucially important.

Never forget that I love you, it said.

He'd forgotten already. What they'd shared was an illusion. Cassie and her family weren't living in the real world. In the real world, angels didn't exist and God didn't care.

His head throbbed, his eyes stung, his arms and legs felt heavy as if he'd been dragging them around for hours. The hole in his chest threatened to suck his soul into nothingness. He might welcome a little oblivion right now. It would be better than hurting so bad.

He shot off a quick text to Mom. She'd want to know.

Austin Stetson passed away after surgery this afternoon. I can't talk about it right now.

I'll call you when it doesn't hurt to breathe anymore.

There was an almost immediate response.

My heart is broken. When you're ready, call me and we can cry together. P.S. It will always hurt to breathe.

Zach put down his phone, buried his face in his hands, and wept.

It would always hurt to breathe.

He woke up on his uncomfortable sofa and tried to clear the fog from his head. Someone was knocking on his door and calling his name. His apartment was pitch black. How long had he been asleep? An hour at most.

He groaned as he got up and hobbled to the door. Was there some sort of fire? The pounding sounded urgent enough.

He opened the door to a frowning Blair, who stood in his hallway holding two brown bags. "They told me what happened at the hospital. I'm really sorry about that little kid. I thought Chinese might make you feel better."

In his half-asleep haze, Zach felt something stir to life inside him. Blair was pretty and available and comfortable. And man, he needed some comfort right now.

She wouldn't try to talk him into believing in God. She wouldn't judge him or make him feel guilty for not measuring up to all those holier-than-thou's out there. She didn't expect anything from him. No virtue, no convictions, no commitment.

Everything was so easy with Blair. With the rest of his life so hard, he wanted easy.

And he was so tired of the fight.

He let out a breath. "You wanna come in?"

Her lips slowly curled into a smile as she glided into the apartment with those electric hips and set the bags on his metal-filing-cabinet coffee table. She flipped on the light switch and studied his face. Maybe looking for a chink in his armor. Well, she'd find plenty of chinks. "You look terrible."

"I feel worse."

"I hate it that people have to die."

"Yeah."

Puckering her lips sympathetically, she took his face in her hands. "I know how to make it all better."

Easy. Being with Blair was so easy. He gently snaked his hands around her waist. "Just don't talk to me about God."

She laughed derisively. "The last time I went to church was Easter ten years ago. I don't believe in all that stuff."

Neither did Zach anymore. He and Blair were perfect for each other.

That thought put a bitter taste in his

mouth, which he quickly swallowed. He didn't even need to coax her. He relaxed his arms slightly, and Blair slid into his embrace as if an irresistible force of gravity had propelled her there. Their lips met in a long kiss that should have heated the passion inside him. Instead, he felt nothing.

"I'm glad I checked out of my hotel," Blair cooed.

"Me too." He kissed her again, hoping to ignite some sort of spark. No luck.

Blair, on the other hand, seemed to be on fire. Her breathing was shallow and rapid, and her lips couldn't have been more eager. "I bet you've never done this with that Amish girl."

Zach winced. Why did she have to remind him? Cassie's kiss might have been the most pleasant sensation he'd experienced in his life, but that was over. Cassie was an illusion. Her faith was an illusion. Her God was an illusion.

He clamped his arms around Blair and doubled his efforts. Surely he could use all that desire he'd bottled up for weeks and make himself feel something for Blair. He kissed her again and again, tangling his fingers through her hair and pulling her uncomfortably close.

Blair sighed with pleasure, slid her hands

down his chest, and found the top button of his shirt.

Zach stiffened as realization slammed into him like an air bag in a head-on collision. How crazy had Austin's death made him?

How could he have talked himself into thinking he wanted this?

Being with Blair was wrong. Unconditionally, absolutely, dead wrong. And he couldn't do it.

He wouldn't do it.

Blair eyed him doubtfully as he pulled away from her and wrapped her hands in his before she could unfasten any more buttons. Dishonorable and cavalier wasn't who he was anymore. As much as he wanted to lash out and hurt Cassie and God and himself, something deep inside him went to battle for his soul and refused to give in to temptation.

The devil-may-care doctor who had once been Blair Baker's perfect match no longer existed. He'd come too far in the last few weeks, and he wouldn't be going back.

"Sorry, Blair," he said. "I forgot myself for a minute."

"I thought you finally remembered who Zach Reynolds really is."

He nudged her away. "You caught me in a moment of weakness, but I'm not doing this. It's wrong, no matter how sad I am about Austin."

Blair nibbled on her bottom lip and narrowed her eyes. "I can make you forget."

"No one can make me forget."

Blair didn't surrender, but the fire in her eyes dimmed. "I think you've lived among the natives for too long. Their hokey religion has rubbed off on you."

He looked away as a fresh wave of pain almost knocked him over. "I don't believe in their hokey religion." Nothing he could say would make her understand. He quit trying. "I just don't want to sleep with you, Blair."

She tried to mask the hurt that flashed in her eyes. "Okay, I can respect that."

He could plainly see that *respect* had nothing to do with it, but he wasn't about to argue. She'd backed off. That was all he wanted. "You should probably go now."

"I've got nowhere to go. I checked out of my hotel, remember?"

"You better check back in."

How did she manage that orphaned-little-girl expression? "Can't I stay here just for the night? I'll sleep on the sofa and keep my moral depravity to myself." A drop of bitterness tinged her tone. Just a drop.

Zach huffed out a breath. He was too

exhausted to persuade her otherwise. "Don't expect anything."

She gave him a ghost of a scowl. "I would never."

Refusing Blair's Chinese food, Zach left her to fend for herself and stumbled to his room, his only object to sleep and forget. He fell into bed like a man already dead. He was. He would never feel alive again.

CHAPTER TWENTY-FOUR

Cassie pulled into the parking lot of Zach's apartment building, parked her car, and took a deep breath. She didn't know if she'd be welcome or not, but at the moment, her feelings didn't matter. Yesterday, Zach's profound suffering had etched itself into every line of his face. Austin's death had devastated everyone, but Zach had shared something extremely close with Austin. It was as if Zach had died right along with him.

While he'd supported Jamie at the hospital, he had gone out of his way to avoid Cassie. She understood his reaction. She had tried to nurture his faith. Austin's death had crushed it. He had lashed out at her because he was looking for someone, anyone, to blame. He needed something sturdy to hang his grief on. He had found Cassie.

All she had wanted to do was help him rekindle his faith. But had she unwittingly destroyed it forever? She hadn't been able to give him the answers he needed, and now his doubt had swallowed his faith whole. If he rejected God, it would be no one's fault but hers. She should never have presumed to try to tell him anything about life and death and the love of God. She'd done a terrible job of it.

The thought that Zach might have stopped loving her stole her breath. Could a change of heart happen so dramatically? And could she hope to make him love her again?

He suffered terribly, and she couldn't let him suffer alone. He might be too angry to accept her comfort, but she had to try. The thought of Zach sitting in that tiny apartment, grieving and lonely, was more than Cassie could bear. So even if he rejected her, she would do what she could.

Her own heart felt like a solid piece of lead. Not only was Jamie her friend, but Cassie had visited Austin several times in the hospital. He had wheedled his way into her heart with his passion for soccer and life and his innocent honesty in the face of death.

She got out of the car with a pint jar of maple syrup and a heaping plate of orange–macadamia nut cookies, Zach's favorite. Even on the worst day, he would give her a smile for an orange–macadamia nut cookie. He joked that they were about a thousand calories per cookie. She teased that she was trying to fatten him up.

Ten o'clock. She hoped it wasn't too early. He'd been dead on his feet yesterday. She didn't want to wake him, but she also knew he had a shift starting at noon. He'd probably be awake.

She walked up the stairs to his apartment and quietly listened at his door for any sign of life. The sound of something sizzling in a pan — bacon maybe — told her that he was stirring. At least she wouldn't wake him up. It was definitely not a normal kind of day. Zach never made breakfast. He never made lunch or dinner either. Well, there wasn't much he could do to ruin bacon unless he burned it.

With her heart clomping around in her chest like a giant in army boots, she knocked on the door. She gripped the plate of cookies tighter as she prepared for anything, including having the door slammed in her face.

Nothing could have prepared her for this.

An icy hand clamped around her throat, and she couldn't draw a breath.

Zach's old girlfriend Blair the Beautiful opened the door holding a spatula and wearing nothing but Zach's pink button-down shirt. It covered enough of her legs that she probably wouldn't be arrested for indecent exposure, but left little to the imagination about anything else.

Blair looked Cassie up and down as if inspecting someone who'd come to the prom wearing jeans and a T-shirt. "Can I help you?"

Cassie's stomach clenched, and she thought she might be sick. "Is . . . is Zach here?" She didn't know why she even asked. She had absolutely no desire to see him now.

"He's asleep." Blair smirked. "But he's got a smile on his face."

Cassie wasn't about to hyperventilate in front of Zach's girlfriend. She had to get out of there. She had to get out now.

Eyeing Cassie casually, Blair twirled a lock of hair around her finger. "You're that Amish girl, aren't you?"

"I used to be Amish."

"You definitely look better without the ugly gray dress and bonnet." Blair held out her hand. "Are those for Zach?"

Cassie looked down at the cookies. She'd forgotten they were in her hand. "Yes," she said, handing them over but fully expecting Blair to toss them in the trash as soon as the door was shut. "And this." She handed her the jar of syrup. Five gallons of sap wasted on Zach Reynolds.

"It looks delicious," Blair said apathetically.

Cassie couldn't stand there one more second. "Have a nice day," she said because she couldn't think of anything else.

Certainly not "Tell Zach I came by" or "I'll call him later." She wasn't going to call him later. She wasn't ever going to call him again.

She turned around and walked slowly down the hall, holding her head high in case Blair watched from the door. She practically skipped down the stairs although she'd already heard the door to Zach's apartment close. She wanted to burst into tears, but tears would have to wait until she made it to the car. She quickened her pace. She wouldn't be able to hold them in much longer.

From the very first, she had known what kind of man Zach Reynolds was. Why, oh why hadn't she trusted her gut and avoided being taken in by his dazzling smile and cute nose? Zach had proved to be just like all those other guys out there who only had one thing in mind. All his talk about virtue and purity and Sir Galahad was just a ruse to eventually get the naïve ex-Amish girl into bed.

And she'd played right into his hands. By the time he'd finished working his little act, she'd almost begged him to kiss her. He must have been overjoyed that he finally got somewhere with this tight Amish goody-goody.

She climbed into The Beast, slammed the door, and rested her head against the steering wheel. She hated for the world to be like this. Except for the Plain people in her community and her family, there were so few godly men out there, and even fewer who wouldn't ultimately disappoint her. Zach, who had seemed so eager to change, so eager to be a better person, had shown his true colors when a crisis came.

She lifted her head and rubbed at the dent the steering wheel had made in her forehead. She'd been fighting with herself for so long, wanting to be part of the outside world while clinging to her Amish values. As Zach had shown her in dramatic fashion, it couldn't be done.

So. What to do now?

Go back to ogling professors and intellectual graduate students who thought she was a fool for even believing in God? Or return to her Amish faith and give up the fight, surrender to the pull she'd been feeling for years? As a member of the church, she wouldn't have to steel herself for battle every day. She wouldn't have to worry about fighting off guys who wanted to use her or get her heart broken by handsome doctors with a weakness for orange–macadamia nut cookies.

A sob escaped her lips. She was so tired. Tired of the struggle with her family. Tired of being a disappointment to Norman. Tired of breaking her mamm's heart. Tired of never being good enough because she wasn't truly one of them.

The car groaned loudly when she turned the key. She pulled out of the parking lot past Blair's sleek new Lexus. Too bad she hadn't noticed it before. She could have saved herself a lot of embarrassment, plenty of heartache, and a plate of orange–macadamia nut cookies.

She drove straight to Mamm's house, which sat at the end of a secluded lane lined with climbing rosebushes.

Mamm answered the door with a spot of flour on her cheek, and it looked as if she were about to launch into a criticism of Cassie's blowsy hair. Cassie immediately flung herself into her mamm's arms and cried as if her heart would break.

Mamm softened as she wrapped her arms

around Cassie and rubbed her back soothingly. "There, there. It can't be bad as all that."

"Mamm," Cassie said through her tears. "I want to come home."

CHAPTER TWENTY-FIVE

Zach dragged himself down the hall to the exam room.

How long had it been since Austin died? Two weeks? Three? He remembered going to the funeral, but he couldn't remember how many days had passed since his world had come crashing down. Again.

At the funeral, the pastor had talked about Jesus admonishing his disciples to suffer the little children to come unto him, and how Austin had hopes of a better resurrection. Only concern for Jamie had kept Zach from getting up and storming out during the sermon. How could the pastor talk about hope for resurrection when God hadn't even given Austin or Zach's dad hope for a long life?

Zach lifted the chart hanging on the door and walked into the room where his next patient waited.

He wished he'd called in sick today.

Anna Helmuth sat on the exam table with a delighted twinkle in her eye as if she were about to take a trip to Disneyland. Zach couldn't have been less happy to see anyone, including Blair. Anna's presence dredged up not only several painful memories of Huckleberry Hill, but also the profound sense that he'd lost something important that he'd never get back.

But it wasn't as if he wanted it back. The angel with the pink dress and the curly golden hair was nothing more than an illusion. He preferred to live in the real world, thank you very much.

"Dr. Reynolds!" Anna said, as if she loved him with all her heart.

He forced a professional smile onto his face, which was the only smile he could manage these days, and shook Anna's hand. Felty sat next to her on the table, but thankfully, Cassie was not with them. Even though he didn't believe in God anymore, he almost said a prayer of thanks that she had been wise enough to stay away. "Anna, it looks like it's time to get you back on your feet. How is the foot feeling?"

Anna raised her eyebrows as if to scold him. "Don't get me wrong, Doctor. The home health nurse is a wonderful girl named Erika, but she isn't you. I promised

457

myself that we wouldn't let you starve. How can we feed you if you won't come over?"

"Working at the hospital keeps me busy," Zach said, staring at Anna's chart so he wouldn't have to look into her dancing blue eyes that seemed to see things he'd rather keep secret.

Anna reached out and squeezed his arm. "You've lost weight, Doctor. Too much. Come for dinner tomorrow, and I'll cook my famous Indonesian Beef Stew. It's a vegetarian dish."

"I'm sorry, Anna. I'm finishing up my first year of residency in a couple of months. I have to spend a lot of time at the hospital."

Anna looked as if she were concentrating on a difficult math problem. "What if I had Cassie make cookies?"

Cookies.

Every muscle pulled taut. Oh, she'd made cookies, all right. A heaping plate of orange–macadamia nut cookies that he had chucked into the garbage can as soon as he saw them. He didn't want her cookies. He didn't want her sympathy. And he most certainly didn't want her religion.

He tried to ignore the mountain of guilt that buried him every time he imagined that scene at the door with Blair in all her half-dressed glory. She thought it was so cute to dress up in his clothes. To Cassie, the pink shirt, the leggy brunette, and the realization of what she *thought* Zach had done must have been a slap in the face.

Well, Cassie Coblenz, join the club.

She'd given *him* a slap in the face when she had assumed that he had actually slept with Blair. If nothing else, that little incident at the door had made it clear to Zach what Cassie truly thought of him. All those weeks of his trying to be a good man, and she had still assumed the worst. She had never really believed in him in the first place.

He wasn't about to enlighten her on what had really happened or not happened with Blair. Let Cassie think the worst. They'd both be better off that way. She could go on feeling hurt and betrayed by what she thought he'd done to her, and he could go on feeling deceived and betrayed by Cassie and God.

He was through with Cassie. What did he care if she thought he was sinful and worthless? He would never live up to Cassie's ideal of a godly man anyway.

Still, letting Blair into his apartment had been a mistake. With all her talk about "no strings attached," she certainly wanted to tie some pretty strong knots. That morning after bacon and pancakes with homemade maple syrup, he had told her that they were really and truly over and that he wouldn't be answering her texts or phone calls ever again.

Despite his resistance the night before, Blair had stormed out of his apartment, proving that she had expected something more permanent from him despite all her protests to the contrary.

He had regretted brushing her off yet again, but he'd already felt so rotten about Austin's death that one more thing to feel rotten about didn't make much of a dent.

He removed the bandage from Anna's foot and pressed his thumb lightly into the nicely healed scar. Anna's foot looked better than new.

"Cassie's in a very bad way, Doctor. Don't you think you could spare even an hour this week to come take a look at her?"

"Is she sick?"

Anna furrowed her brow until the wrinkles piled on top of each other. "Well, she is quite pale and keeps her head down a lot."

"And she's started going out with Elmer Lee," Felty said.

Anna nodded. "Yes, Elmer Lee. She must be sick."

Zach tried not to sound intensely interested. "She's dating Elmer Lee?"

"As soon as Cassie moved back home, her mamm pushed her into baptism classes."

A lump of coal stuck in Zach's throat. "She's going to join the church?" He'd seen Cassie at the funeral, wearing a plain navy blue dress and a prayer kapp, but he'd figured that her mamm had bullied her into dressing Plain like she always did. The thought that Cassie had chosen to join the church was too disturbing to contemplate.

"And," Anna said, leaning forward as if to share a juicy piece of gossip, "Elmer Lee has been eating at Esther's place three nights a week."

Zach clenched his jaw and kept his face passive, as if he couldn't care less that Elmer Lee was worming his way into Cassie's life or that Cassie would be miserable being Amish.

It was none of his business. She had made her choice. Just because he had let her go on believing the worst didn't mean that he was responsible for her decision.

Could Anna and Felty hear his teeth grinding together? There was no doubt that Cassie had decided to rejoin her community because of him.

Fine.

Maybe he'd helped her realize that it was the only place she truly belonged. A timid girl like Cassie who never stood up for herself and never rocked the boat would fit in just fine with the Amish. Let her believe that Amish people would never disappoint her. Let her think that God loved her.

"Anna's been trying to talk some sense into her," Felty said.

Zach narrowed his eyes and tried to breathe normally. "I don't understand. You don't want her to be Amish?"

"Cassie needs to carve out her own path, not take the one that's laid out before her," Felty said. "Her decision springs from a broken heart." Felty stroked his horseshoe beard and eyed Zach as if he could fix this mess.

The lump almost choked him.

Her decision springs from a broken heart.

Zach snapped off his latex gloves. "Good as new. Come back in six months, and we'll check to make sure it's still doing well."

Zach flinched when Anna slid off the exam table. With her short legs, it was a long way down. She landed on her new foot as easy as you please. That woman was going to break a hip someday.

"I was afraid of this," she said as she bustled to the large canvas bag sitting on one of the chairs. "It's going to take something spectacular to lure you back to Huckleberry Hill."

"I'm really busy . . ."

Anna pulled a strange circle knitted with pink yarn from her bag. "This is a steering wheel cover for your car. It will keep your hands from freezing on cold winter mornings," she said, handing it to him. "I used Cassie's steering wheel to get the size just right."

It would fit perfectly, then.

"Anna, I can't accept this."

She ignored him and returned to her bag. She searched around at the bottom before she pulled out what she had been looking for. It was a red knitted square, probably two inches by two inches. "This is a blanket for your turtle. I remember you telling me that you have a turtle. It hasn't died yet, has it?"

He shook his head.

"I made it red so that the turtle wouldn't think it was lettuce and eat it."

"Anna, this is very kind, but —"

She flashed a sparkly grin. "Now, Doctor, don't you even think about refusing. I've knitted my fingers to the bone for you and Cassie." Next, she pulled a stunning navy blue sweater from her bag. The pattern on the front looked like someone had woven braids right into the sweater. He didn't deserve such a gift. He didn't deserve Anna's generosity or Felty's kindness. He'd broken their granddaughter's heart and been a complete disappointment to religious people everywhere.

"I thought about making it pink because I know how much you like pink, but this blue seemed more manly, and you're going to need wonderful-gute manliness if you want to compete with Elmer Lee." She handed him the sweater. He handled it as if it were made of glass. "Try it on, Doctor."

"Right now isn't really the time."

"Take off your white lab coat and try it on. If it doesn't fit, I'll have to take it home and fix it."

Reluctantly, Zach took off his lab coat and pulled the sweater over his head. The neckline was high with a slight V-neck. The long sleeves hugged his wrists at exactly the right spot, and the fabric stretched across his chest like a snug glove.

Anna clapped her hands. "I was afraid with the way you're wasting away, it might drown you."

"It's beautiful," Zach mumbled, because there was truly nothing else to say.

Felty studied Zach's face and seemed to wilt like a flower in the heat.

Anna, however, looked as if she might

burst with delight. "We want you to wear it when you come to dinner on Friday night. And you can even wear the pink shirt underneath if you want."

Zach didn't think anything could make him feel worse about himself than he already did, but Anna's kindness pushed him so low, he was lying facedown on the ground with a mouthful of dirt.

Frowning, he motioned to the chairs in the exam room and sat down on his rolling stool. "Anna, Felty, please sit."

Felty took Anna's hand, and they sat together.

"Anna," he said, placing a hand on top of hers. "I've never been given such a beautiful sweater before. I am truly touched by your kindness. But these wonderful gifts won't lure me back to Huckleberry Hill."

Anna turned to Felty. "I knew I should have brought a pot holder."

Zach chuckled in spite of himself. "Pot holders won't do any good either. After Austin died, I said some things . . . I made Cassie believe some things . . . that hurt her very much, and even if I wanted to see her, she wouldn't want to see me."

"Don't you believe in forgiveness?" Felty asked.

Zach lowered his eyes and shook his head.

"I don't believe in anything anymore. I don't belong with people like you or Cassie. Faith guides your life. In many ways, you are your faith. That's not how I live. It would be like trying to mix oil and water. Cassie hates me for the way I am, and I can't stomach the simple trust she puts in God. We're just too different."

Felty's eyes softened with moisture. "We're sorry about the little boy. We lost three of our own little ones yet. It hurts deep."

Zach paused. "You lost three children?"

"Jah," Felty said. "And we think about them every day. Don't we, Banannie?"

Anna's smile faded, although it didn't disappear completely. "Every hour."

The ache in Zach's chest flared painfully. "How do you stand it?"

Felty leaned toward Zach. "God will wipe all tears off all faces someday."

Zach pressed his hand to his forehead. "I wish I could believe it."

"I wish you could believe it too," Felty said. "Because it's true."

Zach pulled off the sweater, smoothed it out, and folded it carefully. "So you see why I can't take this."

"Stuff and nonsense," Anna said. "I made it for you. Elmer Lee is not getting his hands on it. You're the one I've chosen, and I'm not changing my mind, no matter how persistent Esther and Elmer Lee are."

By the set of Anna's chin, Zach could see it would be futile to argue. He would fold up the sweater and put it in the top of his closet so that it would still be brand new when Anna decided she wanted it back in a couple of weeks.

"Denki," he said.

Was there a good reason he used Pennsylvania Dutch? Nobody but Cassie thought his attempt at the language was cute.

Anna stood, and Felty followed. "Thank you, Doctor, for fixing my foot. I feel like a better person because of it." She got on her tiptoes and gave him a kiss on the cheek. "You are a gute boy. Never forget that."

"It was a privilege to get to know you, Anna."

Her eyes danced. "I'll go knit some pot holders, just in case."

Chapter Twenty-Six

A knock at Zach's office door startled him. He must have fallen asleep staring at his last patient's chart. It was lucky his shift was over. He needed to go home and catch some sleep. He already walked around the hospital as if he were dead, but he didn't need sleep deprivation to make it worse.

He didn't have the energy to stand and go to the door. "Come in."

Jamie opened his door and raised her eyebrows tentatively, almost as if she didn't dare venture past the threshold. Zach shot to his feet. "Jamie, come in," he said. He grabbed the back of his chair and turned it around. "Sit down. How are you? Is everything okay?"

Of course everything wasn't okay. She'd lost her son three weeks ago. Things were never going to be okay again.

She reached out her arms and gave Zach a bracing hug. "It's good to see you, Dr.

Reynolds."

"Call me Zach." He motioned toward the chair again. She sat down on the folding chair opposite his rolling one. "You sure you don't want the softer one?"

"I'm okay."

He sat and faced her, propping his elbows on his knees. "Can I do something for you?"

"I had to drop by the billing office to work out some payment stuff."

"How can I help? There are assistance programs if you can't afford the hospital bills."

She shook her head. "Austin's dad has really good insurance, and he's insisted on paying all the stuff the insurance didn't cover. I was just working out the details with Lynne to make sure that's all settled."

"Good."

She placed a gentle hand on his arm. "I haven't seen you since the funeral."

"Do you need me to do something for you? Anything you need, I'll be there."

"Marla says you're having a hard time with Austin's death."

Zach bowed his head. "Aren't we all?"

"We are all grieving, Zach, but Marla says you're paralyzed."

Why had Jamie come? It hurt like a shard of glass in his mouth to even talk about it.

"They told us that if you can't handle death, you shouldn't be a doctor." He laughed bitterly. "Some doctor I've turned out to be."

"It means you're human, Zach, and personally, I'd rather have a doctor who is devastated by death than one who handles it easily. It means you care. I much prefer a doctor who cares."

"We're a good match, then." He attempted a smile, but his voice betrayed him.

Jamie squeezed his arm and something shifted in her expression as if she'd made a decision. "Austin wouldn't want you to spend the rest of your life mourning him."

Maybe not. But maybe Austin would have wanted to still be alive. Zach kept his mouth shut. He wouldn't upset Jamie with his bitterness.

She took a deep breath. "Your dad is deceased, isn't he?"

Zach drew his eyebrows together. "Yeah."

She sat back and folded her arms. "I've been debating whether to tell you of an experience I had. It's very precious to me, and I don't want you to minimize it."

"You've lost your child. I would never minimize that."

Jamie pursed her lips. "On the night of the funeral, I had a dream. I think it was meant for us."

"You and me?"

She nodded. "Only for us."

"Why?"

"Because God wants us to know."

Zach felt the hair stand up on the back of his neck. "Know what?"

"Something that happened in my dream. I was walking in a grassy field. I could actually feel the soft grass beneath my bare feet. I smelled roses and lilacs, and I heard birds singing. It was a beautiful place. More beautiful than anything I've ever seen before." She tucked a lock of hair behind her ear. "Austin came running toward me. He was dressed in a spotless orange soccer uniform."

"Barcelona," Zach mumbled.

"He had the biggest smile on his face and said he couldn't stay long because the boys were getting a game together, and they needed him to play center mid."

Zach's eyes stung. He folded his arms across his chest and resisted the urge to tell Jamie that it was just a dream. Sure, it was a nice dream, but it was still just a way for her brain to release stress after an excruciatingly hard week.

"I asked Austin if he was happy," Jamie said. "He told me yes because he could run and play soccer like the other kids, and he didn't have any pain, and he got to be with Jesus every day." Her eyes glistened with tears. "He had a soccer ball and did some tricks for me. Before he got sick, he was working on balancing the ball on his head. It was the first trick he showed me."

Zach clamped his eyes shut and wiped away the tears that squeezed through. A mere dream shouldn't call forth tears.

"There was another man who came," Jamie said. "He looked like you. Same strong build, same blue eyes. His hair was dark brown. I don't know why, but I had the distinct feeling it was your dad."

No, Jamie. Don't do this to me. Don't speak of hope when there is no hope. An illusion isn't truth no matter how hard anyone wants to believe in it.

Zach bit his tongue and fought back the tears. Just let Jamie have her say and then he could get away from here. Thank goodness his shift was over.

"Austin called him Pop, although he was a young man."

The word stole Zach's breath. "Pop?"

It was just a coincidence. Pop was a pretty common nickname. Wasn't it?

"The three of us strolled around the meadow. We crossed brooks and played tag around the trees while Austin pointed out flowers and birds and butterflies. There was a hollow tree where Austin kept his treasures: his soccer scarf, an orange beanie, and a long, jagged rock. He said that Pop loved to collect fossils, and they'd been digging for days to find a shark's tooth. Pop had given it to him as a present."

An invisible force crashed into Zach and knocked the wind out of him. "He had a . . . fossil?"

Jamie studied his face. "Pop said, 'Tell him I'm happy and that someday he'll understand all the reasons I had to leave.' Again, I can't be sure it was your dad, but when he said 'him,' I knew he was talking about you, even though he said he had two other sons."

Everything seemed to stand still, even the air in his lungs and the blood in his veins. Zach sat motionless as Jamie's words set his heart aflame.

How could Jamie have known about the color of Dad's hair or his lifelong nickname or the fossils?

His whole body seemed to catch fire.

It hadn't been just a dream.

Pop Reynolds, the guy who earned his nickname from drinking too much soda as a kid, was alive. Zach's dad was alive beyond the grave and so was Austin.

But that wasn't all. Austin was happy. God

hadn't forsaken a sick little boy, and He hadn't abandoned any of them.

Tears rained down his cheeks, and he bawled like a baby. Jamie scooted her chair forward and hooked an arm around his neck, like a big sister giving her kid brother some love.

"I guess you believe me?" she said.

"I guess I do," he blubbered.

She pulled away and grabbed a handful of tissues from her purse. He wiped his face but kept right on crying, so it was kind of like mopping up a spill on the *Titanic.*

"I miss him," he said.

"Are you kidding? I cry a dozen times a day just thinking about my son," she said. "But I know he's with God, and God has a purpose for all things. And He loves us. Bad things happen. It doesn't mean God doesn't love us."

"But why do people have to die?"

"Someday we'll know the reason, just like your dad said. You just have to have faith. Do you have faith, Doctor?"

Zach swiped another tear from his eye. "Not much."

"If it's the size of a grain of mustard seed, it's enough."

"I've got a lot to learn."

Jamie pulled another handful of tissues

from her purse. "And you've got some fences to mend." She stared at him until he met her eye. "With a certain Amish girl."

Zach's heart stopped beating for a second time. Cassie.

He groaned in pure agony and buried his wet face in his hands.

The corners of Jamie's mouth drooped. "You love her."

"Yep. Bad." He trembled just thinking about what he'd lost.

"Then tell her."

"I told her she was naïve and blind. You should have seen her face. I might as well have hit her."

Jamie patted his leg. "You're not the first person to let grief overtake your judgment. Go talk to her. She has the most forgiving heart in the world."

"It's too late," Zach said. He felt as if he'd swallowed a handful of gravel. "I didn't just yell at her. She thinks I did something . . . something that can't be fixed."

Jamie narrowed her eyes. "She wants to rejoin the Amish."

The heaviness in Zach's chest grew until he had to struggle for every breath. "Yeah."

"Nothing can separate us from God's love, Zach."

"Cassie's love is a different story."

Jamie gave him a weak smile. "If anyone can convince her, you can. You got Austin to sit still for an IV. Your powers of persuasion are enormous."

"Not with Cassie."

"Especially with Cassie. She loves you something fierce."

Zach sighed and rubbed the back of his neck. "Not anymore."

"But you love her?"

"Yeah."

"Then go make it right."

CHAPTER TWENTY-SEVEN

Cassie had the most unnerving feeling that someone was watching her. She lifted her head and let her eyes travel down the aisle. Nobody there, just shelves full of bulk candy and dried fruit. Elmer Lee stood next to her, staring at a small container of mints. Was he curious about the calories?

Norman and Linda had come with Cassie and Mamm to the Lark Country Store. The store had just about everything an Amish customer could want, from all sorts of groceries to hats to books to clocks that played church music on the hour.

In the store parking lot, Elmer Lee "happened" to pull up in his buggy at the same time Cassie's family had pulled up in Norman's buggy. What a surprise. It wasn't as if she didn't see Elmer Lee three or four times a week already. Mamm was pulling out all the stops to make sure there'd be a wedding come September.

Cassie tried to happily oblige. After all, she wanted to marry a godly, kind man, and as Mamm reminded her daily, she was nearly an old maid. Older, single boys like Elmer Lee were as scarce as hen's teeth. She should be grateful that Elmer Lee hadn't been taken yet.

Still, in moments of weakness, Cassie daydreamed about holding hands and stealing kisses beneath the maple trees with Zach Reynolds, not Elmer Lee. She put down the package of dried apples she held and raised her fingers to her lips. Her heart raced at the memory.

She was glad she would never kiss him again. Zach didn't believe in God. She couldn't make a home or a life with anyone who didn't love God. And she certainly couldn't love someone who professed his undying love and slept with an old girlfriend a few hours later.

Several times a day, she replayed that horrible memory over and over in her head. The recollection of Blair barely wearing Zach's pink shirt made her ill.

She felt a single tear slip down her cheek and immediately slapped it away. It would do no good to let Mamm or Elmer Lee see her self-pity. She'd already cried enough tears to fill a bathtub.

"Did you find what you want?" Elmer Lee asked.

"Not yet. I need milk chocolate chips."

"My mamm wants birdseed," he said. "I'll meet you at the front."

Cassie nodded. Why did she have to meet him anywhere? They had arrived at the store at the same time. That didn't mean they were together.

She ambled down the aisle until she spotted the chocolate chips. The store had a wide variety to choose from. Milk chocolate, semi-sweet, mint, and peanut butter. She stared at the packages without really seeing them. How would she ever finish her shopping when she felt so distracted? How would she ever get on with her life?

She snapped her head up as that feeling of being watched returned. The aisle was empty except for her. She must be going bonkers.

She jumped as someone laid a hand on her shoulder and turned to see Zach Reynolds in all his beautiful glory standing there with a crooked nose and sad blue eyes. She almost had a stroke.

"Cassie," he whispered. "Can I talk to you?"

She furrowed her brows in confusion. "What do you want?"

He glanced around and put his finger to his lips. "I've been to your house four times. They won't let me see you."

Cassie pressed her mouth into a rigid line. Was Mamm trying to protect her or control her?

Zach looked positively desperate as he glanced behind him once again. "I've left ten messages on your cell phone."

"I'm taking baptism classes, Dr. Reynolds. I don't use a cell phone anymore."

He seemed to disintegrate before her very eyes. "Don't call me that. Please don't call me that." She flinched when he curled his fingers around her upper arms. "Cassie, I've got to talk to you."

"There isn't anything to say," she said, extricating her arms from his grasp and taking a step backward.

He acted like a wounded animal, frantic and wary. "There is everything to say, and they won't let me talk to you. Anna told me you might be here this afternoon. I've been waiting for an hour in hopes of catching a glimpse of you."

Mammi told Zach she'd be here? That traitor.

He leaned closer. He smelled of some irresistible cologne that made her heart clatter around in her chest. "I'm crazy in love with you and if you don't forgive me, I don't think I'll ever smile again. You see, I didn't —"

Cassie glanced behind her. She was not eager for the scene that was sure to follow if Mamm and Norman discovered her and Zach Reynolds whispering in aisle four. She sighed and ordered her heart to be still. She wouldn't let the doctor rob her of reason. "I've already forgiven you. Now go, before Mamm sees you."

"We couldn't have your mamm getting angry." Did she sense a touch of bitterness in his voice? He closed his eyes momentarily, and she saw the muscles of his jaw twitch with tension. "Cassie, what can I do to make you love me again?"

The question conked her on the head. "Love you? Why . . . why would you want that?"

He grabbed her hand. She pulled it away. "Cassie, please, come with me. Just for an hour and let me explain."

He'd hurt her deeply, but she couldn't be insensible to the ache she saw in his eyes. Maybe he truly felt sorry for what he'd done.

She shook her head. Sorry or not, she wouldn't ever trust him again, wouldn't ever believe in his promises, wouldn't open her heart. Offering Zach second and third chances had only gotten her into trouble.

"I . . . I can't, Doctor. I came in for chocolate chips, not a therapy session."

His face grew as ominous as an impending storm. "Cassie, this isn't you." He fingered one of the dangling ties of her kapp. "I can't bear the thought that my stupidity compelled you to rejoin the Amish."

Cassie lowered her eyes. "The Amish are good, decent people."

"Of course they are. But this life isn't what you want, and I feel horrible that I let you believe something that sent you running back here."

"You simply reminded me of the way the world really is. And it's a world I don't want to live in anymore."

She heard Norman behind her and whipped her head around. "What are you doing here?" Norman came barreling toward them as if Dr. Reynolds were a thieving fox out to steal the chickens.

Without hesitation, Norman got toe-to-toe with the doctor. The doctor didn't look like he had a lot of fight in him, but he stood his ground. "I told you to stay away from Cassie."

"I need to talk to her."

"She doesn't want to talk to you."

"You won't let her talk to me. What are you afraid of?"

"Afraid? I'm afraid of losing her. We lost her once to the world. We refuse to lose her again because of some handsome Englischer who fills her head with nonsense but only wants to drag her to hell."

Cassie held her breath. Norman's face turned bright red, and the sweat beaded on his forehead. With his loud voice, he would soon draw the attention of everyone in the store.

"Norman," Cassie said. "Keep your voice down and let the doctor leave. He doesn't mean any harm."

Norman pointed a finger in her face. She leaned away in surprise. "Keep quiet, Cassie. You don't know of what you speak. He is an evil man."

Cassie glanced at Zach. With his eyes blazing with indignation and his powerful fists clenched at his side, he was poised to answer back, that was for sure and certain. But she saw something else too. She saw a man who made house calls to an old Amish lady because he knew that his presence gave her comfort. She saw someone who chopped wood and milked cows in an effort to be helpful and tried to learn how to knit just to make an old lady happy. She saw a man who played FIFA with a sick little boy and wept bitterly when he had died.

She didn't see an evil man.

She turned to face Norman and shot daggers at him with her glare. "Norman, you are my brother, but I am ashamed of you today. You have forgotten that we must treat all men with charity and forgiveness."

"Not him," Norman said.

Cassie dug in her heels. "All men."

"And women too," Zach murmured.

Cassie turned and eyed Zach. He looked so handsome, so formidable standing there as if the world would stop spinning if he didn't hold it up. "Denki for always defending me. You don't need to do it anymore. I've got my family."

As if on cue, Elmer Lee, Mamm, and Linda seemed to converge on them from three different directions. Elmer Lee regarded Zach with alarm written all over his face.

Linda came from behind the doctor and smiled. "It's always nice to see you, Dr. Reynolds."

Mamm hurried down the aisle and wasted no time on small talk or dirty looks. "Time for us to go," she said, hooking her elbow around Cassie's and fussing like a mother hen gathering her chicks under her wing. "You must make those cookies for the gathering tonight yet. So much to do."

Cassie let her mamm pull her down the aisle and away from Zach. She turned back and managed a weak, unconvincing smile. "Doctor, I've made my choice. We don't need to talk. You don't need to explain yourself. We are from very different worlds. I've come to terms with that fact. I hope you can too."

She turned her back on him and hurried down the aisle with her family flanking her on all four sides. Norman led the way. Mamm held tight at her right. Elmer Lee walked beside her on the left, and Linda brought up the rear. It made her think of the Secret Service guarding the president.

None shall pass.

Too late, she realized she'd left without the chocolate chips. She certainly wasn't going back for them. She'd settle for snickerdoodles. Snickerdoodles and Elmer Lee.

"Call me Zach," she heard him say behind her. She'd never heard greater despair.

CHAPTER TWENTY-EIGHT

Cassie ladled the last of the syrup into the pint jar. Titus, her faithful helper, wiped the rim with a damp towel and screwed the lid into place.

"All done for another year, Mammi," Cassie said. A hundred and twenty pints of maple syrup lined the shelves in the cellar, and five more cooled on the kitchen counter. A good year for syrup. The sap had run for nearly five weeks.

Mammi stood on the opposite side of the counter so as not to be in the way of the syrup canning. She was making sandwiches of some kind, though Cassie had no idea what substance sat between the two slices of bread. Since the doctor had given her the go-ahead to move about, Mammi had abandoned her knitting altogether and had started cooking. Pies, cakes, meatballs, fish patties, Jell-O with hot dogs, and a Mediterranean dish called couscous had all been on the menu in the last week. Cassie was sort of glad she didn't live here anymore. Another meal of fried chicken livers might just put her in the hospital.

"I'm glad you could come this morning to finish the syrup," Mammi said, cutting five sandwiches in half and arranging them on plates garnished with wilted parsley. She picked up her frosting piping bag with the ruffle tip and squeezed out a mushy purple substance onto each plate. "Mashed red beets," Mammi said. "Don't they look like lilacs? Just in time for spring."

Cassie studied Mammi's flower creations. They looked more like shapeless globs of lumpy purple paint, but who was Cassie to discourage Mammi's creative side? "They look very pretty, Mammi."

"I love red beets," Titus said, but the toothpick quivered between his lips as he eyed those sandwiches.

"What kind of sandwiches are we having for supper?" Cassie asked, almost not wanting to know. Sometimes it was better to eat Mammi's food and ask questions later.

Mammi seemed pleased with herself. "Spam," she said. "I chopped it up very fine and added pickles and mayonnaise and olives."

It didn't sound too bad. Dr. Reynolds

would have called it a recipe for hypertension, but at least it wasn't chicken intestines or something even less edible.

She shouldn't have let Zach cross her mind like that. It took a few breathless seconds to calm her racing heart.

"It's too bad Dr. Reynolds can't be here to eat with us," Mammi said.

So much for banishing Zach from her mind. Cassie gave in and let her heart gallop wildly around the meadow.

"Why can't he come over?" Titus asked. "Cassie doesn't mind."

As a matter of fact she did mind, but she gave Titus a pleasant smile anyway, as if she were completely indifferent to Dr. Reynolds.

"The doctor tries to stay away when Cassie comes over. Doesn't like to make her uncomfortable or stir up trouble with Norman and Esther." Mammi glanced at Cassie. "He knows how the arguing upsets you."

Yes. It was better that he stayed away. Keep the peace at all costs. Besides, she would be baptized soon. Better not to associate with Englischers.

She held her breath as the familiar heaviness pressed into her chest like a carpenter's clamp. The feeling got worse every time she thought of being baptized. Wasn't this what she wanted? She would find peace and virtue in the community. She would finally belong.

So why did she feel so out of place?

"Titus," Mammi said, without taking her eyes from Cassie, "go tell your dawdi and Norman that supper will be ready in thirty minutes."

Titus looked at Mammi's sandwiches and drew his brows together. "Isn't it ready now?"

"Oh, Titus. Don't think about it too hard. Just go out and don't come back for half an hour. There's plenty of redding up to do at the sugar shack. Polish the kettles or something."

Titus shrugged and put on his coat. "Norman doesn't like the way I do copper."

"Tell Norman that if he gives you a lick of trouble, he'll get no supper yet."

Cassie glanced at the squishy Spam spread in Mammi's sandwiches. Unfortunately for Titus, Norman would probably consider going without supper a blessing.

"Okay, Mammi. I'll go get them."

"But not for thirty minutes."

Titus narrowed his eyes. "I need a stopwatch." He strolled out the door and closed it behind him.

Mammi wiped her hands on her apron.

"Now, dear, we need to talk." She came around the counter, grabbed Cassie's hand, and led her to the table to sit.

"But, Mammi, I need to wash the pan."

"Dirty dishes will keep." Mammi sat next to Cassie and cupped her hand over Cassie's cheek. "Now. How to get you smiling again."

Cassie tried for an amused, carefree laugh. "I smile, Mammi."

Mammi winced. "It's almost painful to watch." She laced her fingers together on the table. "It wonders me why you want to be baptized."

Her answer felt too rushed. "I belong here. This is the community I'm comfortable in. Here, people will never disappoint me."

Mammi raised her eyebrows and grunted. "If you believe that, you haven't met David Eicher. Or Rachel Shetler, with her superior little *hinnerdale.*"

Cassie traced a pattern on the table with her finger. "The Englisch men can't be trusted."

"So you're running away?"

"Not running. Choosing."

"Choosing a way of life that you rejected once before?" Mammi tapped her finger to her lips. "Why did you leave in the first place?"

"It doesn't matter."

"Look at your mammi's face, and tell me it doesn't matter."

Cassie breathed a deep sigh. "There are so many things I love about the Amish way of life. The close circle of family, the mothers caring for their children and neighbors caring for each other. I love the quilts and canning and auctions."

"You forgot to mention knitting."

Cassie surrendered a half smile. "And knitting. I like the unencumbered life of devotion to God. People actually try to live what they believe."

"That is why you wanted to come back. Why did you leave?"

Cassie propped her chin in her elbow. "I knew that no matter what I did, I'd never be able to please Mamm or Norman or the church. When I stood up for myself, Mamm called me proud. When Norman criticized me, Mamm said it was because I needed correction."

"Your mamm always meant well."

"I know, but I didn't want to live like that, always being told that I was wicked or vain or stiff-necked."

"You are the least stiff-necked person I know."

"I'll humble myself to the ground to avoid

an argument, to be sure. And there was my education. I couldn't see how being myself and using the talents that God gave me could be a sin. The rules are strict and unbending. I never understood how wearing pins instead of buttons would get me closer to God. I'm sorry, Mammi, does that offend you?"

Mammi fanned the air with her hand. "Three teams of horses and a roomful of bishops couldn't offend me. Living the Ordnung is not for everyone. What I want to know is, have any of your reasons for leaving changed?"

Cassie knew the answer. It was the one she'd been wrestling with for weeks. "Nothing has changed really. Mamm is happy to have me back, but her happiness seems more like gloating. Her gute pleasure will evaporate the minute I do something to displease her."

"There is an Amish boy who wants to marry you. That's a reason to be baptized."

Cassie massaged the spot just above her right eye. The thought of being bound to Elmer Lee for life gave her an excruciating headache. She didn't love him. She could always be sure of his goodness and fidelity, but she couldn't spend the next sixty years wishing she'd chosen something different. She had tried so hard to pretend, but she just couldn't do it.

She groaned and plunked her forehead lightly on the table. "Mammi, I don't want to be Amish."

"I know, dear."

"Are you disappointed in me?"

"Of course not," Mammi scolded. "It takes a brave girl to walk the path God wants you to walk instead of sitting down in the middle of the road and giving up."

"I don't know if I can go back. I feel as if I'm trapped between two places. I don't belong in either."

"Stuff and nonsense. There are good people everywhere if you just give them a chance. You're too quick to judge. Like with the doctor. You were getting along so fine, and then you dropped him like a hot potato."

Mention of the doctor tightened the clamp around her chest. How could she go back to the real world? Zach Reynolds was there.

"Maybe the doctor will surprise you yet," Mammi said.

Cassie pressed her lips together. She didn't want any more of the doctor's brand of devastating surprises.

Mammi got up from the table. "So when will you tell your mamm of your decision to leave?"

Cassie groaned again. "Never."

"You could take out an advertisement in *The Budget.*"

She huffed the air out of her lungs. "I will tell her tonight, but I might be moving back in with you in the morning."

Mammi's eyes twinkled. "We would be thrilled." She opened the jar of green olives on the counter and skewered one with a long toothpick. Then she stabbed the olive-topped toothpick into one of the sandwiches. "Titus has fifteen minutes left. I hope he remembers."

"He's a wonderful-gute cousin," Cassie said, going to the sink to wash the ladle and pan.

"Such a good boy. He's been here every day helping with the syrup." Mammi skewered another olive. "And Dr. Reynolds has been here all the days that you haven't."

"I know," Cassie said, lowering her head. "He wants to learn how to make syrup."

"When he doesn't have to work, he comes in the evening to study the Bible with Felty. Such a good boy."

Cassie hadn't heard that. "How can that be right, Mammi? He told me he doesn't

494

believe in God anymore."

Mammi's eyes twinkled like a strand of Christmas lights. "For three weeks."

"What?"

"He was an atheist for three weeks. But he recovered."

Cassie gripped her sticky ladle as if it were a lifeline as her heart knocked behind her rib cage. Zach had found his faith again?

Mammi stabbed another sandwich, probably to make sure it was dead. "Yesterday they were reading that story in Judges where the woman drives a tent stake through Sisera's head. I thoroughly enjoyed it. We get so little excitement around here."

"I don't understand," Cassie murmured. "He was so mad at God when Austin died. He . . . he did something terrible. How can he just come back from that?"

Mammi popped an olive into her mouth. "He may have lost his faith in God, but you've lost your faith in God's ability to change people's hearts."

Mammi always said the most profound things at the most unlikely moments.

"He found a way to make peace with the little boy's death," Mammi said. "And now he's hungry for the word of God. He comes to our house, eats three plates of food, and devours the scriptures with Felty. I'm hoping to put some meat on those bones yet."

Cassie turned to stone, stunned by what Mammi had just told her. Zach studied the Bible *and* ate Mammi's food? Wonders never ceased.

Mammi stabbed her last sandwich with a toothpick and studied Cassie's face. "And now I think you're ready for this." She came around the other side of the counter and reached for a blue porcelain canister that said "Sugar" on it. She lifted the lid and pulled out an envelope. "Zach asked me to give this to you."

Cassie set her sticky ladle down and took the envelope from Mammi. Her name was written on the front in Zach's quick, short strokes. Her heart marched double-time.

With slightly sticky, trembling fingers, she opened the envelope and pulled out a letter. Zach's writing filled two pages front and back.

My dearest Cassie.

Dearest Cassie?
He didn't hate her. He didn't hate her! Her knees went weak.

"Sit down, dear," Mammi said. "I'll make you a cup of *kaffe.*"

"No, thanks, Mammi." Mammi's kaffe

tasted like paint thinner.

My dearest Cassie,

Please forgive me. I know you've asked me to stay away, but I won't be able to sleep at night if I don't at least make an attempt to tell you what's in my heart. You said I don't need to explain myself, but I do. Even if you never read this letter, I need to write it down.

I first must thank you for defending me against Norman at the country store. It is a sign of your pure heart that you would stand up for someone who has hurt you so deeply. It was another reminder of how small I stand when I am next to you.

Cassie almost protested out loud. How could he say that about her when she couldn't even offer him forgiveness?

About the night Austin died. I am ashamed that I wanted you to hurt as much as I was hurting. So I let you believe something that wasn't true. Blair slept over at my house, but I did not sleep with her.

The air stuck in Cassie's lungs. Could this be true? It didn't matter. She knew instantly that she would have forgiven him with all her heart.

I let you believe that I slept with Blair because I wanted revenge. I got it. I can't even look at myself in the mirror knowing how badly it must have hurt you. If it makes you feel better, know that I have suffered beyond anything I could have possibly imagined.

The thought of Zach's suffering didn't make her feel better at all. Surely he must have known that.

I can only beg for your forgiveness, but would never blame you if you can't give it.

Through all the turmoil of Austin's death, God has shown me the way back to Him. He has set me free. My Redeemer lives!

The only other thing I must tell you is that I love you with all my heart. I will always love you, even when you marry Elmer Lee and have twelve children and grow pumpkins in your garden. You will always be my angel.

I'm sorry if this upsets you, but I wanted you to know that no matter what

I said in the despair of the moment, I never stopped loving you.

Yours always,

The Fallen Sir Galahad.
Or Darth Vader — who was also a
knight (Luke saved him in the end.)

Cassie smiled through her tears. Zach wasn't one to be serious for long. It was one of the many reasons she loved him.

It was a good thing she was already sitting down or she might have fallen on her face. She clutched the letter to her breast. She loved him.

Mammi watched her and sported a wide grin.

"How long have you had this letter?" Cassie said breathlessly.

"A week or two."

A week or two? Zach had suffered through a week or two, not knowing how she truly felt? "Why didn't you give it to me sooner?" she asked, with a tinge of scolding in her voice.

Mammi shrugged, still with that persistent twinkle in her eye. "You were mad. I was afraid you'd rip it up."

"All this time wasted. Mammi, how could you?"

Mammi giggled. "Now, Cassie. I've had a

lot of experience with this sort of thing. You have to trust that your mammi knows what she's doing."

She had to get to Zach as soon as possible. She wouldn't let him go on grieving for one more minute. She loved him. He was her Sir Galahad, her Darth Vader, and her Da Vinci.

She jumped to her feet and ran down the hall to her old bedroom. "Are my Englisch clothes still here?" she called over her shoulder.

"Jah. I had a feeling you'd be back."

Cassie closed the door to her room and found a pair of jeans and a T-shirt. Not her most stunning outfit, but she didn't care. She had to see Zach immediately. She took the kapp off her head and pulled the bobby pins from her hair, letting it tumble to her shoulders.

She took off the plain green dress and apron, stockings and black shoes, and pulled on her jeans, T-shirt, and boots. Zach liked the boots.

Even though she was in a hurry, she pulled the mascara tube from the top drawer and chastised herself for not buying a cheap mirror when she had the chance. It was almost impossible to get her mascara right using Mammi's microscopic hand mirror.

After taking one last, hopeless look at herself, she found her cell phone at the bottom of her sock drawer, turned it on — yeah! It still worked — and sprinted out of her bedroom, saying a prayer of thanksgiving that she hadn't sold her car yet. It was parked in its usual spot in front of Mammi and Dawdi's house with a For Sale sign in the window. Thank the Lord, it was old enough that nobody had wanted to buy it.

"Mammi," she panted, "remember when I gave you my car keys for safekeeping?"

Mammi stood with her hand out and an eager smile on her face. Cassie's keys, complete with Sir Galahad key ring, dangled from Mammi's fingers. Cassie snatched up her keys and gave Mammi a big hug. "Denki, Mammi. Wish me luck."

"I don't believe in luck."

Cassie raced out of the house and jumped into The Beast. The ignition made a mournful, sickly sound as if it were hibernating and didn't want to be disturbed. "Come on, honey," she coaxed, patting the dashboard and giving it a little gas. She tried three, four, five times, then pounded her head against the steering wheel and groaned. It had been sitting idle for nearly five weeks. What had she expected?

She had no choice. She dialed Zach's cell number. She had to tell him she loved him. Now. No answer. Growling in frustration, she sent him a short text before jumping out of the car and going back into the house. "Mammi, the car won't start."

Mammi raised her eyebrows. "Is the knitted steering wheel cover on? That might warm it up."

"Yes, but it won't help."

Mammi never seemed ruffled about anything, even though Cassie was about as ruffled as she could get. "You'll have to take the buggy."

Titus, with Dawdi and Norman in tow, burst into the house as if he were late for a very important meeting. He looked at Mammi doubtfully, probably wishing for that stopwatch.

Mammi propped her hands on her hips. "Titus, you're five minutes early. All of you go back outside and count to three hundred slowly."

A thundercloud parked directly over Norman's head as he looked at Cassie's very un-Amish outfit. "What's this?"

Cassie didn't want to waste one second trying to reason with her brother. "Norman, I'm not going to be baptized."

He narrowed his eyes. "That's foolishness.

502

Do you want to break Mamm's heart all over again? Change into some decent clothes this minute."

Guilt felt like a shard of glass in her heart. Norman was right. If she left a second time, Mamm would be crushed, Elmer Lee would be disappointed, and Norman would be angry. She didn't want a confrontation with Norman, but she didn't have time to be meek. Nor did she have time to placate him. She loved Zach. She had to see him immediately.

Cassie squared her shoulders and stood toe-to-toe with her brother. "Norman, I'm not going to be baptized. I'm not going to wear the kapp again, even when I'm visiting you and the family."

"You won't be allowed in my house," Norman said.

"That is your choice, not mine."

Norman stood as rigid as a maple tree. "You will go to hell."

"God is my judge, not you. I will take my salvation up with Him." She turned to Titus. "My car won't start, and I need to get to the hospital immediately to see Dr. Reynolds. I've got to tell him I love him. Will you help me hitch the buggy?"

Titus lifted his chin and flung his toothpick out the open door. "I'd never let a broken car stand in the way of true love."

CHAPTER TWENTY-NINE

He was jogging around an empty, maze-like building trying to find a way out. Elmer Lee suddenly materialized, punched him in the nose, and handed him a cookie. Then Cassie, who always appeared in his dreams dressed in white, floated down the hall and came to a stop in front of him. "I love you, Zach," she said.

Before Zach could respond, Elmer Lee took her hand and they walked out of the window together. He tried to follow them, but instead of floating like they did, he fell and the ground rushed at him before he jerked awake and sat up in his bed.

He looked at his alarm clock. Three minutes before noon. He'd only been asleep for three hours.

He realized what had woken him up when he heard three sharp raps on his door. Didn't anybody use the phone anymore?

Okay, that wasn't fair to whoever was on

the other side of that door. He'd turned his phone off so he could get some sleep. Apparently, a long nap was not meant to be.

Not that he slept all that well when he could catch a few hours. All his dreams were of Cassie, and he often woke up mid-dream with grief and regret clawing at his chest.

He stepped into the pants he'd taken off three hours ago and shuffled out of his room to the front door. If it was important enough to come over, it was important enough to answer the door. Unless of course it was Blair, and she'd better not be within a hundred miles of Shawano.

He'd better make sure, just in case. "Who is it?"

"It's Jamie."

Zach quickly slid the dead bolt and opened the door. Jamie could wake him whenever she wanted, especially today. She looked horrible. Her hair was half-in, half-out of her ponytail, and her eyes had that look that told him a migraine was starting. She strode into the room as if she knew exactly where she was going and then paced as if she had no idea where she was.

"Is everything okay?"

"Zach, I've been trying to call you."

"My phone was off," he said, reaching into his pocket and turning it on so he didn't miss anything important. It looked as if he already had.

"They called me from the hospital because they couldn't reach you. There's been a terrible accident."

Zach smoothed his fingers through his hair. "Do they need an extra doctor? What happened?"

"Cassie's been hurt."

Zach might as well have been lost in one of his nightmares. He couldn't breathe, he couldn't speak, and nothing made sense no matter how hard he tried to concentrate.

He stumbled into the emergency room and stood in the waiting area as if expecting instructions about what to do next. The room was empty. Not even an attendant sat behind the admitting window. A TV hummed quietly in the background, playing the noon news for an invisible audience. Zach had never noticed how dark and antiseptic the emergency waiting area looked with its fake potted plants and rack of golfing magazines.

Where was Cassie? Jamie had said the accident was serious. Was Cassie in surgery? Had she already been released? Was she dead?

A tremor traveled through his body, and

his hands shook violently. She couldn't be dead. *Dear Heavenly Father, don't let her be dead.*

He stood in the middle of the room, disoriented and paralyzed by fear. Why had everyone disappeared?

Brian Mills, a county EMT, came out of the door that led to the emergency room. A bandage stretched around his left hand, but it didn't look like a serious injury. He stopped short when he saw Zach and frowned in deep concern. Zach must have looked pretty bad. "Hey, Dr. Reynolds, are you okay?"

Zach planted a hand on Brian's shoulder. "Brian, they brought an Amish girl in here about an hour ago. Was that you?"

"The one in the buggy?"

"Yeah."

Brian nodded gravely. "Some guy was texting and ran into her not three blocks from here. That buggy was so smashed up, it was like pulling her out from underneath a pile of wood shavings." He held up his injured hand. "I got a splinter the size of a pencil."

Zach gripped Brian's shoulder tighter. "What about the girl?"

"Internal injuries. A sharp piece of wood missed her jugular by millimeters. They think she might have broken her back."

Zach was going to throw up. His ears started ringing, and the room began to spin. Struggling for air, he clutched Brian's shoulder more tightly and doubled over.

"Hey, Doc," Brian said, heightened alarm in his voice. "Hey, Doc. Sit down." He practically shoved Zach into a chair and knelt next to him. "You okay?"

"What's the prognosis?"

"She's in surgery. Everything is going to be okay. Just calm down. You're going to be okay."

No, he wasn't, not unless Cassie was okay. Paramedics were trained to reassure patients in dire circumstances. In no case were they to tell the patient how bad things really were. Brian's response only fanned Zach's panic.

He braced his elbows against his knees and took several deep breaths while scrubbing his fingers through his hair. He'd be worthless if he couldn't get control of his emotions. He had to find Cassie and learn how grim her condition really was. He had to keep his head.

"You okay, Doc?" Brian asked again.

Zach took several more breaths and nodded. "I'm okay. I need more information, though. I'm going up to the OR."

"Well, maybe not till you're sure you won't pass out."

Zach held up his hand. "Just give me a couple minutes."

Brian gazed at him gravely. "A friend of yours?"

A friend? How about the girl he loved with every beat of his heart? How about his best reason for living? Even if she didn't ever love him back.

"Yeah. A friend."

"Can I get you a drink of water, Doc? Or a cup of coffee?"

With elbows still resting on his knees, Zach rubbed up and down the side of his face. He was acting more like a patient than a doctor. Clenching his gut, he stood up. "I'll be okay. I'm going to head up to surgery and see what I can find out."

"If you feel like you're going to faint, sit down."

"I will."

With renewed purpose and an oppressive sense of dread, Zach climbed the stairs to the second floor. A beehive of activity near the nurses' station told him immediately which operating room Cassie was in. Three nurses stood with their heads together conversing in hushed tones. They nearly snapped to attention when Zach approached.

"How is she?" he asked Marla. OR wasn't her area, but she was obviously as concerned as anyone about Cassie.

Marla pursed her lips. "I'm not sure. They've given her twenty units of blood, and they said something about a splenic rupture."

The bile rose in Zach's throat.

Marla laid a hand on his arm. "But that's not for certain. I'm just hearing rumors."

"What can I do? Do they need an extra set of hands?"

Marla pinned him with a stern gaze. "Not you, Doctor, and you know it. Dr. Parker and Dr. Desantos are in there. Plus Dr. Halstead. They're the best team we've got, and you need to sit down."

Zach didn't exactly feel relieved, but he felt a little better. Dr. Halstead was a fine surgeon. If Cassie had any hope, it was in Dr. Halstead's capable hands.

He drifted into the waiting room, another one with boring magazines, and sat down. Every muscle in his body tensed like the string of a crossbow stretched to its breaking point. The only thing he could think of to do was pray, and that idea made him flinch. He was afraid he might lash out and say something to God he would regret later.

He pulled out his phone and looked at it for the first time since Jamie had come over. Three texts from the hospital, one from Jamie. One from . . . Cassie?

His heart leaped into his throat. She hadn't made contact with him for weeks.

Will you be my Sir Galahad? I'm not especially fond of Darth Vader.

He couldn't have been more stunned if a bolt of lightning had fried him to dust. Did this mean she wasn't going to join the Amish? Did she still love him? Was it some kind of sick joke from Norman or Elmer Lee?

It couldn't be a joke.

She'd read his letter.

His heart vibrated a thousand miles a minute. Groaning softly, he pressed his hand against his face. Was he going to lose her when they'd only just found each other again? He couldn't breathe. It hurt too bad.

Anna and Felty, plus Norman, Linda, Luke, and Cassie's mamm filed into the waiting room. Jamie followed close behind. Once she'd delivered the horrible message to Zach, she had gone to Bonduel to pick up Cassie's family and bring them to the hospital.

With tears in her eyes, Anna immediately reached out her arms for Zach. She pulled

512

him into her embrace, and although she stood more than a foot shorter, Zach felt like a little boy in the comfort of his mother's arms. There was no solace like a grandmother's hug.

The tears that he hadn't allowed to flow earlier rolled down his cheeks. Let Norman mock him for not being manly enough. He didn't care about anything but Cassie and the utter despair that engulfed him at the possibility of her dying.

"She was so eager to get to you," Anna said. "She almost made it."

"She sent me a text," Zach whispered. "I didn't know."

To Zach's surprise, Esther grabbed on to his hand. "Doctor, they told us Cassie was in surgery. How is she? Did you operate on her?"

Zach wiped his cheek and shook his head. "I just got here myself. They told me she has some internal injuries. She's lost a lot of blood. I'm hoping one of the surgeons will talk to us soon."

"Help us, Doctor," Esther said, her hand firmly around Zach's, her voice trembling with emotion.

"I'll do anything I can."

"I hope I did the right thing," Anna said. "I gave her your letter this morning. She wants to go back to school. She wants to be with you something wonderful. Her car wouldn't start, but she wanted to see you so bad she took the buggy."

Esther's face was a map of painful memories. "What do you mean, Mamm? Cassie never told me such a thing."

"It's true," Norman said. "Right before the accident, she told me she didn't want to be baptized." He inclined his head toward Zach. "It's all his fault."

Zach wouldn't have guessed that sweet Anna Helmuth had an indignant bone in her entire body. "Norman, you'll not say one bad thing about the doctor."

Norman frowned and glanced at Linda. She nodded sternly at her husband, and he closed his mouth.

To Zach's utter relief and dread, Rhonda Miles, the head OR nurse, walked into the waiting room in her surgical hat and scrubs with the surgical mask pulled from her face and hanging around her neck. Rhonda was young, but a crackerjack nurse in the OR. She had brilliant eyes and sharply angled cheekbones. She didn't have much of a bedside manner, but she was a gifted nurse and Zach trusted her completely.

The sight of her stole his breath. Would he be able to bear the news she was about to deliver?

"Are you Cassie's family?" Rhonda asked.

Esther stepped forward. "I'm her mother."

Norman pointed at Zach. "He's not family."

Anna hooked her elbow around Zach's arm. "Yes, he is."

Zach felt as if she'd thrown a warm blanket around him. His eyes pooled with tears.

"Are you Cassie's doctor?" Esther said.

"I'm one of the nurses. The doctors are doing everything they can to save Cassie's life. They asked me to talk to you."

Save Cassie's life. By the way she said it, Zach knew instinctively that it was a moment-by-moment effort.

"How is my daughter?" Esther said.

The lines of Rhonda's face looked severe, as if she were made out of hard, unyielding stone. "She is still in surgery. I'm going back as soon as our visit is over."

"Will she be all right?" Anna asked.

Rhonda glanced at Zach, nodded her acknowledgment of a doctor in the room, then focused all her attention on Esther. "I'm afraid Cassie has been seriously hurt. She's lost a lot of blood. We will do everything we can to save her, but there is a real possibility that she will not survive. You need to be prepared."

Rhonda sounded as if she were rehearsing a carefully prepared speech. She'd given it before.

"What are her injuries?" Zach asked.

"Ruptured spleen, collapsed lung, broken back. The spleen is out, but they can't get her blood pressure up. We're at twenty-five units of blood."

Twenty-five units.

If Zach had been alone in the room, he would have lost it right there, but his demeanor had to give Cassie's family hope, even when hope was slim. Rhonda turned around and walked away, and he almost followed her out the door and into the operating room, just to get a look at Cassie. But no matter how he ached to see her, he refused to do anything to distract the surgeons from their work.

Everyone's gaze turned to Zach as if he could take charge and proclaim that Cassie would live a long and healthy life.

"What can we do, Dr. Reynolds?" Anna asked.

He recognized the helpless, hopeless feeling that overtook them. Like him, they each would have done anything for Cassie, but there was absolutely nothing they could do but wait.

"We can pray," Felty said.

Zach took a deep breath. "Yes. We need to pray." Cassie needed his faith right now, not his doubt. And certainly not his anger. "You can donate blood downstairs. They always need blood." He winced. He couldn't even do that. It had only been six weeks since he'd donated for Austin.

"Will donating blood help Cassie?" Anna asked.

If nothing else, it would be good karma, as Mom would say. "Yes. If they don't give it to Cassie, they can give it to someone else in trouble."

"Let's go, then," Anna said, already heading out the door.

"Don't even think about it, Mamm. You're too old," Esther said.

"I'm not old yet," Anna said, turning on her heels and striding out of the waiting room like an Olympic sprinter in orthopedic shoes. No one would have been able to tell she'd just had foot surgery.

"Wait for me," Felty said. His step was even more sprightly as he walked away. Those two were amazing. Their blood could probably cure all sorts of diseases.

Luke and Linda followed the grandparents.

Norman lifted his pale face to glare at Zach. "Now do you understand why I have been so concerned about my sister? Why I begged her to stay with us?"

Zach clenched his teeth. He couldn't stomach Norman's preaching today. "We can have a frank doctrinal discussion when this is over, Norman. But right now, my only focus is getting Cassie better."

"But don't you see what you have wrought with your worldly influence? She decided to leave the church, and now God is punishing her."

Something inside Zach snapped like a rubber band. He seized Norman by the collar and shoved him violently against the nearest wall. With grief and fear laying waste to his senses, it took every ounce of strength not to pound his fist into Norman's mouth. "Shut up! Just shut up!"

Norman grunted and scowled with every muscle in his face. "You have no right . . . Let go of me. I am a man of peace."

"What you are is a spiteful, despicable hypocrite, and a sorry excuse for a human being." He shoved Norman away from him. "Get out of here. I can't stand to look at you."

Esther surprised Zach again when she laid a gentle hand on his arm. His temper came to rest when he looked into her eyes. "This will not help my Cassie, will it, Doctor?"

Zach took a step back and shook his head.

Esther pinned Norman with a stern eye. "Did the good Lord take your *fater* because he was a wicked man? Are you saying he deserved to die?"

"Nae, Mamm. I did not mean —"

"I know what you meant, Norman, and it does not reflect well on you. God is the only righteous judge of men." She put her arm around Norman's shoulder. "God would never take my Cassie as a punishment. If He punished His children that way, we would all be dead. We are all sinners."

"If she dies, my heart will break," Norman said.

"Mine too," Esther said, her voice cracking. "But we will accept the Lord's will." She wrapped her fingers around Norman's arm and pulled him in the direction of the elevator. "Let's go pray. And then we will give blood."

Zach was torn between prayer and a good battle with the punching bag at the gym. Would his prayers help or hurt Cassie's chances? He felt raw and angry, scrubbed from the inside out with a wire brush. His truce with God was fragile indeed.

There was nothing he could do *but* pray. God already knew how mad he was. Maybe Zach should give God a chance to soften his heart. Maybe God would see Zach's meager offering of faith as enough to save Cassie.

He took the stairs to the little chapel in the basement of the hospital. The room seemed dark and lifeless as if even God had abandoned it. Zach sat in one of the folding chairs and bowed his head.

Jesus said that all things are possible to him who believes. Could his faith save Cassie? If his faith was weak, would he lose her? Did her life hang on the strength of his faith? The thought was almost too horrible to contemplate.

Leaning his arm against the back of the chair in front of him, he prayed. "Heavenly Father, I want to believe. Help me believe. I'll do anything You want if You will just save Cassie. I love her. Please, spare her life."

He wept until he was spent, until every muscle in his body trembled with exhaustion.

After several bleak minutes, someone slipped an arm around his shoulders. He glanced up. Felty sat beside him.

"What does God want from me?" Zach said. "What more can I do?"

"God uses tribulations to strengthen our faith."

"So you mean that Cassie has to suffer to

test *my* faith? That doesn't seem fair. If my faith is to be tested, I'm the one who should suffer."

"That's not what I mean. God doesn't make bad things happen to test our faith. More people are made bitter by trials than are made better. Bad things happen. How we respond to a trial is up to us, but if we let Him, God can teach us something in the process."

Zach leaned his head in his hand. "What am I supposed to learn? I can barely think, let alone open my heart to God."

"You think if you have enough faith Cassie will be healed?"

"Yes. Jesus said it's possible if I believe."

Felty folded his arms. "Do you remember the story of Shadrach, Meshach, and Abednego yet?"

Zach nodded. There weren't many Bible stories he didn't remember. "The king threw them into a fiery furnace, and God saved them."

"What did they tell the king right before he threw them into the furnace?"

Zach pressed at the space between his eyebrows. "They told him that they wouldn't worship his gold idols. They said God would deliver them."

"They said that God was *able* to deliver

521

them. And then they said something that everybody forgets. They said, 'But if not . . .'"

Zach furrowed his brow. "What does that mean?"

"They told the king that God was able to deliver them, but if God chose not to deliver them, they would still believe in Him." Felty tightened his arm around Zach. "You might have enough faith for Cassie to be healed. Do you have enough faith for Cassie *not* to be healed?"

"I don't understand."

"Will you still believe even if Cassie is taken? Because that is the true test of your faith."

Zach wanted to jump to his feet and yell and shout and break every rickety folding chair in the chapel. He would never agree to letting God take Cassie. That wasn't faith. Felty didn't know what he was talking about.

Felty seemed to sense Zach's inner turmoil. "Jesus said, 'Thy will be done.' Can you say the same and mean it?"

Zach thought of Jesus on the cross. He told His disciples He could have saved Himself, but He didn't because it wasn't the will of God. He had the power and didn't use it.

Zach's budding faith had taken a crushing blow when Austin died, but looking back, what had his faith been but a misguided hope that God was his own personal genie who existed only to grant his wishes? And when God hadn't granted his wish, he'd stopped believing.

God had given him a test, and Zach had failed miserably.

He drew in a shaky breath. "Lord, I believe. Help my unbelief."

A tear rolled down Felty's cheek and disappeared into his long, gray beard. "Me too, Lord. Me too."

It was Zach's turn to comfort Felty. He wrapped his thick arms around Felty's thin, eighty-five-year-old shoulders. "Will you pray with me?"

"There's nothing I'd rather do."

"Dear God," Zach began, his voice strong and clear as if God were giving him the words. "I want Cassie to live. I know you can heal her. Please heal her. But if not, I will still believe." He swallowed hard. "Thy will be done," he said, and meant it.

CHAPTER THIRTY

The pain was nearly unbearable. She held perfectly still so as not to make it worse. The left side of her body could have been on fire. Her head throbbed as if it were stuck in a vise, and a sharp pain down her spine almost took her breath away. She was too tired to open her eyes, but if someone knew she was awake, maybe she could get something for the pain.

If someone knew she was awake . . .

Where was she?

Was she dead?

No, she didn't think she'd be in this much pain if she were dead. And it hurt. Bad.

Must have pain medication.

There was nothing else to do. She'd have to open her eyes.

It was dark outside the window and the lights were dim, but she could see enough to know she was in the hospital. Had there been an accident?

Zach Reynolds sat on a chair close to her bed fast asleep. Her heart raced at the sight of him. Oh, how she loved him!

Did this mean he'd gotten her text?

Her text. Her mad dash to the hospital in the buggy. An accident. She didn't even know what had hit her.

She wanted to reach out and smooth the hair from Zach's forehead. She wanted to lean over and give him a kiss. He was so incredibly good-looking and so incredibly good. How could she resist?

Okay, leaning over and kissing anybody was not a good idea. When she moved her head a fraction of an inch off her pillow, the pain flared to life. She groaned softly. No moving for her.

That slight noise startled Zach awake. He looked at her, and his smile could have guided ships into the harbor. "Cassie," he whispered.

"Sir Galahad," she whispered back.

He reached out as if her touch could save him from drowning and slipped his hand into hers. He bowed his head and gently pressed his lips to her fingers. She felt his tears on the back of her hand as his body shuddered and he disintegrated into gut-wrenching, heart-cleaving sobs. He wept as if he'd just walked out of the Valley of the

Shadow of Death.

"Thank You," he said. "Thank You, God."

With her heart overflowing, she held very still and let him weep.

CHAPTER THIRTY-ONE

Zach had been living off little more than coffee and prayer for three days. Dr. Mann had all but ordered him to get some sleep and a good meal or threatened to ban him from the hospital. After he made sure Cassie rested comfortably, Zach had sprinted down to the hospital cafeteria to grab a quick bite. He never wanted to let her out of his sight again.

Only when he had smelled the chicken noodle soup had he realized how famished he was. He'd ended up eating a club sandwich, two bowls of soup, a roll, three cookies, and a piece of pie. Plus a cup of green Jell-O in Austin's honor. He had practically been able to hear Austin giggling with every bite.

After polishing off his third cookie — nowhere near as good as anything Cassie made — he leaned back in his chair and took a swig of coffee. He should call Mom.

A twinge of guilt stabbed him right between the shoulder blades. Mom had probably been pacing the floor since he had texted her that Cassie had been in an accident. He should have called way sooner than this.

He pulled his phone from his back pocket and punched in Mom's number. She answered on the first ring.

"Zach. Finally."

He winced. Mom sounded more than a little annoyed. "Sorry I didn't call sooner."

"No offense, son. I've tried not to be pushy, but really? It's a good thing I didn't hold my breath waiting for your call. I get a text — Pray for Cassie, she's been in an accident. Then four hours later — She's out of surgery. She's going to be okay. I'll call you as soon as I can. It's the curse of a mother with boys to never get the details of her children's lives."

"I'm sorry a text was all you got, but considering my state of mind, you're lucky it wasn't a call from the insane asylum."

"I called all my ladies from church and from the auxiliary. We prayed like crazy."

Zach's heart felt as if it had grown three times larger in the past few days, and it only kept growing. "Thanks, Mom. It really helped."

"How is Cassie?"

"She had a punctured lung, a broken back, and a ruptured spleen. They took out her spleen and put a tube in her chest. Her back had a minor fracture. No permanent damage."

"Thank the Lord for that."

Zach couldn't keep his voice from cracking. "I almost lost her, Mom. I don't know what I would have done."

"I know."

"But you should have seen all the people. Her family put out word that Cassie needed blood, and within an hour there were two hundred Amish people waiting in line at the hospital to donate. I bought every doughnut in town to pass out."

There was a brief silence on the other end. "You sound terrible. How long has it been since you've had any sleep?"

Zach's hand seemed to automatically go to his forehead where the headache had been lingering for days. "I don't remember, Mom. I just . . . I couldn't leave, you know?"

"Of course not, but it would be better if you didn't end up in the hospital yourself."

"Mom, I'm going to ask her to marry me."

An even longer pause. "Are you converting?"

He chuckled. "She's decided not to be baptized after all."

"Well, that's good. I'd probably go years without hearing from you if you couldn't even text."

"I'm wondering if I should wait until she's out of the hospital before I pop the question. I don't want to rush her, but I don't want to wait too long either."

"There's no universe where the hospital is an appropriate place to propose to a girl," Mom said. "Find the most romantic spot in Shawano."

"I'm terrified just thinking about it," Zach said.

"If she has any sense at all, she'll say yes. You're a catch. All the auxiliary ladies think you're hot."

Zach groaned. "Mom, please. Too much information."

Mom giggled. "You can tell Cassie I said so if it will make her more likely to say yes."

"No thanks."

She sounded so close, and he wished he could reach out and get a hug. He felt as if he'd been put through the wringer on Anna's washing machine.

"What are you going to do about a ring?" Mom said. "All your dad's insurance money went to medical school. You're living off hot dogs and ramen noodles."

"I don't know. I thought maybe I could

give her my class ring until I can afford something really spectacular."

"Absolutely not," Mom said. Her voice seemed to echo throughout the entire cafeteria.

Zach chuckled. "Okay, bad idea."

"I want her to have the ring your dad gave me."

Zach felt a hand on his shoulder. He turned around to see his mom standing there in all her motherly wonderfulness. His heart swelled as big as the sky as he leaped to his feet and wrapped his arms as far around her as they would go. "Mom!" he shouted, not caring who he disturbed in the small cafeteria. The tears ran down both their faces as they stood there making up for months of hug deprivation.

"You look terrible," Mom said.

"You look wonderful," Zach replied. They laughed through the tears. "I can't believe you came," he said.

Mom retrieved a tissue from her purse and mopped up her face. "Yesterday, after forty-eight hours of not hearing a thing, I went a little crazy. I hopped on a plane this morning. Thank goodness for American Express."

Zach draped an arm around Mom's shoulder. "I'm so happy, I think I'm going to pass out."

Mom lifted her eyebrows as she eyed Zach. "You might pass out from exhaustion and starvation. It looks like I got here just in time."

"Just in time."

She nodded and rolled up her sleeves. "I'm here to help. Put me to work. And when can I meet Cassie?"

"Let's go see if she's awake. If not, you can at least meet her grandparents. Since the accident, they've been at the hospital almost as much as I have."

"I've been dying to meet them. They've taken good care of you. I owe them my deepest gratitude." She cupped her hand over his cheek. "They brought my son back to himself."

Zach shook with happiness. "Mom, God is good, and I'm never going to leave Him again."

Mom got all soft and mushy around the eyes. "Pop would have liked hearing that."

"He already knows."

Cassie sat up gingerly and let Mamm help her put on the back brace that fit tightly around her like a corset. Then she carefully put on her pants. Mamm frowned but didn't say a word about the jeans or the collared blouse or the white Nikes with fluorescent pink trim. She even knelt down and helped Cassie put her shoes on. In the days following the accident, her mamm had somehow come to terms with Cassie's decision not to be baptized. Mamm hadn't said a word about the church or Cassie's wickedness in all her time spent in Cassie's hospital room. She even cheerfully bore Zach's presence even though he wasn't Elmer Lee. Cassie was proud of her for making an effort.

A near-death experience could do that to a person.

Every moment Zach wasn't working had been spent by Cassie's side. She finally had to put her foot down — which was hard because she couldn't even get out of bed — and insist that Zach go home and get a good night's sleep. He'd done it reluctantly, but she held firm. She wasn't about to let him catch pneumonia on her account.

A few days ago, his mom had come to town, and her presence had helped Cassie rest much easier. Not only had his mom taken over the job of monitoring Zach's sleeping habits, but she had lifted some of the burden from Zach's shoulders. She took shifts worrying about Cassie so Zach could get some rest.

Zach's mom was just as Cassie had imagined her: loving, no-nonsense, devoted to her son and God. She had to have been a remarkable woman to have raised such a remarkable son.

At the times Cassie was lucid, she and Zach had talked about her accident and his newfound faith. He told her of his dream and his despair and Shadrach, Meshach, and Abednego. She told him of her decision to leave the community and her desperation to get to him after reading his letter.

They rejoiced in God's tender mercies. And Zach smiled. A lot.

The visits and cookies and flowers from Amish and church friends never ceased. Mammi and Dawdi were at the hospital almost as much as Zach was, and her brothers and sisters and other relatives visited regularly. The doctor finally had to set strict rules about visitors. Cassie wouldn't have gotten any rest.

The doctor said she could live just fine without a spleen, and some physical therapy on her back was all that was required for her to function normally again. Lord willing, she'd be good as new in a few short months.

"You'll need your scarf and jacket," Mamm said as she took Cassie's hospital gown and folded it at the foot of the bed.

Someone knocked on the door to her room.

"Come in," Cassie called, smoothing down her blouse. Mammi ambled into the room carrying a fuzzy pink sweater. "This is for you," she said, holding out the sweater so Cassie could get a better look.

Cassie sighed and ran her fingers along the tightly knitted yarn. It felt silky soft, like a newborn *buplie*'s hair or a bunny rabbit's fur. The yarn was light, feminine pink that Cassie knew would bring out the color in her cheeks.

"Mammi, this is beautiful."

Mammi beamed even wider. "A beautiful sweater for a beautiful girl."

"Don't encourage vanity," Mamm said, before clamping her lips shut. She looked as if she were biting her tongue.

Mammi raised an eyebrow. "God made Cassie beautiful, like the lilies of the field. Even the lilies wear petals."

Mammi helped Cassie pull the sweater over her head and put her arms through the sleeves. It fit perfectly. The sleeves were long and the neck was high. A modified cable pattern ran down the front of the sweater. The collar of her blouse peeked out of the top and gave her a very tailored look. She liked it. "When did you make this?"

"I whipped it out whenever you weren't around and stuffed it into my bag when you were home. I was sneaky. I knew the doctor would eventually work up the courage to ask you on a date. I had to be ready."

Cassie giggled. Zach had been standing in the hall outside her room this morning when he dialed her cell phone. He had apologized profusely for calling a number she had only given him so he could check on Mammi's foot, then proceeded to ask her on a date. Their first date. He told her he would pick her up at the hospital doors as soon as she was discharged.

Was it bad for her health that her heart raced as if it would trip over itself?

Cassie gave her mammi a kiss on the cheek. "Oh, Mammi. I'm so happy."

"I am too. You're number eight for me."

"Number eight?"

"Number eight match." She counted on her fingers. "Moses and Lia, Aden and Lily, Beth and Tyler, Gid and Dottie, Ben and Emma — they were together once already, but I got them back together. Lizzie and Mahlon — Felty says I can't count them because they sort of got together on their own, but I'm counting them anyway, and Mandy and Noah. Though truly, Mandy and Noah are Felty's match, and I should give credit where credit is due."

Cassie's jaw dropped to the floor. Her mamm's did the same. "It was your plan to match me with the doctor?" Cassie said.

Cassie's mamm looked momentarily indignant. "Mamm, how could you? He's not even Amish. What about Elmer Lee?"

"Now, Esther. You know as well as I do that Elmer Lee was never going to work out for Cassie. Dr. Reynolds is a gute boy, and he makes Cassie very happy."

Mamm's expression softened to putty. She patted Cassie on the cheek. "The doctor is a gute man. He is not the one I would have chosen, but my Cassie deserves to be happy."

"Jah," Mammi said. "And he has such nice hair."

Cassie hadn't really wanted to ride in the wheelchair. She felt like enough of an invalid already. But the nurse insisted. Mamm and Mammi followed close behind as she was wheeled to the elevator and then out the sliding hospital doors.

Zach was leaning on the hood of his car with his arms folded, looking better than anyone had a right to look. Cassie took a deep breath and tried not to hyperventilate.

This man, who had stepped straight out of a men's fashion magazine, was taking her on a date.

He wore jeans and a navy blue sweater that had a pattern eerily similar to the one on the front of Cassie's sweater. Another of Mammi's creations?

He smiled as if he'd never really been happy until this very moment. "Hi," he said.

"Hi."

"You . . . I've never in my life . . . You look beautiful." His eyes shone with admiration as he tried to find the words. He gestured at her sweater. "We match."

She grinned. Mammi was a tricky one.

Zach opened the car door for her. She got into the car, trying not to wince. She was still very tender yet.

Zach grabbed a blanket from behind her seat and spread it over her legs, winking at her as he did. She held her breath and tried to calm her pulse. He'd feel bad if he caused her to have a heart attack.

Cassie waved goodbye to Mamm and Mammi as Zach pulled the car away from the curb and grabbed her hand. "Is this okay? Does it hurt?"

"It feels amazing," she said.

"Yes, it does." His smile was subtle, as if he were trying to contain all his happiness.

"How are you feeling? Can I do anything to make you more comfortable?"

"I'm a little sore, but considering where I've been, I'd say I'm doing well."

He squeezed her hand as if making sure she was still in the car. "I couldn't be more grateful. I'm more than happy just seeing you out of the hospital. I'll do my best to resist the urge to bury my fingers in your hair."

"I should have worn a beanie." She stifled a laugh. Laughing sent a sharp pain shooting through her chest. "So what have you planned for our first date?"

"The first plan is that it's going to last about fifteen minutes. You need your rest."

She frowned in mock disappointment. "I had hoped you'd take me hiking or kayaking. Or bowling is a good first date."

"I've planned something less likely to put you back in the hospital. We're having a gourmet lunch followed by a long nap."

"For me or for you?" She caressed his cheek with her hand. "You look tired."

"Who can sleep when all I can think about is you?" Zach twisted his mouth into a grin and glanced sideways at her as he drove his car up the lane to Huckleberry Hill.

Cassie tried not to grimace. "A gourmet lunch at my mammi's house?" Mammi's cooking was worse than hospital food, and she was famished.

"Don't worry. I did the cooking," Zach said, his eyes dancing as he watched her face for a reaction.

The only thing worse than Mammi's cooking was Zach's cooking. He knew how to boil water and turn on the microwave. She might starve. "Oh, that's nice," she said, trying to infuse her voice with a hint of enthusiasm.

He chuckled. "Don't be alarmed. I made an emergency trip to McDonald's. I hope you like Big Macs."

She smiled. "I love 'em."

He came around to her side of the car and opened the door for her. Then he took her arm and helped her ease out of the car. It was uncomfortable, but she could stand it. He put a firm arm around her back and pulled her close to him. He smelled like hickory smoke. He must have been helping Dawdi with the fire this morning. She resisted the urge to bury her face in his blue sweater and breathe him in. He might think that was a little weird.

"Are you okay?" he said. "I don't mind carrying you."

She nodded and leaned on his arm as they ambled to the house. She'd been off her feet too long. The short walk to the house felt like a 5K. Mammi's kitchen table was spread with a cheery yellow tablecloth and set with lime green plates and fuchsia napkins. A dozen brightly colored balloons hovered over a bouquet of deep red roses in the middle of the table. There was also a large McDonald's bag next to the roses.

"Gourmet lunch," he said, grinning sheepishly.

"You might not believe this, but I love burgers, and the hospital food left a little to be desired." She sat down gingerly, and he sat next to her. "Are we having a party?" She pointed to the helium balloons.

"Yes," he said, "to observe the passing of your spleen and to celebrate the fact that we have matching scars." He pulled down the collar of his sweater to reveal an inch-long scar near his collarbone. She'd never noticed it before.

Cassie still wore a bandage to cover the jagged four-inch scar that zigzagged from her neck to her collarbone where she had been skewered by a piece of wood.

"How did you get that scar?"

He shrugged. "I got cleated by a squirrely forward. Six stitches. The important thing is that we match."

"You haven't got a scar underneath your

rib cage, have you?"

He looked crestfallen. "No, but I do have one where they took my appendix out."

"We're still a pretty good match."

He smiled and gazed at her as if seeing her for the first time. "The best."

His look made her shy and excited and feverish all at the same time. Sir Galahad himself couldn't have been more charming or more wonderful.

Zach's smile disappeared as quickly as it had come, and he looked almost nervous. "Before your next painkiller kicks in, I need to ask you something."

"Okay?"

He slid off his chair and got down on one knee.

Ach, du lieva. She hoped she didn't faint.

"Cassie, I have loved you since the moment I met you. You are smart, beautiful, wonderful in every way. Your snickerdoodles could probably give rise to world peace. If I had lost you, I don't think anything would have been able to save me. Even God's love."

She trembled at the thought. The accident had taken him to the edge of despair. If she had anything to say about it, he would never be there again.

"Will you marry me?" he said, and he

actually looked unsure of her answer. That had to be fixed immediately.

"Can you truly love someone without a spleen?" she said, smiling so hard her neck stitches hurt.

He smiled back. "Can you truly love someone who isn't an Amish guy?"

She leaned over, took his face in her hands, and kissed him swiftly on the lips. "With all my heart."

He actually caught his breath as if he'd seen a glimpse of a heavenly vision. Had anyone ever been as truly in love as she was at this moment?

Zach slipped his hand into his pocket and retrieved a ring. It had a gold band with a princess cut diamond in the center and two smaller diamonds on either side. "It's my mother's," he said. "She wanted you to have it."

"It's beautiful," she whispered.

With shaking hands, he slid the ring on her finger.

A tear made a trail down her cheek. She held out her hand to get a better look. She'd never be worthy of such happiness in a million lifetimes. "It's so much, Zach. A ring this beautiful shouldn't —"

He grinned. "It's too late to back down now. Mom would be devastated if you didn't want it. I don't deserve you, but you're stuck with me."

She laced her fingers with his. "You're stuck with me. Spleen-less and all."

Zach rose to his feet. "Can you stand for a minute?" When she nodded, he took her hands and gently tugged her up. "I want to kiss you in the worst way, but I'm determined to follow the kissing rules. No kissing while sitting down."

"I'm disappointed you're so strict about your own rules," she said.

He groaned. "It's just about killing me."

With restrained eagerness, he carefully slid his arms around her and pulled her to him, bringing his lips frustratingly close. "Am I hurting you?"

"Just kiss me," she commanded breathlessly.

Still handling her as if she were made of glass, he brought his lips down on hers and made her forget the pain. Basically, he made her forget everything except the need to be as close to him as possible. She breathed him in with every breath as the touch of his lips catapulted her to Paris and back again.

Three months ago, she never would have guessed that she'd be standing in Mammi's kitchen kissing frat-boy Zach Reynolds. And now she couldn't imagine life without him.

He was everything to her, and she wanted to spend the rest of the life she'd been so graciously given loving him.

And the kissing wasn't half bad either.

The problem with kissing while standing up was that your knees got weak and you were in danger of collapsing into a heap on the floor and popping all your stitches.

As soon as she got her reason back, she was going to rewrite those kissing rules.

CHAPTER THIRTY-TWO

Felty sat on the workbench sharpening his pruning shears while Anna lounged next to him reading a book. "How long do you think we need to hide in the barn?" Felty asked, tucking his coat more tightly around him.

Anna glanced up as she turned a page. "We need to give Dr. Reynolds enough time to propose to Cassie and give Cassie enough time to say yes. Do you remember what a disaster it was when we interrupted Tyler Yoder in the middle of his proposal? Beth dug in her heels and swore she wouldn't have him."

"I don't think that will be a problem with Cassie and the doctor. Your sweaters did the trick, Annie Banannie."

Anna smiled in perfect contentment. "Denki, Felty. It's nice when people recognize my hard work."

"I hope we don't have to wait in the barn

all day. Two people in love are apt to take their time."

"These things can't be rushed, dear."

Felty finished with his pruning shears and started on the hoe. "What are you reading, Banannie? Another cookbook? The family sure is lucky to have a cook like you. The Helmuths eat better than the prince of Germany."

Anna closed her book, set it on the bench between them, and clasped her hands together as if she were preparing for a very serious talk. "Felty dear, I've decided to take up crochet."

"Crochet?"

She tapped the book in front of her. "If people get too much of a good thing, they don't appreciate it. I think *die youngie* are starting to take my knitting for granted."

"That's not true, Annie. I still see the excitement in the young folks' eyes when you hand out your pot holders."

Anna patted Felty's knee. "Now, Felty, that's because you always see the best in everyone. But I won't be talked out of it, no matter how much you cherish my pot holders. I'm moving on to crocheted dishrags. That will stir things up a bit."

Felty smiled. "And just who are you hoping to stir up yet?"

"We've made a lot of matches in our day, Felty, and some of them proved harder than getting a team of horses unstuck from the mud. But it's time for our most challenging match yet."

Felty put down his tools and fingered his beard. "And who would that be, Banannie?"

"I'm afraid we'll never find just the right girl for him. He's so trusting and sometimes so absentminded, like a turkey in the rain."

"There's someone for everyone, Annie, even Titus. Is that who you're thinking of matching next?"

Anna nodded. "That boy is without guile, and if we're not careful, we might unwittingly match him with a bossy, overbearing girl. It would break my heart to see sweet Titus get henpecked to death."

Felty stroked his beard. "She'll need to be sharp as a tack."

"But we don't want her to ever think she's smarter than Titus."

"Titus is smart enough. He just doesn't flaunt it like some people."

"Such a good boy," Anna said, "but not in an obvious way. I'm going to have to become very proficient with a crochet hook. Shoddy work will not attract the right kind of girl."

"What girl doesn't love a crocheted dishrag?"

Anna sucked in her breath and grabbed Felty's wrist. "Do you think it will be enough? Maybe I should take up painting. I could paint a lovely farm scene on a milk can."

"What girl doesn't love a decorative milk can of her very own?"

Anna pursed her lips. "There are so many ways of attracting a bride for Titus. I could grow flowers or cucumbers. I could cross-stitch a pillow or give her a puppy. Or write a poem for Titus to sing to her." She held up a finger as another idea came to her. "We could give the girl a bale of hay to feed her horse."

"Doesn't seem very romantic yet."

"Now, Felty, I'm thinking outside the box."

Felty took off his hat and scratched his head. "What box are you talking about, Annie-girl?"

"It's an expression that Dr. Reynolds taught me. It means there are no bad ideas."

"All your ideas are good ideas, Annie."

"I hope Titus doesn't mind waiting. It will take me several months to learn how to crochet and paint. And write poems."

Felty propped the hoe against the nearest wooden beam. "Maybe he'll find his own wife in the meantime."

"Nae, that will never do. We can't trust Titus to make such an important decision. You'll have to stall him, Felty."

"Me? What can I do?"

Anna looked skyward and tapped her finger against her lips. "We'll have to think of another surgery. Or maybe we could settle for a root canal."

Felty raised his eyebrows and let his mouth fall open. "I'm running out of teeth."

Anna giggled. "I'm teasing, dear. I know how you hate the dentist." She sighed and took Felty's face in her hands. "I've put you through a great deal in the name of love. Thank you for sticking with me."

Felty wrapped his arms around his beautiful wife and tugged her close. "I would stick with you through a thousand root canals, Annie. As long as we're together, I don't even need teeth."

"That would make it very hard to chew."

"If I still have arms to hold you, I wouldn't care."

Anna settled into her husband's embrace. "Then I'll pray every day that your arms don't fall off."

"I appreciate that, Banannie. I truly do."

Dear Reader,

Huckleberry Hill has become one of my favorite places on earth, and Anna and Felty are like old and dear friends to me. It has been a delightful adventure writing about Anna's antics with her knitting needles and frying pans as well as her good-hearted attempts to find suitable mates for her unsuspecting grandchildren.

I have loved creating these characters and stories for you. I hope you have taken as much pleasure in reading them as I have in writing them.

In 2016, I will be leaving Huckleberry Hill and going a little farther down the road to the fictional Wisconsin town of Bienenstock, where three Amish bee-keepers find love and laughter in my new series: *The Honeybee Sisters.*

Lily, Poppy, and Rose Christner,

known as the Honeybee Sisters in their Amish community, are smart, inseparable, and all grown up. Orphaned when they were very young, the girls were raised by their eccentric Aunt Bitsy, who doesn't behave anything like a proper Amish spinster. The Honeybee Sisters have blossomed into rare beauties, and the boys in the community have begun to take notice. But Aunt Bitsy is determined to scare off all comers with her brusque manner and her handy shotgun. None but the most worthy will make it past Bitsy's defenses. It's going to be a rowdy and romantic summer — harvesting honey from their many beehives and fighting off the boys right and left.

The three Honeybee Sister books will hit shelves beginning in July 2016. I hope you'll come and see what all the fuss is about!

Though I know you'll miss Anna and Felty as much as I will, never fear. Anna wouldn't dream of retiring, not when she still has dozens of unmarried grandchildren to worry about. Not only will a match for Titus test her keen abilities, but her grandson Max never met a girl he could tolerate, and her granddaughter Sarah never met a boy she didn't like.

That should keep Anna knitting pot holders and crocheting dishrags for a very long time.

Sincerely,
Jennifer Beckstrand